Other Books by R.A. MacAvoy

The Black Dragon Series
Tea with the Black Dragon
Twisting the Rope

The Damiano Series
Damiano
Damiano's Lute
Raphael

The Lens of the World Series
Lens of the World
King of the Dead
Winter of the Wolf

Other Novels
The Book of Kells
The Grey Horse
The Third Eagle

DEATH
AND
RESURRECTION

R.A. MacAvoy

PRIME BOOKS

DEATH AND RESURRECTION

Prime Books
www.prime-books.com

ISBN: 978-1-60701-289-4

To Dolly Smith
. . . and with thanks to Mr. Thomas Keu,
for all the grace he lent to Ewen Young

May all be happy.
May all be peaceful, and at ease.
May all be safe.
May all be free from fear.
May all know the truth of their own nature.

—from the Metta Sutta

PART I: Summer and Ewen Becomes a Delog

Chapter One

Ewen Young liked drawing from life. He was good at it.

The drawing of his that the gallery visitor was now looking at was one of his own favorites. Ewen tried not to look at it or the man, but that was not possible.

"I love this," the visitor said. Ewen was the closest person about, but he had to turn toward the man to hear him clearly. "The thing's both a hawk and a man, which is cool, and the man looks like he could be someone in particular. Like a real guy."

"It's Willy. He is a real guy." Ewen pointed to the scrap of paper thumbtacked under the matted drawing. It said: *The way Willy looks at you.*

Another potential customer drew up beside them, holding her glass of mediocre champagne. "He looks to me like an Indian shaman in one of those wooden hat things. That is, if the shaman were wearing a sport jacket."

Ewen didn't know if this was a compliment or not, but at least she was expressing interest. That was good. The whole show was going well, except for the fact he had to be there. He stepped back to allow the two well-dressed art patrons to discuss his work. By their clothes—or by the way they wore them—they were wealthy.

In his red silk turtleneck and black jeans, Ewen's trim figure was utterly compatible with the gallery scene. That was his intent, but really he would rather have been standing in a pail of ice water. Ewen was seeming to be a part of this cultured scene only by light meditation and breath control. He lived daily in a world of paint, of shifting light and the smell of turpentine, but as for the rest of this "being an artist" he'd rather have been standing with his feet in a tub of ice water.

Another woman was regarding one of his larger paintings with such intensity she was squinting. Pulled by her concentration, he strolled over. It was another work he liked, and of which he almost felt protective. He wondered what the stranger saw.

As though answering his very thoughts, she spoke to him. "The eye is led from the rose leaves in the foreground to the red in the back of the garden, and finally to the subject's face. It's so cleanly done I can see the line of shadow from the cloud cutting right across his blue eyes."

She paused and squinted more fiercely. "It's only after you decide his expression is not quite as peaceful as it first seems that you notice his hand is gripping a wickedly thorned branch of the rose bush." The woman turned to Ewen and he saw her squint had more to do with the thickness of her glasses than an angry mood. She was not as nattily dressed as most of the visitors, and her hands were stained with pigment. "I look at this and want to . . . to befriend the man. Is that what you felt when you painted it? Is he one of your sister's patients?"

Ewen blinked. "I'm sorry, but have we met? I have a terrible memory for . . . "

"I'm Enid Buhl. I paint."

Now Ewen blushed and put his hands together behind his back, like a repentant child. "Yes ma'am. You certainly are. You certainly do. I'm sorry I didn't recognize you. How do you know about my sister?"

Buhl shrugged. "Recognize me? How could you recognize me? It's not like we have our photos on the backs of our canvases, eh? And I know of your sister because my husband is in her field. Small world and all that."

"But I've seen a couple of your self-portraits, and they were . . . "

"Without my glasses. I cheated. Love to do self-portraits—the model works cheap and never complains about the pose."

Ewen, who had started to lose his hard-won cool in meeting this very famous and influential artist, found he was beginning to smile for the first time all evening. It was probably a stupid smile. "I—uh— love your work, Ms. Buhl."

"Enid. I think yours is kinda cute too. Tell me about this one."

"This one" was a sketch of very economical lines: a watercolor of a nandina bush with a nuthatch hanging off a branch upside down. "That's from my Chinese-American period," he said promptly.

Enid Buhl sputtered in laughter. "Okay. Good one." Her eyes, enlarged by the thick bifocals, looked at him merrily. "I've been wondering. How did you get called 'Ewen'? That's more Chinese-Caledonian, I'd think."

Ewen ran a hand through his hair. "My parents' idea of a joke. My mother's name was Yuen, so they combined the families with 'Young Yuen.' So, Ewen Young."

"And you didn't hate them for it?"

He considered. "No. Not since I was fifteen or so. But then every teenager is embarrassed by his parents some time. I got off easy."

The great painter snagged a cheese stick off a passing server's tray. "Well, Ewen, I admire your skill with materials. And your vision. Of course, I don't see exactly what you see. It never works that way."

"You're right. I don't even know myself what I see," he blurted out, abashed.

Enid Buhl didn't laugh. She just shook her head and walked on. Ewen started to feel very good about the evening.

Glory, the gallery manager, was able to tell him there was strong interest in at least three of his paintings, and not the cheapest of them, either. The drawings were also popular, even though drawings generally didn't get a lot of interest from these shows. Ewen left her to the business, feeling he had done his job by showing up. Now, having actually met Enid Buhl and been told she liked his stuff, he thought it was the perfect time to leave. Grabbing his leather jacket from the rack, he went out the back entrance into the night.

It was drizzling and dark: a great relief. Ewen drank in the air, a wet fog rising from the warm asphalt; it was almost like the smell of earth. Somewhere close by star jasmine was scenting the wet breeze. He walked down the street in Redmond toward the parking lot where he had parked his Prius. Droplets of rain weighted his hair, causing it to sway with his steps.

He knew, as surely as he knew the sound of his own feet in the puddles, that he was being followed.

There were two of them, quiet-shoed, keeping the rhythm of his own wet feet. He sensed them to be sheepdogs, and felt that he himself was the sheep. He looked ahead for the shepherd.

There, in the next small parking lot, standing between the rows of cars, that shepherd stood. An Asian man—by his slight build and roundish features more likely Chinese than Japanese or Korean, dressed in a rather grandiose rayon sweat suit. He was standing with legs locked apart, hands in his pockets. He was a lot taller than Ewen, and his hair was badly styled. "You are Young," he said, as Ewen halted fifteen feet from him. The man spoke in English.

Ewen's ears were tuned to the padding steps behind him, which came steadily on. "Getting older every day," he said. A gust of wind blew rain into his face. "Tell the men behind me to stop where they are."

The man in front began to smile. He was very confident. "Why should I do that, Young Yuen? How can I give orders to these others, or why would I if I could?" The man had switched to Cantonese. Ewen's own Hong Kong dialect was rusty, but he understood. The two sheepdogs did slow down, perhaps twenty feet behind Ewen, triangulating with the man with the embarrassing lack of taste.

"Because I don't know why you have a problem with me. Are we enemies? If so, no one told me."

The man slouched forward. "Yes, we are enemies, Young, as surely as you are your father's brother's nephew. And his student."

Ewen made a disgusted gesture with both arms, and hung his head. "This is ridiculous. It's the year 2012 and I'm a painter, not Bruce Lee. I'm no threat to anyone!"

"Of course you're not a threat, little man. You're a message." He gestured to the two behind him. There was nothing for Ewen to do but run—straight at the man in front. The taller man jumped into side horse stance and raised a hard punch, but Ewen's diagonal move kept his own face just to the left; Ewen locked his hands around the fist he had just avoided. His momentum carried both him and the fist behind the attacker. With Ewen holding the arm behind the man in a neat half nelson, they both skidded across the pavement in a circular dance, until Ewen kicked one of the man's feet out from under him. He was holding the man up now, an awkward package between himself and the two others.

It was Ewen's intention to use him as a shield, but the man was heavy—one-legged and squirming—and the pavement was slippery. Ewen shouted, "Do you want to see me break his neck? Does he matter to you?"

One of the two shrugged broadly and tilted his head unconcernedly. The other looked from Ewen to his fellow, to the prisoner, who was cursing in two languages and struggling violently. Ewen jerked the trapped arm upward, turning the curses into a scream. The shriek nauseated him; at the same time he felt a tight, sharp thrill in the moment. He saw only the two thugs ahead of him. He felt only the arm being wrenched by his hands.

One of the two turned his back with exaggerated nonchalance and strolled across the shining asphalt to the street. The other—the one who had shrugged—continued to stare predatorily at Ewen, but kept his place. After an eternal few seconds, he too loped off.

"Let me go," said Ewen's prisoner, as though he held all the cards.

"Not a good idea, since you're supposed to be a messenger and I'm supposed to be a message."

The man tried to turn and look Ewen in the face. He stifled a scream and tried instead to stand higher, to relieve the pressure on his joints. Ewen kicked his leg out again and this time the scream was for real.

"Tell me what you want with my uncle."

There was a pause before the answer. "Ask him."

"What exactly were you planning to do to me here?"

The tall man snorted. "Mess you up a little. Like I said. A message. Just mess you up."

"Mess me up . . . permanently?" Asking the question made Ewen feel as if he were in a bad gangster movie.

"No. Of course not. Then how could you tell Jimmy Young? It's him we want."

"Why?"

The man looked down at the pavement and sighed. "Ask him. It's all between the Head and him."

"Head of what?"

"Ask Jimmy Young. You don't get anything else from me."

The excitement of the incident was fading, and Ewen felt he was getting nowhere. "Maybe the police can do better."

"Your word against mine, you stupid Yank."

"Maybe the police will like mine better, Mr. Hong Kong. Are you a responsible citizen? A citizen at all? Legal at all? I bet you aren't."

"You people should learn that sometimes betting isn't worth it. How're you going to get me to a cop? Use your cell phone? Ask me to stand here while you dial? Just let me go. My leg hurts. You know I can't chase you."

Using one hand Ewen patted the man down; it was a rough and inexact process, but he did find a knife. No gun. He was sick of the whole situation, and he released the man, immediately sending him flying with a double punch to the back. Mr. Hong Kong landed on the pavement with a wet sound on his belly.

Then Ewen did run.

Chapter Two

EWEN'S HOUSE was what Realtors like to call a "jewel box." It was small, with two stories and two bedrooms, and everything within was hand-done, including the old plaster. The artistic perfection was marred by the heavy-weight workout bag in the large entryway, the clutter of canvas tarps, and the smell of paint that dominated what had once been the dining room. He had lived in it alone for the past two years, since Karen and he had drifted apart. That was how he referred to it to himself . . . "drifted apart."

As soon as he closed the front door behind him, Ewen took out his phone and called his Uncle Jimmy. James Young was still up. Ewen described the assault at the parking lot and asked for an explanation.

When Uncle Jimmy was finished cursing in two languages, he mildly criticized Ewen's technique as haphazard and inconclusive, but admitted Ewen had survived these mistakes. He finally said he believed he knew what enemy school was responsible. He was no more forthcoming than that—typical for Uncle Jimmy. He said he would have a talk with someone, might get a restraining order, but even if he didn't there would be no more trouble. No reason for Ewen to go to the police. So often the police can't tell the difference between the bad guy and the good guy, and Ewen would then be under their eye. It wasn't good to be under their eye.

Ewen was not happy about Uncle's idea of "having a talk." He also knew restraining orders were useless. Uncle Jimmy told him not to worry. Go to bed. Ewen needed his sleep. Uncle Jimmy needed his sleep.

Before hitting the sack Ewen paced awhile, then went into the other bedroom, where there was no bed but only a small table, a round pillow with a mat under it. On the table was a small plastic Buddha of no particular lineage, and a small painting Ewen had done of his mother when he was twelve. He bowed to both. "I avoided a fight, Mom," he whispered. "You'd have been proud of me."

He crossed his legs and lowered himself onto the pillow, put his hands together at head level and bowed once more. "I take refuge in the Buddha," he murmured. "I take refuge in the teaching. I take refuge in my family, and I take refuge in the great family."

He sat until the events of the night—good and bad—fell into perspective, and then he went to bed.

Mrs. Lowiscu didn't understand why she had to get up early for her sittings, why there were so many of them and why a formal portrait couldn't all be taken care of in a few long sessions of painting. Ewen had explained it had to do with lighting, that he couldn't do it like a photographer with floods and reflectors, and that her children—who were paying the bill—had chosen the light by which they wanted their mother shown. Of course, by the time a family had become established enough, numerous enough, and wealthy enough to desire and afford a portrait of grandmother, grandmother herself was of an age to freely offer opinions. Mrs. Lowiscu thought Ewen should take a few damned photographs in his blessed light and paint from them. Ewen told her he did not work from dead flat images, but from life. Then, Mrs. Lowiscu said he'd best hurry it up because all this early rising and posing might be the death of her.

It didn't bother Ewen. He got along with old people and got up very early anyway. Nothing bothered him unless his subject couldn't sit still.

Mrs. Lowiscu sat as still as a sleeping snake. Ewen hoped that recurring image did not implant itself into his work. Her face itself was very rewarding to paint; the olives and roses of her original coloring had aged to purple and ash. Complicated. Challenging. She had chosen a mauve dress decades out of fashion, but one that had obviously meant something to her at some point in the past. Ewen shaded the color subtly into pink to make her cheeks livelier, but left her old dark eyes alone.

After Mrs. Lowiscu's session, he drove to his sister's workplace. It wasn't quite ten as he parked in its tiny lot. The front garden was filled with flowers and ferns. Pacific Rim Help House had really been a house years before. Built in a pseudo-Wright style, it was still a lovely building, though all the glass made it hard to heat.

The young woman at the antique Chinese desk glanced up from her computer screen. "Lynn," said Ewen. "I'm here for Lynn."

The receptionist responded at though she had never seen Ewen, (who came in at least twice a week asking for his sister). "Dr. Young is with a patient," she said. "Would you like to leave a message?"

"No, Caroline. I'm Ewen, Lynn's twin brother. I'm supposed to be here. Look at your schedule." He reached over the desk and pushed the little spiral binder toward Caroline. "See? Please tell her I'm here."

The receptionist, evidently alarmed by the invasion of her desk and territory, retreated on squeaking chair wheels. She made placatory gestures with both hands and, as a last line of defense, asked Ewen to be seated. Instead, he strode through the tiny, empty waiting room and through a door on which was painted a galloping horse and DR. LYNN YOUNG. (She was "Lynn Thurmond" to the PTA, but still "Young" to the professional world. As Lynn's twin brother, Ewen resented the "Thurmond" just a bit. Except as Teddy's mom, of course.)

Lynn's domain was filled with the smell and sound of running water. A section of the paneled wall had been replaced with rough sandstone. Water ran down it, collecting in a small pool with goldfish. Both the horse-door and the fountain wall were of Ewen's making, and he noticed kids had thrown pennies into the water again.

Lynn looked like her mother. Most people noticed this—if they had seen a picture of Lily Young—but as Mrs. Young had died twenty years before, the resemblance was usually remembered only by Ewen.

Lynn wasn't with a patient; she was at her desk with a tall cup of Starbuck's tilted against her lips. As she heard her brother open the door, she guiltily lowered the cup.

"Just what every psychiatrist needs," she said. "A good caffeine jag."

"If it works for you," he answered. "Your message didn't mention what you needed. Is it Jacob again?"

Although twins, the two did not really look that much alike, except in feature and expression. Lynn Young-Thurmond looked as though a breeze could blow her over; it would take a Category 3 hurricane to bring Ewen Young down. Some clown in middle school had titled them "The Smiling Anime Twins," and though they had changed, the nickname had stuck.

She nodded and dabbed off a latte mustache with a tissue, careful not to smear her lipstick. "He's biting himself again. He asked for you. Are you up for it? I mean—after last night?"

Ewen had been swinging himself into one of Lynn's armchairs, but stopped in place. "What do you know about last night? Do you mean the gallery?"

"No. Uncle Jimmy called me this morning. Told me to be careful. Which was big of him, don't you think? To tell me I ought to be careful because he's got himself into something nasty? That man!"

Once again Ewen was placed between Uncle Jimmy—his teacher—and the rest of his family. "Oh, I don't know, sis. It takes two to make a fight, but only one to make a massacre."

"But you're not hurt, right? I would have known if you were hurt. I'd have woken up."

"I'm not hurt. He scraped a strip off the side of my new Nikes, that's all. Nothing more. But I'm here for Jacob, so let's see Jacob."

Lynn and her brother entered the special room that contained nothing with which a person could hurt himself, unless by paper cut. Jacob Fischbein sat with his feet up on a cushioned chair, his elbows resting on his knees, hiding in his own darkness. Defending himself with his own darkness. He looked up at them warily.

Jacob did not look like the sort of boy who would be biting himself. He looked very normal, healthy, even athletic. This last was true; Jacob was a wrestler at Redmond High, and it was on the mat where he'd stopped being able to hide his unhappiness from the public world.

Jason began speaking in his usual way. "Hi, there Doc. Hi, Doc's Brother. Spare me some change? Mind change? Change of venue?"

Ewen said nothing, but looked around the room for a cushion. He found two, both in a floral pattern, and looking like fat Hawaiian shirts. He dropped them in the center of the room and sat down on one, legs crossed. The remaining pillow lay on the floor in front of him. Ewen did not smile at the boy. He was tired and he knew this was going to be work, but he gave him a comradely glance. He dropped his hands loosely into his lap and took one deep breath. "Okay. Let's get down, Jacob." He closed his eyes.

He heard the rasping of the boy's Levi's. There was a small noise as Jacob's baseball cap sailed across the room and hit a chair. The trick with the cap was a sign of respect, respect in Jacob-language. Ewen did start to smile. He reached out, not with his hand, but his mind. For the first moment of the touch, Ewen was a bit afraid—afraid of Jacob's fears and of Jacob himself. Afraid of the effort involved in opening. Then he just did it. He *opened*.

A small space of damp grass, surrounded by trees. Some of the trees were maple and some were evergreens. To the left was a low wall of stone, limestone, which he could slightly taste. Beyond that was the smell of water. This was a place Ewen had found a long time ago. He scarcely remembered when. He did not know what it meant or how it was that he could get there, but he was now the keeper of it. He felt the bounds, he marked them and fortified them, and now he allowed the mind of Jacob—a bad storm, a bruising wave, a maddened dog, a troubled child—to enter.

Ewen let him in and closed the gate behind him. He defended the borders of this small place that was no place at all. That was Ewen's whole job here. Keeping the borders.

The Jacob-storm entered, hit, and howled against the immaterial walls, but even the branches of the trees weren't bent by it. The wave of Jacob's misery struck against nothing and it vanished. The biting dog—the biting, the always-at-the-edges, fear-filled biting—found nothing to bite. Ewen held within his mind this small, open place where only the boy sat, sat gripping the grass in his fingers, sitting tight as a drum. Ewen himself did not enter with Jacob. This was Jacob's refuge. In a sense, Ewen *was* the place and, in another sense, he wasn't part of this event at all. Ewen's place-making was a huge, simple concentration, just at the limit of what he was able to do, but Ewen sat on the pillow, unmoving, and he kept the boundaries.

Lynn was shaking his shoulder, gently. He felt himself flinch.

"How are you?"

Ewen opened his eyes and squinted at the light. There was Jacob on the carpet in front of him, his head on the other Hawaiian pillow, sleeping like a baby. "I'm tired," said Ewen. "I am really tired today."

The tiredness went away after five minutes pounding on the heavy bag at home. Ewen was now angry, as he had not had time to be the night before. Angry at the Hong Kong idiot with the bad sense of drama and the bad taste in sweatsuits. Angry at the sheepdogs behind him. And, yes, really angry with Uncle Jimmy. No way around that. Now that there was no one in the family present to defend him against, Ewen was thinking Uncle Jimmy was every kind of horse's ass.

He remembered the matches, one after another through his childhood, in which he had been given no choice but to compete. No choice but to win. The classes for which Sifu James Young had never showed up, and for which the responsibility had devolved upon Ewen—who had to show up because Sifu James Young might well not. Always working without pay, because he was family. Well, of course *he* never had had to pay for his training, either. He hadn't *had* to keep going. Mom hadn't been enthusiastic about the whole martial arts thing at all. His real talent, his art, had come from her. Dad would have backed him on dropping out, even though Jimmy was his brother. Especially because . . .

Lynn never felt obliged to follow kung fu. She had been more the ballet type, the pony club type.

Ewen had done it all to himself, to be honest about it. He was still doing it *to* himself. Who was he fooling? He did it because he was good and he knew it, and because . . . because it was grand.

He worked out for forty-five minutes and then once again he was tired, but not in the same sense. He took a shower and went out to putter around in the garden.

Ewen's kung fu curse was Uncle Jimmy, but his garden curse was bamboo. He didn't dislike bamboo in and of itself, but for what it had done during his four years living in the small suburban house. Ewen's grandfather had liked bamboo very much, and had planted different types in both the back garden and front. It had flourished. God, how it had flourished, and so had a feud with Mr. and Mrs. Kelly on one side of the property, who had no love for bamboo at all.

For years, Mr. Kelly had run down errant shoots of bamboo with his lawn mower and Mrs. Kelly had dug up the monstrosities coming up in her annual border. They had blamed the infestation on old Mr. Young, who held the opinion that the Kellys were fortunate to have such graceful volunteers for their very ordinary back yard.

When resentment grew to fury and the county was called, Grandfather had a service come and dig out his lovely bamboo, and he felt he had done more than his duty toward neighborhood peace. The next year his bamboo came back from its severe pruning livelier and more invasive than ever, and the Kellys' resentment grew as well.

When Ewen inherited the house, he had no idea of the battle he was entering. Even though he was not responsible for planting the damned bamboo, the Kellys despised him for it. Despised him and all his doings and let him know it. The Kellys' German shepherd had him marked for destruction.

Ewen had read up on bamboo, gone out to the edge of his property, and dug a ditch three feet wide and five feet deep. In doing this, he used nothing more complicated than a shovel. The ditch took him almost the entire first year of his residency; it strained his relationship with his roommate Karen, and did not improve the looks of the property—which, until it was refilled, had probably not endeared him to the rest of the neighborhood. When the ditch was done he went to Home Depot and bought rolls of long aluminum plating, and lowered them into the ditch, riveting them together as he went, so there was a metal wall five feet deep separating the Young property from that of family Kelly. It should have been enough.

Bamboo, however, does not always send its runners in straight lines, and some had spread to the yard of Mrs. Blick, whose property was behind both the Young and Kelly yards. Mrs. Blick did not pay too much attention to her own back yard, so now the Kellys were also angry with Mrs. Blick and twice as furious with Ewen.

These days Ewen would wait for the Kellys to be out, on the rare occasions they took their dog with them, and he would vault the five-foot fence in between the back yards and yank out any sprouts of bamboo he saw, hoping to eliminate the problem before they noticed it.

This afternoon Ewen was in his front yard, weeding around his little water garden. The shubunkins followed him from side to side, poppling the surface of the water with their hungry little mouths and hoping. Ewen didn't notice them. He wanted to call the police about the attack in the parking lot. The Chinese school vendetta seemed to him a custom more fitting for an alien planet than for the Puget Sound. Maybe those guys the night before *had* been space aliens. He also hoped Uncle Jimmy, like Grandfather, hadn't degenerated to feuding. Uncle was, with all his faults, a good person, and had been Ewen's teacher since Ewen was five years old. But Uncle Jimmy was also undoubtedly getting crotchety, and being at odds with the rest of the Young family did not improve his attitude.

Ewen believed the family trouble had started because Granddad hadn't approved of his oldest son becoming a martial arts teacher. His father had told him as much. Not that his grandfather hadn't approved of the discipline itself—he hadn't faulted Ewen for taking lessons, and was even proud of the boy when he had won his little boyhood awards—it was just that it wasn't the proper way to make a living. It had no future, unless one was intensely practical and with good business sense, which ruled out Uncle Jimmy. Better he should have been a lawyer or a dentist. Ewen, unlike Granddad, knew that being too impractical to run a profitable martial arts studio—his kwoon—meant Uncle Jimmy would have been hopeless as a lawyer. Or a dentist. In Ewen's own semi-practical mind, he was grateful for Uncle's outlaw status; in comparison, it made a grandson foolish enough to be an artist seem like a paragon.

And his outlaw uncle was going to "handle" the situation . . . How? A duel to the death on a Seattle rooftop? Hiring a hit man?

Oh God! Ewen sat back on his heels. He whispered, "I take refuge in the Buddha. I take refuge in the dharma. I take—"

Rinngg!

"—a phone call. I take a phone call."

Ewen sprang to his feet, running for the door, because he knew it was his sister, Lynn, and he knew there was more trouble.

Lynn's voice was brimming with maternal fear. Her son Teddy had been threatened by a strange man during recess. "He called to Teddy over the schoolyard fence and he said . . . he said he should buy white clothes, because his family was going to go into mourning."

"He said Teddy's family was going into mourning?"

"Yes, Ewen. Teddy's sure that's what the man said! I called Uncle but there was no answer. I had to leave a message!"

Ewen's stomach turned over. He dialed Uncle Jimmy himself. No answer except the voicemail. He got into his Prius and drove to Lynn's.

He reached his sister's house, parked, and darted under the three-color, Tibetan-style gate lintel and to the house. He frequently referred to his sister's family as his "Sino-Tibetan relations," a reference to Theodore Thurmond's strong Tibetan Buddhist beliefs, though Theo was a six-foot tall balding blond of German ancestry.

Theo was out on the porch, face strained, his long blond hair escaping its ponytail and hanging around his face. "We can't get hold of your uncle," he said. "The police are on their way."

Ewen swept by him and banged open the screen door. Lynn sat on the living room couch hugging six-year-old Teddy, who was two-thirds the size of his mother. They both looked lost. "I'm so sorry," said Ewen, kneeling down by the couch and trying to fit them both into one large hug.

"As though it's your fault," said Lynn reprovingly, with a little snort. She frequently acted as though she were much older and more experienced than her twin brother. Ewen had always felt this was a result of her medical training.

Ewen began to pace, from the television at one end of the room to the altar at the other. "I should have called the police at once. Not just Uncle Jimmy. I should have known better."

"Who would have thought?"

Teddy lifted his head from his mother's embrace. "Is this like in the movies? Where one Chinese guy tries to kill another because of kung fu?"

Lynn patted her son and said absently "No, dear. They have things like the Pride Fighting Championships for that now."

Hearing that simple statement, Ewen stopped in his tracks. Perhaps Lynn really was older and wiser than he was. "You're right. The idea makes no sense. Uncle Jimmy doesn't even have much of a school! That can't be what it's about."

"It's about his gambling, of course," said Lynn with a shrug. "Uncle Jimmy must have been having another losing streak."

"Oh." The idea hit Ewen like a brick and he simply stood still for a while. "And that's what the guy meant about me being a message?" he finally said. "About some people betting on the wrong things?" He hit his head with the back of his hands. "Yeah, I bet you're right, Lynn. And it would have been no good to break the old man's back—then he could never pay. But a nephew. Or a niece . . . "

"Or a grandnephew." Lynn silently mouthed the words over Teddy's head.

Ewen shook his head vehemently, then said aloud, "I don't think the guy meant anyone was going to hurt Teddy. If he has wanted to harm him, then—" Ewen broke off and lowered himself into the antique chair opposite the couch, the one Theo could not use because it put his knees to his chin. "Hey, why aren't the police here yet?"

"They are coming. This isn't exactly an emergency by their definition."

Teddy, whose attention span was shorter, even for potential violence, wandered over to his newest Star Wars picture book.

"This gambling thing. Uncle gambles a lot, doesn't he? I never heard about it, exactly, but . . . "

Lynn gave him a long-suffering look. "Ewen! Uncle Jimmy gambles endlessly, and on anything, from mahjong, to the ponies, to when a fly on the window buzzes away! Why do you think he's always in debt? Why he can't afford a decent studio for teaching, or some equipment made after World War Two?"

"It's because he doesn't charge much," said Ewen reflexively. "And he's not a business—" He stopped himself. He was done defending his uncle. "How come I never heard about how much he gambles? I'm the one closest to him out of all of us."

"That's why, stupid. Dad doesn't want to break your faith in your dear Uncle Jimmy, who gave you so much of his time and attention. And . . . well, he *was* good to you. And you were so good at it. So Dad told you the reason Jimmy was stiffed in the will and you got the house was because Granddad didn't approve of his career. As if! He didn't want to give a house to a man who would immediately lose it in a poker game."

Ewen's mind was racing and going nowhere. He was out of his chair and pacing again, and then heading for the door. "I'll be back," he said. His sister bounced to her feet and followed, taking him by the arm. "Ewen, the police will want to talk to you."

Gently, he freed himself. "Yeah, when they get around to showing up. Meanwhile, I'm going to find Uncle."

Theo was still watching on the porch. Ewen sprang past him and down the porch steps without touching them. Behind him he heard Lynn's voice, louder this time. "Ewen, stop and take a breath. A deep breath."

"I'll take several," he said, but he kept running.

Uncle Jimmy's neighbor, Madge, told him she didn't know for sure where Jimmy was but probably he was out at The Garage. The neighbors still called the place "The Garage," which was what it had been before he had rebuilt it into his kwoon. It still looked more like a garage than a school.

Ewen took out his cell phone and tried his uncle at his work number, getting only the answering machine. He got back into his car and drove the short block to the studio. The single, rolling garage door was locked down, but the small doorway to its side was cracked open. There was light within. Good. Uncle was there after all. Just ignoring the phone.

Ewen wanted to discuss some things with his uncle. He was perhaps becoming too angry—angry with his whole family for keeping him in the dark, for treating him with kid gloves because he was a "sensitive artist." But he was especially angry at Uncle Jimmy, for making all this deception possible, for maybe endangering little Teddy. He wanted to burst the door open and shout for his uncle, but his long years of training had taught him discretion in the practice hall. He quietly opened the door and walked in.

There was the mirror on the wall, the wing chung-style dummy, the heavy bag, the speed bag, the row of striking pads for the adult students and the tiny set for the children who made up so much of Jimmy Young's clientele. There was the red training mat on the floor for throwing and falling, and there on the mat there was Uncle Jimmy.

Ewen's uncle seemed to have just accomplished a break fall: one arm flung out, one leg bent up. It took a moment for Ewen to make sense of what he was seeing, and as he did, his nose registered the smell of something burnt. "Uncle," he cried out, and ran to the splayed form on the mat, where red had blended with red.

He knelt on the mat and lifted Uncle Jimmy's head. There was a small neat hole above one ear and another, not as small or neat, below the other. There was a dark, wet spot on the front of his green polo shirt. Jimmy Young's eyes were open and drying.

"No!" shouted Ewen, holding the head as though it were something very delicate: something he could hurt or help by the holding. "No!"

The mirror was in front of him. He saw himself in it, holding Jimmy's body. His own head, tilted up like that of a keening dog, looked entirely foreign to him. For a moment he saw the angle only as a painter sees things, a shape removed from personal meaning. He also saw something else—the image of a tall, burly, black-haired man he remembered bringing down on the asphalt not twenty-four hours before. Mr. Hong Kong. Mr. Hong Kong was holding a gun. His nose was bloody. Ewen knew he hadn't hit that nose the previous night. He turned just in time to see the man's eyes narrow over the short sights of the revolver, in time to hear a crack like close lightning, and to feel a blow to his body that knocked him over the corpse of his uncle.

He was walking through a huge hall, or something much like a hall, and there was a light before him, a bright light. It did not seem to be a particularly friendly sort of light—not a very human light—but somehow he knew it. The glow of the light roused Ewen's curiosity, and he wondered how he could express that light on paper. On each side of the light smaller lights were hovering, and in them he saw familiar and comforting things—houses and flowers and people talking. They flickered with smoke like that of a hearth-fire. He had no doubt how to paint these. He stood among them all—the single unwavering illumination and the pockets of comfort—and he tried to decide which was more worth investigating, when a voice filled the place.

It was a familiar voice. He remembered he liked the voice, though he remembered little else, and he tried to make out what the voice was saying. This took some time, during which the soft smoky fireplace lights grew more and more attractive. He felt he was a bit tired and would like to sit down by one of those fireplaces. Then he made out some words.

"Ewen Young, child of a noble house," it said. "Child of the Way. The time has come for you to seek a path. At the ending of your breath, the radiance of the in-between has become visible. This is the essence of reality, the luminous void, the undefiled mind, centerless and abounding. Recognize this, for it is your true state, and rest in it."

"I will instruct you further."

The voice was Theo's, of course, "Tibetan" Theodore. This was his version of the introduction to the bardo—the transitional state of existence between two lives on earth. It was Theo's own translation, and he was proud of it, so Ewen had heard it more than once before. More times than necessary, in his opinion. He had always thought it very wordy.

Ewen looked at the luminescence, the smoky lights, and the featureless space through which he was walking. He turned around and suddenly the whole situation seemed very funny to him. He felt an urge to laugh, but politely restrained himself. He spoke up. "No thanks, Theo. I don't believe I'll be going this time. But thank you for your good advice. I appreciate it." Then he did laugh, and the great, bright open space broke up with that noise.

Ewen woke to great pain in his chest, the smell of disinfectant, and a number of faces gathered around. There was his sister and there was Theo. There also was Dad, who lived all the way down in Santa Barbara. For a moment he wondered where Mom was, but then he remembered she had been dead twenty years.

As he should be, if he remembered correctly. He thought about this, and wondered how long he had been unconscious. He looked around and met the eyes of his sister.

"Oh, Ewen," Lynn cried. "I knew you'd come back." She touched him.

"Ouch," said Ewen. He passed out again.

Chapter Three

THAT DAY, Ewen Young entered the world of morphine. He found it a very rewarding one, although nasty pain got in the way. The sun shone into the hospital room window in the most beautiful fashion—much more easily paintable than the great illumination he had just left—and the plastic bedside water jar was an entrancing shade of red. So was the nurse's lipstick. He told her red was a wonderful color, and she smiled in a knowing fashion.

"That's the dope," she said. "Does great stuff with colors. Don't get to like it too much."

Then there was sleep again, and the pinch of the IV line as he tried to turn in the bed. After more sleep, a man in a suit was standing next to the bed, clearing his throat. Ewen attempted to speak to him, and the attempt really hurt.

"I'm Detective Petersen of the sheriff's office," the man said. "I'm sure you are in pain, Mr. Young, but you really should thank your lucky stars you're here to hurt. They almost lost you. Used the paddles twice, or so I'm told. You've even got burn marks on your chest."

Ewen gazed at the man and in a thread of a voice asked for more morphine. The man, who was tall, dark, and angular-featured, smiled as the nurse had smiled and then he nodded. He pressed the button that called a nurse.

Ewen closed his eyes and soon the nurse was injecting something into the IV line and left. He hoped this would erase the pain, but it did nothing right away.

"Mr. Young, I'd like to ask you a few questions, and it will have to be now because in a few minutes you'll be out again. Okay?"

Ewen found he could move his neck easier than he could inflate his lungs, so he nodded and mouthed, "First tell me what happened."

Detective Petersen gave him a brooding frown. "You don't know what happened? You don't remember anything?"

Again, Ewen mouthed words and hoped the man was good at lip-reading. "I know I was shot. In the chest. I can't breathe much."

"You were shot with a .38, which nicked your heart wall—or membrane, or whatever they call it. In fact, you can say you were actually shot in the heart. That's a story few people have to tell. You bled half out, went into shock. Your sister and brother-in-law found you. Your heart stopped in the ambulance, and then again on the operating table. Both times they could start it again. You must have quite a heart, Mr. Young."

Ewen tried to smile but wasn't sure it had worked. His gift of stupid humor rose unbidden and he found he was whispering "I try to be nice to people." He had actually made some sound. The morphine was making itself known.

"Did you see who shot you?"

"Oh, yes."

Detective Petersen lifted his hands to heaven and his brooding face went light for a moment. Then his manner returned to somber. "I'm sorry, but do you know that your uncle was shot, too?"

"Yes. I found him. He was already dead. Just newly dead. I think the same man did it." Now Ewen had a ghost of his real voice back.

"We can pretty well guess the same gun did it, so odds are good. What can you tell me about this man? Was he white, or . . . or Asian, or . . . "

"He was Chinese. Not American-born. Not from the north. Hong Kong. He was tall: not as tall as you. Big-boned, stocky. He has two bruises on his back and a sore right arm. Also a bloody nose." Ewen's enthusiasm for description outran his breathing capacity and he lay gasping.

The detective stared open-mouthed. "Who the hell are you, Mr. Young? Sherlock Holmes? A psychic? Johnny Smith?"

"No. I just met the guy the night before. He and two other men tried to assault me on the street."

"Tried?"

Ewen didn't have the energy to tell him the whole story. "I ran away," he said, and in his present state, it seemed a marvelously clear and clever thing to say, and not entirely a lie.

Detective Petersen looked at him long and hard, and Ewen could see he was no man's fool. "And you called the police?"

Ewen shook his head and tried to look properly remorseful. "I thought of it, but what could the police have done? I had never met any of the guys before."

"The police might have shown you a layout—mug shots, I mean. But probably, to be fair to you, they wouldn't have. Not if you weren't hurt. But the layout'll happen now; just you wait."

"I will wait right here," said Ewen, and closed his eyes.

This waking, seeing faces and falling asleep again was getting old.

Once it had been his sister; she told him she had known immediately when he was shot, and called 911 from her house. Ewen had no doubts about her knowing; when Lynn was in labor with Teddy he knew because he was sitting in the back office of the kwoon doubled over with cramps. It wasn't supposed to be like this with fraternal twins, but it was with Lynn and Ewen. She was trying to hug him without actually touching him at all when he fell asleep again.

Then came his father. The elder Dr. Young looked more angry than worried, but that was just Dad; he was who he was. And, as a cardiologist, he knew more about Ewen's injury and surgery than Ewen knew or wanted to know. They didn't speak much.

It was night when he woke again, this time needing an attendant's help to turn to use the urinal without dislodging the IV. He tried not to ask for the morphine because he wanted out of this particular fading and shifting reality, but his resolve didn't last very long. His heart hurt.

He called up from his mind a vision of Kuan Yin, the bodhisattva of compassion: she of the great heart. In his mind, as always, her face shifted to that of his mother's. That helped, but after less than half an hour he rang the bell and asked for morphine again. They were willing to give it to him.

In a dream he returned to the place he had been so recently, the luminous place. Theo was telling him all about it—telling him he was the child of a noble family and not to be afraid of the light and he, in turn, wanted to tell Theo that he *wasn't* afraid of it, just not ready to dive in yet. Then he was touring the dream place, where occasional dead people drifted off to the sort of light that most attracted them, and which determined their next birth. He was wondering how to portray what he was seeing in oils without using the old Tibetan style (which never much appealed to him), when he became aware of noise in the hospital room. There was a nurse's aide clutching his bedrails, her eyes very wide, asking, "Mr. Young? Ewen! Why did you tear that IV out of your arm? And where did you leave your bandages?"

Ewen stared at her, uncomprehending and bothered. The shade of the dream was still with him. "I didn't leave them anywhere. I didn't *go* anywhere. I went to sleep," said Ewen, irritated. She stalked off, threatening to tie his hands to the bed rails. Ewen slept again.

In the morning they gave him an ice cube for breakfast, which was just fine with Ewen. He was not hungry. A different aide took his temperature and blood pressure, and this one seemed very pleased by the results. Ewen basked in the pleasure of having passed a test without having studied for it. As he became able to think a bit, he remembered Uncle Jimmy was dead, and began to be sad, not only for the loss of his teacher but also for the belated loss of his own innocence. That he, of all the family, should have not known of Uncle's problem! Problem, hell, fatal flaw. If someone had let him know Uncle Jimmy was a compulsive gambler, perhaps he could have had some influence, could have prevented matters coming to this. Or more likely, he reflected, he could not have. Perhaps saying he hadn't known was just denial. There had been all that avuncular teasing—"I bet you fifty cents you can't kick the tennis ball before it hits the ground." Or, "You better win this match because I'm betting on you!" Could Uncle Jimmy have really been betting on Ewen's little kid tournaments? How bizarre. Good thing he had done well—*usually* had done well. If he had known he was the object of money, he would surely have blown every little match.

As he was thinking on this, the detective from the day before came in, this time with a shorter, blond fellow. Each of them was toting what looked like a big photo album.

"These," said Petersen, "are layouts. I'm going to lay them by you on your bed. No, don't raise your head; we need you alive for this."

The blond man shot his partner a reproachful glance. "Don't worry, Mr. Young. I'm sure you're entirely out of danger."

Ewen almost laughed. "Sure. Unless the same guy sneaks into the room and shoots me again. Like on TV."

"Not likely," said Petersen, deadpan. "We have better scriptwriters." He opened a book and held it above Ewen's head. "These are men who match your description and have sheets in the Seattle area. Asian men."

"Tall Chinese man is what we're looking for," Ewen corrected the detective, who in turn looked skeptical of the very concept.

"This might take a while," said the other detective.

It took approximately three minutes. "That's him," said Ewen, lifting his unencumbered arm to point. "In fact, it looks more like him than most photos look like their subjects. I'd have to say that's a great likeness."

"Hah. Spoken by one who knows about painting likenesses," said the tall detective, surprising Ewen considerably. Then it occurred to him that detectives do research.

"So, who is he?"

Detective Petersen winked. "Tell you later," he said, gathering up his albums. Both detectives seemed very pleased. On the way out the blond turned and said, "God bless you and keep you, Mr. Young."

"Thank you," answered Ewen. "And—uh—you too!"

That was a very stupid thing to say to the guy, thought Ewen, once he was alone again. He felt embarrassed. But the cops on television never said, "God bless you and keep you."

Ewen did a small fraction of his usual morning meditation, which was difficult while being on drugs and flat on his back. He kept thinking what a stupid response that had been to the blond detective: "And you too!" He kept thinking of how he hadn't known or tried to help Uncle Jimmy. He was occasionally visited by images of Kuan Yin. Or was it his mother? His heart hurt.

Chapter Four

DESPITE THE AIR CONDITIONING in the station, Detective Rick Petersen had the window by his desk wide open. His partner, Gideon Ryde, who had no window, had rolled his chair over, and was typing on a laptop. The day was so rare, so beautiful, that both men occasionally stopped and stared out at the sun, mesmerized.

Gideon Ryde spoke. "Hey. D'ya think we'll get him, Rikki-Tikki-Tavi? The shooter?"

"Don't call me that, unless you want to get called 'Giddy Ryde' again. And yes, I think we've got Chow."

"It's just Young's word. And things can get complicated when it's among the Chinese."

Petersen snorted. "Ewen Young is about as Chinese as I am Indian."

"Okay, so you don't wear braids and his ancestors came to America before most of mine did."

"Yeah."

"Yeah, but still," said Ryde, "it can get complicated."

Mr. George Blundell was not having a beautiful day. He was, in general, a worrying man and not one for appreciating beautiful days. He did, however, take a certain pleasure in the attitude of the employee standing before him. Chow was sick with fear.

"Young Yuen is alive, yes," said Chow. "If being hooked up to things that breathe for him is alive. He is just parts, now. No problem."

"Just what? Parts? Parts of what, may I ask?" Blundell rolled his soft desk chair around behind the desk, as a standing man might pace, or a tiger stalk. Blundell chose to wheel.

John Chow knew his English did not confuse Blundell. His English was better than Blundell's, because he did not have the mumbling American accent. He knew he was being mocked, and there was nothing he could do about it.

What he did not know was that his boss thought Chow's "English" accent was phony and stuck-up. As though he thought he could convince people he was a Brit, and not Chinese at all. These two men could, merely by speaking the same language, offend each other all day long.

"Parts for other people, Mr. Blundell. He is dead for all he means to us."

"So is Jimmy Young, Chow. Dead as a doornail. Where does my forty thousand dollars come from now? Do we ask his brother the cardiologist to pay us back? Perhaps we just pass the hat. You are familiar with the expression 'pass the hat'?"

Chow was not, but his fear of his boss was giving way to anger. "You know why I killed old Young! He was ready to talk. And the nephew, too . . . He could have recognized me. Now there is no one who can identify me."

"Goody for you," said Blundell, lacing his hands over the paunch that concealed his abdominal muscles.

"Goody for you, too," answered Chow, and he left the room, almost, but not quite, slamming the door behind him.

Blundell watched him go, and for him the day was still not beautiful.

Ewen was sitting up, and the effort this took made him crabby. He tried not to show his crabbiness to his visitors, who were telling him what a lucky man he was to be alive. He personally thought he might have been a luckier man not to have been shot at all. He was also depressed at the thought of the long recovery time awaiting him, and how weak and flabby he would surely become before it was all over. He had never even broken a bone before, and couldn't recall a time when he had been weak and flabby. He hadn't known how ego-involved he had been with his body. Well, he was. So there. And, on top of everything else, he had missed Uncle Jimmy's funeral,

Perhaps that wasn't such a bad thing, really.

None of these things needed to be said to his sister. Lynn could read the set of his eyebrows easier than another might read a book. With Theo, who was there too, Ewen had to be more careful to conceal his mood: especially since Theo had done his best to lead

Ewen through the bardo, and Ewen had been rude enough to refuse and turn back.

"You know what the doctor told us this morning, bro?" asked Lynn, and then answered herself immediately. "He said that you have the blood of four different people in you. Five, including yours."

Suddenly Ewen felt himself plural—more than plural—his blood vessels carrying a throng of genetic messages like the messages carried on old-fashioned telephone lines. Sometimes—in those pre-cellular days—one could hear other people's phone conversations, like wind, behind one's own talk. Back when they were children they had occasionally entertained themselves with this flaw in the phone lines. Now Ewen himself had become an old-fashioned party line. This struck him as being more interesting thought material than the constant refrain of his luck.

"I wish I knew who they were," he said, in his thready voice. "I wish I could . . . "

"Thank them?" ventured Theo. "Of course you do. But when they gave blood they already knew . . . "

Ewen interrupted him crossly. "No. I want to know them for my own sake. To know what—I mean who—I'm made of."

"That you never will," said Lynn, peacefully. "Or maybe, those foreign parts of you are all you ever *will* know about yourself, according to Zen. But realistically, I don't think we can find out for you. Unless there is a legal or health issue resulting from donated blood, there are big privacy restrictions."

Ewen wasn't satisfied. Privacy restrictions concerning his inner self? Why did he meditate if not to confront such restrictions?

After a few more minutes, Lynn and Theo left, but he thought about his immigrant blood for another hour.

That night Ewen found it hard to sleep; every position was equally uncomfortable. When he did sleep, he dreamed immediately and clearly.

He was in a small apartment with a glass-door opening to the balcony. On the walls of the apartment were pictures of a small dark child: studio shots, collages, snaps tacked to the wall.) On the floor were scattered the toys of a toddler, including a red-wheeled pull toy of a wooden caterpillar, complete with bouncy antennae. The door to the deck showed red geraniums in pots on the rail, and a small bamboo in a pot in the corner. Some vague feeling of responsibility for the bamboo led Ewen to unlock and open the glass door, and once he was out on the balcony he began to be worried that the geraniums on the rail might fall, because the apartment was quite high up.

A passerby could be killed if one of the pots fell and struck him on the head. Ewen moved to put one of the plastic pots on the floor of the balcony, but could not move it. He had some difficulty making contact with his hands. A second glance showed him the container was firmly attached to the rail by a bolt with a thumbscrew. He walked back into the living room, and there was a woman standing in the hall leading to the living room, her robe clutched tightly to her chest with one hand. She was a dark-skinned Asian woman, or perhaps half Asian and half black. Not someone he knew. Suddenly the wrongness of his being there struck him. He lifted both hands into the air in a sign of surrender. "I'm sorry. I didn't mean to intrude. I'm dreaming . . . I won't hurt you."

The young woman flattened herself between Ewen and the door to the other room. She hissed, "Who are you! Who *are* you! How did you get here?"

"I'm Ewen Young," he said, with the cold calm of dreams, but now doubting this *was* a dream. "I don't know how I got here. I should be in the hospital." She threw a framed photograph of the child at him, but it made no impact.

The apartment and the woman went away. Ewen awoke, crying out, his heart beating like thunder. The nurse's aide rushed in and after a brief check berated him once again. Not understanding why, Ewen looked down at his left forearm, where the IV had been tethered. There was nothing there, and no sign the needle had been torn out. The IV tube lay in a coil on the mattress next to him, in a small damp spot, which was not bloody in the slightest.

"If you have to *go* so bad, you just let me know! Even if you don't want anybody to watch you, I can put the jug in your hand and leave the room. And if it's . . . something else, well we can work that out. You're hurting yourself this way!"

Ewen caught his breath. "I'm sorry, ma'am. It isn't that. I don't think it's that. I had a nightmare."

"A nightmare in which you tore out your IV line?"

Ewen showed his left forearm. "It doesn't look like I tore it out, does it?"

She examined his arm, and then the end of the IV line, lying in its bed of limp tape and damp sheet. "Well, you're not bleeding, at any rate. But if you don't stop this, they *will* tie you up."

Ewen sank back onto the bed: very, very tired. "No, they won't," he said, and mumbling to himself he added, "I don't think they'll be able to."

She snorted. "So that's the word of the great kung fu master: they won't be able to. You'd be surprised." She left the room before Ewen could explain that that wasn't what he had meant.

He wasn't sure what he *had* meant.

The next morning there was a lot more pain. Ewen, abashed, asked for more morphine but was told *that* was over. They gave him pills. They also took out the IV line and allowed him to put on a robe so he could start to get out of the bed. It seemed strange and unfair that only a few days after he had been shot in the heart (or in the wall of the heart, which must be close to the same thing), they were now asking him to sit up and put his feet off the side of the bed, telling him that soon he would be standing by himself.

And soon he would be going home, they said. This made him feel trivial as well as in pain. When his sister came in, he was in another bad mood, which, of course, she already knew.

"I brought you something," she said. "Something to play with." She was wheeling the something behind her in a big blue suitcase.

"It's a game, Ewen, a computer game. I use it with a lot of my patients." Without waiting for a response she positioned his over-bed table with one hand, while unzipping the bag with the other. "It's fun. It works on biofeedback."

"I'm trying to avoid all feedback from this bio at the moment," he grumbled, trying to maintain his attitude of grumpiness in front of his twin. It was not possible. She placed a small plasma screen in front of him and began plugging things in to several metal boxes she had laid out on the floor.

"It'll be fun; believe me." When he still looked unconvinced, Lynn put on a look of mock severity.

"You're not allowed to mope around any more, Ewen, because you have been officially declared a delog by Theo's Tibetan advisors. You've got to act impressive."

"A 'delog'? God! What's that? Uh—it isn't some kind of god, is it? Or anything like that? With blue skin and lots of eyes and . . . and maybe flies out of its body at night . . . ? Please tell me it isn't."

"Not a god. Not even a tulku. A delog is just one who has returned from the dead. Without being reincarnated, I mean. And it's always for a reason."

He looked at his sister uncertainly. "And *you* believe that, Lynn?"

"Well . . . it's certainly true that you were technically dead, and you aren't now. And of course I believe there's always a reason. For everything. It's just that it's usually too complicated a reason to understand. Sooo . . . " Through her obvious weariness, her grin was still shaded with mischief. "'*My Brother the Delog.*' Like the title of a TV show."

"Fine. From now on I'll sign my paintings 'Ewen D. Young.' They'll call it my 'Post-revolver Period.'"

Once Lynn had set up the equipment and given him instructions, he found the game *was* putting him in a better mood, despite all his crabby intentions.

It was very different from what he knew of computer games. He could work his skin's galvanic response and heart rate variability and a few other buzzwords from his sister's world to find his way through fantastic animated streets, and considered his performance level praiseworthy. He wondered if this had anything to do with his new ability to exit the hospital bed in the middle of the night. He wondered if he dared share this experience with Lynn. If there was anyone on Earth he could talk to, it was his sister.

But no. She was a shrink, after all, and now she was saying she was sure he could have done better in the biofeedback if his body was not fuddled with drugs. Definitely no.

Ewen continued on, opening magical doors on the screen and freeing an animated falcon from a cage. He was still trying to shoot a computer-generated bow at a target without hitting one of the

CGI yaks roaming the hillside, when they brought him red Jell-O at noon.

"Cheer up!" said Lynn. "It could have been green." Ewen felt he'd had enough of his smiling Anime Twin. They were nothing alike anymore.

Later, while he was alone, still playing games with the machines, he was startled by a heavy thump on the door. The door swung open to reveal his father, shuffling backwards into the room as he laboriously turned a small tree in his arms. It was a bonsai: gnarled, complex, very beautiful, and heavy. Dr. Young stepped toward the bed, peered around the shrubbery at the bedside furniture, which was cluttered with computer and biofeedback equipment, and at the windowsill, which was far too narrow for the pot. At last he dropped to one knee and sat the thing on the floor. He rose, one hand braced against his lower back, and turned to his son. "Birnam Wood to Dunsinane hath come," he said with an aggressively wide grin.

Ewen was still wide-eyed and beginning to shake his head from side to side. The movement became faster. "No. Dad! Don't let that be what I think it is. Don't let it be for me."

Now that Ewen was suitably distressed, Dr. Young felt free to return to his more usual cool equanimity. "Yes, it is for you, and you should feel very honored. This thing—I mean this beautiful bonsai—must be at least as old as you are. Hell—as old as I am."

"I know," said Ewen, shrinking under the blanket. "And I will be its slave for the rest of my life. Why, Dad? Why would you do this to me, sick as I am?"

This banter was what Ewen and his father used to replace intimacy. They exchanged nothing closer.

Now Dr. Young seemed positively jovial. "Me? Have more respect. This is from your uncle's kwoon. I guess it is actually more in memory of James, but you're the official caretaker. Now don't go on about it. Think what this must have cost!"

"I know what it must have cost; you know the care they need is like that of a newborn child—only they never grow up. And Dad—Ryan Watanabe's father raises these things. Which means Ryan Watanabe's father is going to know if I let it die. I'm sunk." He did sink, back onto the bed, breathing with difficulty.

After a moment, he revived enough to ask, "So, what'd *you* get for me, Dad?"

"Two nights without sleep," said his father. "And a lot of joss and prayer. Why are you asking? What should I get you? What do you want? A real, gray elephant, rather than this white one? A new girlfriend?"

Ewen winced at the old joke. His family believed he had taken a vow of celibacy. They were wrong; he just had not had any long-term relationships in the last two years. Nor much in the way of short-term ones, either, but that was his own business. Then he had an idea that might serve to distract his father, something difficult and something he really wanted.

"I do want something, Dad. But only you can give it, and it'll be really hard."

Dr. Young looked wary. "Go on."

"I'd like you to forgive Uncle Jimmy."

Dr. Young's face went stormy for a moment, then slid into its usual smoothness. Ewen, the portrait painter, did not miss either expression. "Of course I forgive him," said Dr. Young. "He is dead! Do you think I could hold a grudge against my dead brother?"

Ewen dropped his eyes from his father's face. "I think it's possible. I'm not saying you hold grudges especially, but . . . "

"Yes, you are," said Dr. Young. "And maybe, yes, I do. It's unfair that you ask that of me after this horror he led you into, and after all those years of our trying to cover for him. And paying his debts with money that should have gone to your and your sister's education . . . "

This information startled Ewen. "I didn't know anything about the money. We got by. We got by just fine."

Ewen's father placed himself firmly in the visitor's chair. "We got by only because you weren't really interested in education."

Ewen was outraged. "So what's a BFA?"

"Trade school," answered his father, with mischief.

"Ewen, your mother and I worked like horses. And before all that work could make a difference—before I had time enough to give her the life she deserved—she died. All the while James . . . "

"Also worked like a horse. Sweated like a horse. Do you think a martial arts teacher sits back and lets his students feed him peeled grapes? I'm eternally sorry about Mom dying—everyone says I feel it *too* much—but I don't think the money mattered so much to her. She loved life; she was young, and she wasn't looking to slow down and rest. Uncle Jimmy didn't cause Mom's cancer."

"And as for me, do you think I've been training all these years instead of studying medicine or law because I'm lazy, too, or to act out adolescent rebellion? So I could win fights with other kids, or pick up big plastic trophies?" Ewen stopped, because his breath had let him down again.

Dr. Young stood up, slightly alarmed. "Ewen, calm down. You've not recovered enough that you can afford to race your heart like this. I'm sorry if you thought I believed you to be lazy. I never, ever, believed you were lazy. Or rebellious. Well, not too rebellious, anyway. You were always a good kid. Too serious about this spiritual stuff, maybe, maybe just a little too unworldly. So is Lynn. You both got that from your mother's side of the family."

This was an old complaint. It was true that May Young had been the only real Buddhist in the family—until her death and the changes it caused—but Ewen also considered his mother's mother, a hardheaded businesswoman who owned a chain of restaurants. His maternal grandmother had not been "unworldly" in any respect. He managed to keep his face straight only with effort, and calmed down and listened.

Ewen's father, evidently reassured his son had done himself no harm, sat down.

"I never quite understood your dedication to fighting—especially since you don't seem to be the fighting type. You seemed to be under James's spell, somehow. We saw you as innocent, almost gullible. I admit now there were good things we didn't understand about James, just as there were . . . other things about James *you* didn't understand." Dr. Young stood beside his chair, with the heavy-shouldered attitude of a bull beset by spears. His shoulders lowered.

"I will work on forgiving my brother."

The nurses were amused by the busyness of Ewen Young's hospital room. Usually when so many people came to visit, it meant a person was on the edge of death. They were glad to believe this was not the case with Ewen Young. He was just a popular guy.

Of course, the police detectives were in a different category. There was a lot of conversation in the staff room about the shooting, Ewen's very close escape, the murky background of the attack, and the possible association with mysterious Chinese villains. One orderly on loan from Gastro suggested that Ewen Young himself was a member of a Tong, or was even a snakehead. The nurses stared him down.

"Irwin, do you have any idea what a snakehead is?" asked the Floor Nurse. Irwin had only the vaguest notion, but he wasn't about to admit that.

"They're . . . they're slavers." When the staff continued to stare, he added, "White slavers, I mean."

"Well, that lets out our Ewen," replied the nurse, and the subject was closed.

Inside that busy room, another biofeedback game was going on, with Ewen and Lynn sharing the finger sensors. Ewen himself was becoming an expert at the game, despite his shortness of breath, but when he played with his twin they were masters.

"Of course, you've played this before, Lynn," said Theo, who was (despite himself) a little envious.

"Not as much as I should have," answered his wife in a cool, detached voice. "Always too busy." Her eyes were half-closed, and her mind was somewhere within the game "event."

"We're all always too busy," added Ewen, in the same tone. They were making it rain in the game, and the sound filled the room. Then the two now-familiar detectives entered the room and, with reluctance, Ewen saved the game with their task uncompleted.

His three visitors were not at all reluctant to see them, for they had only dealt with these detectives once before, and the police were, to Lynn, Teddy and Theo, still exotic.

"I'm glad to find you all together," said Detective Petersen. His voice was very deep. "But perhaps it would be better if the little boy went out to play for a few minutes."

"I'll watch him," added the blond detective. "We don't want to frighten little Theodore with talk about . . . the crime."

"Our son knows about death," said big Theodore, standing boldly. "I run a hospice."

Teddy looked from one grown-up to another, vastly amused by this interchange. "I *could* go out and play," he stated hopefully. "Or you could go out and I could play the computer?"

Everyone smiled. Theo sat down again. Gideon Ryde sat down on the floor next to the boy, wrinkling his suit jacket. Rick Petersen remained standing. "We've got some more photos, these of people we have reason to believe worked with Chow. We plan to move in on the guy today and it would be a help in holding others if you could identify any of these. Don't speak unless you're sure, of course, but if you *do* remember any faces . . . "

Teddy asked Petersen loudly, "Are you an Indian? I don't mean like from India, but a real Indian?"

Petersen winced and swayed a bit, his thoughts cut off. Ryde leaned over and stage-whispered to the boy "Yes, he is an Indian, Theodore. But he doesn't like people to talk about it. Especially when he's discussing important things."

"Being an Indian is important, isn't it?" Teddy asked the room at large.

Ewen took the plastic-sleeved photos and examined them closely, hoping to bring attention back to business, since talk of his genealogy clearly bothered Petersen. "I don't remember any of these people, and, as you know, I'm usually pretty good with faces. I look at faces as possible projects. That's how I see Chow, as a possible . . . hey!"

Ewen had looked up, but not at any of them in the room. He looked intent, then concerned, then alarmed. "Chow! No." After a moment he raised one hand and pointed it at the air. "Wait!"

In another moment Ewen vanished.

He was there and then he wasn't there. There was an empty bed, with the covers still lightly sinking down. There was silence, broken only by the squeal of a gurney going down the hall and Detective Ryde sliding up the wall to his feet. Then Teddy stood up and bounded to the side of the bed. "Wow, Uncle Ewen! That's neat!"

For the slow count of five no one else in the room spoke. Teddy turned to his father. "I bet you could do that, too, Dad. If you wanted to, I mean."

Chapter Five

EWEN HAD been here before. He had been here always. The luminosity, undifferentiated, complete, was before him, and he could step into it because that was simply his nature. But as he regarded it, he remembered the shape of his life so far, and it did not seem to be finished—also, he saw another shape beside him. This shape was everything the light was not. It was fear, it was anger, and it was ugly. It emitted a fog of desire to push away—to push away from everything. In this strange space it seemed to recede in all directions. Ewen looked at it with his artist's eyes and saw a flower withered in bud, the sepals gone hard, and the petals thick and frozen. He recognized it as the man who had shot him, John Chow. He could have drawn Chow in either form; the angry man or the hardened bud. His immaterial fingers twitched to do so.

Now he saw more—he had a distant vision of Chow himself being shot. It had been in the head, as he had shot Uncle Jimmy, after Uncle had been badly wounded from a distance, and was no more of a threat. And, for an instant, Ewen even saw the face of the man who had shot Chow, a pale face, smooth, and slightly red about the eyes. Then that face was gone. The distant vision was gone.

The thing before him was not Chow anymore, not man nor bud at all, but a force of rejection that moved willfully away from the light and toward a darkness that had not been in the great space before: a darkness it created as it traveled away.

Ewen's thoughts were cool and removed, but he felt he was witnessing a great, cosmic mistake: one that he could perhaps rectify. He went up to the thing that had been a man and said, "No need to do this. No need at all." It turned to him and, for a moment, there was a shadow of Chow's face, which met Ewen, or whatever he saw as Ewen, and it recoiled in terror. The Chow-thing began to spin away faster, creating confusion where it went. Ewen turned away to take a breath, or something like a breath, to avoid taking in this contagion, and then he turned back again and followed the thing.

He spoke. "It's all right. I've been here before, and it's all right."

"I thought you were dead!" screamed the Chow-thing.

"I—I was dead and you are dead now. It's all okay. Don't—don't spin out of control. Don't be afraid. Come back where you were. You'll find there are better places to go. I was there. It's okay."

Chow closed harder. "Sure, and you just want to help me. Sure you do."

Ewen shrugged his shoulders. He felt no anger. No attachment at all to the situation, but merely a distant compassion. "Why wouldn't I? You're dead. We all die, friends and enemies. That ends being enemies. Believe me—here I am not your enemy, and I don't think I *could* lie to you. Not here." Ewen paused and thought. "I'm sure Theo would say that. Theo's my brother-in-law. He'd say that being afraid or angry is the only thing that can do you damage here. Or maybe just refusing to see clearly. I'm no scholar but I know that much." He pointed back toward the luminosity, which was fading in the distance. "Come back with me."

"You think I believe you! Like I believe this whole thing is happening? Go to hell!" The Chow-thing jetted away toward darkness and a confusion that made Ewen's eyes hurt.

"Wrong thing to say," murmured Ewen. He went back to the ground luminosity, warmed his hands in it, gazed a moment and said to it, "Not yet. Not yet."

The five people in the hospital room had reacted in their individual ways. Little Teddy Thurmond had begun to understand this had not been an action expected of Uncle Ewen by the rest of his family. Teddy's father was chanting, his face slightly pale. Detective Ryde in the corner was also praying. Different prayers. Lynn was still sitting on the bed, looking intently at nothing, with her head tilted, and listening—it seemed—to something no one else could hear. She did not seem upset by her brother's disappearance. The tall detective was watching with the rest of them, his face alert, composed and waiting, when Ewen came back.

He was sitting where he had been when he disappeared, with his gown rumpled up. He looked into each face intently, one by one. He glanced down, with the sudden thought that his hospital gown had not come back with him, and was relieved it had. He rearranged it for more modesty and pulled a sheet up to his waist. When Ewen finally spoke, he was careful with each word. "Please tell me what happened here—in your own eyes. Tell me what *you* saw."

Again, it was Teddy who spoke. "You went '*poof!*' Uncle Ewen. You weren't there. Then you came back."

Ewen thought about this, licking his lips. "Was I gone long? No, I can see by the way you're all standing that I wasn't gone long."

"So where were you?" asked the tall detective, quite calmly.

"I was . . . in between . . . " Ewen wrinkled his nose in a thoughtful manner, trying to explain. "Uhh . . . What can I say? I was there before, when I was shot, but I didn't take it seriously. I mean I didn't think other people could notice."

He sighed. Thought. Spoke again. "It's not a place like this is. Get Theo to explain. He knows more. But—" and he looked at Lynn with some satisfaction, "this explains why the nurses have been so upset with me. They thought I'd been tearing out my IV and walking around."

Lynn just shook her head.

Theo, though, was ready to explain. "I *thought* this was what had happened. Ewen was in a bardo realm—he must have learned how when his heart stopped those times before, and yet he still came back. He came back from the bardo. Actually, all realms are bardo realms, in betweens, as Ewen said. Life's a bardo. The next life will be a bardo. But the bardo we usually think of is that one in between life and death, or more exactly, between life and another life . . . "

"Okay. Thanks," Petersen said shortly, with a curt slash of one hand. Theo shut up.

"Life is strange," said Petersen. "Washington State is strange. King County is especially strange. We can't go anywhere with that right now. Before you went '*poof*,' Mr. Young, you said Chow's name. What did you mean by that?"

Ewen took a long, labored breath and sank back against the headboard. "It was Chow who went '*poof*,' Detective. He's dead. I saw him. As I said before—been there, done that. I thought I could help him. I don't know why I bothered. But he wouldn't listen to me. He ran away—went dark. Where he went I wouldn't follow. Not for Chow, I wouldn't."

Gideon Ryde stood very close to Ewen, shouldering Theo aside. "Where he went? Where he went? You *saw*, Mr. Young, you saw him go to hell?"

Ewen attempted a laugh. "He told *me* to go to hell, Detective. That was the last thing he said."

"But you didn't."

Ewen's strained smile faded utterly. "Not so far."

Petersen simply asked, "Chow is dead?"

"Yes, sir. Just now."

Petersen took out his cell phone and dialed. Getting no reception, he strode out of the room. Gideon Ryde followed. At the door he turned back and put an envelope in Ewen's hand. "I meant to mail this to you, but since we're here . . . " Then he, too, was gone.

"I want this kind of thing to stop," said Ewen. "I wasn't made for this kind of . . . of . . . "

"Magic," said Theo firmly. Ewen nodded and let that description stand. He opened the envelope and stared. At last Lynn asked him what it was.

"It's a sympathy card," said Ewen. "For Uncle Jimmy."

Late the same afternoon two things of note happened; Ewen had a scan that showed his heart was healing very well, and John Chow's body was found dumped in a parking lot near Qwest Field. He had been executed by a bullet in the back of the head, just as he had executed James Young.

Detective Rick Petersen entered Ewen's room as Ewen was eating dinner: real food. "Good thing for you you're in a hospital bed in the middle of a busy hospital," he said in his very deep voice.

Ewen looked up, chewed and swallowed. "You mean you found Chow?"

"Exactly as you said. Killed about the time you pulled your vanishing act. Tell me, just for my own satisfaction, Mr. Young. Did you kill John Chow?"

"No." Ewen had been expecting that question.

"Did you have any hand in his death?"

"No. Not unless he was killed because you were looking for him."

Petersen smiled slightly. "And would you be willing to take a polygraph test? Purely for *my* satisfaction, of course. I can't really demand it of you."

Ewen looked pleased at the prospect. "No problem. If it were Lynn you were asking, I bet the polygraph wouldn't mean anything. She's a psychiatrist and uses all these biofeedback programs in her practice. She probably knows how people fake them: spies and such. But me—I only started doing that biofeedback stuff in the hospital, in a computer game. I'll do a lie detector test for you, but I think you'll have to bring it into the hospital, and I don't know what the bandages around my chest will do to it."

Petersen shrugged. "I have no intention of putting you on a polygraph. I just wanted to know what you'd say."

"I think it'd be fun. And I *am* very bored. I'm thinking maybe tomorrow I can go home."

The tall man looked doubtful. "I wouldn't count on it, Mr. Young. It hasn't even been three days yet, and you flatlined twice. And of course, disappeared once."

"Three times, I think," said Ewen thoughtfully. "Disappeared three times. Twice to the 'in between' and once to some lady's apartment. The nurses keep accusing me of pulling out my IV and going to the bathroom by myself. I swear I never did."

He met Petersen's impenetrable eyes. Suddenly Ewen grinned. "You have to understand, Detective; the only reason I'm not knocked flat on my ass about all this supernatural stuff is that I'm already flat on my ass. Not used to being weak as a kitten. Not yet used to being still alive. But whatever is happening to me, I think I'm gaining control. Maybe next time I can keep my clothes in order. Drag my IV behind me into the otherworld. Better yet, maybe it'll never happen again at all."

"Some people would really dig it," said Petersen. "Popping in and out between worlds."

Ewen shuddered. "Scares the shit out of me."

Petersen gave him a tight smile and then glanced back toward the door. "But don't get your hopes up about going home tomorrow. You might be disappointed. And if you *do* go, please let me know first." Petersen paused a moment. "I mean, if you go somewhere other than 'in between'."

"I know what you mean," said Ewen, and he returned to his dinner.

Lieutenant Kopek dropped his hand on a pile of the papers covering his desk. "Another of your *hunches*, Petersen?"

"Well, yeah. Just a hunch."

"And the hunch told you to contact the Medical Examiner's office in case a body matching that of John Chow turned up. Just two hours before it *did* turn up."

Petersen slid his weight onto one hip and looked calmly into the lieutenant's blue eyes. "Think, Lieutenant. Assuming James Young was the original intended victim—and I think that makes all kinds of sense—and assuming it was his gambling got him in trouble—and according to the family *that* makes all kinds of sense—then his death was a bad decision. Very bad, from a lender's point of view, as now he cannot collect his debt, whatever it is."

"The threat to his kid—I mean his niece's kid—wasn't sensible, either."

Petersen stood, imperturbable. "Yes, it was, Lieutenant. It's the follow-up that wasn't. That's why I thought Chow—the guy whom Ewen Young identified as his assailant—had blundered. Blundered so badly he had become a liability. So it made sense he would be eliminated."

"The guy *whom, whom* blundered," repeated the Lieutenant, narrowing his eyes at Petersen. "What a gift for words! Just like Shakespeare. Well, you're the poet, aren't you, Ricky? According to Ryde, anyway. The literary man." Kopek gave Petersen a look of complete malice. "And aside from your inspiration, I suppose there's no private source of yours to go with this hunch?"

Petersen shifted his weight again and looked at nothing in particular. "Sir. If there was a source to this idea . . . it was not of this world." He snickered as he said this, to make it sound like simple sarcasm.

Kopek tilted his head right and then left, cracking his bull neck. "Christ, Petersen. I get enough of this crap from your partner, with his Bible and Book of Mormon. I don't want that kind of shit from you, too. You can play your cards as close to the vest as you want, and if you make the collar, then okay. But if you don't . . . I'll let you both hang in the wind as easy as the next guy. Remember that."

Petersen had not needed the reminder. He disliked the lieutenant, and he despised the way Kopek mocked his partner. But Petersen was sensible. He didn't envy the lieutenant or want the lieutenant's job. What he wanted was to find bad guys. He needed that in his very soul, as a hound needs the chase. He was willing to accept almost anything as true, if it led him to the bad guys. Petersen *was* a poet, and a good one: published and polished. He hated the department knowing it. He barely forgave Giddy for letting the word slip.

But no matter. He went back to his threadbare office chair, to think. He propped his feet up on the windowsill.

Chapter Six

"YOU *CAN'T* GO HOME," said Theo once again, reasonably. "You can barely make it to the hall and back without help. What will you do— sleep by the toilet and eat delivered pizza?"

"What's wrong with that as a lifestyle? Millions of Americans . . . "

"Can get off their butts if they need to. You, on the other hand, are not lazy but badly injured."

Ewen found himself in an obstinate mood. "I will not stay here one more day. I refuse. And I don't have the money to afford twenty-four-hour nursing care, so it's obvious I can just . . . "

"Come to Sangye Menla," Theo finished for him. "It's perfect. It's meant to be."

Ewen swallowed what he had been about to say. "To a hospice? But Theo—the idea is that I'm *not* dying."

"Everyone is dying," said Theo, with some ponderosity. "Dying every moment of their lives. And it's no big deal for you to stay there. You're family.

Dying every moment . . . Wasn't that just like Theo? Even in his stubbornness, Ewen could think of no place else to go.

Had his brother-in-law not run a hospice, there would have been no chance of Ewen getting released, not only because of the severity of the wound and the need to recover from surgery, but because many in the hospital felt a sense of ownership in this remarkable medical success. Theo, however, had taken in many patients in worse shape than Ewen, and done well by them; as well as could be expected. Even the trauma specialist who felt Ewen's life was her own doing felt she could safely let him go.

The head nurse had her reservations. "Mr. Young—you *have* to remember you can't be using any of that judo any time soon."

"Judo?"

"No punching and kicking for at least a month, and I'd say two if I thought I had any chance of getting you to cooperate."

Ewen was leaning on the bed, trying to explain to the orderly what clothing he wanted to wear home. "You do me wrong, ma'am. I've never felt less inclined to throw a kick in my life." He chose the green T-shirt Lynn had brought to the hospital along with other easily donned items. "Am I allowed at least to draw? Lying flat on my back, of course?"

"You can finger paint for all I care," answered the head nurse. "Go ahead. Make a mess. And when you're on your feet again, I'll let you do a sketch of my bea-uutiful face!"

Ewen turned, looked at her intently, and then nodded. In her turn she blushed. "I didn't really mean it, Mr. Young. You know that."

"But I did."

Years ago, Ewen had begun his painting for Sangye Menla trying to make the works as peaceful and reassuring as he could, only to find that his wilder and more spontaneous sketches and painting were better received. As one man had said, "I'm dying. I don't have time for timid stuff." Now there was very little timid stuff in the rooms of the dying.

Ewen had once had no idea how pervasive a thing that dying could be in the business of daily life until Lynn had married Theo. Ewen secretly referred to his brother-in-law as "The Tibetan Brother-in-Law of the Dead."

Over the past few years, he had grown accustomed to his sister's devotion to the cause of mental and emotional suffering, and the constant rotation in and out of their lives of the dying people in Theo's hospice.

Now he knew about it all in another way. Lying on a bed by the window with an Ellis Peters mystery novel propped carefully on his body and a summer rain falling outside, Ewen wondered, somewhat uneasily, whether he ought to start conversations with the folks going about their business around him—tell them death wasn't so bad, once the pain stopped. Tell them not to turn their backs and spin away, as Chow had done. But he was embarrassed at the very idea.

That's what Theo talked about, and he did so at whatever length a person would listen to. And Theo had studied it; he had the map of the place, so to speak, and from Ewen's limited experience it seemed to be accurate. One patient, Francine Bellows, who was a middle-aged woman with bone cancer, had asked him how he was doing, but her words had seemed to Ewen more courteous than curious. He said he was doing fine. And he was.

But no kicking or punching for at least a month.

Sangye Menla was on the Ridge, outside the city of Redmond, a block from the Thurmonds' house. It lay in an acre carved out of the Douglas firs. It was very pretty, with red geraniums making splashes against the green shrubbery. Despite Ewen's warnings, Theo had planted a grove of black bamboo, shielding the hospice from the road. The bamboo seemed be behaving itself. On the front porch, outside Ewen's window and within easy eyeshot, was the terrible bonsai.

There were more nurse-practitioners than doctors working here, but today Willy Sherman was on duty, a special sort of doctor whom Ewen had once caught helping to change a bed. He could see and hear Willy across the hall, with his hawk-like face and tenor voice, sharing a joke with someone just outside Ewen's sight. Ewen had discovered that Dr. Willy had come to the hospital the night after Ewen's surgery.

"Would have tried to get in on the operation had I known in time. Never seen such a wound. Would have been interesting." Dr. Willy talked in short bursts, too busy for nouns.

It was strange that Ewen had been catapulted over the border of life and death in time to meet Chow, but had failed to help his uncle. Of course he had been busy being shot at the time, but Ewen wished—if he'd had the choice— he could have assisted Uncle Jimmy. But maybe Uncle Jimmy hadn't needed any help. That was the better thought. Uncle Jimmy hadn't needed help. Not with the afterlife, at any rate.

Ewen's mystery novel fell back from his hands. He emitted a tiny groan and settled back to sleep.

Mr. George Blundell was not hooked on cocaine. He could take it or leave it. Right now he chose to take it. He had certainly been pissed-off when he killed that moron Chow, but it wasn't the coke. No, it was sound business. He chose to snort another line. Now he had to write off the Young debt, of course, but that wasn't big time.

He had been a fool to hire a fool. Chow, with his stupid "fighting arts." It always came down to a gun in the end, so why bother with the middle? Blundell suddenly saw very clearly that he *wasn't* a fool after all, because how could he have known exactly how much of a moron Chow was? Even a Chinaman usually had more sense than to try intimidating a fighter in his own ring, as Chow had done to Young. That's just not gonna work. The guy's gonna fight. You're gonna have to use the gun, which was what made Chow the moron. Not Raymond Blundell.

With Chow, Blundell had done what he had to do. You can't leave a moron running around breathing with so much he could say about you. And say to anybody—such as the police. Which is what this moron did, when they caught up with his moron ass.

Blundell was still pissed off at Chow. He was now *really* pissed off at the younger Young, because in spite of all Chow had said, Ewen Young was not spare parts; he had lived, and that was a stupid miracle. That was why Chow had to die. Blundell snorted another line and enjoyed being really pissed off.

Gideon Ryde was trying to explain to Allie, his wife, what had happened at the hospital the day before. It was difficult, and in fact it couldn't be explained, so he had to trust Allie to see the truth beyond the impossibility. She didn't doubt Gid's veracity or his vision, but when he narrated what Theodore Thurmond had said about the in-between, she looked not doubtful, but worried. "It sounds sort of . . . pagan?" she ventured.

Ryde sighed. "Well, I think it was pagan to a pagan, but that doesn't mean it was pagan in itself. It wasn't pagan to me."

Allie, who was a policeman's wife, said, "That'll do."

This visitor was totally unexpected. For some reason, Ewen hadn't thought of his former girlfriend, Karen, since being shot. Not at all. He felt instantly guilty on the matter. She only lived in Tacoma, after all.

She walked in uncertainly, and sat on the edge of the bed, as beautiful and blond as ever. Paler than ever. "Ewen, forgive me, I was out of state. I only just heard."

"Forgive *you*? For what? I could have called. I should've. Forgive me for scaring you—I mean, if you were—"

"Scared? Out of my mind! I can't believe this happened to you, of all people. I guess it was that damn uncle of yours . . . "

"Enough of that," said Ewen, sharply, and then wondered why, once again, he was being backed into a corner defending Uncle Jimmy.

"I'm sorry, Ewen. It doesn't matter, anyway. The only thing that matters is that you get better."

Karen looked exactly the same. Ewen found he was wishing she'd changed her hair, at least. He felt he was trying to talk across a gap of two years and of two moments; he didn't know her at all now, but at the same time he felt he could slide very quickly again into the smooth intimacy of a couple that had lived together for three years. "I am getting better," he said. "Better every day. In a month I'll be on my feet again. No problem."

"But in the meantime," said Karen, diffidently. "If you need someone to take care of you . . . I could take some vacation . . . "

Ewen hated that phrase: "take care of you." He especially hated it coming from Karen. "Aren't you still with Hugh?"

She hesitated. "Yes. Yes, more or less. But if you need me . . . "

"Thanks a lot, Karen, but I'm being taken care of up the old wazoo. It would be a shame for you to use up vacation time, and leave Hugh alone, when it's Theo's pride and passion to hover over me. And then there's Lynn."

She smiled, sort of. "Yes, there's always Lynn. You're two of a kind."

Things had gone too far in only a few phrases. Too painfully far. "I'm really sorry, Karen. Forgive the way I'm talking. It's just the drugs they've got me on. I never know what I'll say next. I appreciate your offer, but, really, I'm being well looked after."

She took his hand in hers, impulsively. He almost flinched at the surprise of it, and at the memories. "But if you need anything, Ewen. Anything. Call me. The number's the same. I'll come running."

"Thanks, Karen," he said, and let his eyes droop, miming sleepiness. He heaved a great sigh. He heard her steps toward the door, and then: "Hey, Ewen. I hear you're doing really well. The painting business, I mean. Not about getting shot."

He mumbled something deliberately incoherent. "The painting business" indeed. That's what had really separated them. The painting business—which wasn't really a business at all, not to Karen. That and "the martial arts business." Ewen had been expected to go down in flames, because he rejected all Karen's serious advice. (Karen, the department store buyer.) *Surprise, Karen!* He hadn't gone down in flames. He had done quite well.

He had only gotten shot in the heart.

Ewen found his drowsiness was not all invented. Perhaps not invented at all. Before he fell asleep he wondered what Mrs. Lowiscu—who sat like a sleeping snake—made of it all. Perhaps she was still sitting there, waiting.

Dr. Willy soared into the room, his eagle-like nose lifted intently and his arms laden with sheets, which he dumped at the foot of the bed. "I see you had another visitor, Picasso. You'll have to start sending them to Mr. Parrish. He hasn't had a visitor all week. Now, though, we're going to get you up."

The "we" was only Willy, but the getting up was still brisk. The doctor got Ewen under one arm and heaved him to his feet. Those feet seemed to have forgotten the feel of weight on them. They tottered down the hall between selections of Ewen's own paintings, and he was not too proud to hold on to the doctor's elbow and hand.

Chapter Seven

Detective Rick Petersen had an informant who knew a lot about the business of gambling crime in King County. He told the detective that Chow was not a casino employee, but was connected to a big guy named George Blundell. "Blundell the bookie?" Petersen asked. "I haven't heard about him in a while."

Finerhan danced from foot to foot as he held out his hand to passers-by for spare change. Panhandling was not really his occupation; giving information was. But he didn't mind the spare change, either. "Blundell ain't no bookie. Not no more. He bankrolls bookies. He bankrolls crack. Bankrolls all kinda stuff. Problem is, he's a cokehead himself. Makes him hard to work for, ya know?"

Finerhan had graduated high school and finished a year of community college. He had once possessed all the words necessary for grammatical speech. One after another he had dropped them onto the streets and the sidewalks and never bent to pick them up again

"You used to work for him?" asked Petersen. "Blundell?"

Finerhan shrugged. "Naw. Not so much. But that's why he killed Chow. Pissed off, ya know? And, hey! Maybe that's why Chow killed Jimmy Young? Maybe he's on coke and pissed off, too. Whatever, lissen to me: this stuff I'm givin' you is good and true. Blundell's your man and you gotta watch your ass, 'cause he's an icehead, too."

Petersen sighed, put his hand into his pocket, and gave the dancing Finerhan quite a bit of spare change.

Later that night all the spare change was gone, and Finerhan was feeling ticked-off that Petersen hadn't given him more. It had been good and true information and Finerhan had deserved more. He told one of his connected bar buddies that the cops knew Blundell was connected to Chow, and they were gonna get him for the hit, which was all also good and true. (Finerhan's business *was* giving information.) He had enough sense remaining not to say he had been the one who tipped the cops off. Instead, he said that one of Jimmy Young's own people had figured it, which wasn't good and true, and in fact Finerhan didn't know who Jimmy Young's people were, or even if he had any, because Finerhan had never met Jimmy Young or even heard of him before this week. Still the information got him some more spare change. Finerhan knew he deserved it, and Finerhan was quite the cokehead too.

Dr. Willy was thinking about Mr. Parrish, who was shaking and cursing. It had been longer than one week, actually, since anyone had come to see the old man. Parrish was tough as nails. He was fighting death hard, and fighting his fellows harder. The nurses would only enter his room in pairs, fearing the strength of Parrish's still huge arms. So far, he had thrown nothing heavier than a vase, but that had sailed far, and had Dr. Willy been the kind of guy to care about flying vases, or even flying bedpans, he would have exited the room by now. "Don't you want the pain medication, Thurgood?"

"Pain medicine? You don't give me enough freakin' pain medication to do anything!" Parrish tried to rage, but ended up coughing instead. "I'm a big man. I've got big pain! I hurt like freakin' hell!"

Willy leaned against the wall, arms folded over his polo shirt. "But what *can* we give you if you keep tearing out your IV? Would you prefer constant needles?"

"I hate your freakin' needles. I already look like a mosquito's masterpiece!"

From behind Dr. Willy, Ewen Young cleared his throat. "You know, Doc, IVs have a habit of coming out by themselves." Ewen was leaning against the wall, but he was standing. By himself.

Parrish went on. "Just give me pills—two pills. Four. A dozen. Dammit, a shot of bourbon, already. Why do I have to live like I'm already dead, when . . . " He lost his train of thought, and his large, gaunt chest rose and fell like a bellows. "When I just want something . . . something."

Ewen slid weakly past the doctor. He was staring with great concentration at Parrish and tilting his head slightly, as though he wanted to be sure exactly what he was seeing. Parrish looked up, still panting from his coughing fit. "What're you lookin' at?"

Ewen only shook his head and kept staring. Parrish said, "You're the guy . . . " Another spell of angry coughing. "You're the guy they say died. Died and came back again."

"I guess that's what they say," said Ewen, distantly. Parrish roused. "Well that's crap. You're dead, you don't come back. You come back, you weren't dead. Got it?"

"Okay. Then I wasn't dead." Without invitation, Ewen sat down on the bed in the small space not taken up by the big man's frame. He crossed his legs and leaned slightly forward, touching Parrish's temple with one finger. There was a tiny crack in the air, as of static electricity, and Ewen pulled his finger back while Parrish glared at him. "That a joke of some kind?" Parrish demanded. Ewen shook his head, stared some more, and then, more confidently, touched him again.

Dr. Willy watched, glad for any respite from the sound and fury. He saw Ewen's face tighten, and watched as it seemed to age, while Parrish blinked and rubbed his eyes. Willy reminded himself that Ewen was a patient, too, and was probably more fragile right now than he looked, perhaps more fragile than Parrish. He pushed away from the wall and stepped closer, only to see the two men sitting motionless, no longer touching. It seemed as if both Ewen and Parrish had fallen asleep. Then, it was as if a shimmer appeared in the doctor's vision, a loss of focus, and he could not clearly see the men on the bed. This loss of focus was a thing that happened to him frequently, working with the dying. Sometimes he developed a sudden allergy and had to blow his nose and wipe his eyes. Disdaining to take off his glasses (he might be seen) Dr. Willy merely squinted and the disturbance went away. He thought to wake Ewen quietly, to tell him to leave now that Parrish was sleeping, but decided to let it be and went out of the room to continue on his rounds.

Ten minutes later he saw Ewen leaning against the wall in the hallway, between two of his own paintings, breathing heavily. "You okay, Picasso? What did you do, put Mr. Parrish into a yogic trance?"

Ewen looked very tired. "No. I don't know anything about trances, Doc. I just kept the boundaries. That's all I know how to do." Ewen walked carefully down the corridor to his own room, looking back once to say "When he wakes up, I bet he's still gonna want his shot of bourbon."

"I'll tell the attending when I leave," answered Dr. Willy.

Chapter Eight

THE NEXT MORNING started badly for Ewen. When he woke up, even before heading to the bathroom, he glanced out the window only to see that one large branch of the bonsai had snapped, hanging like a broken arm along the trunk. He felt unreasonable panic. Stopping only to empty his bladder, he padded barefoot onto the porch and lifted the intricate little bough. It hung only by a strip of bark. If it could somehow be patched, he thought . . . sewn back, like an amputated finger. But that wouldn't work; there was the phloem, xylem, and whatever else that made a tree. He knelt on the wooden floor in his cheap blue hospice pajamas and bit his nails. "Oh no," he whispered. "Oh shit, oh shit. I'm done for."

Mrs. Swann was sitting there in a rocker. She hadn't slept well and had been there since dawn. "Well, young man, you must be very attached to that little tree."

"I hate it!" he blurted. "It's a white elephant!" Mrs. Swann merely rocked. "But it was a present, and took a long time to grow, and the guy will probably come looking for me . . . "

"Come looking for you?" she asked in some alarm.

"I mean come to see me, and he'll see this."

"Hide it," suggested Mrs. Swann, and Ewen thought for a moment. He had never heard a more brilliant idea. "But hide it where?"

She rocked meditatively. "In the closet. Visitors here never look in the closet."

"But . . . there's no light in the closet. It'll die."

"You hate it," Mrs. Swann said reasonably.

Ewen decided to hide it in the closet. While he was toting the tree down the hall (and it was both awkward and heavy), Mr. Parrish strode toward him, rolling like a sailor on the deck. He was not attached to a rolling pole and dangling bag for a change. He stared at

Ewen's burden. "That thing!" he spat. "I nearly broke my leg on it last night. It's dangerous."

"You broke the bonsai?" Ewen's voice shaded into menace. "You broke the bonsai? You admit it?"

"Hell! Damn thing nearly broke me!" Parrish's shoulders rose and his hands clenched. The two stared at each other along the length of the hallway like two gunfighters on a western street, both in blue pajamas.

Ewen spoke first.

"Grab the other end of this," he said.

They hid it in the closet.

Before stumping back to his room Mr. Parrish stopped and turned, as though he'd remembered something—as though he wanted to say something—but then stood silent, eyes narrowed, shaking his head slightly. He said, "Oh, by the way, I guess if you complain loudly enough around here, you can get what you want."

Ewen made an interrogative, noncommittal sound.

"I finally got that shot of bourbon."

Ewen's father came by at eleven. They did not talk about his brother. They did not talk about the shooting. They talked only about the bonsai.

Ryan Watanabe came by at noon, and they talked about Uncle Jimmy's funeral, about seeing Jimmy's ex-wife, who had come up from Santa Barbara, and about how the school was holding together. It was a strained conversation, but then any conversation with Ryan was strained, as he was a creature of motion and not language. It was impossible to read what Ryan thought, except by the way he shot one fist into the opposite open palm. There was some emotion there, though of what kind Ewen could not be sure. Ryan took a lot of reading.

The tree was not mentioned, even in passing. Ewen did not trust this silence and he sweated. While Watanabe was still there, Detective Petersen showed up, allowing Ewen to take leave of his uncle's student. Police business and all.

Watanabe left, uncertain himself what had been so odd about his visit. He never could read Ewen. After thought, he attributed it to post-traumatic stress disorder.

In fact, the tree had not been mentioned because his uncle's bonsai meant less than nothing to Ryan Watanabe. He didn't remember there was such a tree.

Detective Petersen was surprised at the warmth and excitement Ewen showed at his arrival, and wondered if perhaps Ewen Young didn't get many visitors. That would have been a shame, since it seemed Young was a friendly sort of guy. Nonetheless, his voice as he spoke to Ewen was neutral—almost chilly. Petersen was a poet, but not a warm or fuzzy one.

He told Ewen they had a suspect in Chow's murder, a man named Blundell. Petersen was putting a police car out in front of Lynn and Theo's house and was considering one outside of the hospice. "But since it's less than two blocks away, I was thinking we could make do with one. What'd you think, Mr. Young? You're an alert kind of guy. Will you let me know if someone or something feels wrong to you?"

Ewen stared hard. "A car at Lynn's—Lynn's? Now?" He stared, uncertain, and he thought. "Do you think this Blundell might hurt them? Why? What do you know, Detective?"

"Know? Nothing. I just get feelings, Mr. Young. Gut feelings. Considering what I've seen, you probably know all about gut feelings."

Ewen nodded and thought again. "One car should be enough."

As he walked out the door, Detective Petersen turned and asked how Ewen was feeling.

"Alert," answered Ewen.

That evening Mrs. Swann went downhill. Everyone in the place knew this because of the number of family who came to visit. Ewen was sketching, trying to make as little noise as possible, when he was asked to visit her. This summons took him unexpectedly and his mood sank; he was tired and didn't want any more preternatural or even emotional experiences.

The number of people and the amount of worry in the room had made the air sour, but as Ewen pressed his way toward the bed, old Mrs. Swann had a smile for him. "Ewen! It's late to ask, but I would like you to draw me something."

"Sure," he said, "I'll just go get my stuff."

"Oh! I didn't mean of me. No. I meant of the tree. In the closet. Sketch the tree in the closet."

He stared, uncomprehending for just a moment, and then saw faint smiles on the faces of the Swann family. "She was just now talking about that tree," someone said. "The white elephant tree."

Ewen darted back and dragged the bonsai half out of the closet, catching the leaves on a pair of his jeans. Nothing broke. For fifteen minutes he sketched in charcoal, and in his imagination he put the tree deep in the closet, its leaves still shining despite the darkness. Spraying the sketch with fixative, he got caught in the fumes; coughing, he shook the sketch dry, and ran back to Mrs. Swann's room.

A woman in her fifties, maybe a daughter, held it out before Mrs. Swann's face, and the dying woman smiled again. "Thank you, Ewen," she said, and added, "May I keep it?"

He said, "Yes," meaning, as they both knew, *for as long as you can keep anything*, and he backed out of the crowded room. He lay back on his own bed and hoped Mrs. Swann would have no other need of him, because he was very tired. He was already asleep when Mrs. Swann died.

She had no further need of him.

Ewen peered out the window at the police car, which was barely visible. He was ready to get out of this place. Living among the dying was just too much. It could do you in. He worried he would become obsessed, like Theo, or that he would become inured to it, like his father. He thought that thirty-two was too young to be living this way. He had some "wild-and-crazy" points left to use up, which had accumulated for too long in his quiet life, and he wanted to spend them all. Today, if possible.

He put on his clothes—tight jeans and this time a red T-shirt, to show how young he really was, and how wild and crazy—and decided to tell them all he was going home. He felt so full of himself, or so frightened, that he tried to shadow-box for a couple of minutes, and then sat on the bed, heart pounding, feeling less energetic but equally uncomfortable about something or other—and feeling stubborn.

He was brushing his teeth when he got the call from his sister. It was not a call on the telephone. He spat into the sink, looked at his shocked face in the bathroom mirror, and said, "Oh crap."

In the hall he ran into Parrish—literally. The weight of the big man slammed him into the wall, but he kept his balance and tried again to run past. Parrish grabbed him by the arm and was dragged along.

"Lemme go. Lemme go," shouted Ewen. "Gotta go."

Parrish grinned. "Bathroom's that way," he said, but his expression changed as Ewen kept going, pulling Parrish along with him as a terrier pulls a tall man. "Whoa. Whoa, fella. Ain't you the guy with the hole in his heart?"

Ewen took a second to release the man's grasp, running backwards as he did so. "Not now! Let me go!" He took a huge, gasping breath and ran on, through the quiet lobby, where someone was toting out the last of Mrs. Swann's things, and into the door, which gave before him. He was in the lawn, on the driveway, and now realized his feet were bare. The gravel was slippery, but he did not feel its sharp edges. There was noise behind him, catching up.

Parrish hollered "Where the hell we goin'?" Ewen didn't have breath to answer. His mind was clear. It all had to do with his sister. Parrish had him by the arm again, but not to slow him down. "Where we goin'?" he shouted once more.

They were coming to the police car, which was parked halfway between the hospice and Lynn's house. The driver's side window on the car was shattered, and Ewen found himself stopping before it, looking in at the shattered head of the uniformed officer behind the wheel.

An enormous drum was pounding in Ewen's ears, and for a second there were no thoughts, but only the knowledge that the asphalt beneath his feet was very hot.

"Shit!" said Parrish, seeing the dead policeman. "Shit, goddam!"

Ewen started again toward his sister's house, first dragging Parrish with him, then, as the big man saw their destination, being dragged by him. "Shit!" said Parrish again. "Shit, goddam." Ewen had no air to spare for speech.

There was the front garden, so much messier than that of the hospice. A whiffle-ball. A whiffle-bat. Teddy's plastic tricycle, lying on its side in high grass. The old rose bushes in which Ewen had once painted a blond man with his hand bleeding in the red roses (a man now dead). He clambered up the peeling stairs to the door, which was locked.

"I don't fuckin' believe you!" came a voice Ewen didn't recognize, followed by a slam against a wall. It was a noise too loud to have been made by Teddy's little frame, and too small to have been made by Theo's. Ewen didn't need the sound to know what was happening. He stood with both hands pushing against the door, and then was pushed aside himself by Parrish, who threw his weight with huge commitment against the panels. Ewen knew the door, and its locks and hinges, and the state of his own strength. He had an idea, but was not sure it would work. "Going in!" he said, not particularly to Parrish or to anyone, and he disappeared from the porch.

"Goddam!" said Parrish, staring around himself. "Shit, goddam!"

Ewen was inside. He saw them all: Lynn, Theo, and Teddy, but not as he was used to seeing them. They were brilliant in color—hurt and brilliant. Theo was on the ground, bleeding brilliantly, but aware, and Lynn had slid down the wall, breaking the plaster. Her mind was concentrated like a beam of light upon her child. Teddy shone like a young sun, with his hand in his mouth and his face swelling like a melon. In the middle of it all stood a man Ewen had never seen before, a big, heavy, red-faced man with an aura that looked like an ugly lava lamp and a gun in his ugly hand. Ewen tried to knock the gun away, only to find he was not material and could not touch the thing.

"You are *not* living through this, bitch!" The ugly man waved the gun at Lynn and then at Teddy, and his ugly mind was whirling. The sight of him nauseated Ewen. He felt his own spirit sink within him and as it did so, he gained materiality and moved again. He now had enough body around him to confront the man, who must have been the one Petersen had called Blundell.

"You're the one not living through this!" Ewen shouted, and he punched the man in the throat. The blow was good—focused—but not as strong as he had expected. The huge sound of his heart pounding was back in his ears. It shook the room. Even Lynn, even Teddy, even the stunned mind of Theo seemed to hear it, for they all turned toward it.

Blundell put his hand up to his neck, as though uncertain what had happened to him. His breath whistled and blood started to erupt from his nose and lips. His eyes focused on the form of Ewen before him and he mumbled with loathing "Oh, not you! The fucking cause of it all!" Blood spattered as he spoke, some of it landing on Ewen and some of it passing through him.

Ewen stored away the strangeness of that statement—that he was the cause of it all—thinking it might be important later. Later, it might make sense. He struck at Blundell's gun hand again and this time succeeded in whipping the long arm around in a circle. He was still not strong enough. He shouted, making little sound, and in his anger he willed himself back to the real world once again, physical among the physical once again.

The room was getting more real by the moment, but by the same moment he was also wearing out. Blundell, coughing and staggering, his breath wheezing through his cracked windpipe, aimed the gun at little Teddy, who was curled in the corner, sucking on his hand. "One more move out of you, you fuck, and the kid comes apart." His voice was ragged, but clear.

"How will that help you?" Ewen cried, hearing his own voice as from a distance. The big drum of his heartbeat in his ears was getting louder as he solidified; as he came down. Now Ewen was *there* enough to see that Blundell's face was beet-red, and his eyes were dry and staring. Drugs, thought Ewen. Coke? Meth? Ewen had no idea. But he knew that it didn't matter to this man that shooting Teddy wouldn't help him, or that shooting the cop hadn't helped him. There was no hope to be found in reason right now. Ewen leaped between Blundell and Teddy, but at that same moment Blundell himself turned away to follow the sound of the great drum. Everyone seemed to be listening to Ewen's heart-drum, but then the drum shattered the door off its hinges . . . and it hadn't been his heart after all, but Mr. Parrish's fists, and Mr. Parrish staggered into the room.

The two big men were much of a match in size, but Parrish had cancer, whereas Blundell had a Beretta. They grappled for a moment and Blundell managed to aim the gun at Parrish. From behind, Ewen punched him double-handed in the back, just as he had punched Chow the week before. Not even a week before. The gun went off into the wrecked door and then Blundell, brought to his knees, managed to right his aim. He shot again. Parrish went down, but he was dragging Blundell to the floor with him. The gun was hidden between the two men.

Ewen, completely material now and completely winded, leaped into the air and came down, adding his weight to the blow he struck Blundell in the back of the neck. More blood spat from the man's broken throat to his mouth. The gun went off again, turned back upon its owner, and Ewen witnessed Blundell's ugly spirit spinning away. He saw it retreat from the room down a dim passageway that had not existed before, and something in it called to him.

The in-between called to him.

Ewen turned away from it. He stepped over Blundell's body to Parrish, who was lying flat with a hole in his blue pajama top and a big, idiot grin over his face. His eyes met Ewen's. "Shit. Goddam! That was great, kid! That was just what I needed. Better than bourbon."

"It *was* great," Ewen answered. "Because of you, it was great."

Parrish gave him a nudge with one big fist. "Hell, it was great all around." The fist dropped and Parrish's light retreated. This time, Ewen followed after.

It actually felt good to get away from his body this time, because that body was fairly used up, and Ewen, by now, had almost become accustomed to the ground luminosity. He knew what to do, what to say.

But to his immaterial surprise, he found he was some place else. He was in the small place with the damp grass and the trees set round—the place that had been his only magic before this week's catastrophe—where off to one side there was a little stone wall, with a trickle of water flowing beyond it. He was in his own place, where he kept the boundaries, but where his own feet had never stood before. There he stood, in the middle of his own fantasy. Mr. Parrish stood beside him, but without a hole in his chest, and not in the hospice blue pajamas. Mr. Parrish was wearing Levi's and a denim jacket, and he seemed in considerably better shape than he had been before. "Hey, hey! I know this place. Remember kid? I came here with you one time. Yesterday."

Ewen sighed. "I'm thirty-two years old, Mr. Parrish Not a kid. And, yes, I know this place. I made it."

Parrish looked only amused. "You made it? Who are you, God?" He started walking, his hiking boots swishing through the green grass.

"No. I mean I saw it once and I use it. For years I've used it. It's a place to go, and to take other people."

Parrish kept going. "So, then tell me—where are we? Where're we goin' this time? This time I don't feel like sitting like a lump."

Ewen walked behind him. "Where we *are* is a park near Santa Barbara, where I grew up. Where we're *going* I have no idea."

"Santa Barbara. Santa Barbara. Never been to Santa Barbara. Sounds nice. But why here? Why did you use this place?"

Again Ewen sighed. "Because I was a bummed-out teenager when I found it, that's why! Do I need a better reason?" There was so much Ewen didn't want to say to Parrish about his being a bummed-out teenager.

"And you were a real pissed-off sonna bitch when you were a teenager, right?" Parrish was in a good strong mood.

"Wrong," said Ewen, feeling really irritated by the memory. "Not a son of a bitch at all."

"Too bad," said Parrish, who had almost reached the edge of the ring of trees. "And what's on the other side, here?"

Ewen opened his immaterial mouth to say it was a cemetery—that he had spent his best teenage hours sketching in a cemetery—but he felt too embarrassed to speak. Parrish's big hand reached into the cedar trees and pushed aside the heavy foliage, but instead of the manicured lawn and the rows of flat headstones, laid out like chocolates in a box, Ewen saw only more trees.

"Pretty good," said Parrish, and he reached down to pick up a backpack that hadn't been there before. "Looks like a big place. And I'm in the mood for something big, after all the candy-ass shit I been goin' through." Something sloshed in Parrish's jacket pocket and Ewen saw it was a silver flask. Parrish stepped into the woods, his heavy boots pressing down the moss on a path Ewen had never seen before. "You comin'?"

Ewen peered into the cathedral forest, and thought: *The woods are lovely, dark and deep* . . . but he was alive. He was not quite thirty-three years old and he was alive. He shook his head.

Parrish did not seem surprised and did not encourage Ewen. He was tightening the strap on his pack. "Bye, kid. See you around," he said.

Ewen let go of the boundaries once again, and found himself panting on the floor of Lynn's living room, watching his sister press a wad of cloth against Theo's chest. Theo was propped up against a wall, blinking, his gaze fixed on the face of his wide-eyed son. There were two dead men in the room, both of them large. There was the sound of a siren in the distance. Teddy flung himself against Ewen, shouting. "Uncle Ewen! Uncle Ewen!" His face was sadly swollen, but he was not crying. "Did you see what happened? Everything happened! Daddy got shot. A strange man came in and he got shot. And then another one! Did you see?"

"I saw," said Ewen. "I saw a lot."

PART II: Winter and the Cold North Light When the Nights are Very Long

Chapter Nine

EWEN WOKE UP in cold dread, but he could remember no dream. It was four a.m. He swung out of bed as though he were being chased, hearing his pulse pound in his ears. He meditated for an hour, trying to keep himself in a state of attention, not hiding from his mind's and his body's distress. It was not pleasant sitting, but he soldiered on for the hour, because he felt that getting up before the timer would be putting him on the slippery slope to forgetting his practice entirely. He was always worried about that slippery slope, because he didn't think he was one of those natural meditators one reads about. He had only started after his mother died, and only because she had valued meditation, and he wanted to do something for her. That had been twenty years ago, and one might think the whole thing in the past and done by now, but he still meditated.

He had his paints and easel in the car before the sun was well up; daylight was getting later and later as winter wore on. He arrived at the client's house just as the R.K. Bolt, Inc. CEO emeritus Richard Bolt finished dressing. He spread his drop cloths once again—the household staff was always cleaning up after him. He replaced the cardboard he had leaned against the south windows to even out the light. Bolt came into the solarium and, as always, asked if he might order breakfast for Ewen. As always, Ewen demurred.

"Too early, eh, Young? For me, too. Can't get those gastric juices working until eleven." Bolt looked once more at the photo taken before the first sitting, to help him get the position right. "Don't know why you can't just do it from the old Kodak. Save us both trouble."

"The photograph," Ewen said, "doesn't know what's important."

They remained in the solarium for an hour or so, when there came a huge, distant growl from outside. In another minute, rain began pattering on the windows. Bolt took a long breath. "Winter's coming," he said, with an air of outsized profundity.

For the last month, Ewen's senses had been telling him winter was coming, and his artist's eyes had already informed him the light of the day was not peaking very well. That was simply how winter was in Washington State. Low light, very short days and lots of rain. It meant a necessary adjustment in the mind, which was done gracefully by most Washingtonians. Ewen came from Santa Barbara and for him it required more effort. The rain meant he was done painting for the day.

He was not done working, however. After he got home, he spent an hour or so catching up on some bills and listening to NPR, until it was time for the weekly school meeting.

Weekly school meetings were a necessity because Ewen refused to consider himself the head of the kung fu school that had been Uncle Jimmy's. Each Friday he reminded the rest of the school that his was an interim position: that he had no talent for organization, no training to be a teacher, and absolutely no interest in the job. Every Friday the students in the school claimed they had no other option than Ewen.

"You're a Young," insisted Ryan Watanabe. "This is the Young style of kung fu. Without you the lineage would come to an end."

This would make Ewen laugh outright. "James Young had five teachers, two of them in Hong Kong, two in L. A. and one in Santa Barbara. None of them were named Young or related to anyone named Young. The 'lineage' you talk about consisted of one man, picking and choosing what he wanted to learn."

"Two men," suggested Perry Janaway, with a sly grin. "Two makes a lineage. A tradition."

"Tradition!" sang Barbie Cowell, cutting a few steps from *Fiddler on the Roof*. "But, hey, Ewen! What are we supposed to do? Disperse and start over in other styles? I, for one, refuse to do that! I'm too old to start over."

"We're loyal to you, Ewen," said Ryan. "Think of this like the presidency."

"Like the *what*?"

"The presidency. Anyone who wants the job is probably not the kind of man you should elect as president. Therefore, you are perfect for the role."

Once again Ewen suggested that they simply go on without a head—sort of a community school—and once again they all protested that a martial arts school couldn't be a democracy.

Forced by the weight of public opinion, Ewen would again cave in and remain a dictator.

That evening he got another call from Karen, to tell him she was no longer with Hugh. She told him so at great length, while he stared at the back yard, eyes unfocused. It seemed to him sometimes, in summer, that he could actually see the bamboo grow. When he had hung up it occurred to him he should have told her she was not going to be "with" Ewen again, either. He was not a choice to return to when better choices failed.

His thoughts slid back to the school. He should have told them all he was not a choice to make when better choices fail—or die. How could he be a teacher when he himself did not *have* a teacher? He missed Uncle Jimmy more than any of them. Not so much his personality, which had been somewhat . . . tart? No. Sour. Sour was the word.

What he missed was simply his uncle's being there. He missed Uncle Jimmy's eyes looking at him. (Look at me, Uncle Jimmy! Uncle Jimmy, look at me!)

Ewen, on impulse, rummaged under his desk through the wastebasket, looking to see whether anyone or anything had invited him out this Friday night. He was still head down, finding nothing, when the doorbell rang. He popped up so fast he almost hit his head against the keyboard tray.

The house was utterly still and the only light on was the one beside the desk. It was all very dark and he had heard nothing before the ring. He heard nothing now. With a memory of last night's sleep terrors, Ewen approached the door. He felt oddly formal, almost fated, as he stood by the door (not directly in front of it) and asked, "Who is it?"

The voice, always surprisingly deep, said, "Petersen."

Ewen put his hand to the knob. It felt very cold in his hand. He opened the door to find the detective standing there alone, a tall dark stripe against the faint streetlights.

"Have you been watching the news, Mr. Young?"

"No," said Ewen, mystified. He stood unmoving for five seconds; only then did he think to invite the man in. Petersen walked in and closed the door behind him. He did not move toward the living room.

"Another priest has been killed," he said. He stood still as a statue, as though prepared to wait for a response all night.

"I didn't know any priests had *been* killed," said Ewen. "I have no idea what you're talking about." He thought to add, "Please, sit down."

Petersen folded himself into a chair, his long, big-boned hands on his knees. Ewen took a seat on the couch opposite, and the two men sat in the low light of the lamp and stared at each other.

"You don't watch the news, Mr. Young? Or read the papers? Check the Web?"

Ewen shrugged. "Not lately. Lately's been sort of crazy, Detective."

"In more ways than one. I thought you might know about this, because this one was a Buddhist."

Ewen felt a bit irritated. "I don't really know any Buddhist priests, Detective Petersen. Unless you count Theo."

Imperturbably Petersen asked, "And what would you call yourself, Mr. Young?"

Ewen felt himself break out in a sweat. "Oh, God! Not a priest. No! No! Not even a Buddhist, sometimes. Just a guy out to make a . . . a living."

He saw Petersen's dark eyes glance at him, shifting in a thoughtful way. He wondered what on earth Petersen was thinking now—what he was thinking, ever. The man's face was not readable, not even for an artist like Ewen.

"Have you gone anywhere interesting lately, Mr. Young? Any dreams that might be more than dreams?"

Ewen's neck hair began to prickle. "Last night I . . . didn't sleep well. But that's all. No dreams. Nothing strange has happened since that—thing—at my sister's house last summer. I'm hoping that's all over."

Petersen tilted his head, ever so slightly. "I can sympathize with that. But won't Mr. Thurmond be disappointed if you stop visiting the bardo?"

"I'll disappoint Theo any time I feel like it. And as for visiting the bardo—I find the iffy part—the uncertainty—is the coming back. And right now I'm not ready to give up on this incarnation."

"I'm not asking you to give up on anything. Or risk anything. But how about visiting a crime scene? As an artist, if for no other reason. New material to add to your rose gardens and portrait backgrounds. Different."

Ewen, listening to Petersen, was of three minds. Part of him thought this "new material" an appalling idea, part of him thought it really neat, and the rest was simply embarrassed. "I am not psychic, Detective Petersen. I don't have psychic flashes. Something happened once, but it's over."

Petersen stood. "Well, maybe. And probably this is a waste of my time. But is it a waste of yours? Come on—it's Friday night and you're sitting here in the dark. What better thing do you have to do?"

Ewen was about to answer that he wasn't just "sitting in the dark." He was going through his financial records. But that sounded very, very lame. He got to his feet.

As Ewen followed Petersen out the door, locked it and set the alarm, an energy grew within him that said this was by far the best thing to do with his night. Compared with thinking about Karen, or about the school, or about the fact that he had not found any invitations in the paper scraps of his week, this was great stuff. It was starting to rain again, which was only to be expected this season, and the streetlights were fuzzy with wet air. He sailed over his flight of steps without thinking, as always, and the leap won him a startled glance from Petersen. It reminded Ewen he was not expected to act like an adolescent any more.

But at this moment Ewen didn't care what the tall detective thought of him. He could hear the rain patter on his hair and Petersen's leather-soled shoes creaking over the walkway. His senses were awake in the dim light, and he was content.

The car was ordinary: a dark sedan, as he had heard the cars of the FBI were. The only other time he had traveled with the police was in a black-and-white, just this summer, when Blundell had tried to kill his whole family. That trip had not been exhilarating. This one was.

He snapped himself into the seat belt and asked Petersen who smoked.

"Don't know. It's not my car," answered Petersen. "And, of course, it's not Gid's car, either. The department shuffles them around as it sees fit, and sometimes the users are rude enough to stink them up."

Ewen looked around at the bland interior and wondered how many strange things had happened inside this car. Inside it or nearby. "And where is Gid . . . Detective Ryde, Detective?"

"Gid's doing really useful things for the department right now," said Petersen. "Or he's gone home to his family. Sometimes . . . " Petersen's face glowed slightly from below, from the instrument panel, "Sometimes Giddy keeps the fort and lets me do a crazy thing by myself. Now and then."

There was a slight smile on that angular face. A real smile. Ewen stared, surprised. "And I'm a crazy thing?"

The smile blinked out. "No sir, Mr. Young. If I thought you were in the least bit crazy, I wouldn't have asked you to do this. No. It's just the idea that is crazy."

"I agree," said Ewen.

They drove south on 520, past Bellevue. Rain spattered on the windshield, and the freeway lights made a thousand prisms. Ewen wasn't sure where they were anymore, and when, after a few more turns, their veering into an off-ramp pushed him sideways in his seat, they emerged onto an unlit road and he was entirely lost. "Where are we, Detective Petersen?"

"Issaquah."

"There's a Buddhist temple in Issaquah?"

"Didn't you know?"

"We're not all the same, Buddhists."

"Well, you'll see."

Against the charcoal-gray sky, he saw the building's long curving roof lines rise up like the branches of a hemlock. It had a pagoda roof. There was a large doorway, black in the night, but probably painted red, and over it lines of yellow crime-scene tape, which Petersen pushed casually upward. He had a key, and rattled it into the lock, put his shoulder to the big door and pushed.

Inside, the light was bright to Ewen's night-adapted eyes. There was a smell of wax and oil and of something sweeter. Sweeter, but not nice. He found he was looking at an enormous gilded Buddha, tall as a two-story building. Around it were smaller statues, of many kinds and shapes and figures, all also gold. Without thinking, he slipped his shoes off. "Vipassana," he said.

"That's what I hear," said Petersen. "And what does vipassana mean to you?"

Ewen looked around him, at the shadowed splendor, and the stark, carpeted floor. "Exotic," he answered, and then, coming to attention, added, "It's a school. Owes a lot to tantra. Originally from the north of India, but . . . "

"I know. But what does it mean to *you*, Ewen? Mr. Young."

Ewen turned to look at Petersen, and found the detective had not taken off his shoes coming into the temple. "It means nothing at all to me, Detective. I've never, to my knowledge, met a vipassa . . . vipassana person in my life. I know they do some heavy meditation; that's all."

"And what do you think of this place?"

Ewen looked around, from the Buddha to the deity to the offering lamp, wherever the light allowed. "Cool! It's like a movie!"

Ewen saw Petersen's eyes flicker, and the white of his teeth. "Cool it is. Nothing else?"

"I *said* I'm not psychic!" Petersen nodded. "I never believed you were. Please come with me."

From the grandeur they passed into a very ordinary room that was half kitchen and half office. Petersen flicked on the light. There was a light dusting of dark powder on the desk, with smears dotting it, and there was more bad smell. The smell was not very strong, but it was much the same as what Lynn and he had smelled on their trip to Hong Kong, ten years before, while hiking down a picturesque road. There they had come upon a road-killed hog, sparkling with slivered headlight glass and dragged into a ditch. The temple ceased to be cool to Ewen, and this adventure was no longer so neat. Petersen led on.

There was a hall of narrow doors, standing open. A bathroom, a storage room, a bedroom with an empty bed frame. A bad, bad smell.

They entered into a room like the previous bedroom, except this had a mattress on the frame, a print of the blue Medicine Buddha on the wall and an enormous amount of dried blood everywhere. On the carpet was scattered matter that wasn't blood. It was awful.

Petersen stepped into the room carefully, standing on a runner of plain newsprint paper. "They spent most of the day doing their blood forensics in here. Sort of superfluous, wouldn't you say?" He motioned for Ewen to come in.

Ewen took a careful step forward, and was hit by a blow harder than any he had received in his life. The weapon that attacked him was frozen, was blind, and its name was fear. He heard his breath explode outward through his nose. He heard himself whine. He fell through long blackness, dizzy and without purchase, and he remembered all at once what his dreams had been.

He screamed. "I . . . I can't . . . "

Out of long habit, he called up the meditator—the watcher—in his mind, to try to understand this thing which was annihilating him. The watcher he called up appeared in reality and he was standing beside himself in the dim light, staring at his own expression of shock and horror. As he watched his own form, its horrified expression seemed to soften, to become aware of something. It turned and looked at him.

He turned and looked at himself.

Ewen felt there was something not right about this image. It was a trivial thing, but it was not right. The difference caught his attention and calmed him a bit. He studied the form. Was it in the hair? The eyes? Suddenly he knew the picture was right after all, and that his own idea was in error. Ewen was used to seeing himself in a mirror, and a mirror is reversed, left to right. He found this observation very interesting and he noticed that he was not afraid anymore.

Out of the corner of his eye he saw an arm waving. A finger pointing. It was the detective, Petersen, though in this strange darkness it took him a while to remember who Petersen was. Petersen seemed to be speaking to him. Perhaps he was shouting, though no sound came through. He pointed first at one Ewen, and then another. Fascinating: Petersen, too, could see the other Ewen. Then Ewen saw he was pointing intently from him to the first Ewen: the one he had seen look so afraid. It looked like Petersen was commanding a dog to come here. Come here.

Ewen stepped forward and went. He stepped into his body without feeling any obstruction and he turned around, fitting it to him like a complicated coat. He waited for some great change to happen in him, but the only change was that be began to sway on his feet. Petersen reached out to grab him.

"God! You feel like ice," he said.

"Cold in here," said Ewen. Petersen pulled him back out of the room. "What just happened in there?" he demanded, almost angrily.

Ewen thought about it. "Well, I've been having these dreams, and now I remember . . . " He stood there, head down, forehead wrinkling.

"Now you remember what?"

Ewen sighed. "I forget again."

Petersen drove him home. Ewen's hands and feet were cold. He felt very removed from the moment. He remembered this was called "shock." After ten minutes in the dark car, the detective spoke. "So. This wasn't your usual trip, was it?"

"What's my usual trip?" Ewen found his voice was shaking.

"Well . . . It wasn't to your brother-in-law's heaven, was it? Nor to hell, either. Though for a moment I worried . . . " Petersen's dark gaze did not move from the road ahead, but his voice was not entirely even. "It *was* a bad scene. I'll give you that. Bad crime scene, I mean. Not just what happened with you."

"I don't remember much about it," said Ewen. That was only half-true. He wished he remembered less.

Petersen talked. Perhaps just to keep Ewen with him.

"It's the fourth murder like it. A Catholic priest, a guy who used to be a Catholic priest, an Episcopalian, and now this."

"And I never heard about any of this? I mean, I don't watch the news much, but . . . "

A car swerved in front of them, and Petersen tapped the brakes. The offending vehicle was a white Subaru, much like Ewen's own car, and the driver blithely scooted across three lanes of traffic and made its exit lane at the last moment. People leaned on their horns all around them. Petersen eyes didn't even flicker. Ewen glanced over, slightly awed at this casual expertise.

"The first two were in Alberta, the third in B.C. This is our country's first visit. The scenes all looked like someone was mauled and then chewed up by a family of bears."

"Papa, mama, and baby bear?"

Petersen glanced over. "Yeah." He waited for a response, and when he got none he added, "So. You think there was something odd, there?"

"Odd as in supernatural?"

Petersen shrugged. "Any kind of odd."

Ewen cocked his head at the tall detective in curiosity. "Didn't you sense it—feel it? The cold? The blind darkness? The . . . the . . . "

"No I didn't," said Petersen. "And I don't want to learn how."

"Me neither," said Ewen sadly.

Petersen took Ewen home and watched from the car window until he'd gotten into the house, like a polite guy on a first date. He sat there for five minutes afterwards, staring as the lights went on in Ewen's house, one after another. Evidently Ewen Young was not ready to go to sleep. Petersen didn't blame him. He shook his dark head in the darkness and drove away.

Chapter Ten

EWEN WAS STILL a bit shaky as he began to work on Mr. Bolt's portrait the next morning. He had done his early morning meditation, only to find he was sitting with a mind lightly laced with fear. He sat and watched the fear for half an hour—it was like the light ornament of frost on a windowpane—and when it didn't seem to change much, he unfolded himself, took a shower and gathered his painting tools.

The light today was very gray, and he had no problem with leakage from the south windows. It was all north light today. With his brush, he applied methodical thin glosses of oil over his opaque background, making the skin translucent. The small brass globe Bolt wanted included in the picture shone like gold under Ewen's brush, like a small sun. He wondered if perhaps the brass ball was more of a symbol than a decoration: not so much of Bolt's importance to world trade, but that he simply had brass balls. Ewen didn't dwell too long on the thought; he just painted the globe. While he painted, a favorite Donovan song went endlessly through his head:

Color the sky Prussian blue.
Fleecy clouds changing hue
Crimson ball sinks from view
Wear your love like heaven . . .

The song improved his mood quite a bit.

"I want to see it now," said Bolt after there was too much wet oil for Ewen to continue and the sitting was over.

"It's not done yet, Mr. Bolt. It won't look like you. It'll just be a pattern of colors and you'll be disappointed."

Bolt cleared his throat in a commanding fashion. "It's a pattern of colors that I'm paying for, and so I will look at it."

Ewen tried to be very polite to subjects. Subjects were not usually as rude as Mr. Bolt. "Suit yourself." He stepped away from the canvas.

Bolt stared, narrowed his eyes, and took a slow, contemplative breath. "Oh, I can see myself coming out of there. It's just fine. I was . . . concerned I might be all pink cones and wavy lines. You know—modern art."

Ewen considered. "Well, Mr. Bolt, it *is* modern art in the sense that it's being made today. Cubist style, for example, isn't modern anymore, but it still exists. If a person wanted a portrait in Cubist style, I'm sure there are artists happy to paint it for him. I even did a few Cubist things myself, in school, to see what it was all about. I must have seen things differently from the Cubists, because I didn't want to continue the effort." He was cleaning brushes as he spoke.

Mr. Bolt raised his head from the painting. "You went to school? For this?"

Ewen stared. "Yes, I went to school. Four years of art school."

"Instead of going to college, you mean? Or was it after college?"

Ewen breathed deep and slow, but he could not stop his teeth from grinding. "It *was* college, Mr. Bolt. I have a Bachelor of Fine Arts degree."

Bolt snorted. "Huh. I thought you just sort of picked it up, here and there."

Ewen thought of a dozen responses, none of them polite. He said, "Some artists are self-taught, but that's not the easiest or best way to go. Back in the days of Michelangelo and DaVinci, students were apprenticed for years and years, starting by grinding pigments and stretching canvases."

Bolt looked at him with one eyebrow up and a lopsided smile. "Michelangelo and DaVinci, eh? Heard those two were sort of . . . light in the heels. That right?"

It took Ewen a few seconds to understand the reference and then he went from confusion to irritation to simple surprise. "Mr. Bolt— you're hacking at me, aren't you? This whole conversation is . . . "

Bolt pointed a finger. "Gotcha. It's the least you deserve, after making me sit there with itches and twitches and flies on my nose."

"Flies on your nose?"

"Gotcha again."

Next in his day came the Saturday children's classes at the kwoon, which were usually a delight. Barbie Cowell assisted with the six- to eight-year-olds, in which there was a lot of running and whooping and gold stars pasted on foreheads. A girl named Neave was seven, and the most coordinated of the lot. The boys tended to end up in giggling heaps on the floor, often on purpose.

Eight-to-eleven was a larger class, and many of them originally had been sent to Jimmy Young because of behavior problems. Uncle Jimmy had been good with these kids, and Ewen was trying to be the same. They had been a subdued lot after Uncle's murder, and some never came back. But most did, and there were even new kids. Ewen couldn't think why.

After the classes, Ewen was home in front of the TV, too tired to go out, and stuck with his own company. He picked up a pad and tried to work up some impromptu sketches, while watching an old *Law and Order* rerun. They came out more like doodles. When he glanced down, he noticed a face, one he hadn't done on purpose, obscured by some sort of screen of bushes, or trees. It was not a pleasant face. He snickered at himself; *Crouching Tiger, Hidden . . .*

Hidden what?

Ewen had had enough. He bounced off the couch, arms raised in guard, though he did not know against what. The bad smell of the temple from the night before was in the air. Death and incense. He took a deep breath of the stuff. He decided what was hidden would be discovered sooner or later, and he would rather it be sooner. On his own terms. He leaped up the stairs, four at a time, and did a SWAT team assault kind of meditation.

Cross-legged, he sat in anger and in the fear that crept into his mind. It was no longer fear without a subject, without pictures. It had the bloody room he had seen last night as a base image, and the subject was himself being ripped apart. He was being ripped in two, and staring from a dizzy remove at this own lost self. Ewen increased his energy and called up what he thought could be his strongest weapon against fear— the light beyond dying. The "ground luminosity" of last summer's strange trip. The light of awareness.

Even that light became terrible to him. It was—after all—death itself and Ewen did not want to die. In every atom of his being he did not want to die, and what was staring at him from behind the screen of his mind wore death as its own ornament. Ewen's heart lurched.

"That's it," he said to the room at large. "I'm staying in this spot until I'm through with this." With these words his confusion ran out of him, and he was alone. For a long time, he was alone. Then, after hours of sitting, at one sudden moment the fear went away.

Immediately after that, the doorbell rang. It was dark in the meditation room and getting very cold. Ewen untangled his legs and jumped up to answer the door. His numb legs failed him and he fell flat on his face. Lifting himself by the doorknob, he stumbled into the hall and down the stairs with the banister under his arm. At the foot of the stairs he used the hanging heavy bag to swing himself toward the door.

Again, like last night, it was dark in the hallway and there was no sound from outside. He propped himself with one hand against the wall to the right of the doorknob and felt shooting pains begin in both legs. The after effects of the lotus posture. He flicked on the porch light, and, taking a deep breath, he opened the door.

On his doorstep stood a woman and a dog. The woman was striking, her long hair dark with blondish highlights and her face strong and interesting. Very interesting. She stood well, as though she might be a martial artist or a dancer. He didn't know her. The dog he first mistook for the Kelly's German shepherd, but no—this dog was larger and furrier. It looked at him intently, eye to eye, and after a moment let its tail thump, once, against the porch.

"That's very odd," said the woman. "Rez doesn't like strangers."

"German shepherds don't generally like me," he replied and then brought his meditating mind closer to normality. "Can I help you?"

"Well, yes," she answered. "I'm hoping you can." She stared intently into his face, without embarrassment. "I *think* you can."

"Come in," said Ewen, stepping back from the door. It was not like him to invite strangers into his house, especially after dark. But she was very . . . interesting. They came in: the woman and the dog. He flicked on the overhead light.

Under the incandescent lamp, she was not merely striking but beautiful. Her hair was mingled dark and blond, her skin a bit tanner than Ewen's own, her cheekbones and nose strong without being sharp, and her eyes were the hazel brown that contains flecks of shining gold. Her mouth was generous and only touched lightly with lipstick. The names of colors—rose madder, viridian, sienna, golden ochre—ran through Ewen's mind. He repeated them twice, silently, like an incantation. He knew he was staring.

The dog's tail thumped once again, this time against the hall carpet. It recalled Ewen partly to himself. "So . . . how . . . er, who . . . ?"

"I'm Susan Sundown," she said. "Dr. Susan Sundown. A veterinarian." As if that explained it all. After another moment she gave a small sigh and said, "Ricky never mentioned me?"

"Ricky? Is he one of the new students? I don't remember all their . . . "

"Ricky Petersen. 'Rikki-Tikki-Tavi,' as Gid calls him. After the Kipling story, you know. Because what he does is 'run and find out.' "

"Detective Petersen? Ryde calls him that?" The idea of that tall, saturnine man being known as Rikki-Tikki-Tavi struck Ewen almost speechless.

"Yes, of course. He's spoken of you, so I thought perhaps he might have mentioned me to you."

Ewen waved toward the couch, and sat himself down in a chair opposite. She sat and the dog sat on the floor at her left side, in military precision. "No," said Ewen. "Detective Petersen has never said many unnecessary words to me. All business. I assumed he didn't talk much. To anyone."

She smiled with her lovely mouth, but only for a moment. "Rick actually has a lot to say. He's a poet, you know. Published in fancy magazines. " She smiled again, with a sort of uncertain pride. Ewen got the feeling this woman was not, herself, a poet. "He's talked about you and your sad experience last summer. And about your . . . abilities."

Ewen was profoundly uncomfortable with this. "About last night, too? About what my *abilities* did to me last night?"

She nodded. "That's why I'm hoping you won't tell him about my being here. He didn't want me to come." Her gold-flecked eyes narrowed. "In fact, he *forbade* it. As though he has the power to forbid me anything!" She glanced back to him. "But of course it's up to you whether you want to tell him we came to see you. I can't exactly *forbid* you anything—can I?"

Ewen slowly shook his head from side to side. "I'm not likely to be having a chatty conversation with Detective Petersen in the near future." Nor would he be likely to call him Rikki-Tikki-Tavi, should they have another occasion to meet.

She settled back into the couch and the dog thumped its tail for a third time. As though that third thump was a charm and now completed, the woman said rapidly "It's about my great-uncle, the shaman. He's gone missing."

"Your great-uncle the what?"

"The shaman. Tribal medicine man. You know what that means. Don't you?"

Ewen felt slightly stoned at this moment, perhaps as a result of his long meditation. Or perhaps the conversation was really as strange as it seemed. Dr. Sundown went on. "He lives over in Idaho, on the rez." The dog suddenly stood and put her head forward onto Sundown's lap.

"Not you, Rez," she said absently, and stroked the large head. "The Nez Perce Reservation. We're Sahaptian."

"Oh," said Ewen. *Nez Perce. Sahaptian.* He looked at the hazel-eyed part-blond woman before him and held his tongue.

"Last week he went out to talk to the cedars and did not come back. I spoke to Ricky about it, because of the connection with the murders of holy men in Canada and here."

"Holy men?" Ewen tried to draw the connection.

"Yes, exactly. Holy men. If you knew Uncle Sid, you'd have no doubt about it. Everyone knows he's a holy man, and what's more, his medicine is very strong. He didn't have a heart attack or get pulled down by a cougar. Not Uncle Sid."

"But you still think he's in trouble?"

"I think he's dead. I know it, really. Something bad got him. I feel things sometimes, and this is one of those times. You're one of the few people I think can understand that."

Ewen made a noncommittal sound.

"I think it was the same bad thing that got these others. Ricky can't help me, because he's King County and has no jurisdiction, and Idaho law enforcement won't take his being missing seriously. They assume one more Indian disappeared in the snow while on a bender. Even the tribal police are useless, and they should know better."

"And you think *I* might be useful?"

"Exactly."

Ewen sighed and scratched his head. "I didn't do so well last night. Did Ricky tell you that?"

Her gaze didn't falter. "He said you can feel the thing. I need that. But I have some strengths of my own, too. I could have gone Uncle Sid's way in life. I just wanted to be a horse doctor more. The 'other' medicine. What I need is help, and all I've got right now is Rez. She's the best, as dogs go, but even Rez can't speak human. I need another human, and one with power. When Ricky mentioned you, I knew it was meant to be. I need you to go with me to Idaho and find out what happened to Uncle Sid!"

Ewen wanted with his practical side to believe this woman was crazy. Things would be simple if she were just crazy. But she was connected with Petersen and there was nothing crazy about that man. Besides, Ewen himself knew she was not crazy, and he sat there and stared from her hazel eyes to the wolfish eyes of the dog. Very similar eyes. He gave a sigh that lasted forever.

Another uncle. Why another uncle? Most people rarely think about uncles at all, and here his life seemed to be revolving around them. *When bad things happen to good uncles.*

"Maybe it's not related to the other cases, doctor. And if it is, I don't know what I'll be able to do about it. I don't know about monsters, except the Tibetan kind, and that's only because of my brother-in-law."

"He's Tibetan?"

"German," said Ewen, absently. "German-American. And maybe the murderer is just a man. Or a monster of a man. And what if we do find it? Him?"

She shrugged and patted the dog again. "For that we have Resurrection, here. And from what Ricky says, you're pretty handy to have around, too."

He glanced at her in alarm.

Chapter Eleven

Ewen slept badly that night, half-convinced he had let himself get involved in the schemes of a schizophrenic woman. The only thing that kept him from deciding to cancel the whole thing was that this woman was connected with Detective Richard Petersen, who was definitely not schizophrenic, and to whom he definitely owed a debt. There was also the fact that he could not deny there was something very nasty and very real going on in the world out there. The previous evening had proved that.

Besides—the Indian veterinarian was a very attractive woman, and if she was a little bit odd, at least she already knew he was, too. He fell asleep on that thought.

The next morning he finished the final sitting for Mr. Bolt's portrait. The rest of the painting could be done without a sitter. He spent the rest of the day arranging people to take on his classes at the kwoon. Though he was the school dictator, he found it very difficult to find subjects to do his bidding. Finally, he called Ryan Watanabe, Barbie Cowell, and Perry Janaway, and simply told each of them they were going to be the head of this or that class. Then he hung up on each. He hoped Ryan—an enthusiast—would not drive some junior student to rip a ligament. He knew that Perry would spend half the time mugging around and telling lawyer jokes—but that was okay; lawyer jokes had never ripped anyone's ligament. Barbie would do fine. Barbie had also had classes dumped on her before, by James Young. Now, thought Ewen, smiling, he really was carrying on the family tradition.

He cut his grass for what he hoped would be the last time this year. Should have done it weeks ago. He called Lynn, and since he couldn't successfully lie to her, he told her only that he was going out of town for a few days and would explain later. She took it in stride. Teddy demanded to speak to his uncle, as he required more explanation. Ewen did the best he could.

Ewen fed his fish. He packed his bag.

Dr. Sundown had said she would take care of the flight expenses, but he did not intend to let her shoulder all the financial burden. After all, he was the man and she was . . . What? Damsel in distress. Let it be that. Just damsel in distress.

When she showed up in a very ancient and dirty GMC Suburban, complete with dog, he knew she could not have the sort of money to purchase two last-minute round-trip airline tickets to Idaho, plus canine passage. He was glad he'd been to the bank. He slid into the passenger seat and reached for his wallet. He felt a soft weight on his left shoulder. It was the nose of the dog. He glanced at her without moving his shoulder and heard the single thump of her tail.

"That is *really* unusual," said Dr. Sundown. "Resurrection does not like strangers. Mostly she doesn't like anybody."

"More unusual than you think," said Ewen, who felt absurdly complimented by the dog. "German shepherds *never* like me. There's one in the neighborhood that has his eye out for my hide."

"You're safe as long as we're around." Dr. Sundown heaved the big old car out onto the road. "Rez will take care of you."

He thought about the name, and about himself. "Why do you call her Resurrection? Did she come close to dying, maybe? Did her heart stop and you brought her back?"

Susan Sundown shot him a glance of too much intelligence. "No. Perhaps it's you who should carry that name. In fact, I think that should be your Indian name. I'll have to talk with Grandma, but . . ."

"My *what*?"

She ignored the interruption. "Rez is called that because she's a cadaver dog. She finds the dead."

This information took Ewen's thoughts in a strange direction. He felt removed from the car, the easy local traffic of Redmond, the beautiful woman beside him. The amber eyes of the dog stared into his, in complete ease.

As Ewen Young breathed in and out, looking at the dog, Dr. Sundown asked, "Why are you holding your wallet? I mean, you've had it in your hand for over a minute and haven't moved. Are you going to show me your ID and registration?"

Ewen breathed out heavily and returned to the matter at hand. "Sorry. I need to give you money for my fare. I went to the bank this morning."

He was prepared for a wrangle about the money. He was not prepared for her to say, "You can pay for gas, if you like. But I won't know how much that is till we're there."

"We're driving?"

"No. Why should we drive when I've got a plane?"

She's got a plane, thought Ewen. Easy as that. "Got a plane." This woman is going to fly us over the state of Washington and into Idaho in an airplane of some sort—probably a small "puddle jumper." I am in a movie, he thought, and he sank back into his seat and felt himself grinning. I am in a movie, and it's an adventure movie and we're going to find a monster. The grin died away.

Once before Ewen had been in a private airplane. He had been a sophomore, and his roommate had had a brother with a single-engine plane. He remembered how much noise the thing made, and how uncertain the angle with the ground seemed. He had been scared blank by the experience.

This time, with Dr. Sundown at the controls of her Cessna and Rez in harness behind them, he felt nothing but a brilliant amazement: at the mountains piled beneath them, at the snow and the dark bitter tree-line, and the feeling of bodiless freedom as they shifted course from north to south, and at the long expanse of wild Washington State as it passed beneath. Today fear was far estranged.

Susan Sundown was wearing faded jeans and a flannel shirt. She wore them well. On her feet were cowboy boots, very pointed and scuffed, with tall heels.

"You're looking at my boots," she said.

"Yes. I like them."

"These old things?" she asked in a teasing voice. They *were* old things. "You know why the toes are so pointed?"

"Style?"

"Not hardly. When you lose your stirrups, the points make it easy to find them again. That can be important."

"I can imagine," said Ewen, and added, "but I've always wondered why cowboys wear high heels. No gowns, but high heels."

Susan giggled. "They make it harder to slip your foot all the way through the stirrup and get caught." After a moment, she added, "It also expresses your confidence that you're not going to have to walk home. Cowboys used to buy their boots very tight, for the same reason. I guess it all comes down to vanity.

"And, if we're talking about vanity, I have to give in to it and claim that my great-grandfather was once the rodeo king of the country. The biggest Indian rodeo king of all time. His name was Jack Sundown."

Ewen leaned back and smiled at this. For a long time there was no sound but that of the engine, and the breathing of the big dog behind them.

"You're not saying much," said Susan Sundown. "Are you just the quiet sort?"

"No," said Ewen. "I talk a lot. But I also like looking out the window." He looked for a long time, very relaxed. So far he really liked this movie.

They came down outside Tacoma to fuel up. For the first time in his life Ewen saw the ground come up straight in front of his eyes, and he worked to remember it: the sight and the moment. It would be necessary to use diagonals on canvas to round the lines of perspective, but not too much or it would look silly. As he thought about it, they landed and came to a stop, a bit more sudden than he had anticipated. He swayed in his seat-harness and the dog, in her own harness, let out a little grunt. Ewen was still grinning when Dr. Sundown leaned over to remind him he had offered to pay for gas. He scrambled for his wallet.

"It's a good thing I called before leaving," she said. "Gram isn't at the Rez at all. She's at a powwow by the Tamástslikt of the Confederateds."

"The Confederates?" said Ewen.

"Confederated Tribes of the Umatilla. That's the Walla Walla, Cayuse, and Umatilla. They've got a big cultural center. For whites to see." Dr. Sundown shot a guilty glance at Ewen and amended it. "For nonnative people, I mean. So we're heading toward Pendleton as soon as I clear a plan."

"That'll be nice," said Ewen serenely. He had very little idea what she had just said.

He wished he had brought pastels, because the view of Oregon from close above was priceless. All he had was the little sketchbook he called his idea book, and he drew idea after idea into it, with marginal abbreviations suggesting pigment. Susan Sundown glanced over occasionally, with respectful interest, but the pages held no more meaning for her than Confederated Umatilla did for Ewen. Resurrection slept.

Outside Pendleton they hit some updrafts, and the plane bounced and sank, bounced and sank. Ewen was not subject to motion sickness, so he drew on. The dog slept.

Cows raised their heads as they passed—the plane descending lower and lower. That was a neat angle. Could one paint cows contemplating an airplane? From the plane's point of view?

The wheels hit the ground with a considerably larger bounce, and Ewen lost his pencil in the air and caught it again, staring at the tiny airstrip before them. Dr. Sundown, although busy with the landing, did not miss this.

"You caught your pencil in the air," she said. "You were looking out the window and you caught your pencil in the air."

Ewen nodded and pressed his face against the glass, looking at the grass stubble, the dirt, the small, square building, and the lively faded red windsock. "This place is great!" he said.

"Is it?" Susan looked at the dingy little airport doubtfully. Then she looked at her passenger, who was hopping out of the plane, swinging his little bag on his shoulder. "I'll have to learn to see it that way."

Ewen had forgotten this trip was about monsters. He had forgotten about cold fear and dismembered priests. He knew only he was having a great time. He watched Susan chock the plane and busy herself with a dusty tan Buick parked by the shed. It had primer spots on the near fenders. It looked mistreated but not quite abandoned.

"Is this legal?" asked Ewen, more from curiosity than concern. She was pulling the key out from under the floor mat.

"Oh, sure. Raymond left it for me. He was one of my patients when I worked out here. Or, I should say, his cows were." She got in the car and he followed, hauling his small sack with him. The old car groaned to life. The floorboard emitted a slight fragrance of exhaust. Ewen kept his window open. Puddle jumper to rattletrap, he thought. Nice line, but for a poet, not a painter. He glanced again at the beautiful doctor who was driving and wondered what else here was for a poet and not a painter.

"I've never been to a powwow," he said, to make conversation.

"Why would you?" Dr. Sundown answered. "You're not the kind of whi . . . I mean, non-Indian who knows about powwows."

Ewen took a deep breath of the wet Oregon winter air and said, "Lots of times I go places you wouldn't expect. Like the Assyrian picnic last spring. Assyrians in Washington State! I did drawings and I gave them away. I also went to a Mormon Stake children's day. If you give away sketches of faces, almost no one cares who you are."

Susan thought about this. "Nice. But if you give them away, what do you get out of it all?"

"I don't forget what I draw," said Ewen, still looking out the window.

"And do you want to sketch people at the powwow? The dancers, maybe? The kids in costume? A lot of photographers come . . . "

He shook his head. "No. That's for another time. This is for you. For your grandmother. Your granduncle. About the . . . thing."

"The wendigo?"

"What? I'm sorry?"

Dr. Sundown sighed. "I think it's a wendigo. It's an Indian kind of thing. They're from up north. They're very bad. But I shouldn't have even brought up the idea. I've got no way of knowing."

"Wendigo," said Ewen, taking some time over the word. "We can call it that. A wendigo."

The first thing he noticed as they approached was the beat of the drum, a big, soft thump that popped his eardrums like the effect of a change in altitude. The community center itself was nothing much: three large rooms with fluorescent lighting and vinyl floors. They were filled with people, many of whom were children who ran through the groups of adults like schools of small fish through reefs. Some of the people, children and adults, were dressed in what Ewen thought of as costume and others in what he thought of as cowboy. Just inside the door he pulled back to make a scan of faces. There was every sort of face: sharp, round, light, dark, some with a lot of make-up, and some without many teeth. His fingers twitched, creating memories.

"Come on," said Dr. Sundown. She plucked his sleeve to pull him through the first room, which was largely open, to the next, where the drumbeat sounded. Ewen heard the drum as a heartbeat and remembered last summer. Parrish. The door. His attention faded for a moment and he was surprised at the force with which Susan propelled him forward. He stopped to meet the glances of other surprised people and apologized before being pushed on.

As at any social event, the doorway between rooms was blocked with people talking. Ewen had only a glimpse of a woman in a tremendous display of turquoise and silver talking with a man in buckskin who was wearing an improbable tailpiece, when he was pulled into the room with the drum.

"She'll be with George Thibedoux. He's up for Best Drum of 2012. Just wait here till I find her," said Susan Sundown, and she left him standing against a wall.

In the middle of the room were dancers: sweating, sparkling, gloriously dressed. Four older men sat in one corner, bending over one old drum. Ewen, forgetting his promise, grabbed for his sketchbook. It was not to draw the dancers, but to draw the four old men.

Susan pressed her way around the edge of the dance to the musicians' platform, and tugged on one drummer's leg. Ewen saw him glance down, not missing a beat. They spoke for only seconds, and then she was snaking back again. She saw the sketchbook and respectfully stopped, but he slipped it back into his pocket.

"Find out something?" Ewen asked.

She took him by the hand and led him through the crowd again. People still clotted the doorway. As they stood, waiting for a break in the crowd, one young man of the cowboy variety saw Ewen, shoved himself away from the wall, and approached Ewen with a friendly but speculative stare. "Californian?"

Ewen was startled. "Yes." *How'd he know?*

"Modoc? Pima? No, not Pima . . . "

"Santa Barbara," said Ewen as he was once more dragged away.

"What was that about?" asked Susan, as she led him into a more open room with the smell of food.

"Guy somehow knew I was from California," said Ewen. "But I don't remember meeting him before. And I usually do remember."

"Strange," said Susan, not really paying attention. She had found her grandmother.

When Ewen saw Grace Sundown he thought for a moment he was again looking at Enid Buhl, the great artist. It was not that this woman resembled Buhl in any usual sense; it was the way in which she looked at Ewen.

She was very, very old. Her face was a fine mesh of wrinkles and she was darker than her granddaughter, but she had the same flecked brown-hazel eyes. There was still some black in her hair.

"So," she said, looking at him. "You will be able to find my brother? His spirit, maybe?"

Ewen opened his mouth in alarm, but Susan spoke first. "I think maybe he can, Granny." Then she turned to Ewen. "I didn't tell her that about you. She doesn't—didn't—know we were coming. It's just the way Granny is."

"I have no idea whether I'll be able to find your brother, ma'am," said Ewen, flushing. "It was Dr. Sundown's idea to bring me here. I haven't found people . . . " and here he paused, not knowing whether what he was saying was the exact truth. "I haven't found *missing* people before."

She eyed him speculatively, as though he were a car for sale. "It may be you can," she said. "Try for us. But try carefully."

Susan Sundown said, "Granny, I've been thinking that maybe it's a wendigo."

"Wendigo?" The old woman's eyebrows rose, making her forehead crinkle. "I don't think so."

"How can you be so sure?"

Ewen felt a complicated line of energy between these women, made of more than family affection. He took a small step backwards.

"I'm not sure. But I'd look first for Bear Woman."

"A woman!" Susan seemed scandalized.

"Bear Woman," corrected her grandmother, looking at her sidelong and severe. "Remember, Susie, it was *you* who didn't want to study the old traditions. You could have. You have the power in you. But you chose to be a vet. Very worthwhile occupation, too. But you don't know as much about spirit as you think you do. You don't know about Bear Woman, and now you should!"

Susan's expression hinted her grandmother's opinion was one she had heard before, but her tone was respectful. "Tell what I need to know, Gran."

"First, she doesn't like men at all. Specially men who would enter the spirit world. Next, she likes to tear things apart. Those things you heard about from your policeman—those are the signs of Bear Woman, all right." The old woman sighed, glanced at Ewen and then back at her granddaughter.

"And besides all that, Susie: I have to tell you that you look like a stupid Indian who has had an accident with the bleach bottle. What are you doing with hair like a surfer girl?"

Dr. Sundown turned her head away, half-embarrassed, half-angry. "I think a person ought to be able to do whatever they want with their hair."

Ewen had drifted away for a moment as Grace talked about Bear Woman. Drifted away into a cold place. Now he came back. "I think her hair looks great," he said with conviction.

Grace Sundown looked at Ewen carefully. "And if your sister dyed her hair blond?"

"My sister *has* dyed her hair blond. And blue. And red. And . . . how the hell did you know I have a sister?"

She smiled. "You just told me." Then she smirked and added, "Most people have a sister. It wasn't Indian magic." Grace Sundown turned from them as another elder with massive silver earrings put a hand on her shoulder and began to speak into her ear.

Susan and Ewen grabbed tortillas stuffed with something meaty from a woman at the food tables and ate them as they worked their way back to the front door. Ewen's didn't taste as he'd expected. He stopped to take notice, and she saw his face. "They're mutton," said Susan. "The Dine brought them. A specialty. Don't you like it?"

"Now that I know what it is, I do," he replied, dribbling juice onto the tile floor, and onto his shirt. "Sometimes, you just have to know." He passed closely along the wall, because now two women in huge colorful shawls were swirling in the middle of the room, to the delight of the crowd. Susan swallowed and cleared her throat. "The one on the left is a possibility for Best Shawl Dancer. Of 2012."

"You're right up on this stuff," said Ewen, appreciating the show of color. "Do you dance, too? Or play something?"

"No," said Susan Sundown. "I happened to read it on the Internet."

It seemed their detour to Oregon was over already, for Susan pulled him onward and through the door. "Okay, back to the airport."

"That was a quick stop," said Ewen.

"I just wanted Gran's advice. With Gran, it has to be in person. And not her advice on my hair!"

Outside, in the parking lot, he was wondering what to do with his sticky hands, as the little napkin that had come with it was used up. Susan said, "Oh, oh. Watch out." At first he thought she was talking about his mess, but then he noticed she was looking down the row of parked cars.

There were five young men there, leaning against cars. They all looked pretty much like cowboys except one who wore a stud in his lip. They were staring at the two of them, in a sort of above-all-of-it fashion.

"Watch out for what?" whispered Ewen. "They're not doing anything to us."

"Not yet, they're not," said Susan. "But if they start making comments, don't respond."

"Of course I won't," answered Ewen. "Why would I?"

She went on as though he hadn't spoken at all. "Just leave them alone. Those guys have obviously been booted from the powwow for being drunk. They may be looking for trouble."

"Well, I'm not," said Ewen. "I'm just looking for a napkin."

"They may make racial slurs."

"Against Santa Barbarans?" Ewen grinned as he said this. He wasn't looking at the men, but he was definitely seeing them. Seeing things was his life's training.

One young guy in a red shirt pushed himself away from the car, smiling broadly. "Hey, chickie, chickie, chickie!" he called.

Dr. Susan Sundown kept walking, staring straight ahead. Her stride was stiff, her eyes fixed ahead. Ewen ambled behind her. The man in the red shirt, who by his glassy eyes certainly was drunk, looked from Susan to Ewen and back again. Ewen thought, well, here comes the ethnic slurs. From a Native American against a Chinese. The thought was hilarious.

"Hey, brother," said the guy. "Why'd you have to bring a white girl to the powwow? Aren't Indian girls good enough for you?"

Ewen stopped to reboot his mind, but Susan Sundown didn't stop. She spun sideways with a roundhouse punch to the man's jaw that dropped him flat on the pavement.

"Oh hell," whispered Ewen.

In the next few moments, nobody moved. One man, about six feet away from them, with a bottle in his inside vest pocket, gave a large belch, which echoed in the silence. Ewen stood between Susan and the men, with his arms out in both directions, as though he were the referee in a prizefight. He hoped no one *would* move.

Another tall guy on the other side of a truck, the closest to Ewen, decided that he should do something. He pushed himself onto the truck's hood, stood up and stared. As he stood there, he considered the situation and decided to become angry. He became very angry. He hurled himself forward with full commitment, aimed straight at Ewen . . . who did nothing in response except duck.

The fellow came over Ewen's back with the liquid grace of the really drunk, and Ewen rose up, in order to slam the man on his chest as he sailed above. His assailant flipped over and came down on his back, instead of his head, as he might have otherwise. Ewen had done this merely to save the man from major injury, but now there were two young men lying flat on the pavement, put there by Susan and Ewen. "Oh, hell," mumbled Ewen again.

Someone came up behind Susan Sundown, outraged, cursing. At the same moment, the man with the bottle, older and heavier than the others, took the malt liquor out of his vest and hurled it at Ewen, who dodged it. Behind him, Susan slapped it away from her head. It bounced off her hand and straight into the nose of a fourth party, who had been standing by inoffensively. This man, too, went down bleeding.

"Oh hell," said Ewen for the third time.

The man who had thrown the bottle now demanded his attention. He tried to rabbit punch Ewen, who was forced to trip him and spin him around, so Ewen missed seeing the last man of the five come up behind Susan, wrap his arms over hers, and lift her from the ground. He called her a bitch. He called her some other things.

Ewen heard the struggle and turned toward it, almost missing the fact that the man between them had thrown another punch at him. It grazed his face, stinging,

Susan, however upset and confined she was, had not missed seeing this. She lashed out one pointed boot with full force and caught Ewen's attacker at the base of his tailbone. The man let out an agonized cry and fell in a ball, holding his rear end. In the moment of distraction that followed, she viciously kicked her captor in the shin with her heavy heel. He let her slip. There came another few moments in which no one moved. Then Ewen grabbed Susan by the hand and shouted, "Run!"

He found he had to drag her along. "Why run?" she asked. "We've got them all down!"

"I know! I know! That's why we're running."

"Huh?"

"From the police, you idiot—I mean, Susan. We're the bad guys here!"

She began to keep up with him, though with her boots it was difficult. "What do you mean? They're drunk. They . . . "

"They did nothing but call you a white chickie. I don't think the police will find that just cause for laying a man out. And then there was the man hit with the bottle." Ewen paused at a street corner, trying to remember which way led to the airport.

Susan pointed out the direction. They turned a corner and continued along the street, now walking, but very quickly. "But we didn't throw the bottle," she said. "And there were five of them and only two of us."

"All the police need to do is look at my driver's license and they will see I'm not a Santa Barbara Indian . . . "

"A what?"

"Never mind. But if they look me up they'll find out I run a school of kung fu . . . "

"I didn't know you did. Run it, I mean. Ricky never said . . . "

"Let's just go," said Ewen. "Let's just go."

Ewen was tense as they readied the plane for the next leg of their journey. He watched Rez, released from the hold of the plane, gambol around in a carefree manner. This seemed surprising for a dog of her somber occupation, but Ewen was in no mood for play; he was preoccupied with listening for sirens in the distance.

"Remind me," he said to Susan, "never to offend you."

"Oh, I will," she replied. She seemed pleased with herself. She threw a stick for the dog, who caught it in the air, lay down, and ate it.

When they were aboard again and she had begun taxiing down the runway, he breathed a sigh of relief. "What would you have done if the police asked you why you clobbered the guy?"

Very soberly she said, "I would have told them it was a part of my native tradition."

He stared. "And is it?"

Susan began to smile, and the smile grew to a giggle, and the giggle to loud, raucous laughter that reddened her face and caused tears to start and her nose to run.

Ewen watched this with fascination until the contagion of laughter overtook him. She braked the plane. "Give me a minute. I can't take off with my eyes running this way."

Rez shared her owner's mood. Being unable to laugh, she barked instead and tapped her front paws in a stiff staccato on the floorboards.

Eventually they stopped laughing and were off and in the air. "So, where are we going now?" asked Ewen.

"Oh, haven't I told you? Of course I didn't! Well, we're going east to Idaho, where Sid was lost, just outside the reservation. There's an old forest up there with some red cedars in with hemlock. It's an unusual thing—to have red cedars in the high country. It's special. That's where Uncle Sid went to pray; he would talk with the cedars."

"And what if he's still doing that, and all your worry is for nothing?"

"Then I'll be a very happy vet," she said. Her eyes did not show belief.

They flew over the black-green countryside, dusted with snow, and then over white mountains so bright under sunlight they hurt the eyes. Wind in the mountains caught the small plane and knocked them about somewhat. Rez threw up once. The large animal harness in the back shivered and swung.

"Your life is so different from mine," murmured Ewen, glancing at the woman beside him. "The closest I get to nature is pulling the bamboo shoots out of the yard."

"Bamboo! That sounds very civilized, very cultured."

Ewen grinned. "My neighbors don't think so."

"But that and the painting, and that house you live in. All seems perfect to me. Very small scale and perfect."

"I'm a small scale sort of guy," said Ewen. "And you haven't even seen my painting."

She shrugged. "Just as well. I'd probably say the wrong thing: admire it for the wrong reasons. But Ricky says you do really pretty pictures."

"Thank Ricky for me," said Ewen, dryly.

"I can't. Then I'd have to admit I went to your house after he forbade me."

Ewen thought about this for a moment. He was displeased by her reference to Detective Petersen, and especially to his authority over them both. "He doesn't have the right to forbid you things, Susan. Remember? You told me so."

"No. But he told me secrets. That implies a certain right. Still, I need to find Uncle Sid, and I can't get those guys in Idaho to believe he's a part of this series of killings." She leaned back and cracked her knuckles.

"Fact is, I can't get them to believe Sid is a holy man. He's just an Indian, after all." The bitterness sharpened her voice.

"Tell me, Ewen. Do you have trouble in your life about . . . about being Chinese in a white country?"

He considered. "Is it really a white country anymore? You couldn't guess it where I live. And what do I know about trouble, really? My father's a doctor. So's my sister. My grandfather left me a whole house, free and clear. My biggest problem is being a disappointment to Dad. And I'm not really that, any more, since I've got a reputation."

"Sounds great. But you did get shot."

He laughed uneasily. "By a Chinese."

She hesitated. "So everything about your life's okay? Even when you travel into the land of the dead?"

There was silence for a minute, and Susan hurried to say she didn't mean make him talk about that, but he interrupted. "I'm just thinking about what to say . . . I only did that a few times. And I hope it was just . . . a thing that happened and is over."

There was more silence. He hadn't really talked about the events of the summer for months to anyone. Not even to his sister. Lynn was still afraid, thinking of Teddy.

Now, high over the northwest mountains, Ewen felt able to talk again. To talk about magic to a magic Indian. Ewen took a big stretch and cracked his neck left and right. "It's dangerous, going between. Dangerous and tempting. I didn't really know what I was doing, or seeing, or if I was going to get back."

He met her hazel eyes. "I like to be in control of myself," he said. "That's what martial arts are all about. And painting, too, I guess. When . . . all that happened . . . I was totally *out* of control, and I didn't like it at all."

"Oh, jeez!" Her eyes were wide. "And then I show up on your doorstep! I should never have asked you to do another crazy thing!"

Ewen shrugged easily. "You're not asking me to go between worlds. Nothing crazy. You're asking me to help find your Uncle Sid. You think maybe I can see special things. Only problem is, I doubt I'll be any good for that. I don't want to disappoint you, but like I told Detec—your Ricky—I'm not John Edward or Miss Cleo."

"Who are they?"

"They are supposedly psychics."

"Never met them."

"Used to be on television?"

"Don't have one."

Very different, thought Ewen. He looked at the profile of the beautiful Indian woman and wondered if they would be too different after all.

Chapter Eleven

EWEN LOOKED DOWN at the passing hills; white-dusted, the forest, lit white from beneath, and the mountains that were glaring white. His eyes dazzled.

Something was going to happen soon. No matter whether he made wisecracks or kept still, and no matter if he asked for explanation or did not, something was going to happen. His heart skipped a beat—a thing that had never happened to him before this summer.

Of *course* something was going to happen. They had come for something to happen, in the woods, beneath the cedars, with a dog leading them, fogging the frosty air around her. Perhaps that something would be only disappointment for the woman, but it would be something. Ewen felt for the presence of his recent fear, as though searching the mouth for a sore tooth. So far, so good. Sunlight brought a warm smell from Susan's long, long hair as she sat beside him, and he thought, perhaps something was already happening.

By the time they landed the light was beginning to fail, and the dirt patch they landed on would only be considered an airport by use of imagination. The plane stopped in a neat 180-degree turn, which Ewen hoped was intentional.

"Sorry we're so late," said Susan, popping the door open and sliding to the ground, stiff and numb with cold. "I didn't allow enough time for the side trip."

Ewen slid out on his side. He heard his spine pop as he loosened his muscles. His breath hung in the air. He looked at the deep woods nearby, where the sunset made a fence paling of the Douglas firs. There was no sign of habitation except a square wooden shed, padlocked. "Where can we go in the dark?" he asked. "Is there a car somewhere? Do you have a flashlight?"

"Of course I have a flashlight," answered Susan, walking around the nose of the plane. "No car. But would you really be confident about going into the woods after dark?" Her wide eyes seemed to say she didn't know if he would be confident or not, or whether he ought to be or not. Was he Superman or was he a fool?

Ewen knew he wasn't Superman. "You're the guide," he said. "And so, the boss."

Her eyes widened further. "I guess I am. I'll have to remember that." Resurrection thrust her nose into Susan's gloved palm and whined. She glanced at the dog and straightened her shoulders. "Of course I am. I mustn't get fancies out here. After all, wendigos are only a kind of creature. People have more power than any other creature."

Wendigos, thought Ewen bemusedly. *But what if it's Bear Woman? Do people still have more power?*

Susan was still getting used to remembering she was the boss. She delved into one of the cargo holds. "Then, lady and gentleman, as your guide I can assure you we are set. We have sleeping bags. And space blankets. And food. Even toilet paper and a trowel. Yes, we're set."

After moving to Redmond from Santa Barbara, Ewen had thought he had encountered cold. Now he decided he had not. The beef jerky did not warm him, and even the bean soup heated over a Sterno fire had only a temporary effect. The gloves he had brought were acrylic and had been fine for shopping in Redmond Town Center in winter, or even clearing his garden in winter, but here they were laughable.

There was frost sparkling on the tips of the dog's fur. She looked at him bright-eyed and he envied her. He remembered a Jack London story in which a man attempts to stave off freezing by plunging his hands into the warm body of his husky. But first, he would have to kill him. In the story, he did not succeed. As Ewen had these thoughts, Rez stood up, stiff-legged, and stalked away from him.

Ewen walked out onto the dirt of the landing strip, which was frozen, and began to do a series of exercises aimed to raise his chi energy. They had always worked at home, and to his surprise they even worked here, as long as he kept doing them. "Don't get sweaty," Susan called; she was seated in her half-zipped sleeping bag, looking utterly comfortable.

"No danger of that," he answered. His coat, too, was acrylic pile. It did fine in Redmond.

When it was completely dark, he returned to the plane, guided by the light of her heavy halogen lantern. "Too bad there'll be no moon until midnight," he said, bouncing up into the body of the plane.

Susan gave a one-sided smile. "I'm surprised you know about the moon's phases, Ewen. Being a city guy and all."

"I get up early. And do you think of Redmond as a city?"

"Big city."

The sleeping bag was very warm. It was not acrylic. Susan had cut cedar boughs, dragged them onboard, and layered them under the bags. He crawled into his, only taking off his coat afterwards. He was very close to the woman. And the dog. He said, "I smell roses."

"Hand lotion. You really need it out here. Want some?" Ewen turned it down. He watched his breath mingle with hers (and the dog's) in the cabin air. Being large enough for livestock transport, it was a good, solid cabin, but not lushly heated.

Susan shifted in her sleeping bag. "Sorry there's no TV," she said.

"I don't watch it much," he replied, somewhat defensively.

"Oh. Then we've something in common." He glanced up, and wondered how many of his own thoughts were echoing in the woman's mind. He thought of Detective Rick Petersen. Ricky. He thought of his last date, which had been with Perry Janaway's sister, Penny. The girl had been fun, and hot in many ways, but she had asked him to share some blow she happened to have. Perry must still be wondering why he had never asked his sister out again. He'd have had fits about the cocaine.

"Tell be about your . . . your magic," he asked Susan. "If it's not offensive of me to call it that."

"Offensive to call it magic? As opposed to what?" She turned to him and her teeth glimmered in the failing light.

"Well—Theo, my brother-in-law, thinks of what happened to me as religion. He wouldn't like . . . "

"Magic! Religion! It's all just ways of understanding life." Susan let out one of her big laughs. "I'm happy to call it magic."

"Sometimes I can make things happen. Little things, or they're little to most people. When I was a girl I could call hawks. And deer, sometimes. And sometimes I just know something has happened. Just know it."

"My sister's like that. But just with me. We're twins."

"I didn't know that. Cool! I'd like to have that kind of closeness with someone . . . "

"It's not *that* kind of closeness," he said, uncomfortably, though he wasn't sure what he was uncomfortable about.

"But I chose not to follow up on that aspect of life. I chose vet school. That," she made a wriggling gesture, hidden in her sleeping bag "was a big and very useful magic. Like you chose painting." He could see the whites of her eyes moving over his face.

"It wasn't really a choice. I was born to paint. Until I was shot, I never had anything *really* strange happen to me. I just painted and did martial arts. And martial arts were just, well, a hobby. I haven't competed since high school."

"But you do that Buddhist meditation stuff. Ricky says you're really good at it."

He guffawed, briefly. "Meditation isn't really something you're *good* at. You just sit there!"

"It's all Chinese magic to me," said Susan, teasingly. They traded grins in the lantern light.

Resurrection paced over, yawning, making a crackling frozen cloud with her breath. She thumped herself down between Ewen and Susan and gave a great sigh. The dog was so big he couldn't see Susan at all over the top of the mass of fur. There was silence.

Ewen took the hint and rolled over. Sleep surprised him instantly.

Susan Sundown had a harder time falling asleep. In the quiet of the cabin there was nothing to keep her embarrassment at bay. She realized she had hauled off and hit a man, simply because he offended her self-image. Calling her white. And it was just after Grandma had teased her about pretending to be white. Susan cursed the impulse that had made her highlight her hair.

But Ewen Young had liked it. He had said it out loud, and Ewen was a well-known artist. She knew that because she had had a friend look him up online. Susan saw a few of his paintings on a web site and thought they were very pretty. She knew she should call them something more special than "pretty" but she didn't know the words.

Ewen himself was pretty special. He moved like . . . she stopped to find an image in her mind. He moved like an animal, but that wasn't saying anything much. A tortoise was an animal.

He moved as if he were underwater; that was it. Only nobody underwater could move so fast. She had only seen him in action for a few seconds, and at the time she was busy kicking and being furious, but she noticed. And the way he bounced onto the plane from the ground, with both legs together, all the time talking about something else and not noticing her staring . . .

And he hadn't ragged her about starting the fight. Not much, anyway. He hadn't gotten pissed at her, though now she could see she had put him in some danger of the law. His hands and feet being lethal weapons and all.

Now that she thought about it, he hadn't thrown one of those lethal weapons. She had done the kicking and punching, and she *had* been pretty good at it, too. Even if she had to be embarrassed later, the fighting together was a plus. She wasn't ashamed of her performance.

Her nose was being tickled by Rez's coat. Susan was well aware why the dog had plopped herself between Ewen and Susan. This wasn't the first time the dog had gotten in between her and a possible romantic opportunity. Susan had always had mixed feelings about this, and at the moment they were growing decidedly negative.

Chapter Twelve

BETWEEN ONE MOMENT and the next Ewen was fully awake. He sat up, listening, peering around in the light of a new-risen moon, and the black dread came up in him. He disciplined it as he had before, but it welled up again. This time the object of fear was not in his mind.

It was outside.

He examined the darkness and now it was painted with the faces of bears and monsters. They were quite realistic, for—as he knew—they had been painted by his own imagination. His heart was pounding, and he felt a shred of fear that it might break open from the old scar of the summer, and out here there would be no medical science that could put it whole again. This thought, too, he disciplined.

Beside him Resurrection stood, stiff and lean, like the statue of the wolf suckling Romulus and Remus, and her growl echoed through the cabin like the engine of a Harley.

Susan gasped, sat up and whispered, "I had a nightmare . . ." and then, "Oh God. Oh shit! It's here."

The dog shot a deep amber glance at her human and her growl rose into a series of thunderous barks. She backed into Susan, straddling her.

"It's fear," shouted Ewen over the barks. "It's only fear."

"You goddamn well bet it's fear!" Susan cried back and she was shaking. "That doesn't mean it's less dangerous!"

Ewen leaned over and touched her over her heart. "Step away from it," he said, very slowly. "Let it move past you . . . I've been in situations like this before," he added gently. *Once,* he added silently. *And then it took Petersen to haul me out of it.*

Better not to tell her that part. Someone had to be cool and calm. Someone.

She looked at him, her face edged and delineated by the light of the moon, and she put her hands to her own breast, over his. Her shaking slowed. The voice of the dog, which had risen to a siren's wail, also slowed, deepened, and again became a threatening roar.

Susan glanced at her dog and took an immensely deep breath. "You're right. I gotta get over this. There's something here and I can't punk out this way now. Or ever. I'm the boss and it isn't fair to Rez."

Ewen almost grinned as she echoed his thoughts. She pushed his hand away from her and turned around in her bag, reaching beneath her for the cedar boughs. She pulled one free. "Here," she said. "Rub this on yourself. Your hands. Your head."

Ewen was busy: looking and listening. Feeling. But though he had no confidence in Susan's own Indian magic, he saw that Susan needed something to do. In moments such as these, something to do made the difference between fight and panic. Ewen rubbed the soft needles into his hands and hair, and then wiped his aromatic hands over his face. It smelled good. Felt good. Not as good as a sharpened broadsword would feel in his hand, but good. He looked at Resurrection, who was now bounding repeatedly over them, from one side of the cabin to the other. Her eyes were shining, but she still growled.

Ewen wiggled out of his bag. He put his hand on the door latch. "I'm going to get out of here," he said.

Susan's eyes widened. "Out there? Bad idea! Ewen, that's a very bad idea."

"If something comes, I've got no room to meet it in here," he answered, and he popped the door open and jumped out. What was actually in his mind was: *It will follow me. It always follows men. It's probably been following me since I went to the temple. I* won't *lead it in here.*

Outside it was very cold and crystals of ice sparkled on the dirt of the runway. The crackle of his own breath made Ewen strain for any other sound. He walked away from the plane, feeling his body heat sucked up by the night. Whatever it was, the cold was its ally.

Standing under the moon, Ewen did a breathing technique taught to him, not by his fighting uncle, but by Theo the pacifist. Tibetan snow-meditation. Heat-yoga. He raised the heat in his belly and sent it down his arms and legs. He felt it like a fire in his limbs. Hearth-fire. He looked about and waited.

The thing approached Ewen from behind, but when he leaped around, it was behind him still. This presence was not just fear: it was a lightless center that moved the air around it, and scraped over the ground. Ewen darted to a large tree and put his back against it. The thing spread slow fingers of itself around each side of the trunk, coming again from behind.

Across the runway stood another tree, its cascading branches reaching almost to the ground. It was a cedar. On an impulse, Ewen sprinted the width of the bare earth, slipping and sliding on the ice. He ducked under the spread of the tree, which was fragrant even in the frozen night.

It came straight for him and under the moonlight he could see it, though it tricked his eyes. It had a head of dissolution, of rotting death. It turned his guts to water and his stomach cramped.

The vision came into his mind of a drum made from a human skull Theo sometimes played. It had seemed a tasteless act to Ewen, once. But he remembered Theo saying to young Teddy, "It's what we're made of, son. We come and we go. It's all okay." Ewen visualized the rotting face as only a different form of the skull by Theo's altar. A different form of his own face. The cramps in his stomach loosened. He moved a step away from the cedar trunk to see the thing better.

Behind him he heard Susan chanting something he did not recognize and the low howl of Rez. "Rub the cedar oil on your hands," she called to him. "I've put magic in it."

Susan's Indian magic. Ewen felt a moment of pity for her and then remembered how pitiful his own story would seem to any number of people, had he been brave enough to share it. He hadn't been brave enough, but now he rubbed his hands together. "Susan's magic," he growled with as much authority as he could muster.

And the thing moved away from him. For a moment he felt almost euphoric, but then he saw it was turning toward the airplane. This was not what he had intended, whether Susan's magic surpassed his own or not.

The dog, howling, charged out of the plane to meet the heavy rotten thing. Wolf-like, she slashed with her teeth at the decayed flesh and her momentum carried her right into the blackness within it.

"Rez!" screamed Susan. She jumped from the plane and ran forward.

I am the boss, she had said. And, *It isn't fair to Rez.*

Ewen bellowed "No!" and he, too, ran from his place of safety. He saw the dog pitched out of the mass of darkness. Rez spun in the air and came down on the runway, skidding on the frozen ground. "No! No! It's me you want!" he shouted. "I'm the holy man! I'm the man of power!" He was so frantic that he didn't even hear himself shouting these absurdities. He ran and skidded, and came to the plane with legs spread to catch balance, sailing like a snowboarder over the ice.

Susan stood over the limp form of her dog, with only a cedar bough for weapon. She shook it in front of the encroaching shape of horror and she shouted, "You cannot come here! You cannot come!"

The thing turned its head back toward Ewen. "Throw me a branch," he called to her. "Throw me a cedar branch. Magic it!" Without hesitation she reached back into the cabin and brought one out: a long and sturdy thing. She threw it at Ewen and the cedar bough made a lazy circle in the air toward him. She threw well.

The thing—the rotten monster—extended one heavy limb in a swipe at the spinning cedar. There were long, chunky claws at the end of its arm, if arm it was, but they did not reach the branch. Ewen grabbed it from the air and hefted it. This weapon was front-heavy, but then so was a broadsword. He tore a few of the lower twigs from it and strode toward the monster.

Which then took the shape of a bear—a bear not out of nature but straight out of Ewen's worst imagination. It was much higher at the shoulder than Ewen's head. It was black; it reeked and it roared.

Bear techniques, thought Ewen. *I should have learned cedar broadsword against a monster bear. I missed that class.*

It raised an arm the size of Ewen's body and swiped its spiked claws at him. He leaped back and came down in a high-back stance, with his weight on his rear leg, and as the claws swept by him he lunged, sweeping down and to the right with his feathery weapon.

The monster screamed. It reared up, so very, very high, and then struck with its other arm.

Now Ewen was no longer seeing the branch as a piece of rough wood and needles. He was seeing a Chinese broadsword, and he was very comfortable with a broadsword. He continued the sweep up, making a circle, and sliced into the other arm as it came at him. There was even a little red flag at the end of his broadsword. For some reason that gave him confidence.

The bear-thing stood like a man—a giant—a building—and it came down at him with all its terrible mass. Ewen bounced back, and found he was stopped by a heavy bough of his cedar tree stronghold and could go no further. The thing came down over him.

An image rose in his mind, and it was not one of broadsword work, or of martial arts at all. "Sam Gamgee!" he cried and flattened himself on the ground beneath the falling terror, his "broadsword" propped straight up beside him against the earth.

It was huge blackness and weight and fear, but the fear in it was not all his own fear. The shriek he heard was deep and deafening, and it was not from him at all.

He saw nothing for a while.

He felt himself being slowly dragged by the collar. He felt warm wetness. It was the dog, licking his face. He heard Susan's voice. "Oh thank God! Thank . . . thank The Cedars! You're all right."

"I'm a little sore," he said calmly, thoughtfully, polling the regions of his body. He slowly sat up. Resurrection was all over him, licking and whining. The wolfish dog's joy could not be expressed by her tail alone, so she wagged the whole of her body. Susan was less effusive, but her eyes shone. "I'm sorry I couldn't carry you back to the plane. The best we could do was pull you along. You might have had injuries to the head; I couldn't tell, but out here you were going to freeze if you didn't wake up, so . . . "

"Whoa!" said Ewen. His head *was* sore. "What about the monster?"

"It's gone."

"Gone? You mean dead gone, or . . . "

She sighed. "No. It crawled away. Rez tried to follow it, but I called her back."

"Good thing, too. It's a real bitch." He giggled, and it hurt. "No offense meant, Rez." He clambered up, clumsily. His hands were numb, and he had to put his feet down by guess. He accepted her help back to the plane.

Susan zipped him back into his sleeping bag. She cracked open a plastic hot pack, and wrapped it around his hands. "Well, Grandma was right and I was wrong. It was Bear Woman."

Ewen found himself giggling again. "How do you know it's Bear *Woman*?"

"I'm a veterinarian, remember?" She began to start the little stove. "I'll make some soup, okay?"

"Soup's always good after a battle with a monster in sub-zero conditions," said Ewen through numb lips.

Susan wrapped her open sleeping bag around her legs, like a blanket. "How did you learn that magic, Ewen? I mean, the cedar-power runs in my family, but to turn a cedar branch into a sword . . . ?"

"You saw it as a sword, too?" He was very surprised. "I thought that was only a trick with my mind."

"It was a sword," she said. "And the thing was a bear. A prehistoric cave bear, I guess. Why not? These spirits have been around at least as long as we have." She seemed to be as much excited as frightened by the whole event. Ewen looked at her white eyes and white teeth shining in the moonlight and wondered what kind of woman he'd discovered.

"I think it looks like what it wants to," he said. "Whatever it gets from our minds to scare us."

She looked at him out of the corner of her eye. "And have you a bear phobia? I doubt it. I think it *is* a bear."

"And the cedar branch. Is it still a broadsword?"

"It's nothing," she replied. "It's gone. With the Bear Woman."

By the time he finished his soup he was calmer. Tired. "Thank you for the Indian magic," he said. "I'll never doubt it again."

"I didn't know you *had* doubted it."

"Well—how could I know? But it wasn't anything Buddhist that fought off that thing. And it wasn't *Chinese* magic." He glanced at her sidelong.

She smiled, with a gentler expression than her usual smile. "Still, we don't have Nez Perce battle swords. With flags on them! And then—magic was only half the battle, tonight." She held up her own steel cup. "Here's to the warrior!"

Then she remembered the cold nose pressed into her side. "The warriors!"

Though the exhilaration of survival faded, for the rest of the night they sat and listened, and did not sleep. They did snap open more hot-packs, and opened their bags and zipped them together very cozily. Susan put a blanket around him as well; a blanket arranged in between the two of them, but they held each other closely for the rest of the dark hours. Resurrection did not object at all.

Chapter Thirteen

THEY WAITED for the sun to be high in the trees before venturing out. Ewen felt light-headed after the long, strange night, almost pleasantly so. He wondered when the full effect of the experience would hit him. Susan looked thoughtful. The dog was full of play, and of fight. "You could wait here by the plane," Ewen offered. "Rez and I could take a look through the woods."

Her glance went from startled to offended. "You and Rez? What would you do by yourself in there? Even with the dog. Even supposing that she *would* follow you and leave me here . . . ?"

He took a deep breath and blew out a cloud of frozen mist. "I just meant maybe one of us should stay here in case we meet something. In case we don't . . . "

"Come back," she finished for him. "Then what? I'd have two people and a dog to look for instead of one uncle. We'll all go. I'll track."

Track what? Ewen wondered, gazing out over the acres of windblown snow.

At one end of the runway there was a small, snow-obscured road leading through the woods, and after about fifteen minutes high-stepping through the snow Susan, stopped and looked to her left. Without pausing, Resurrection plunged into the bank of snow at the roadside and disappeared into the trees. "She knows this place," said Susan confidently. She and Ewen followed.

The cedars made a dark forest, but enough snow had filtered through the boughs to cover most of the ground with white, which reflected the light back up against the undersides of the soft, flat needles. Ewen looked wonderingly up. He had never seen a green both so dark and so bright. It was immensely fragrant, despite the dry air.

Susan said, "I think we should keep our voices down." She pointed to an encrusted bough at one side of the trail. "There's a great weight of snow. As the day gets warmer, a lot of it may start to slide. Vibrations, like talking . . . "

"I get it," whispered Ewen.

"Oh. And avoid brushing against branches as you go by."

"I get it."

Rez plowed in front of them, making their going easier. With the clouds of her steaming breath, she looked like a very small locomotive bearing down the winding trail. She seemed immensely happy to be driving through the cold woods. Her tail was wagging in high, sloping rhythm.

Ewen strode closer to Susan and spoke into her ear. "She doesn't seem to have been effected by last night's battle. She was thrown pretty hard."

Susan smiled, her full lips glossy with Chapstick. "She's a dog. Every day is new to her. But that doesn't mean she's forgotten. Her nose will never forget that . . . thing."

"Neither will my eyes." He walked on beside her, silent for some minutes, and then asked Susan if she had seen anything other than a bear in the monster.

"Yes. I saw old Death," she said very softly. "That's her *other* face." She was silent a moment and then whispered, "And Ewen, I think it would be better not to think of her as a monster. Not like King Kong is a monster. Or Godzilla. Those you can kill with bombs, with airplanes. It would be a mistake to think of Bear Woman as one of those. Stopping her will require other means."

They walked on, crunching, a few moments more and Ewen murmured, "And that's why you wanted me here. You think I have those other means." His voice was filled with doubt.

"After last night, how can you ask?" Susan let out a great sigh and stopped in place. "Ewen, I was almost sorry to have asked you to come, because she is so dangerous. Horribly dangerous: but it's too late to stop now. Not too late for Rez and me, but for you."

Ewen smiled. His lips smarted in the cold air. "You mean it's got my scent? I knew that already. I've had dreams."

"Exactly. I think it would have been dangerous for you even if we hadn't come to your door. There was a reason that Rez was thrown out of the darkness alive. There was a reason the thing did not immediately take me, though I was less defended. Bear Woman desires to kill men. She has always hated certain men: men she can't use. She killed her own brother, that's the tale. And she hates shamans, medicine men, men with power. She hates you, Ewen."

He was taken aback. He had forgotten his call to the monster of the night before. He resisted the thought of Ewen Young as any sort of spiritual "master." That was something out of Theo's world. He himself wanted to be "master of the mat." Or "pigments master."

He cleared his throat and tried to explain in a whisper. "You give me too much credit. What power do I have, really? Martial arts? That and five bucks will get you a pretty big cup of Starbucks. Or do you mean the power to paint? That's nice work, if you're in fashion. How long I'll be in fashion I don't know. But if you mean the weird stuff, the going in and out . . . the things like the branch turning into a broadsword? That's not any power of mine, Susan. That's something that happens or it doesn't, and I'm not sure it isn't making me *less* powerful . . . "

"I don't mean the cedar-broadsword, Ewen. Not even the kung fu, though that really kicks ass—forgive the expression. I mean power over yourself, Ewen. Body, mind, spirit. Power over yourself. That's what you have. She'll never have such power, not over her own feelings, and not over yours. That's why she hates you." Susan paused, breathing hard. "Whatever you believe about yourself, Ewen, believe that she hates you. I saw it. So did you."

He could think of nothing to say. He suddenly noticed his fingers and toes were cold. He, too, believed the thing hated him, and he had no idea what to do about that. The dog, seeing them facing each other tensely, breathing their emotions into the air, moved softly between them and engaged in a complicated whining conversation with their smells. Placating them. Making peace.

Slowly, Susan began to smile. "Yeah, girl. You're right. You're usually right."

"She says let's get on with it," said Susan, and stepped onward, ripping the snow with her boot soles.

Susan and Ewen looked down at Rez's head, dusted with snow. He began to walk forward in the snow.

Chapter Fourteen

SUSAN WAS whispering again. For a woman who was constantly warning Ewen about noise, she spoke a great deal. "This is a sort of natural avenue in the trees. Uncle found it years ago. The cleft in the hill here is probably what made it possible for the red cedars to grow. Really special. It's a shame it isn't part of the reservation because then we could protect . . ."

The dog broke in, commandingly. She did not bark or whine, but made a complex noise that sounded amazingly like human speech. Her nose was up and so were her hackles. Then she lowered her head and began to stride forward, rolling her heavy shoulders. Susan fell in behind her. In a soft and somber voice she said, "Rez is the boss, now. She has the senses and we're blind."

Ewen came last. He understood what Susan meant, but he did not feel blind. His own senses went out in all directions. Sight was treacherous along this trail, glaring white and draped and spotted with green shadows, but it was still usable. His ears gave him the sound of the dog breasting the snow and the easy bellows of her breath. He heard Susan's feet stepping down into the dog's cleared path with delicacy, making little disturbance. He could hear his own boots following hers. Over all this was a dry hiss of blowing snow, drifting into their tracks even as they were made. No bird called. He felt the cold on his face, and he closed his eyes, turning his head left and right for some reminder of the corrupt shadow that was so much darker than that of the trees. He felt nothing of that darkness, but suddenly he felt the presence of the woman in front of him, and he felt the beginnings of her grief.

And more than this, he felt Resurrection, whose heavy body and single-minded soul aimed straight ahead. She was an arrow that knew its target. She was indeed the boss at this moment, and without warning Ewen found himself seeing from inside her mind. He reeled and caught himself against the bough of a cedar, causing snow to drop all around them.

He could see Susan ahead of him, but imposed over that he could see what Rez saw. He got his balance back, but did not lose that double-centered vision. Very strange. Very strange.

Through the mind of the dog, Ewen became aware of that which awaited them under the snow, some five hundred feet ahead along the path. He felt it through her. Smelled it.

He reached for Susan's arm. "Stop here. Please. Just for a minute. Let me go ahead with her."

"Why would I want to do that?" She shook off his hand. "I know Rez and I know where we are along the path. I can guess what she must be smelling. I was prepared for it." She turned to him, her eyes wide. "But how are you . . . ?"

He tried again. "Maybe it's not as easy as you think. I know how you must feel; how I would feel if it was my family out there. And the dog—she's saying it's very bad."

"She's saying this to you? You know how *I* feel?" She swivelled in tense anger at what she thought was arrogance on his part, and she then met his eyes. Her own went still wider. "You *do know* . . . what . . . what *is* it you know? That you're seeing?"

Ewen swallowed heavily. "Your uncle, I guess. About four hundred feet away. He's buried in the snow. You can't see anything at all from the surface. He's . . . scattered."

Susan uttered a great sigh that froze crackling in the air. She made tight fists inside her mittens. The dog slowed, then stopped, and turned to her master. Intensity was in her form and her gaze. "Rez is saying I should follow," said Susan, and she went on.

The avenue opened up into a rough circle, in which there was nothing to be seen except a heap of snow-coated stones in the middle, and a few bare twigs of brush sticking up. "This is the sacred circle he found," said Susan woodenly. "We think it must be old." Resurrection made a quick cast around her and then, with a strange dignity, she sat down. She made no sound. Her tail did not wag, but her amber eyes met those of her master and shone.

Ewen knew what was under that white carpet. He didn't know how he knew it, unless it was somehow through the dog, but he could smell it, hear it, even taste it in the back of his throat. He stood in place with one hand folded over the other and watched Susan start to brush the snow away.

How perfectly preserved was this brutality. How ruby-pink the snow. Ewen shook his head slowly and looked at Susan instead of the remains of her great-uncle.

She had put her mittened hands over her face. "Leave us here," she said quietly. "Please. Just for a few minutes."

He found it odd that she said "us," and not "me." He was not sure whether she was referring to the dog or to Uncle Sid. Or both. "I really don't think I should do that," he replied, shifting his weight from one chilled foot to the other.

"We'll be safe."

"Well, will I?" He tried not to make the question sound sarcastic.

She took it simply. "Don't go far. Just out of the circle. And only for a few minutes."

He retreated, but continued to watch her. He could feel the dog's mind, but not Susan's and he was concerned. He saw her take off her mittens, and pull a short, thick stick of faded green from her parka pocket. She also took out a small Bic lighter and applied the flame to the end of the stick, which lit and smoked. She waved the stick in the cold air and the flame went out, leaving slow embers and much more smoke. She pointed it around the circle, and said something Ewen could not make out. Then she splashed the smoke over her own head and Rez's plush back.

The smell came to him, and though it was not incense as he was used to it, he remembered vividly his mother's funeral, and the cauldron-sized burner of sand, gleaming with the light of joss sticks. He hadn't thought of this for all his adult life.

Recollecting himself he listened to the woods: snow, here and there, dropping from the branches, wind hissing over dry snow. Far away, the heavy bounce of a mule deer. From a few yards out there was a tickle of sound—the slight scratching which he knew to be the feathers of an owl shifting on its perch. He felt the owl's sleepy picture-thoughts. He heard mice under the snow around him, with their tiny, self-involved thoughts. Within the open circle, there was no sound or feeling of anything alive but the woman and the dog.

Ewen was not happy about this new extension of his senses, wondrous as it was. He breathed calmness as well as he could.

Throughout her ceremony, Susan Sundown had not stepped out of her own first tracks, and the dog had sat motionless. Now she reversed herself and stepped back to Ewen. She said nothing to him, but flipped open her cell phone and punched out a number. After a minute she tried again, and then shook her head. "No reception." Her voice was almost normal. "They'll think I shouldn't have burnt the smudge stick. Crime scene and all. Too little 'police-affiliate-dog-handler' about it—too much . . . Indian."

"I think they'll understand," said Ewen, though he didn't really understand himself.

She cleared her throat. "Ewen, I'd like you to go out to the road again and dial nine-one-one. I've used the phone from the strip back there before today and there was reception. I'll wait here."

"No! That's crazy, Susan. I'm not going to leave you alone out here! It's out of the question."

"It wasn't a question, Ewen. Someone has to stay with the . . . body. That's how it's done."

"Then let it be me. I'll stay."

Susan's eyes widened. "No, Ewen. Not you. There's too much you don't understand!"

In frustration, he slammed his fist into the nearest cedar bole, and little showers of snow fell all around. "There sure is! That's why I can't go," he said. "I'll just get lost in the woods. City boy—remember?"

"Not with Rez to guide you. Plus the footprints."

"She won't go with me and leave you here. You know that. And the wind is blowing in the clearings. Wouldn't take much to get me lost."

Susan Sundown was losing her temper. "Bullshit. And she'll do what I tell her to!"

Ewen was losing his temper too. "I won't just do what you tell me to!" replied Ewen. "If someone's got to stay here, it'll be me."

The dog butted herself between them and tried to whine some sense into them. Ewen shut out her thoughts. "How 'bout we leave Rez, then, if she'll stay that long for you?"

"Because it'll violate the . . . the crime scene. I know she won't touch the body but the crime scene people can't take that on faith."

He was on the edge of saying he couldn't see what good any of them could do for old Sid by staying, and they might as well all go, but right now, with Susan's face streaked with frozen tears, that didn't seem a tactful thing to say. So he thought fast and said, "Nothing bad will happen here today, in the daylight. I can feel it. I can hear the deer feeding out of sight in the trees and I can hear the mice under the snow. Today I can hear and feel a lot and I know there is no danger from Bear Woman. Trust me."

She looked wary but a bit impressed. He added, on impulse, "Just leave me the smudge stick." When she still didn't answer he said, "Leave me Rez, then. If you're sure you'll be okay finding your way without . . . "

"Of course I will," she snapped. She pulled out the extinguished incense and the lighter from her pocket. "I'll have to wait for the police out there, but they'll be quick about it, because a body's involved. And the weather's good for copters." She turned to the dog, and looked intently down. "Rez. Guard!" She slapped her hand over Ewen's as she gave the command. Rez's wolfish amber eyes shifted from one to the other and she whined.

"Just do it!" The dog lay down.

Susan set off into the tracks they had left and was out of sight within a minute. He stood beside the unhappy dog for another few minutes, then knelt beside her in the snow. He closed his eyes and was immediately back in her simple but disciplined mind, seeing the images within the dog's thoughts: the retreating back of Susan, the smell of her anger and her stifled grieving, the loneliness of her marching back under the shadow of the branches. To Resurrection's thoughts he added a suggestion of his own: following Susan. Keeping her safe.

The wolfish dog whined and wiggled, but there was a wall between her mind and his suggestions—the wall of her training, which was also her self-respect. Ewen put one hand against the heavy-maned neck and added urgency to his request. He let leak a bit of his own fear for Susan Sundown. Rez sprang up quivering, and Ewen sensed one new image-thought added to the mix. *SHE isn't seeing me,* thought the dog. *I'm hiding. SHE isn't seeing me and so I'm not disobeying.* With this new certainty, Rez was off, spraying snow around her.

Ewen squatted there and grinned to himself, because there was so much that was human—no, universal—in the way the dog justified her disobedience. And in the present tense.

So dogs think in the present tense.

Then he stood up and followed Susan's tracks to the center of the circle.

He didn't look down; he knew everything about the body parts already. He put one hand out to the stone cairn at the center of the clearing and put his mind in order. It had been months since he had attempted the particular act he was about to try, and he had never done it before by calm choice. He bowed his head and whispered into the crackling air, "May all beings be happy. May all beings be kind. May all beings be safe . . . " He broke off the meditation and said, quietly but forcefully, "Sidney Sundown. If you can hear me now, I ask you to speak with me." He waited one more moment in the quiet snow and then he stepped over the boundary.

The light rose up and he was in the presence of the in-between once more. It beckoned to him. Ewen moved neither toward it nor away. He stood there and waited for something to happen, and what happened was that the great brilliance sank slowly into a small glow, and into a campfire. He found he was standing in the same place in the cedars, one hand still touching the cairn. The difference was that it was not winter and he was not alone. Beside a fire of aromatic burning wood sat a man, very old and very beautiful.

"I've been waiting for you, son," he said to Ewen.

The old man was wearing a flannel shirt and baggy old Levi's. He stood up beside Ewen easily without needing to use his hands. His face was very like that of Susan's grandmother. Like that of Susan herself.

"You were waiting for me? Waiting for *me*?" Ewen asked him.

"Yes, you, young'un. I'd hoped you'd show up since the day I came through here. I waited for you. There was another man came along a few days ago, thrown out of the world by the same wickedness as I was, but he moved right on. Moved smartly! I don't know what his hurry was."

"Maybe he was your kin?"

It took Ewen a few moments to understand. "Oh, no. Not him. I never met him. He was a Buddhist priest. They don't . . . believe . . . in waiting. They want to get on to the next thing. That's what I was always taught. That you shouldn't be dead and hang around where you'd lived before."

The old man shrugged. "Don't know why not. It's not like there's a lack of time or anything."

"He wasn't kin," Ewen said again. "Just Chinese."

The old man grinned slyly. "And here I was thinking he was Santa Barbara Indian." Ewen stared stupidly for a moment, then burst out in a sputtering laugh. It made the little fire dance, just as though it were a real fire. Perhaps it was a real fire. Ewen was feeling sure about less and less. "You've been watching us," he accused the old man.

Old Sidney Sundown just shrugged again, though by the wrinkles at the corner of his eyes he seemed to be appreciating his own craftiness. But his mouth went serious as he said, "I want you to be careful, son. About that thing last night. What you fought was only its shadow. *Only its shadow.* It has worse powers than turning into a big bear alone in the woods. Its real badness is over the souls of men, and the biggest part of it has already gone on to the coast, where it got that Chinese fellow."

The spirit poked its little fire thoughtfully with a stick and sparks rose. "It uses live men as its hands when it can, and those will be harder to fight, maybe, than the shadow. I could've fought the shadow, if that's all it sent after me. But," he added, "it wasn't all. Still, I got no complaints. I had a good, long life."

Ewen watched the firelight on the spirit's face and tried to remember why he'd come here. What was important to know from old Sid Sundown?

"You say 'it.' Your sister said it was 'she.' Bear Woman. I need to know what it is."

Sidney Sundown spat into the embers of his fire. "I call it 'it' because I wouldn't give it the respect to call it a lady. And even though it hates men, it's quicker to use them than women to do its purpose, 'cause it locks onto their hate. Men are better for hate, when you come down to it. But the thing itself is just an 'it.' A very, very old 'it.' And remember, Ewen—Young Yuen—that just as you're learning things about it, it also knows things about you. It has an image of you locked in keeping where its heart would be, if it had a heart. But that's why I'm here, waiting for you. To tell you that you have two advantages over it. First, it doesn't know your true name."

"I have a true name?"

"You know you do. Everyone has a true name; usually they just need to be told it. You are Raven, He-Who-Goes-Between-Worlds."

"Raven? Isn't that just a bird like a crow?" Ewen felt an absurd sting of disappointment. "Can't I be something else? I don't know if I've ever even seen a raven!"

"Oh, you have. And they've seen you. But it don't matter. Raven is who and what you are. Raven goes between; that's a fact well known. And you always were a messenger. Even before you got shot and bounced around with dying, you could pull things from other worlds into your own. You made pictures of them for people. Now, sometimes, you can do more than make pictures.

"You don't need an old Indian to tell you this. But what is important is that this thing doesn't know much about you. It can't. Though it's good at killing, it can't go easy beyond the border of death. I doubt it knows that anyone can come and go—like you can." The beautiful old man smiled. "You've got a leg up there, son."

"A leg up. Great. And what's my second advantage?"

"You know *its* true name."

Without having to think about it, Ewen said, "Fear. Fear is its true name."

Sidney Sundown smiled. "There you go, son. Right the first try." He sighed. "I wish I'd had the teaching of you, Ewen. I do wish that. Then you might have been more than a messenger."

Ewen was stung. It was in his mind to tell Sundown that he had had teachers. Good teachers and in plenty. But he looked at the old man's eyes and the set of his jaw and then he, too, wished he could have learned from Sidney Sundown.

The man went on. "But call my sister when you get a chance. She's no one's fool. And even my little Susie, though she's as stubborn as a pony picking at a gate, she was born with power." The old man smiled softly. "And I guess she can kick like a pony, too." He sounded quietly proud of his granddaughter. "You can kick ass in the living world, Ewen; you're real impressive there, but over here—well you're going to need help, son. All kinds of help. Not just spirit world help. Don't turn any help down."

"I won't," said Ewen. "That's why I came over here to see if I could find you."

The old man nodded. "Well, good. You did. Now go home."

And Ewen was back standing in the snow. Feeling cold.

The world was very bright for Ewen as he waited for Susan and the authorities. He was thinking hard: hard enough that even his feet were warm. With his gloved hands he was playing with a ball of snow. First he heard a helicopter in the distance, and then Rez came loping in, her tongue lolling. She looked at him sidelong, as conspirators do, and then she sat herself down in the same hole in the snow in which Susan had told her to stay. Five minutes later Dr. Sundown came, leading a party of Idaho State Police. She saw Ewen squatting where she had left him, and saw the dog and the dog's footprints. She cast a cold eye on both of them, but the most of her ire was directed to Rez, who greeted her master by thumping her heavy tail into the snow, in a duplicity that was (at the very least) human.

The crime scene police set up an encampment outside the ring of cedars, close to where Ewen sat. They moved into the circle as cautiously as archaeologists gridding a site, and there was a great flashing of cameras.

Susan Sundown stood beside her erring dog and Ewen, trusting neither. She was winded and underneath the professional calm of her face was great distress. Ewen wondered how best to help, when she looked straight at him, and more closely, at the compressed ball of snow he was fiddling with.

"That . . . " she said. "That's Uncle Sid's face. Holy gods, you've really caught him. It's perfect." She reached for the small head, and he relinquished it to her.

"I knew you were an artist, but this . . . " Suddenly Susan looked at him in wonder. "You *saw* him! You must have seen my uncle!"

"Yes I did," Ewen answered, lacing the fingers of his crusted gloves over his knees. "I spoke to him."

"What did he say?"

"He said . . . well, he said quite a lot. He said to be careful. He said the thing wasn't a she but an it. That it wasn't worth calling a lady. That what we saw was only its shadow. That it did its worst work through the minds of men it poisoned and held. That we had to be ready for more bad stuff. And that I should not reject any sort of help."

It was on the tip of his tongue to come out and say that Uncle Sid had told Ewen that he was simply not very powerful, as spirit power went. That he was just a messenger. A raven, of all embarrassing things. It was not the humiliation of it that made him keep that secret, but the fear that the information would cause her to lose hope. After all, he was her only champion, unless you counted the dog.

Instead, he continued, "He said he had things he could have taught me, but it was not too late for us, even now. He said that I should listen to your grandmother. And to you, though you are . . . are as stubborn as a pony picking . . . I don't remember. Picking at something."

"Picking at a gate," she finished for him. "He always used that expression. About me, anyway. But he said you should listen to me? To me?" She looked confused and distraught. "What do I have to say? I'm a veterinarian!"

"He said you had power. More than me, actually. And—oh—he also said my true name was . . . "

She shoved her mittened hand into his face, "Don't! Don't say it. Not even to me. Especially not to me. The true name is secret, and I could fail you. I could be misled and spill it to her."

"To it. He said 'it.' Remember that. It's no lady. And I know its true name, too. I think it can only help if I tell you that."

Her face went severe as a blade. "Yes. Tell me its true name."

He opened his mouth to say the word, but was stopped by some instinct. "I think you know it already. It's better if you think of it yourself."

She stared at him, while lights flashed and men took careful steps behind her. "Bear Woman? No, that's no name of power. Everyone knows Bear Woman." She stared at Ewen, who gazed down at the little, ephemeral portrait head of snow. He thought how snow was like flesh. How perfect. How quickly gone. "You were there last night, Susan. You fought it as hard as I did. And Rez. What were we fighting?"

Immediately she answered "Fear. Its name is fear." And then she giggled, with a touch of hysteria. "We have nothing to fear but fear itself!"

"That's as true as anything I've ever heard," murmured Ewen, resting his chin on his hands, watching the technicians particularize the very violent death of Sidney Sundown.

Chapter Fifteen

THE THREE OF THEM were taken out of the cold in the police copter, leaving Susan's plane in the frozen field. After a brief, noisy flight, they landed near a small police station and were escorted inside. The warmth in there was wonderful.

They were not told anything directly, only glared at. Ewen was getting used to this particular police glare, but so far from home it was more disturbing. Still, from overhearing the various officers and technicians Ewen got the idea the local police already had guessed that the old man had not been killed by an animal. Susan, who had missed the conversation with her dead uncle, looked at Ewen in revulsion at descriptions of blade length, angle of approach, and of footprints layered deep in the snow. Booted footprints.

Ewen leaned close. "You were right when you told me old Sid could have taken on the shadow we fought. He said to me that it prefers to use men for its weapons. The next violence—if there is more—will come from people it has . . . seduced."

"Seduced? Seduced how?"

He shrugged, uncomfortable and tired in the wooden chair in the hall of the tiny police station. "Seduced by fear. What else does it have?" His mind was very weary, and working slowly, but he managed to say, "You know how often people are seduced into doing terrible things because they are afraid."

Susan's eyes were rimmed in red, and she was focusing with difficulty. Staring at him. "No one on Earth was ever afraid of Uncle Sid."

Ewen closed his own eyes and pulled his feet up onto the seat of the chair, locking them in place over his knees. This was better on his back. He didn't answer her.

She observed him sitting in full lotus and gave a small, lady-like snort. She slid from tears to a sly smile. "So you're a real Buddhist.

Impressive! But can you do this?" And she slid from her chair down to the vinyl flooring and sat in perfect balance on her stocking heels. "Can you do this?"

"Not at the moment," murmured Ewen, and smiled drowsily. "I'm too tired." Susan clambered back next to him.

She leaned her head against his shoulder, which, because of the position, was very stable. "What did he sound like, Ewen? To you. What was Uncle Sid's voice like?"

Ewen thought about it for a few moments. "He sounded a lot like an old Gary Cooper movie."

"That was Uncle Sid," she said, warmly. "Oh yeah. That was him!" and she yawned and collapsed onto Ewen's shoulder. The dog at their feet, also yawned, and Ewen settled into a state that was neither sleep nor wakefulness, and let the time go by.

Beautiful woman. He thought in unexpected contentment. *And fine lady.*

My lady? Ewen came entirely awake for a moment. He remembered "Rikki-Tikki Tavi."

I hope so. I hope we are not too different.

The sky was darkening before the police let them leave, and they had both told their simple story numerous times, and separately. Ewen had not mentioned the battle with the bear shadow, nor having talked to Sid Sundown. He could not know whether Susan had been as circumspect. By the time the interviews were over, Susan was asleep on her feet, so even if the state police would have driven them back to the plane, it would not have been reasonable for them to fly. Instead, they took a ride to the nearest public accommodation, which was a bed and breakfast inn, and were booked into one room together. The bed was covered in a down comforter and it was a lovely night. It would have been lovelier had they not been exhausted.

In the middle of the night, Ewen was wakened by a great, rolling thump, and saw that Resurrection had leaped onto the comforter, and was settling down at the foot of the bed with a deep, human groan. She did not lie down between them. Ewen looked over at the huddled shape under the covers beside him and wondered. In the end, he simply watched her sleep.

They were allowed to leave in the morning, with the clear understanding that they would return if called. Susan and Ewen ate breakfast at a pancake house, where she could keep an eye on Rez, who was sitting outside the window with her leash loosely draped over a parking sign. She sat with the attention of a Buckingham Palace guardsman, and every time either human met her eyes her heavy tail thumped once, as in a ritual.

Ewen, whose hand was tracing outlines on the clean surface of one of the large napkins, said, "I've never really seen a German shepherd that looks like her."

Susan smiled, looking down at her plate of eggs. "She's a shepherd by courtesy."

"Come again?"

"They would never accept a part-wolf as a police tracking dog, would they?"

Ewen darted a quick glance at Resurrection. "She's a wolf?" He didn't really know how a wolf would differ from a German shepherd.

"Not entirely. Not even mostly. She's what she is."

After breakfast, they caught a ride to the landing strip; where they also required a battery charge for the plane's engine, which had sat out there in the cold all that time. In a few minutes they were in the air, headed for the nearest small landing strip with a gas pump and then for home. After they were well above the trees and the blowing snow, the sun danced on the wings from behind, and shone on the eastern sides of the mountains.

"I ought to say I'm sorry for dragging you into this," said Susan. Her eyes were unreadable behind the dark glasses she wore against the snow glare below.

"But I hope you're not. Sorry, I mean," said Ewen, unsnapping his safety harness and leaning towards her.

"Well, no. But bringing you into danger. Helping it get its sights set on you. For that I'm really sorry."

Ewen pulled his feet up onto the seat without noticing. He hated to sit with his legs dangling. "But remember; Sid said it was already fixed on me. You didn't make it happen."

Reflected glare bounced off Susan's aviator glasses.

"And remember, also, that he said I should learn from you."

Her mouth dropped opened. "Yeah. He did. But learn what?"

Ewen settled back. "Tell me all you know about Raven."

"About the bird? Size? Habits?"

"Stories."

Susan looked at him curiously and shrugged. She talked about Raven for about forty minutes as she flew the plane. Ewen wasn't at all sure he liked what he was hearing. "So it's a trickster? Fair weather friend to humanity? Liar?"

"Or maker of the world." Somewhat timidly Susan asked, "Did Uncle Sid call you 'Raven'? Exactly that?"

Ewen wiggled uncomfortably. "Yes. Just a big crow."

"Well—don't be offended by a name *he* gave you. Be proud! And I wouldn't worry a lot about the reputation of Raven; it's different among the different tribes. What's important is knowing that Raven can be of use to you. 'Cause one thing about Raven; whatever the story, he always knows what's going on."

"I wish I did," said Ewen.

The found a place to land for gas. They flew out of the sunlight and through a lot of rain.

It seemed strange to be back on a Seattle pavement with Susan. Last time he had stood there with her he was still thinking of her as Dr. Sundown. Last time was barely two days ago. They got into her beat-up Suburban and drove 520 out to Redmond, the windshield wipers on high and the smell of wet dog coming from in back. Ewen tried to think of what would come next.

"I don't think it would be a good idea for you to be alone right now," he said to her.

She shrugged. "I won't exactly be alone. I'm a vet," she answered. "I've got a lot of calls to make. Nobody else is going to be available and people—horses and dogs, I mean—may die." As she noted the stubborn set of his jaw she added, "But when I'm done with work, I guess I could get my calls forwarded to your place."

There was a pause. He said, "I'm not sure that's a great idea, either."

She raised both eyebrows at him and he hurried to explain. "Susan, you know what's going on. Where I am is not exactly the safest place for you to be."

She sighed. So did the dog. "Well, I don't really have any other choice right now. It's your house or my own solitude."

Ewen considered. "There's Detective Petersen . . . "

She sputtered. "Stay with Ricky? And here I thought you and I were doing so good together! Besides which—Ricky's never home. He's a cop. And what exactly could Ricky do against that thing in the woods? Shoot it?"

What better thing can I do about it? Ewen thought. But he was ridiculously glad to be preferred as Susan's protection.

By the time they reached Ewen's house the rain had stopped again. Or perhaps they had simply driven out from under it. His garden looked much the same as it had, which surprised him and reminded him again that he had only been away for a short time. Next door the Kelly's dog was out on its tether: a leash attached to a large steel screw they anchored in the lawn when they wanted the dog out of the way. As Ewen stepped out of the car, feeling his bones creak from long sitting, it saw him and began to bellow, spinning in a circle around its metal constraint.

Susan was out of the car on the other side, ignoring the ruckus. "Oh," she said. "You've got a little pond. I didn't notice it before." She, too, was cracking her spine and neck in relief. The gesture was so tomboyish in the beautiful woman that Ewen grinned. He remembered the cowboy boots in action.

The tenor of the dog's barking changed suddenly, and Ewen saw it had managed to pull the screw out of the sodden lawn. It was going for Ewen.

This was not the first or even the second time this had happened. Normally he would have hopped onto the roof of the Suburban and waited for someone to come and claim the animal. But there was Susan to consider, and so he stayed where he was. He feinted with one arm to draw the dog off the line of his body.

Softly, silkily, Resurrection stepped between Ewen and the charging shepherd. She stood there and looked calmly at the Kellys' dog.

It sat down suddenly on its haunches, leaving ripped streaks in the wet grass. Its momentum had carried it onto the driveway that divided the properties. It sat there at the end of its muddy skid marks, mouth open, tongue lolling and ears flopped sideways. Then it began, circumspectly, to turn sideways and back off. It backed halfway across the lawn, then turned and lollopped onto the front porch of its own house and lay down before the door.

"Have you got fish?" asked Susan, standing on one of the rocks beside the water. "Oh—I see. Those cloudy-colored goldfish. Very nice."

Ewen followed her line of sight and saw the little shubunkins nibbling at the surface. "I tried koi, but they got eaten by . . . " He stopped in mid-sentence, shaking his head in disbelief. "Susan, did you see what just happened here? That dog was charging me, and . . . "

"Rez stepped in. Yeah. That's part of her job."

"But the dog didn't even try to fight. He looked like an idiot. He ran off. I've known that dog for two years and he's a monster." Ewen bent down to Rez, who had lost all interest in the neighbor's dog. He touched her respectfully. "You are something, Resurrection. You are really something." He looked up at Susan. "I never had a dog. What on earth did she say to him?"

"She said 'go away'." Susan had also lost interest in the Kellys' dog. "Now, I've never wanted a goldfish," she added. "But out here in the open, they might be nice to keep. How often do you feed them?"

Ewen grinned from ear to ear. He shook his head in wonder. He put one hand around the woman's shoulder and the other on the dog's head and led them into the house.

The day began to twist differently an hour later, as Ewen was alone and unpacking. He got a phone call from Detective Rick Petersen, who was not a happy man. "What the hell were you doing in Idaho, Mr. Young?" he began.

Ewen felt a surge of ridiculous guilt, immediately submerged in anger. "That's not really your . . . " he began, and then reinterpreted Petersen's question. He cooled down. "We were looking for Susan's Uncle Sid," he answered with less vehemence, then added, "You knew she was going, didn't you?"

There was a pause before Petersen answered. "I didn't know she was taking you."

Ewen stalled for a moment, remembering Susan saying she was told about Ewen and his peculiarities as a secret. He didn't know how he felt about the detective. "She had to do something, Detective Petersen. She thought I could help find him."

Another pause was on the other side. "And evidently you could."

"I think it was Rez who found him. I was just . . . along for the ride."

Petersen groaned. "A ride with Resurrection. Did you get bit?"

Ewen was startled by this and felt a bit of mischief. "No, but I might have, except for her."

"Susan?"

"Rez. When I got home, the neighbor's dog charged me, ol' Rez stepped in and showed him the error of his ways. Without even growling at him."

"I believe that. That wolf-dog is a terror."

Now Ewen felt full of male mischief. "She's a pussycat, Detective. A cocker spaniel. She's Benji."

He thought he heard Petersen mumble, "I could show you scars," but it might have been his own imagination.

Petersen did say, "So you had no more trouble: not like a few days ago. You know what I mean."

Was it only a few days ago? "Not like then. There were some drunken cowboys—I mean Indians—but nothing she couldn't handle."

"The dog?"

"Susan. That woman's a terror." Then Ewen sobered a bit. "Detective Petersen, I think there is still danger."

"Damn right there is. We've got a serial murderer: at least one, and he's traveling. Do you know something more—something the police don't?"

"Nothing I could tell the police."

"You can tell me."

Petersen was right; he could tell him. Petersen had stood by Ewen last summer and covered for what could not be explained by logic. And Petersen had stood by him just a few days ago, in the middle of horror. Ewen had been so flushed with his (possible) victory over Rick Petersen in the game of love that he had forgotten that that stern and dignified man—also called Ricky—had stood his friend.

"Yes. Okay. Here it is. There's a monster. Susan's grandmother calls it 'Bear Woman,' but Sid says it's no lady. He calls it simply 'it'."

"Sid is the one who's dead?"

"Yes. I spoke to him yesterday. He waited for me at the spot in the cedars."

"Waited for you? The dead man?"

"Yes. He said the Buddhist priest had been there briefly, but wouldn't wait."

Petersen spoke very carefully. "Waited for *you*, Ewen?"

"Yes. For me. He said the thing uses people to do its bidding. It locks in on fear."

"Like it locked in on you?"

Ewen regarded his nasty memory for a moment and then answered. "Yes. But it won't lock in on me anymore. Not *that* way. I'm sort of immune to it that way. I got over the fear after the . . . thing at the temple."

Petersen snorted. "I think it could scare the living shit out of me. From what I saw."

"But it didn't, Detective. It didn't scare you. That's important. It didn't. And I owe you for that. Big time."

The silence spread out so long Ewen suspected they might have lost the connection. Then Petersen spoke again. "What else did the ghost say?"

"That the thing will try to kill again. That it wants me."

"Oh, shit!" Petersen was actually shouting into the phone. Ewen had never heard him shout. "Oh, shit. I was afraid of that. And I got you into this."

"No you didn't. I was already having dreams. And besides—that wasn't a bad thing. Or Sid doesn't think so."

"Yeah, well—what does he know? He's dead." The sarcasm was heavy.

Ewen spoke with sudden passion, "And I'm the one who's not, remember? How many times should I be dead, now? Three, maybe four? I'm not entirely unprepared for something like this." He wondered how much of this story Petersen would swallow, considering that Ewen himself felt nearly powerless. "But I'm worried about Susan. She came up against the shadow of the thing in the woods. She used a power she called 'cedar' against it. She survived, but now it knows her. And it knows Rez."

Petersen cursed again. "I can help against the serial killers. Maybe. As well as anyone could. But against a shadow in the woods . . . "

"She's going to stay here with me for a while. I know it's not safe here, but where *is* safe right now? And Detective—I've got to ask you . . . about Susan . . . "

"What's between the lady and myself?" Petersen chuckled. "Hell if I know. Ever knew, really. I have the disadvantage of being only a human being."

"And what am I? Chopped liver?"

"No. I just meant you're not a dog, or a horse, or . . . " Then Petersen made a startled noise. "It's like that?" There came a seething pause. "I should have guessed when you talked about the dog like that." Another silence, and then, "Well, what do you want us to do about it—pistols at sunrise? That lady goes her own way, Ewen. Remember that. She always has."

"I will," said Ewen, and added, with a tiny barb, "Rick."

The house was very quiet, after hours of the noise of prop engine and highway. Ewen sat down to think, and as often happened when he was intending to think, he found himself sketching. The sketch turned into a larger drawing, which he blocked out, sized, and prepared for paint. What had begun as an effort to remember one face, seen only for a brief time, became three faces, which were a series of variations upon one another. He was lost in the differences and in the similarities of eyes when the phone rang. He knew immediately who it was, and answered, "Hello, Lynn."

"What on earth happened to you a few nights ago, Ewen? And then about a day later? I called, but there was no answer. I would have called the police, if I had anything to tell them except I knew my brother was in trouble." Dr. Lynn Young-Thurmond was not the sort of woman to get emotional on the telephone, but Ewen felt every nuance of her voice.

"I'm sorry, Lynn. Something did happen, but I'm okay. I was in Idaho. I didn't think to call." Ewen realized how unusual that had been. All the strange events and he hadn't thought to call Lynn, his twin.

"Who died?"

Ewen smiled at the baldness of the question. "No one that night. A man did a couple weeks ago. In Idaho. A . . . friend wanted me to go along with her to . . . identify the body."

Of all his relations, Lynn was the only one who never chivvied Ewen about female "friends" or lack thereof. The only one who had never pressed him about his mysteriously disappearing relationship with Karen. "So. Why were you going to call me?"

Not *when*, but *why*.

Ewen trapped the phone against his shoulder, leaned back in his chair, and wiped vine charcoal off his hands. "I was actually going to call Theo. I need some advice."

"About death or Buddhism?" This question was more obvious. Those two subjects were the only ones about which Ewen could possibly need advice from his brother-in-law. "Not that it's any of my business, of course . . . "

"It's about both, really. Is he there?"

"No," she said uneasily. "Someone's just died at the hospice. Why don't you call and leave a message?"

"Will do that. And give my best to Teddy."

"Teddy's always got everyone's best," answered Lynn and she hung up.

He did not have to leave a message at the hospice, because Theo came to the phone immediately. That meant he had either finished the clear-light portion of his bardo readings, or the patient had been one of those who specifically requested he did not. Usually the dying were kinder to Theo, and allowed him to mutter in a corner of the room even if they were Baptists. "Theo," Ewen began. "What do I do about a demon?"

There was only a moment of silence. One didn't easily flap Theo. Not about things to do with Tibetan Buddhist. "Tell me more," he said, and Ewen told him, from the beginning—from the night terrors he had suffered the last few weeks to the encounter with the dead Mr. Sundown. Theo listened silently and when Ewen was done, he remarked, "So this Sidney Sundown waited for you. In the bardo. For a week or more. That's quite special, you know. Difficult."

"Well, Theo," he said grinning. "One man's bardo isn't another man's bardo."

Theo grunted. "But it's still the bardo, and this man must have been quite a yogi. To be able to wait without distress."

"About the demon, Theo . . . "

Theo sighed and thought. "Well, you can't kill it, of course."

"I was afraid you'd say that."

"It's just common sense. It's not alive. It never was. How can it die? Remember what Padmasambhava did to the wild spirits of Tibet? You've seen their faces. They were quite scary."

"I've seen the faces."

"He turned them around—from being malignant to being protective spirits of the dharma. That's what they are now. That's why it's such a holy country. That's why . . . "

"Theo. Theo. You expect *me* to enlighten the monster? I'm not Padhma-whoever."

He heard his brother-in-law breathing on the phone. "Maybe I'd better take a hand in this," he finally replied.

Ewen had not even considered this possibility. He thought of gentle, scholarly, slightly obsessive Theodore Thurmond and his family, which was also Ewen's family. "*No!* No, Theo. You've got a wife and kid. Listen—I've already got a sort of . . . inoculation against this thing. And Sid said it was for me to do. What I want from you is just advice. Let's say I can't get the thing to accept the Four Noble Truths. Can't even get it to accept Jesus as its personal savior. What else can I do to stop it killing?"

Theo was silent longer this time. Ewen heard him scratching his beard. "Send it away, I guess. For a time—a time in the spirit world might be a very long time in our human terms. There are a number of rituals for doing that. Many are Bon—animist rather than strictly Buddhist—but I could lay my hands on them pretty quickly. Or you could."

"How?"

"On the Internet of course. But I'm thinking. If this spirit is known to the Indians, they might well have better knowledge of how to control it."

Ewen was pleased to hear Theo admit as much. Ewen's brother-in-law needed to become more ecumenical. "I've got some sources on that already. I just wanted your advice."

He heard Theo fiddling with the phone. Talking to himself. Then: "I wish I'd been there. By the landing strip. I don't mean instead of you, Ewen. I don't have your particular gifts. But I've never seen a destructive spirit, except inhabiting a human body. Plenty of those in the world. But speaking of that threat, what are you going to do about the humans it corrupts? Its 'hands'? The ones that killed the shaman? Shouldn't you at least call the police?"

"I—uh—that's taken care of, Theo. Petersen knows. And I'm going to take certain precautions."

"I hope you get better police protection than we did last summer."

"I'm hoping for much better protection," said Ewen, remembering. "And—uh—please don't talk to Lynn about this. She doesn't need another thing to worry about."

"You know I can't stop her from knowing," said Theo. "I won't have to say a thing and still, she'll know."

Ewen hung up the phone and began to make plans.

Chapter Sixteen

THAT EVENING was a senior class, and these were generally smaller. Only seven students showed up. Ewen had the difficult task of singling out three of them to stay for a meeting without offending the others, but he managed to get Ryan, Barbie, and Perry alone in the office afterwards, saying he wished to discuss how classes went in his absence.

Ryan was stretching in the way only he could stretch. Ryan did yoga and tai chi and a bit of savate as well as kung fu. Ryan seemed to have very little else in his life besides martial arts. "Good class, sifu," said Ryan, who was the only one who ever called Ewen "sifu"— Chinese for *teacher*. "Nice and aggressive. We don't get enough multiple attacker stuff. Not against weapons."

"I'm glad you liked it," said Ewen, not smiling.

"So what's up, Ewen?" asked Barbie Cowell, who was also not smiling. "You don't really need to know how classes went for the couple days you were gone. Why'd you happen to ask the only senior students without family responsibilities to meet in secret?"

Ewen must have been staring, because Perry Janaway, leaning back in an office chair, his long legs on the desk, grinned and added, "Yeah, bro. We're not stupid." (Perry was the only one who called Ewen "bro.") "And we know something's come up, with you flying away to Idaho for the weekend. I happen to know you don't even ski."

"It's something like last summer, isn't it?" said Barbie, calmly. "When you started to find your strange powers."

"What strange powers? I mean, what do you know about what happened to me last summer? I didn't . . . "

"We know Uncle Ewen went '*poof!*'" added Perry. "That kid Teddy is amazing."

"And the perfect spy," said Barbie, complacently. "Because he doesn't even know he *is* a spy. So tell us. What is it you need?"

All kinds of help. Don't turn any of it down.

So Ewen didn't. He told them.

He told the whole story over again for the second time that day, and although the narrative became smoother each time, he felt it less and less real. He doubted that even these friends could believe a tale he could scarcely believe himself. When he finished, the three were staring at him. Nothing was said for a few seconds. He felt like a total fool.

Then Ryan said, quite seriously, "Tell me about this Bear Woman. Her chi force. What was it like?"

Ewen blinked. "Its chi force? It was a kind of big, black, bear chi force, I guess. How else can I answer that?"

"It is probably blocked chi force," said Ryan Watanabe, folding himself thoughtfully into a pretzel. "Perhaps formed from the structure of that mountain valley. Perhaps the fear of people in that rugged area has gotten caught over the years. Violent feng shui. It needs to be rechanneled."

Ewen slowly shook his head. "Ryan, sometimes you are just too Chinese for me to understand, even if you are Japanese."

Perry rubbed his face in his long hands. "But besides the bear-things, there are humans involved in this, right?"

"It was humans who killed Sidney Sundown."

"And you want us to help you stand against it all," said Barbie.

"Like in *Buffy the Vampire Slayer*," Perry suggested. "We be the crew!" Perry was completely unconvincing when he put on his "street" accent.

"Please, no," said Ewen, weakly. "Not like that."

Ever practical, Barbie Cowell asked, "Then like what?"

"Just with whatever spare time you can give me, at night mostly, to help me protect Susan—Dr. Sundown."

She nodded. "You got it," said Ryan and Perry together.

Barbie, already planning, said, "I'll take first watch tonight."

"And I'll take double broadswords," said Ryan, straightening himself on the floor mat. "Or, no. I don't have any real edged broadswords. I'll use my katana."

"Your katana! How strangely Japanese of you," said Barbie, dryly. "Are you going to allow us to use weapons, Ewen?"

He snorted. "Barbie! Will I *allow* you? I am the one asking you for help. Not giving you a test! And the thugs who killed the priest last week had machetes. I don't know yet what they used to kill Sid.

"Guys, I'm asking a real terrible thing from you. You could get killed. If I knew any other way to protect Susan . . . "

"This is the perfect way," said Barbie. "I'll be there tonight."

"Policeman at the door," said Perry, apropos of nothing, and the others looked puzzled. But from where he was sitting, Perry could see out to the front door. "There *is* a policeman at the door," he repeated.

Petersen, thought Ewen, and he bounced to his feet. But when he got to the glass door in the front of the school, he saw it was a uniformed cop. No. Two uniformed cops. His stomach flopped at the sight of them and he scrambled to unlock the door.

They were looking oddly at him, too, and after a second he realized it was because he was wearing a flamboyant red tunic with a wide sash wrapped around the middle. He was also still sweaty from class. And behind him stood three others dressed in other variously florid uniforms, also sweaty and very intent. No wonder the cops stood together, unsmiling and wary. "Susan," asked Ewen, and his voice cracked. "Is she okay?"

"Are you Mr. Ewen Young?" asked the older of the two, ignoring his question.

"Yes," answered Ewen, feeling numb.

"We'd like you to come with us, Mr. Young."

"First, tell me: Is Susan Sundown okay?" Ewen held to the doorjamb for support. The two policemen watched his hand uneasily. "We don't know anything about that, Mr. Young. We're here because of the German shepherd. Do you know anything about it?"

Because of the dog? "That dog would never go anywhere without Susan. Dr. Sundown. Have you looked for her?"

With a perfectly blank cop face, the older one said, "We'd like you to come with us, Mr. Young." He took out a pair of handcuffs and said, "Turn around, please."

From behind Ewen Perry spat, "What the fuck!" The other two growled and shifted their positions. The police, seeing this, went solid as stone.

Ewen was purely mystified. "Why those? I *want* to go with you."

The police were still looking at Ewen's outraged "posse," and they were very wary. "Now, sir, we can be perfect gentlemen about this, or we can simply arrest you and take you to the station. If you make it hard, and we need to use force, we will. If you people behind him make it difficult, we can get more cops. There's a lot of us available, you know. More than there are of you."

"But, Mr. Young," added the younger cop, "we don't want to arrest you and take you to the station. We want to take you to the crime scene . . . "

"The crime scene," whispered Ewen, and all the color drained out of the world. He turned his back and let them cuff him. They led him to the police car and he slid into the unpadded back seat. The one who tried to guide his head in found that even with his hands locked behind him Ewen Young needed no help with balance.

The three students, still in their uniforms, ran for their keys, following the black-and-white like hounds on a trail.

On the porch, Ewen tried again to get information out of the officers, with no success. Once in the car, he worked on his breathing, forming concentration out of his own distraction, and when they pulled to a stop in front of his own house, he was fairly collected. It was dark, but neighbors stood about in clumps, outlined in their own doorways. The rain still fell.

The Kellys were out in company, standing on their driveway, wearing slickers. As the police officer opened the door for Ewen, large, bald Mr. Kelly strode forward and called Ewen a very foul name. The cop stood between them, holding Kelly off, but Mrs. Kelly pushed between, the cop's grip was lost and Kelly swung a heavy punch at Ewen's head.

Ewen dodged without knowing he was dodging. He was looking, astonished, at the Kelly children, who were red-faced, weeping in the rain. While one cop held Ewen by the elbow, the other began a bellowing match with Kelly. Ewen was marched up the glossy drive of his house and to the porch stairs, past the weeping kids, who scrambled back from him as from a monster. Rain began to drip from the wide tunic sleeves of his uniform as he was led up the porch stairs.

There, against his front door, was the body of a big dog, skinned and gutted. Blood had been rubbed over the screen door and smeared into the coconut mat. Still attached to the heavy neck was the long chain lead, which ended in a muddy, steel corkscrew: the lawn tether.

Ewen felt his heart take two huge beats and then settle. "This is the Kellys' dog," he said, knowing he sounded stupid. "Not Rez. It's not Susan's dog."

"We know it's the Kellys' dog, Mr. Young. We were hoping you could tell us what happened to it. Why it's here."

He shook his head. "I don't know. I didn't do it."

He heard Kelly from the base of the stairs, shouting, "Sure you didn't, you fucked-up cultist! Just look at him! And those others, standing by the street in their crazy robes!"

Ewen tossed his head to get the wet hair out of his eyes and looked down at Kelly. "Cultists? What cult do we belong to, the kung fu cult?" A cop dragged Kelly away again.

"Undo those. Let him go," echoed a very deep voice and long legs ascended the porch stairs. Ewen looked up at Detective Petersen's dark face and started to sneeze.

"You sure . . . ?" began the cop holding him, then took one look at the detective and hurried to obey.

"What happened here?" Petersen directed his question at Ewen.

"I don't know. I just got here," he replied and sneezed again. He wiped his wet shoulder over his wet face. "I've been at school all evening."

The cop spoke up. "Someone says they saw him kill the dog." Both Ewen and Petersen looked sharply at the cop, who pointed to the driveway. "The little girl."

Petersen took the flight of stairs in two steps and went over to the Kellys' angelic-faced nine-year-old daughter. "You saw this man kill your dog?" The little girl backed away against her mother's slicker. Petersen's face was not naturally child-friendly.

"Go on, speak," said her mother and shoved the girl forward. "Tell him what you saw."

"They had a fight," said the girl.

"Who had a fight? And when was that?"

"Don't be so rough on her," said Mrs. Kelly. "You're scaring the child."

Up the driveway came a shorter figure, blond-haired. It was Petersen's partner, Gideon Ryde. Petersen immediately gave up his spot to Ryde, who squatted easily down, his suit jacket hem soaking up rainwater. "Hello, kiddo," said Giddy. "I'm sorry about your doggie. What happened to him?"

She pointed at Ewen. "They had a fight."

"He killed him," prompted the mother. "He killed Wreck."

"Rex?"

"Wreck. That crazy guy finally did it." Mr. Kelly bellowed. "He's wanted to for a long time, and . . . "

"And I'd like to talk to your daughter, if you don't mind." Ryde smiled at the child. "Now, sweetie, tell me just what happened."

The girl warmed to Giddy Ryde, as children always did. "They had a fight and the other dog chased Wreck home and he hid on the porch."

Ryde pointed. "This man's porch?"

"No! I *said* he ran home. Our porch."

"And that was when?"

She sighed at grown-ups' hopeless stupidity. "Earlier."

"And then what happened?" Ryde's smile was not returned by the Kelly girl.

"Then I let him in."

"But how did he get on Mr. Young's porch, kiddo?"

She turned her head left, she turned her head right. Then she shrugged.

Petersen had been with the dog. Now he returned to the group. "Whoever took out that dog was a hunter. Or a trapper. A very professional job. Have you ever hunted, Mr. Young?"

"Never. And I never touched that dog."

Mr. Kelly mumbled "Cultist!" but no one was paying attention.

"Let's go inside and talk about this," said Petersen. "Go in by the back door, please."

Ewen went with him up the drive, and when the Kellys tried to follow, Ryde headed them off.

Petersen brushed past Ewen going through the kitchen door. He pulled a large Smith & Wesson from his jacket. "Give us some light," he said, and Ewen flipped the kitchen switch. "Everything look as you left it?"

"So far."

He went from room to room, letting the detective lead the way. Every room was as he had left it. Petersen saw a large, tall shape in the hall and found he had drawn down on the heavy bag. They went upstairs, into each of the small bedrooms and the bath, and then returned. "Fairly neat for a bachelor pad," remarked Petersen. He turned on the table lamp in the living room and sat down. "So tell me, Ewen, why do you think . . . " Petersen's voice trailed off, and Ewen saw he was staring at the big sketch on the French easel: the one of three faces.

"Susan!" Petersen said, and he stood again and walked over. He looked closely from one face to the others and shook his head. "I suppose that's her grandmother? I've never met her, but the resemblance is there. And the other?"

"Sidney Sundown."

"From a picture, or is that . . . the ghost?"

"It's from when I met him. Yesterday. And I'm not sure you ought to call him a ghost, because he wasn't visiting this place. I was visiting him."

"So you were the ghost?"

"Detec . . . Rick. Have you heard from Susan? When they said it was about a dog I was afraid it was Rez they were talking about. And I'm still worried."

"Called her on her cell phone as soon as I heard about this. She's doing emergency surgery on a horse with stones. I left her a message not to show up here until this thing was worked out." Petersen returned to the couch and sat in the light of the lamp, his lean face made craggy by shadows. "I've also got a uniform sitting in the hospital waiting room. A good man. So tell me Ewen—what's the story here?"

Ewen reminded Petersen about their earlier phone conversation: coming home with Susan, and Rez quieting the charging German shepherd without a growl. Petersen nodded. Then Ewen told him about the four o'clock children's class and the senior class at six. He did not describe his meeting with the three students after. It would be a bit much to expect even so understanding a police detective to accept the idea of a "Buffy crew."

"They came to the door, asked my name, told me to turn around, and put cuffs on me," said Ewen, still in wonderment.

"They arrested you?" asked Petersen, furrowing his forehead.

"No. They just cuffed me and drove me here. Mentioned the dog and wouldn't say anything else. I don't understand it, Rick. What'd I do to get them so down on me?"

Petersen grinned. The expression transformed his usually dour face. "Partly it was the looks of that pooch on the porch," he said, "but I imagine most of it was because you scared them."

"I was perfectly polite."

"Yeah, but everyone sees action movies. Especially cops. We love 'em. And there you were, tricked out in all that Chinese splendor and looking so, well, Chinese."

"Santa Barbara Indian," replied Ewen, and at Petersen's questioning look he just shook his head. "So who killed the dog, Detective?"

Petersen leaned back. "I don't know. Someone who doesn't like you, Ewen? Or someone who didn't like the dog? And by the way— why do the Kellys hate your guts? Are they racist, or fundamentalist Christian, or . . ."

"My grandfather planted bamboo," said Ewen.

Petersen was nonplussed for only a few moments. Then he leaned back his head and roared with laughter.

"And as far as the dog's enemies, that's the whole neighborhood. I could see him getting poisoned, or shot with a pellet gun, but not . . . not this."

"Not this," Petersen agreed, sobering. "Susan told me she thought this might have been done by the men that this thing, this bear spirit of yours, had possessed. How does that sound to you?"

"Sounds absolutely loony. But I suspect she's right. Except that Theo would call them corrupted rather than possessed. And it seems they're hunters?"

Petersen described how neatly the carcass had been skinned, leaving only the face and ears attached. How the gut sack had been removed with minimal mess. And he shared with Ewen what he knew about the condition of Sid Sundown's body, which seemed to have been dismembered by blades and subsequently damaged by the forest animals.

"That part isn't exactly true, Detective."

Ewen remembered vividly sitting in the snow, sensing life all around him except for within that dreadful circle. "I think the animal damage came around the same time. Normal animals are too frightened. I think it was it—the thing."

Petersen sighed and leaned back, cracking his knuckles behind his head. Ewen could see flickers of amber in Petersen's eyes as the lamplight touched them.

Petersen was an Indian too, they said. Why should both he and Susan have amber in their eyes? And in the dog's too. Ewen slowly returned to attention.

"I have seen very strange things in the woods around here," Petersen muttered. "Hell, in the towns, too." His glance sought out Ewen. "Once I saw a white deer jump the road in front of the car. Gid saw it too. I can almost swear there was something shining between its antlers. A cross, if you can believe it! Just like on the Jägermeister label . . . I saw that. Me—not some shaman."

"Sounds neat."

Petersen gave a tight smile. "It was. But most of the strange things I come across day to day aren't so neat. This is the place with the Green River. Bundy's old hunting grounds. I find it a dark place. Maybe that's just because I'm a cop." He looked up at the ceiling. "All this stuff puts me in a strange position, you know? What are you supposed to do when you're a cop and the bad guy is a bug-eyed monster? I can't put that in the reports. And I can't get the amount of assistance I would like to have to protect that wild woman, Susan. Or you, for that matter.

"But," he continued, lifting his head toward a sound in the back. "I've got Giddy Ryde. He's my partner and a man of prayer." Petersen said this with no shade of irony. "And I think that's him coming in now."

The slight blond man came through the house, making his own survey of the place. "Nice picture of Dr. Sundown," he said of the drawing on the easel. "But you left out Resurrection." He sat down on the couch beside Petersen.

"I think Ewen here has a pretty good alibi," drawled Petersen.

"The Kellys will be so disappointed," answered Ryde. "Though I think I had begun to convince them that if it had been you, you'd have dumped the body on their doorstep, not your own." He placed his hands neatly on his knees. "The children are upset, of course, but not really grieving. I don't think anyone in that house really liked Wreck."

"Wreck?" asked Petersen, eyebrows raised. "With a *W*?"

"As in automobile wreck. I gather that's what he did to the house. But none of them claim to have heard the dog make a sound all evening."

Ewen felt an impulse to tell Ryde that was because the dog was dead. Under no other circumstances would Wreck have been quiet that long. But he thought of that horrid corpse on his doormat and kept his mouth shut.

"We'll have to canvas the neighbors, of course, but a good many of them are out there on their porches now, and yet no one comes forward to say they saw or heard anything. Which is strange."

"And I'm assuming this is tied in with the murder last week, and the one in Idaho." Ryde turned to his partner. "Lieutenant Kopek is going to have trouble accepting the connection, you know."

"No way in hell he will ever believe in this thing, Gid. Not even in killers specializing in holy men, let alone in a demon inspiring the whole thing."

"I, on the other hand," said Gideon Ryde, "believe very firmly in devils. And speaking of things devilish, shouldn't we let in the three 'devil worshippers' out there who are soaked and freezing their heads off?"

It took Ewen a second to follow Ryde's question. "You mean my guys? They're still out there?"

"I think they would have stayed out there until you came out. Or until doomsday."

"Do let them in, Gid," said Petersen. "That is, unless there's something Ewen doesn't want them to know about this."

"I have no secrets," murmured Ewen. "That wasn't my idea in life, but as it turns out, I have no secrets."

The three were cold, and though they had been sitting in their cars for most of the time, still damp with rain and sweat. Barbie Cowell's face was blue and her teeth chattered. Ewen ran for towels and blankets while Petersen, very mildly, began verifying Ewen's alibi. When Ewen returned to the room he heard Petersen repeating the word "Bear Woman," and the three students were responding with their own individual and inept attempts at pretending not to understand.

Ewen doled out the towels and blankets. "He knows all about the demon," he said, pointing to Petersen. "I told him this afternoon." When all three stared warily, he added, "These detectives were the good guys last summer."

Chapter Seventeen

When Susan Sundown drove up to Ewen's house, she took in the single police car still in the driveway and the yellow police tape. She ran, Rez beside her, to the back door, which was opened very politely by Gideon Ryde.

She was surprised to see a scene of almost Christmas-like coziness in the living room, where a number of people in red, black, and green were sitting at leisure, one a woman wearing a terry-cloth turban above her Chinese tunic. Detective Rick Petersen was on his knees by the fireplace, teaching Ryan Watanabe how to start a fire without matches. Ewen was pouring cocoa from a large pot.

She looked from one to another, and at last said to Petersen. "You still carry that flint and steel in your suit jacket?"

"Of course," he replied, glancing up only for a moment. "I treat gifts with respect."

Ewen watched and listened to this, looking for personal signals between the two. The only thing he picked up was that Rez had begun to growl, deep and quiet. For an instant he sensed Petersen through her nose and did not like what he smelled. Then he wrenched himself out of the dog's mind.

The night had certainly not gone as planned in the school office. It was almost midnight before the detectives had finished their questions, their door-knocking circuit of the neighborhood, seen off the single crime scene investigator they had rousted for something as minor as a dog killing, and prepared to go. Ewen asked them to stay for one more thing.

"I want to go next door and talk to Mr. Kelly," he said. Petersen lifted his eyebrows but Gideon Ryde thought it was a great idea. "I just want you to be here in case he goes off on me again."

"This is the man who thinks you're a devil worshipper?" asked

Barbie, now starting to sound seriously congested. "And that you killed his dog?"

"I think that's a great idea," said Ryde. "I'll go with you."

"Gideon the peacemaker," said Petersen. "Better you than me." When they left the house Petersen was once again feeding the fire and Rez was still quietly, growling at him.

The Kellys' door was discolored and gouged by dog claws. One of the porch posts had been seriously gnawed on. There was a light on, so Ewen knocked, softly. He hoped a child wouldn't answer the door and scream at the sight of him. He heard the TV and knocked again, a bit louder. There was a rustling and then the porch light came on and the door opened. It was Kelly himself. He looked surprised to see Ewen and not pleased. He also looked very tired.

"Mr. Kelly, I'm hoping you still don't think I killed your dog."

Kelly took a deep breath. His angry eyes did not quite meet Ewen's. "No, I guess not. Everyone says you weren't here." Then he looked up sharply and said, "But I think it's your fault Wreck got trashed. "

"How?"

Kelly didn't see Ryde approach the porch in the darkness. "Something to do with the gangsters your granddad was mixed with. It's the second time we've had violence here in a year and it's all around you. I don't like that. I've got kids."

Ewen suddenly felt very sorry for the man. "I know that, Mr. Kelly. I'm sorry. All I can say is that I don't have anything to do with gangsters and never have. My grandfather was a compulsive gambler, and that was how he got killed. I don't think that has anything to do with your dog. I'm very, very sorry about Wreck."

Kelly rolled his eyes. "Oh, don't bother! I know how you felt about Wreck."

Ewen took a slow breath. "No, Mr. Kelly. You know how your dog felt about me. I never wanted him hurt. I never wanted your children upset."

"And what're you gonna *do* about it?" Kelly's face was growing red.

Gideon Ryde stepped forward. "We're leaving a car right there in the driveway, Mr. Kelly. We'll be keeping a man here while we sort this out. Mr. Young, here, can't do anything about what happened. I hope you can see that. Craziness like this could have happened to anyone."

"Yeah?" said Kelly. "But it happens to him, duzzen' it? And we're stuck living next to him." He closed the door in their faces.

Ryde sighed and put his hand on Ewen's shoulder. "He was upset. It's understandable. Don't take those things to heart, Mr. Young."

Ewen *had* taken those things to heart, but he said, "Hey! It's okay, Detective. He didn't call me a cultist once."

Ewen tried to get Barbie to go home. He argued that the car outside meant they were safe for the night. He explained the proficiency of Rez. Barbie remembered her promise, however, and balked. He fed her Nyquil (not mentioning it would probably knock her out) and fixed her up on the bed-couch.

Susan was also feeling stubborn. "I got you into this, Ewen," she said. "Would have been fine if I had just done what Ricky said and left you alone."

Ewen was getting tired of these discussions. "If what your grandmother said is true, I was already on this thing's hit list and if you hadn't been there, I'd have had no warning. Besides—Rick got me into it first.

"Now we've got you feeling guilty about getting me involved and me feeling guilty about getting the Kellys involved . . . "

"You *are*? That's just silly."

" . . . and I'm sure 'Ricky' is somewhere right now feeling guilty about getting any of us involved. I think we should call a moratorium on feeling guilty."

Susan showered and came out to find Ewen not in the living room, where Barbie Cowell had begun to snore, nor in the main bedroom. She walked uncertainly into the darkened spare bedroom and only after her eyes adjusted did she see Ewen Young, sitting in a corner, legs folded in the way she had teased him about, eyes open. He was still as a stone.

She went into the master bedroom and lay down on the bed, but on top of the covers, lest she be presuming. A few minutes later he came in and lay down beside her, pulling the spread gently down and over her.

She woke up.

When Susan woke in the morning, she was alone in the bed. With a blanket wrapped around her and her hair in a snarl, she went looking for Ewen. He was not in the guest room. The bathroom door stood open. She went down the stairs and found him in the living room, with his legs spread out and close to the ground, his whole body making sweeping, circular gestures around him. His eyes were half-closed. His hands were smudged gray and there was a black streak across one side of his face. When he noticed her he finished the exercise in one smooth whip of the body and smiled. She returned the smile slowly, because she was dazzled by his movement.

What dazzled Ewen was the image of a tall, splendid Indian woman wrapped very naturally in a blanket, her hair as wild as the ocean. At the completion of the form he bowed, looking straight at her.

"What's that?" she asked uncertainly.

"It's called 'Dragon.' It's a training form. A code. Made up of a lot of self-defense moves, hidden in a dance."

"Could I learn it? Eventually?"

He laughed. "You could learn it today, Susan. But it might disappoint you." She turned her head to one side, questioning. "Nowhere in the form does one use a boot kick to the butt-end," he said. They smiled at each other in the silliest way. Not moving from the bottom of the stairs she asked, "What do we do now?"

That could be taken in so many ways.

"Think about things," he replied, wiping more charcoal across his smudged face with his hand. "About the enemy, I mean. I don't have to think about . . . the rest."

Susan grinned at him, and with her large, generous mouth the grin was intoxicating to Ewen. He realized he was in love: in love so deeply there was no surface to it. He thought maybe he had been near this level once before, but had only brushed it. It occurred to him that if he had died this summer, or even this past weekend, he would have never known such a feeling, and he was grateful.

"What is it?" Susan asked, coming closer. "The way you're looking at me. That expression."

"What expression?"

"You look . . . you look like Yoda."

This took a long time to sink in. "You know," she explained. "Yoda from *Star Wars*?"

"I know Yoda," he answered, and they both broke out in the usual giggles of people finding themselves deeply sunk in love. Rez yapped and leaped into the air, her wagging tail striking the heavy bag in the hall, making it swing.

The moment of grand idiocy ended.

Later, after breakfast had ended, and Susan had left for her day's work, Ewen sat back down at the kitchen table to think. He had a lot to think about and he knew he was at a disadvantage, because he couldn't wipe the grin off his face.

Feeling like this, he thought, I could enlighten the Bear Woman. But would he feel like this if the thing threatened Susan, or even her dog? Hostages to fortune, he said to himself. I have shackled myself with hostages to fortune, tighter by far than last night's handcuffs.

What should he do now? Barbie had been sent home with a bag of Ling Chi tea and strict instructions to stay in bed until she had fought off the cold she was obviously coming down with. When the late winter sun rose, maybe in an hour, the police car in the drive would be called away. Then what? He couldn't sit there passively waiting for the killers to make their next strike.

Ewen did what he could. He slipped on a pair of rubber boots and went out in the rain to ask the police officer whether he preferred tea or coffee. He worked out a bit. He tightened up his sketch of the three faces. When he saw daylight outside the window he picked up the phone and called Grandma Sundown at the number in Oregon.

"I hope I didn't wake you up," he began, and the woman laughed. "Not at my age. I don't need much sleep. And maybe I'll get Sid's body back today. Probably not, but I want to be ready to bury him."

Ewen took a deep breath. "Mrs. Sundown, I'm Raven. Your brother said so."

Hundreds of miles away, the woman lifted one eyebrow, hearing Ewen give her his sacred name so casually. "And how was he doing, when you saw him?" she enquired placidly.

"He was doing very well. In fact, he looked great," he answered, happy to be able to say that.

"I never thought different," she said in a matter of fact tone of voice. "So you're Raven. Don't know why I didn't see that myself, but then Sid was always sharper than me. I guess you want to know how Raven fights Bear, then."

"Yes. Exactly," said Ewen, and so she told him.

It was after nine when Ewen went out to spray the blood off his porch. It would take more than a blast of the hose, but he got the worst off the front door. To the left of the door was something white showing through the pattern of holes on his black, tin mailbox. He had brought in yesterday's mail upon returning with Susan. He picked the paper out. It was block printing in pencil and said Go Back Where You Came From. Thoughtfully, he put it in his pocket, and went down the stairs.

He went down to feed the fish . . . but the fish were all dead, because the guts of the dog had been dumped into Ewen's little pond. He felt sick to his stomach. As he turned away he found himself being looked at by the Kelly daughter, who stood on the driveway wearing a yellow slicker. He maneuvered himself between her and the pond, and walked forward, forcing her back a few steps.

"Hey, Sheila. Why aren't you in school?" he asked, in order to have something to say.

"Daddy kept us home today. To keep us safe. He's home, too."

Ewen wished Daddy hadn't done that. He was conscious of his house as a place of contagion, and himself as the center of it. "Let me walk back with you," he said. "I'd like to talk with your daddy."

"We're going to bury Wreck today. In the yard. He's in a box. Mommy says we can't have a new puppy, because Wreck wrecked the house. Daddy says not all dogs wreck the house. They had a fight about it."

"I can understand both sides," said Ewen.

Daddy himself came out before they reached the door. "Sheila! What do you mean running out here by yourself? Did I go to all this trouble so you could walk out in the rain all alone?" He looked up at Ewen, opened his mouth, but said nothing.

Ewen spoke quietly. "I agree she shouldn't be out here alone, Mr. Kelly. I also would like to speak to you. If you have a moment."

Kelly did, and he shoved his daughter through the door and closed it behind him.

Ewen told him how he had found the organs of the dog in his pond, and asked if they wanted them for the funeral. "I guess so," said Kelly, leaning against the door. "If I can get them in the box without the kids seeing. This funeral business, you know, is mostly for the kids."

Ewen nodded and led Kelly to the little pond, with all the white bellies of the fish floating, amidst the dark shapes that came out of Wreck's insides. "Wow," said Kelly, looking down wearily. "They really played hell with your pond, didn't they?"

Ewen shrugged. "It can be fixed." Then he took the scrap of paper from his pocket. "Now, Mr. Kelly, I need to know if maybe . . . maybe one of your kids might have left this in my mailbox. I need to know because if it's not, I have to tell the police. But if it is, we can just throw it out and no harm done."

Kelly read it and his face darkened. "You think my kids would write something like this?" He glanced up and met Ewen's guarded eyes for an instant. "Hell! You think maybe *I* wrote this garbage. Don't you? You think I'm some kind of racist."

"No," said Ewen. "I didn't think it was you. I just needed to know before I called the police. And it's funny. Where I came from is a very nice place, and sometimes I wish I were back there."

"Where?"

"Santa Barbara. California."

Kelly almost smiled. "Yeah. Great weather."

The two men stood face to face and looked calmly at one another, and to give weight to the remark, drizzle began to fall again, speckling Mr. Kelly's glasses.

Ewen cleaned the pool and put the dog's remains into a garbage bag, which he left by the corner of his house, where Kelly could pick it up unnoticed. The bodies of his shubunkins, turned from calico to gray in death, he put into a smaller bag and dumped in the garbage. He ran the hose into the pond, to change the water entirely. When this was all over, he thought, perhaps he would stick to mosquito fish.

There was a phone message, and he took a calming breath before playing it, but it was just Richard Bolt, letting him know that his daughter had really liked the painting so far. He thought how universal it was, that people whose portraits he painted told him how someone else liked the work. Rarely that *they* did. Perhaps it was because they thought it would be self-flattery. Perhaps they felt they should then pay him more. Whatever it was, it made him happy that someone had liked the painting.

He could not reach Petersen, but Gideon Ryde answered the phone. Ewen told him about the message in the box, and asked if he thought it meant anything. Ryde waited a while before answering. "Yes, Mr. Young. I believe it does. In fact, the same message, word for word, was found in the mail of the two victims in Canada. That they were to go back where they came from."

"And where did they come from?" asked Ewen, thinking they couldn't all be Chinese.

"Well, the first one—the Catholic priest—had been born in Italy. The other one, who was a Methodist, had come from Maine. From Maine to Ontario province. Not a huge leap." Ewen heard a rustle as Detective Ryde shifted the phone at his ear. "Actually, Mr. Young, I doubt these messages are what they seem. It may be they're a way of putting us off the scent. Making us think the attacks are simple xenophobia. I don't think they are."

As reasonably as he could manage, Ewen asked, "Then what are they?"

"Bad men attacking good men, Mr. Young. When you come down to it, that's what it's all about."

On impulse Ewen said, "And what about yourself, Detective? You're deep into this and you're a good man. Aren't you?"

Ryde laughed. "I try to be!"

"But you have a family. Kids. What do you do about the danger?"

"I pray, Mr. Young. I pray. There's danger everywhere, Mr. Young. We're in the hands of God." After a moment he added, "I'll send a man over to get that note."

Chapter Eighteen

WHEN SUSAN RETURNED that evening, Ewen had roasted a chicken. She laughed because it wasn't what she had ever thought of as Chinese food. He replied that it became Chinese food the moment he ate it. He offered a bit of meat to Rez, who politely declined, to his surprise.

"Don't be offended," said Susan. "She knows I would give her hell if she accepted." He wiped his hands on his napkin and did not try sneaking treats again.

Afterwards she made another fire in the fireplace: the second in two days and the second he had had all winter. She made it with flint and steel, using char-cloth as tinder. The kit she kept in her pocket was much like the one carried by Petersen, and that sight was a bit unsettling to Ewen. *That lady goes her own way, Ewen. Remember that.*

Spread out on the carpet in front of the fire, she told him legends about Raven, and he, in turn, tried to describe what it was like to pass between worlds. Then he remembered the note in the mailbox—GO BACK WHERE YOU CAME FROM. He told her about it.

Susan stared, then giggled. "We've been trying to say as much to all you whites—you non-Indians—for hundreds of years."

"And so the woolly mammoths said to you, before that," he replied, and they began to get silly. Not at any time during that evening and night did they discuss the men who were trying to kill them, or what they could do about it. The night was quiet until Sheila Kelly ran out into the front yard, screaming.

Susan woke up precipitously, but as she thrashed around for a robe she was aware of Ewen already darting out of the room. As she scrambled down the dark stairs—stairs that were not her own—she heard Rez's battle cry, and the dog was downstairs flinging herself against the closed door. She put the dog to heel, made sure Rez was listening to her, and opened the door herself.

Under light of a distant streetlamp, Susan could see the child, dressed in pink pajamas, both hands to her mouth, sobbing. She had wet herself. Ewen was standing at the driveway, wearing only his BVDs, looking, for once, indecisive. Then he stepped toward Sheila just as her father erupted from the door. Susan hurried barefoot down the steps to the path and onto the drive.

"It was in my room!" the little girl cried. "It was right there in my room with me. And I couldn't move!"

"Well, you *did* move," said Ewen, getting down on his knees before her. "You did manage to move after all. So . . . so it's all right."

Kelly bulled forward, hands clenched, not knowing quite who the enemy was. Ewen looked from Sheila to her father and reached out for the little girl very, very slowly, touching her on the side of her tousled blond head. Susan ran up to stand beside them, to be a buffer between the two men.

Sheila's eyes met Ewen's. "It was a monster," she said, and she closed her eyes and folded her legs and sat down, the damp part of her pajamas resting on the damp grass. She closed her eyes, yawned, and gave a little smile. Ewen was still touching her head, and his eyes were also closed. He sat back on his heels and only then took his hand away. Sheila's mother came over to pick up her child and couldn't manage to lift her off the ground. Kelly himself picked her up and looked wondering at her sleeping face.

"I guess she had a bad dream," said Susan. She kept her hand on Rez's head, because the dog, obediently sitting beside her, was emitting her very quiet growl.

"Scared the shit out of me," said Mr. Kelly to Susan.

"Me, too," she replied, giving him a social smile. Engaging him. Wanting him not to look down at Ewen and wonder about the touch. She gave Ewen a little prod with her toe, lest his trancelike behavior started to give Kelly something else to worry about.

Ewen opened his eyes, took a deep breath, and yawned. " 'Scuse me," he mumbled, stood up and walked back into the house.

Now there were lights on other porches, and other people in bathrobes peering. Kelly took his daughter into the house and Mrs. Kelly, sparing one wondering look at Susan and her immense dog, followed her husband.

Susan found Ewen sitting on the couch. "What did you do?" she asked. "You touch that girl and she stops screaming and falls asleep? What kind of power . . . "

"She didn't just have a bad dream, you know," whispered Ewen. "It's very close. They're very close."

"How do you know? Did you see what she saw? When you touched her head?"

"I saw a monster, all right. I . . . don't want to talk about it right now. That tired me out."

She sat down beside him and put her arm around him. His body was chilled. "Okay. Okay, love." She had not used that word before. "Just tell me what you did."

He leaned back. He had never tried to explain this thing he did, not even to Lynn. With Lynn he had never had to. "I have a picture of a place stored in my head where I can . . . get away from things. I can share it with other people sometimes. I do it for some of my sister's patients."

She considered this. "Could you do it with me?"

"Not just now," he answered dreamily. "The place is occupied by Sheila. Besides, you don't need that place at all. It's for damaged people." Then he, too, added the word "love."

Next morning Ewen woke and checked in with the police. He was unable to get Petersen: was told to leave a message. He next tried Petersen's cell phone number and let it ring and ring. There was no response. He did the same for Ryde, again leaving a message and letting the cell phone ring. This was very odd, but he kept his composure and saw Susan off to work, with Rez marching beside her. As soon as they were gone, he called his three students.

"It's going to happen very soon," he said. "And somehow I don't think we're going to have much help." None of them asked for explanations.

By nine-fifteen, all three were there: Barbie with a reddened nose, but looking alert; Perry with a weight sagging in his jacket pocket; and Ryan with a double armful of martial arts equipment.

He had light kicking-slappers, a set of sparring pads, and a long zippered bag.

"What's all that?" asked Ewen.

"Where would you hide a leaf?" Ryan Watanabe returned.

"I wouldn't hide a leaf!"

"You would hide a leaf in a forest," said Ryan, as though Ewen hadn't spoken. From the bag he emptied a pair of training broadswords, a blunt tai chi sword, and—wrapped in silk—a breathtaking katana.

"My father had to buy it in this country," he said. "In Japan they weren't allowed to own them in the fifties."

Ewen thought about this. "And you were worried the police would stop you for having this? Won't they stop you for using it, if you do?"

"Hey, bro," said Perry from the other room. " 'Rather be judged by twelve than carried by six.' That's my motto. Not very popular with most other lawyers, though." He added, "I don't guess you're sure about when this . . . strike will hit?"

Ewen gave a great, rattling sigh. "Soon," he said. "Not soon by days. Really soon."

"In daylight?" asked Barbie, only slightly froggy.

Ewen shifted left to right. "Soon," he said.

But he didn't expect it would be in fifteen minutes.

Sheila Kelly was out of the house again; he saw her through the front window. "I didn't think he'd keep them home from school a second day," he said to no one in particular. "I wish he hadn't." He went to the door to meet her, because she seemed to be heading toward his porch again. As he opened his front door two Dodge vans pulled up to the far side of the street. Men poured out of them: too many to count immediately: men dully dressed in grey sweats, T-shirts, camouflage jackets . . . Some were wearing fatigue caps, some baseball caps, some bareheaded. All were openly carrying weapons. They did not look at all real. Sheila saw them and stopped in place. She had her knuckles in her mouth and was biting down on them. Their eyes tracked Sheila and they jogged toward her.

Ewen burst out of the door and leaped over the porch stairs. He started to pick the girl up and then thought better of it. He waved his arms at the men, as one would wave to distract a dog, or a bear. One of them raised a rifle. Ewen picked up and threw little Sheila to the side, towards her front door, and at that moment he heard the whine of a bullet past his ear. He ran up his driveway, zigzagging, stealing glances over his shoulder. When he saw they were following him and not Sheila, he gave up zigzagging and ran like hell.

He darted into his back garden, and as he leaped over one carefully placed and well-tended mossy boulder, he heard the crack of lead against the granite. There was nothing that he could do about Sheila Kelly now. Nothing he could do about any of his friends. Two more bullets spattered against the wooden fence behind his yard just as he reached his severely kept border of black bamboo and vaulted the six feet of the plank fence into Mrs. Blick's yard. The untended bamboo on this far side was so thick he almost bounced back against the fence, and he slid down to the ground as more bullets made specks of light appear amidst the boards above him. He thought, *Am I deaf, or are the bullets that quiet?*

He decided it was his hearing. He decided it was shock.

There was a scramble on the other side of the fence, and the boards warped inward as heavy boots scuffed up the height of it. A man in a fatigue cap appeared over the top, blinking against the leaf cover and aiming his rifle before him. Ewen reached gently up and pushed the barrel aside. As the man hung there above him, legs spread for purchase, Ewen punched him hard in the balls. The man lost his fatigue cap and his rifle and came down in a tangle of bamboo. There was the sound of another body coming over the fence.

Ewen picked up the rifle. He had once shot a friend's rifle; he pointed at the man's body slowly moving on the ground, and thought that he was finally going to kill a man, and what would that be like? It was like nothing, because nothing happened. The trigger worked halfway and stopped. A second man was coming over now so Ewen took the gun by the barrel and swung it at the head of the crumpled man beside him. It made a noise like a stick striking a wooden drum. In the same sweep of the rifle butt, he clubbed the second man, who was brandishing a machete awkwardly as he came over the fence.

This one didn't go down so easily. He sliced at Ewen, who evaded easily. The bamboo, however, sliced very nicely: diagonally. A voice called from the other side of the fence; it was no one Ewen knew. As the machete man withdrew for his return sweep, Ewen used his rifle to block the blade. He drove on for the man's throat. He hit twice and the man's neck flopped back and then forward. *Now I have killed a man,* thought Ewen, but still the thought meant nothing. He looked around him at the bristle of bamboo and felt as though he was in a tiger trap. But he decided he wasn't going to be the tiger that perished in it. This third man had a rifle too, and again he tried to point it at Ewen before committing his body to the drop. But this was a very confusing place now—this side of Ewen's garden fence—filled with branches and bodies and beautiful, flowing black bamboo. He couldn't get the barrel in line and so the man decided to drop into the yard.

Ewen, standing right in front of him, put out one foot, almost casually, and turned the sharpened stems of the cut bamboo toward his attacker. As the man fell on the stems, they pierced him from the middle of the thigh and up through the groin. He screamed and screamed. Ewen picked up this man's gun and threw it far away into the grove.

He could not hear the fourth man come over the fence because of the screaming, but he saw him come. He felt no more surprise. He seemed to be in the world of the rakeshas—the world of rage demons—and beings like this would come at him forever. He looked for the machete the first man had had, but couldn't find it in the debris. He cursed once and then looked up at the fourth man, wondering what the weapon was that he held in his hand. It was light and made of metal, and painted with the usual military green camouflage—and it took him a moment to realize it was a tomahawk. It was a tomahawk with a spike on one end.

The man swung the spike at him, vertically, between the bamboo stems still standing. Ewen stepped back, figuring out the weapon, and then he stumbled over the machete and went down backwards in slow motion, buoyed up by the trampoline effect of the bamboo behind him. He clawed amid the bamboo, the whole stalks, and the cut ones.

The man in front of him, outlined against the fence, looked like a recruiting poster for the military, from his brawny chest in white T-shirt to the golden stubble of hair on his head. *Someday I might like to paint this,* Ewen thought, and as the big young blond man lifted his tomahawk for the killing strike, Ewen took one handful of the sharpened bamboo-ends and drove them into the inside of the man's thigh. One muscular leg crumpled and the tomahawk's strike went very wide.

Ewen couldn't see well. There was blood in his eyes, but it was not his own. The man's femoral artery was spraying the over entire clearing of broken bamboo and broken bodies. Red. So red. Still he raised his tomahawk again at Ewen, who was standing beyond all emotion, and Ewen stuck a bloody spear of bamboo through the man's eye-socket and into his brain. In another moment a terrific noise burst the air. Ewen looked up.

Chapter Nineteen

PERRY AND BARBIE saw the men coming from their cars only after glancing up to see Ewen burst out the door. Perry went out the front door. Barbie, seeing where the attackers were heading, took the back way. In her pocket she had her weapon—perhaps not the one she would have chosen had there been time for choice, but it was the one she knew best and carried most often.

Barbie leaped over the little back porch and peered down the driveway at two men with machetes, who looked for all the world like soldiers in some jungle. They stepped up to her. They smiled unpleasantly. When she took out six feet of silvery chain with a red flag at the end of it and began to whirl it over her head, one of them laughed; the other grinned. The chain-whip sang. It whistled. When the steel dart at the end of it slammed into the laughing man's hand, he dropped his machete. When it slammed into his eye, they both stopped smiling.

The other soldier-man slashed his weapon at the chain-dart, thinking to break it. Instead, his blade-handle and his hand found themselves wrapped in the chain. He howled in pain and charged at her. Barbie stepped aside and circled another loop of the chain around his neck.

He was strong, with a bull neck. She didn't dare let go, but she heard the man she had stung coming up behind her, and pops of gunfire in the distance. She gave one low, undramatic back kick and broke the knee of the rear attacker. She dragged the man she was throttling away from his partner's reach and kept throttling him. The air was suddenly broken by a huge explosion and she lifted her head in wonder, but she kept on throttling.

Perry went out the front door some seconds after Ewen There were five men still in front of the house, striding toward the drive. Two of them had guns. Perry dashed to cut them out, sheep-dog style, because he was the only one of his people who had a gun. A little .32 revolver. He didn't challenge the guy with the rifle; he simply shot at him as he ran.

He had never shot at a living thing before, or shot while running. It was good luck that he struck the guy at all, grazing him across the stomach. The guy flinched but didn't drop his rifle. He turned to Perry with outrage on his face and aimed. Perry dropped to the pavement and rolled. The bullet went over his body and hit the struts of the porch. The other man had a handgun, side-holstered. Perry didn't wait for him to draw, but shot him full in the chest. The man with the rifle fired again and Perry heard the shot, thought, *Good, he missed again,* and then the pain told him the man had not missed. He tried to lift his gun again and found it oddly difficult. The man he had stung in the belly smiled and aimed with exaggerated care. Then the world exploded in noise. Perry looked up.

He was seeing, and therefore, against all expectation, he was not dead. Perry glanced over to see a man he didn't know at all standing in the middle of the lawn next door, holding a smoking shotgun. The next thing he heard was the collapse of the body of the man who was going to kill him. The mangled body fell across Perry's legs.

It was by chance that Ryan was the last one out the door, and the first thing Ryan saw outside was three men standing on the sidewalk in front of the house. They were advancing upon Perry Janaway, who seemed to be already occupied by men with guns. Two of the trio on the sidewalk had machetes and one was holding an ordinary baseball bat. Ryan leaped between them and Perry and positioned his katana into low guard. The men looked beyond him, at Perry with his .32.

Ryan had to draw their notice. He swept his blade left and right. That did little. "You look like idiots!" he screamed, and when that still didn't seem to capture their attention, he added, "Dirty assholes!"

The three turned to him and the man with the baseball bat said, very calmly, "Go back where you came from." Ryan was mystified by this odd command, but did not let it distract him. He thought hard as the three came on.

In all the multiple-attacker training he had done, the attackers had advanced one at a time, or at least slightly staggered. These three came on as one, as though they were not about to fight but to lift something heavy together. Their faces were strange. Distant. Unfocused. The hair on the back of Ryan's neck stood up. In sudden inspiration he darted over the wet grass to Ewen's fishpond. He knew this pond, for he had helped build it. He leaped the thirty-inch benched wall and landed on the concrete bottom. His feet skidded on algae, but of all of James Young's students, Ryan had the best sense of balance. He saw the men pause and look down the driveway. They moved almost as one. He heard light gunfire.

Ryan shouted more obscenities. He stuck out his tongue. He made rude gestures. The three men advanced upon him.

He saw them come, and they didn't look like real men. He realized his hands were shaking and thought about his breath. He put the katana back into low guard, and immediately realized he had lowered the tip into the water, which splashed around his legs. *I've gotten my father's sword wet,* he thought, and raised the angle just a bit. He heard one man moving around the pond to a spot behind him and one off to the side, but though he could track the man's steps, Ryan became aware there was something wrong with his hearing. He seemed to be almost deaf, and of all his senses only his vision seemed to be working clearly. Even with that he could see only straight in front of him; his peripheral vision was fading. He breathed deeper and dropped lower into an open-X stance. His senses began to return.

The man in front of him leaned forward over the pond's benches, and swung his machete. Without conscious thought Ryan swept up to intercept the blow, where the man's hand met the crude blade. He caught the hand as well. He did not hear the man's scream because he was screaming himself—screaming as though that was the only way to use a katana, as though that was the only way to breathe. Out of the corner of his eye he saw the baseball bat being raised above his head, while the owner of the bat stepped with one leg over the pond wall. Ryan moved from his hips and continued the swing of the katana to meet the bat just where it met the man's hands. The concussion of metal with hardened wood almost loosened the blade in his hands. The man stared for only a moment at the stub of the bat in his hands and then he threw it at Ryan's head. Ryan ducked.

There was a great boom that beat on his eardrums and everyone looked up, except for the man who had lost his hand along with his machete. Ryan saw something moving out of the right corner of his vision and remembered the third man. He continued his long, single sweep of the sword and caught the third man as he climbed into the pond. The katana took him across the middle and he was almost unaware of the contact. The man fell forward and the machete came down upon Ryan but no hand was holding it and the poor steel of which it was made bounced off Ryan's shoulder and slapped the water.

Ryan Watanabe unfolded and reversed his strike. He caught the falling man at the neck and again felt that concussion in his wrists and shoulders. He came back to the man who had thrown the nub of the baseball bat and took off the leg that had come over the pond wall. Then he found himself back with the first attacker, who was squatting on the bench, holding the sheared end of his arm in his remaining hand. He was still screaming. Everyone was screaming.

Having gone through one sweep to the right and return to the left, Ryan finished his simple technique with a pull back and a stab to the front. He did this from habit, without having to think about it. As he felt his sword enter the body of the man with a missing hand, he wondered if he should have done that. Was that a fair strike? The man had stopped fighting by now. He wrenched the blade away. Both Ryan and the man stopped screaming.

The color red seemed very bright to Ryan, as he stood there with three men on the ground spouting blood around him. Blood arced into the fishpond. The water had become altogether scarlet. Drops misted his face. *I did only one thing,* he thought. *I swept right, then back left, retract and stab. That's all I did.* In the next few seconds his true vision and his hearing were fully restored, and he was aware of a large man, whom he thought he recognized as Ewen's neighbor, holding a shotgun by his side, barrel down to the earth. The man was looking at him warily, but without malice.

Mr. Kelly stepped slowly forward. His eyes were wide. He was cautious. "I couldn't get a clear shot at the guys," he said to Ryan, and then added, "Besides. It didn't look like you needed no help."

Ryan wiped his eyes, and his hands came away so red it looked like there was paint on them, and he thought of Ewen, the painter. The fishpond seemed as filled with blood as with water, and on the surface of it floated a small green shape, like the organ of a slaughtered animal. It was the spleen of a dog, but Ryan would never remember to ask about it, and would never know it had belonged to Kelly's dog, Wreck.

One of the attackers was still screaming, but two were lying still from their perfect dismemberment. Looking around him he saw a human head, rolled yards away on the careful, suburban grass. He saw the splayed fingers of a hand. He saw guts spilled out of their living container and saw that his chinos and sweats were brilliant. Brilliant red. He heard sirens approaching and was very angry they hadn't shown up before this. Before he had had to do this—before he had learned this much about himself. He put the katana carefully down upon the pond's side bench and thought, *I honor my father's sword.*

I don't ever want to touch it again.

Ewen climbed back over the fence in time to see Barbie Cowell kneeling on a very large man, methodically throttling him with her chain whip, while kicking at another one who was crawling over the ground toward her on his belly. He passed by this odd scene, stopping just long enough to kick the bull-necked fellow helpfully in the head. "Pull the chain up right under his chin," he advised her. "Better leverage." Then he was running down the driveway again toward a scene slick with blood. Three men were lying in it and one of them was Perry Janaway. As Ewen bent over, his breath caught in his throat, Perry raised himself on one elbow. "'M okay," he said, panting. "Bastard just caught me in one arm. Your neighbor took the guy out."

Then Ewen saw Kelly, standing there with his shotgun at ease, conversing with somebody. He looked like a pheasant hunter on a slow morning. After another few steps Ewen saw who Kelly was talking to, and stopped dead in his tracks.

There was Ryan Watanabe, standing in a pool of blood: a literal pool, bright red. Around him was spread the ugliest sight Ewen had ever seen. It was uglier than the sound he had heard when he jabbed the bamboo spike into the man's brain. Spilled guts, a leg, a human head, and all ruby, ruby, ruby, and very clean-edged. Calmly Ryan was conversing with Mr. Kelly. It took all of Ewen's courage to walk over to them, and as he did he heard police sirens.

Ewen met Ryan's eyes. "How many?" he whispered.

Ryan was swaying ever so slightly. "Three," he said and then added, as out of politeness, "You?"

"I don't remember," said Ewen, although he did. He turned to Mr. Kelly. "How is Sheila, Mr. Kelly?"

"She's fine," said Kelly. "All the clan is fine."

The first police cars pulled up to the house. "You'd better put down your gun, Mr. Kelly," said Ewen quietly. Kelly did so, and they all stood still, Ryan still in the pond of blood, wearing ruby from his hair on down.

Ewen thought distantly that this was the second time in—what?— three days he had been a figure in a murder investigation. Third time in a year. Things would never be right again.

For some reason it was Mr. Kelly who was doing all the explaining to the police. That seem odd, but he didn't interfere.

"These guys: they came piling out of their cars—a dozen of them."

"Eleven," Ewen corrected him, but no one heard.

"First they went at my little girl, Sheila, but I got her into the house. I saw them all chasing my friend Ewen here down his own driveway and I got my gun. Eileen called nine-one-one. I come out and two guys are shooting at this black kid I know—works with Ewen, and they got him down, and I . . . " Mr. Kelly's understanding caught up with his words and he finished. "I blew him away. My God and Mother Mary, I blew him away . . . "

His voice drifted off.

Now police were darting all over with drawn guns. Ewen could see Barbie Cowell standing in the drive by Perry, looking harmless, her chain dart again in her pocket. Ewen raised his voice and asked if there was a detective he could talk to. There wasn't.

"There are four more of them," he said to the man in uniform. "Over the back fence. Four more of the eleven that came out of the vans."

"Dead?"

"Some are." The cop looked measuringly at him. "Dead how?"

"By bamboo."

He was handcuffed. Ewen was handcuffed again: twice in three days. Ryan was handcuffed, very warily, and Mr. Kelly was handcuffed. Perry was not handcuffed because he was shot, and without explanation, Barbie Cowell was not taken into custody at all. She sat on the porch steps, her arms around her knees, watching the police quarter the area, call out the discovery of the bodies over the fence, gather together the few attackers still living and herd them to the other side of the yard from her group.

Ewen heard one cop's exchange with another. "I dunno. All the asshole said was, 'Go back where you came from.' I was born in Seattle. I go home every night."

Ewen wondered if they had told Sid Sundown to go back where he came from, too. How perfect that must have been. He waited patiently for Petersen and Ryde.

Chapter Twenty

"If you had an idea something was about to break, why didn't you let us know?" asked Petersen, not chidingly, but in puzzlement.

"I left a message. I also called on your cell," said Ewen, out of great weariness. "I also called Detective Ryde."

"My cell was on," said Ryde.

"Mine, too," said Petersen. "And I never got a message at work."

Ewen shrugged. "Maybe it's still waiting."

"I wouldn't be surprised if it simply isn't there," said Ryde. And when Petersen glanced over he added, "Oh, I don't mean Carolyn ditched it, or didn't care. I just mean . . . " He waved ambiguously, "Something wasn't right, here."

The understatement was such that Ewen almost began to laugh. Instead he started to hiccup. Petersen looked blankly at him for a moment and stated, "You have made the national news."

Ewen stopped hiccupping. He stopped breathing.

"Yes, I thought that would take care of hiccups," murmured Petersen, "but still you had to know, sooner or later. You are food for the tabloids." Then he said, "You were all together. All your martial arts friends. Were you expecting it to go down like this?"

"Like *this?*" Ewen said, and then thundered, "Like THIS? . . . No. Not like this." He cleared his throat. "I was more thinking we'd have always someone on guard at night. When . . . when Susan might be there."

Ryde and Petersen looked quietly at him, Petersen's hands tented together under his chin. Ryde said "I understand something . . . something supernatural is happening here, Mr. Young. At least I think I do. But we've got to put our thinking caps on and figure out what to say to . . . "

There was someone else striding over the vinyl flooring toward them. Someone with heavy feet. Both Petersen and Ryde suddenly closed down their faces. Ewen looked up to see Lieutenant Kopek, whom he knew just from reputation. "How many men did you kill today, kid?"

Ewen started to stand but Petersen's hand softly held him down. Ewen had not meant the move to seem aggressive, but he sat hurriedly. "I think two, sir. Lieutenant. I think it was two that died."

"With bamboo spears? That a Chinese traditional weapon?"

"They were just growing in the garden," said Ewen, defensively. Kopek, a pouchy, blond man, looked narrowly down at Ewen. "Surprised you aren't lawyered up yet," he growled.

"The only lawyer I know is in the hospital," said Ewen. "He just got shot." Petersen gave him just the slightest shake of a head and Ewen shut up.

Ewen went to jail.

Lynn found him a lawyer, a gray-haired woman who heard his story with wonder, horror, and amusement. He told her about the dog and the note in the mailbox. He told her about the death of Susan's granduncle. He did not tell her about Bear Woman.

"Good thing this is Washington State," she said.

"Why?"

"In Massachusetts, say, they have different attitudes about self-defense." She added, "They probably can't even hold you long. Not with the hardware the terrorists sent up against you."

"Were they really terrorists?" asked Ewen.

"You think *I* should know? The press is calling them the 'Go Back Where You Came From Gang.' There's a lot of talk about cults and xenophobia."

"And what about Ryan? Ryan Watanabe. There were only machetes and a baseball bat against him."

The amusement flickered larger over her weathered face. "Only. And only three. How very unsporting of him to kill them. No. I sincerely hope none of you are going to be in much trouble. In fact, you may wind up heroes."

Ewen stood up in his chains. "Not for that!" he cried. "God! Not for *that!*"

Being in jail was a strange and new experience for Ewen. It was not a bad jail; it was much nicer than the ones he saw on TV, and he didn't have to share his cell with anyone. But he *was* locked in. He sat on his little cot and meditated. It was not a pleasant meditation, but he stayed with it until roused by the man in the cell across from him, who was saying, "Hey, Bud. Hey, Bud. You doin' some kind of protest? Jail house protest?"

Ewen unfolded and looked across at the man, who was wearing a disheveled suit. No tie. His face was sweaty. "No. No protest. Why did you think . . . ?"

"The way you were sitting. I thought maybe you were fasting or something." The guy shuffled his feet and leaned against his bars. "I'm in here because I wouldn't take a damn Breathalyzer test. That's all. Then they take away my tie so I don't *hang* myself. It's my right not to take one of their damn tests."

"I see," said Ewen. He had never studied the matter of Breathalyzers and civil rights.

"What you in for?" asked the rumpled guy.

"I just killed a couple of people." The man froze in position, leaning against the bars, and said nothing. "They're trying to decide whether they think I was right in doing it," continued Ewen. "My lawyer thinks they'll let me out."

The man blinked rapidly and looked Ewen up and down. "I . . . thought that was paint all over your shirt."

"It is paint," said Ewen, soothingly. "Oil paint. These are my work clothes. They took the stuff I was wearing away."

After that conversation, it was quiet in the cell block.

Ewen worried about Perry. He worried even more about Ryan. He would not have wanted to be Ryan, today. He wasn't sure he wanted to be Ewen. He missed Susan terribly. He even missed Rez. After a supper he could not eat he was taken upstairs to be questioned again, and not just by Petersen and Ryde. The gray-haired lawyer was there but objected to very little that was said. It wasn't like *Law and Order* at all. He answered questions until he didn't really know what he was saying, but at least the answers were consistent, because they were the truth and the truth is somewhat easier to say when one is exhausted. And no one asked about anything supernatural. That made it much easier. At last he was allowed to return to his cell.

Next morning Ewen woke up to a corrections officer telling him he could go. No charges had been filed so far.

Ryde led him to the basement garage and offered a seat in a car. Detective Petersen was driving—not his police sedan but his own vehicle—and they went out through the back entrance. Ewen was confused. "Are you taking me home?" he asked. "I hope so. Because my car isn't here, and I don't know how else . . . "

Petersen answered, "I don't know if I'm taking you home, Ewen. I'm not sure whether you want to be home right now. But I'm taking you wherever you want to go. Just now, though, duck down."

Ewen ducked, not knowing why. "Is Susan . . . ?" he asked.

"She's fine."

"Perry?"

"He's out of the hospital already," said Petersen. "And Ryan Watanabe is released. They're not charging any of you—at least not yet."

Ryde turned reproachfully to his partner and said, "And they're not likely to, either."

Petersen shrugged. Like the lawyer, he added, "Be glad this is Washington State, not . . . Massachusetts."

They turned the corner to Ewen's street. "Well, here's your place," said Petersen. "What do you think of it?"

The first thing he saw was the parking problem, as both sides of the street were locked tight with vehicles. Some were police cars but most were vans. Most were sporting satellite dishes on their roofs. Once closer he noticed the amazing amount of crime-scene tape, which was draped like crepe paper at a party, all around his property. There were people gathered in casual little knots, conversing. It looked as though they were expecting a parade. Ewen saw one other thing down his driveway as he was driven by.

"The bamboo," he said. "You've cut it all down. All of it. Back to the fence."

"Not us," said Petersen, smiling. "That was raiders from the outside, trampling our scene."

"Huh?"

Ryde said, "People have snuck in and cut it down. All night it was a battle with them."

"Huh?"

"Souvenirs," said Petersen dryly. "'Genuine Ewen Young martial arts bamboo.' To be sold on eBay."

Ewen ducked down again. He did not object when Petersen kept right on going.

The detective took Ewen to his own house.

Petersen lived in a log house, inconvenient and covered outside in algae and moss. Inside it was spare, unexpectedly clean, and full of books. Ewen sat his dirty and paint-spattered self down on the edge of a couch. The two detectives left him there.

Ewen sat alone with a Coke and a microwave dinner and wondered about the future. He called Lynn and told her where he was. He wondered just how much of all this his sister had been an involuntary party to, both in her mind-connection and from television. Lynn was being watched by reporters too. She said she was spooked, but not by the reporters. He need ask her no more about *that*. She had a police officer parked by the office door, and Teddy was with her, playing in one of the special rooms she had set up for waiting children. Teddy was not spooked; on the contrary, he had to be repeatedly restrained from going out to stare at the police officer.

Next Ewen called Perry's house and got an ear-full from Perry's father, who had worked extremely hard to get his son out of poverty and into a law degree, which he felt was now imperiled by Ewen's shenanigans. Ewen listened to all this silently, feeling his guilt in every word. He was not told where he could find Perry.

Then he called Ryan and got no answer. This was disturbing, but then Ryan couldn't have found Ewen either, if he'd been looking. Too much police protection; and it was the same for Barbie. Out of a perverse curiosity he turned on the TV to the local news, and found out that Ewen Young and the Patrick Kelly family had been attacked by Canadian terrorists. A pretty young woman in a bright red coat stood outside the Kellys' yard in the freezing snow and imparted this information. She was Chinese.

Canadian terrorists. Ewen's mind could not accept the conjunction of those two words. He found he was shaking his head slowly back and forth.

The woman on the television suggested there might be a connection to the Syrians. To the Syrians? Ewen wondered if they had bears in Syria. Was that demon, "Pazuzu" or whatever he had been called, in *The Exorcist* from Syria? He couldn't remember. Ewen started doodling his idea of Syrian demons on a little square sticky-pad.

He heard heels and claws pelting up the porch stair, and in came Susan Sundown and Resurrection. He rose to let her in, but she already had a key. Ewen had never considered that she might have a key to Petersen's house. He rose to greet her.

Her face was bright as sunlight. She said, "You've won, haven't you? It's over?"

He could not meet those shining eyes. "I don't think so, love. We beat the shadow. We beat the Bear Woman's human 'hands.' But we haven't come against the demon itself. For that, it's just a matter of when."

She laid her head on his shoulder in a comforting manner, as though it had been she who had been given the bad news.

Two hours later, after a great deal of close cuddling, Ewen sat bolt upright. He suddenly had a thrill of knowledge. Abruptly he asked Susan to leave. She refused (of course) and when he tried to push her toward the door Rez interfered.

He sat down again cracking his knuckles. "Don't be a damn hero!" he shouted.

"Don't yourself! I'm the one with the power, remember? *Raven messenger*? What are you going to do against it? Flap away?"

There was a very good fight brewing, and Rez was spinning in circles of dismay between them. Then, between one moment and the next, Ewen cooled off. He stared past her into the distance.

"Susan," he began slowly, "I have an idea." There was a half-minute of silence and then he asked, "We need a bear trap. What's a good trap? A good, strong trap that just won't let go of you?"

Susan let go of her anger, and stood silent for some moments. She chuckled. "Sometimes I think my job is that. And sometimes my whole life!" And gazing into her rueful face, Ewen knew he had been given the answer. He knew the whole thing. Once more he asked her to leave, and this time she looked at his face, saw the new and different certainty in it and said, "Okay. For a little while."

Ewen sat alone in the dark cabin. He saw a spider, hanging from a thread, outlined by the dim light of the window. It went up and, then, in its own time, went down again. Ewen was not quite calm, for images of the battle kept sliding through his mind, and everything in those images was lit with horror and tasted of blood. And in the battle just over, the terrible, lesser battle, he had only been risking his life.

He noticed a fall of white outside the back window. It had begun to snow. He went to the window and saw it had already coated the porch, and the boughs of the firs all around. Beautiful, as fresh snow is always.

Waiting was over.

Ewen opened himself up to the in between. He stood on the edge of what was manifest and what was everything else and he shouted, "Bear! Bear, you piece of shit! You stinking turd! I'm coming for you, bear!"

He thought there might be a pause. He thought (hoped) that nothing would happen at all.

In the next moment he was struck off his feet and sailed into the far wall, hitting with a blow that jarred his brain. The world filled with snarling, and with the stink of bear. Everything had all gone dark.

Chapter Twenty-one

EWEN FOUGHT to stay conscious, and with a huge effort he threw himself over the edge, out of this world and into the void. He began to spin, becoming a small crystal in the darkness. The thing that had struck him was sucked after and was upon him now. It was a bear. It was stinking darkness. It had many blank eyes and its soul was confusion. Confusion soaked Ewen and got in the way of everything he had planned his trap to do. It turned his mind to mud.

He saw the luminosity again—*one last time*, he thought—and he tried to do as Theo had taught, to see it as his own nature. Instead it just made him sick. The ground of being seemed nothing more than the ringing pain in his head; the light in it nauseated him. He felt himself running away from the monster and from the light, and from all he could see. He looked for a place to hide.

He remembered this long corridor; he had been here before, but now he didn't remember what it meant. He was running down a hall and there were doors and lights on each side of him. Some were kind lights and some were comforting, but even the most gentle brightness hurt his eyes. And the monster was at his back.

They went on into the dirty dark. He himself was reaching toward the dark, towards a place of some safety, where neither the monster nor the light could find him. A place where he could catch his breath—maybe learn to think again. There were not many doors left in the corridor and it was black at the end.

Then out of one small door white-lit with snow stepped the figure of a man—an old man—and he took Ewen into one hand. It appeared that Ewen was small enough to fit in a hand. In the distance there came a wolf's howl, a sound completely solitary, and the old man said, "Raven. You are Raven."

Ewen recognized Sid Sundown and he recognized himself. He took wing.

The monster behind him—with its wrathful eyes, its breath of contamination and its huge malice—had slowed at the light from the door, and now it stopped, staring in all directions, striving to see a black raven in the dark. It did not look like a bear any more, but like one of those wrathful deities that Theo had hung all over the walls of his house. Protectors he called them, but this thing protected no one; it was all arms, eyes, and teeth.

Raven saw it and didn't care if it was a wrathful deity or a brute beast. He came down like a bullet and took out one of its staring eyes. The monster roared. It swung around with many huge arms, and Raven dodged among them. He went for another eye and missed.

The wolf howling in the distance grew louder; it was a battle cry. Raven was distracted by it. The wrathful deity opened its impossible jaw.

Sid was right. This is no lady.

Ewen—Raven—was sucked into the dreadful mouth of the thing. He darted sideways. The great jaw closed and caught only his black tail feathers. It shook him. Shook a bird.

Raven flapped uselessly in the monster's mouth, but suddenly the monster itself was yowling, and Raven wobbled away with battered feathers. Hanging on to the side of the enemy's face was a dog, or maybe a wolf. It was a big, heavy-coated thing, with wild amber eyes. The monster swung its hideous head left and right, and the dog hung on.

Raven hunts with Wolf, thought Ewen. Someone had said that, but he did not remember whether it had been Sid, or Susan, or Granny Sundown, and he didn't remember at all what it meant. His thoughts were thin threads, not human thoughts at all—bird thoughts—but they were sufficient for the moment. He took out the other of the enemy's eyes.

He felt himself being sucked in again, but this time not into the monster's mouth. This was something much worse. He had succeeded in reaching the end of the corridor, and now realized that had been a great mistake. He had followed Chow after all.

Ewen felt himself constricted. His possibilities died around him and his future was just hell. He squawked like the bird he had become as he saw the three of them—bird, beast, and dog—sinking into a funnel of darkness. The end of the tunnel was not an end at all, but a very nasty beginning. He had a quick image pass though his mind: *Black hole. Nothing gets out of a black hole.*

He fell in.

The walls were stone hard and lit by soiled red, leading with the speed of a skid on ice toward a trap. It was a funnel was made of hatred and the trap at the end was a most terrible womb.

As the future squeezed him, Ewen knew himself to be himself completely for an instant. He was no longer confused and he was no longer Raven. He dived past the enemy to grab Resurrection, a creature who hadn't volunteered to be bait for this, but Rez would not release her grip on the monster. He concentrated on his identity and on hers, and he felt himself grow bigger and stronger with the force of mind. He pulled her with that force, and for a moment he thought he had succeeded, but he shared her mind enough so as she faltered, confused, he, too, faltered, and they slid all together; Ewen, the enemy, and the wolf-dog went into the birth of hell.

This was what he had intended for the enemy. That much was going right. The rest was horribly wrong.

A voice was calling. A human voice. It said, "Rez. No! Stop it!" and immediately Rez let go of the thing.

He was holding Resurrection in his arms. She flailed her legs, helpless. Some part of him knew he should let go of the dog and try again for the surface, but the rest of him knew he would not let go of her, and that it was already too late. They were at a spinning disk: the event horizon of this black hole, this dreadful birth. He suspended all hope. *A long time till my next chance at enlightenment,* he thought calmly. *A long time until another human birth. Oh well.*

It was worth it. Too bad about the dog, but it was worth it.

"Rez! Come!" said that same voice, and without any more fuss they came back, Raven and Wolf. Ewen and Resurrection. They lay sprawled on the floor of Petersen's log house, and he heard the rain drumming on the windows and the roof.

Ewen's head was pressed painfully against the wall. Susan Sundown was standing next to him, holding a rearing dog by the collar. They were both panting. She stared, blinking, from one to the other.

"I couldn't get to you," she said. "I'm sorry, I only pretended to leave . . . No! What am I saying? I'm not sorry at all. I don't know what you had planned, but I stood on the porch and I heard something go bang inside . . . And we came in and Rez broke away from me, and for a long time I couldn't find either of you in the dark."

She ran her beautiful fingers through her messy hair and through her dog's fur. Ewen thought that he could lie there forever and never get enough of the sight. He could draw it a thousand times. He could kiss that hand forever.

"Then I thought I heard Uncle Sid and I got . . . angry or something. I shouted at Rez. I called her and she came. You both came."

"Sure did," he said, and he found he was beginning to weep.

"She's never done this. Not since she was a puppy. She's not supposed to go off like this! She's a recovery dog."

"She sure is," said Ewen. "She brought me back from hell. You both did. You brought me back from hell." He grinned through his tears and rubbed his aching head.

Rick Petersen came home after a long and worried day to find the three of them in a triangle, heads together, the humans side by side on the couch, bent forward. Rez did not snap nor snarl at him. She had not even announced his presence; by this Petersen knew something important had happened. He looked at the human faces to get an idea. It was a wonderful idea and he feared to trust it. "It's dead?" he asked.

"No," answered Ewen. "It's born."

Petersen's face remained impassive, but looked at their expressions and he was warily more hopeful. "Explain."

Ewen made a circle in the air. "I mean we trapped it in an incarnation. So now it's limited: mortal, and in another and much worse world than ours. And by *we* I mean us here. Rez saved me from the thing and then Susan here saved the both of us from something worse. And old Sid, too, though he isn't here. He had a part in it."

Ewen settled back in the cushions, clearly enjoying himself at last. His forehead was bruised and swollen. "And you had your part in it, too, Detective, since this is your house and I made it into my trap." He gave an explosive sigh and stretched his arms over his head.

Petersen stood there, dark, still, his hands in his coat pockets. "And may I ask you how long the thing will be . . . born? You have to understand, I'm a cop, and Redmond is my beat, and no matter what experiences you've had, or profundities you've discovered, my business is my beat. I have to know."

Ewen looked at the man standing there—standing so tall and alone in his own house—and he remembered the house key in Susan's hand and the fire-start kit in Petersen's pocket. For a moment, just a moment, he was sorry things had not worked out for Petersen. For just a passing moment. He answered the question with, "How long is a life in hell, Rick? How long is a life in hell?"

"Usually it seems pretty long. From what I've seen." Petersen still didn't move. "But as long as the thing's not coming back in my time and in my city," he said, "I'm happy enough. He went into his own bedroom and shut the door behind him.

I'm happy enough. Petersen's standard for happiness must be very low, thought Ewen. Much like Ewen's had been just one week ago.

He leaned back towards Susan and said, "Theo would say I should have enlightened the thing, instead."

"Now you're getting full of yourself," she answered. "Remember, you're only Raven. Nothing important. You said so yourself." Grinning, she prodded him with an elbow.

He went back to his own house that night, caring nothing for police tape, reporters, or curious neighbors. He went about his simple business quietly.

No charges were filed against what the media had dubbed the "Kung Fu Dream Team." Again the gray-haired lawyer shook her head and said, "If this had been Massachusetts . . . "

In the next few days Ewen was solicited to give two interviews, one offer coming from the *National Enquirer* and the other from *Soldier of Fortune*. He did not answer either request. He also found a message on his machine, asking him if he was interested in doing a portrait of a small company's CEO in Seattle. This offer he answered promptly.

Two days later Lynn met Susan. It was obvious (to Ewen) that they liked each other, because within ten minutes of being introduced they were both making jokes at Ewen's expense. Although Ewen and Karen had lived together for years, Lynn had never particularly liked Karen.

Ewen did an oil sketch of Susan and Lynn giggling together under a rare, late January sun.

It was well into February before he even noticed the winter season beginning to break. The little crocus and snowbells he had planted in unexpected places in the garden popped into flower.

His "ninja flowers," he had called them.

Ewen's life was good, but it didn't become the endless euphoria he expected after the affair of the Bear Woman was over. He still carried the burden of the school he didn't want, and the Kellys had bought another puppy—a terrier—that barked without let-up. He didn't feel entitled to complain about it.

He loved Susan madly and was also immensely proud of her and all her idiosyncrasies. He was even proud of Rez, (though she continued to invade his mind without invitation,) but things weren't fairy-tale perfect. Susan lived on the other side of Snoqualmie Pass and he lived in suburban Redmond, and the two didn't mesh seamlessly into each other's lives. She had her occupation, and so did he.

He painted her a lot when she wasn't there.

PART III: Spring Arrives and Ewen Goes Over the Border Again.

Chapter Twenty-two

"OF COURSE you're usually right," said Ewen, resentfully. "You're usually right. You're dead. You have an advantage."

Sidney Sundown nodded and poked the fire. "Yes, I have an advantage, but I have a disadvantage, too. I can only sit here and yammer at you. You have to do things without me." (What he actually said sounded more like, "I c'n olly sit heehr . . . ")

"And I can't be your teacher, Raven. You have to find another old man. One that's alive."

Ewen was sitting beside Sid in front of the brushwood fire in a ring of cedars. Sid was sitting on his haunches and Ewen was in half-lotus. That was only a small difference between them, compared with being alive and being dead.

Ewen was also sitting in the middle of an empty kung fu kwoon. He saw both the green trees and the white walls, but his mind was in the forest. "Should I put out an ad in the newspaper?" he said. "Wanted: Old man to guide a small kung fu school, and especially guide Ewen Young."

Sid glanced over. "Come on, boy. Don't your people have any tribal sense? Don't you know where to look for help?"

Ewen grimaced. "Lots of people say we have too much. Clannish. But whether he's Chinese or not doesn't matter. There aren't that many Chinese in kung fu anymore. They're all into wu-shu. To find any teacher with years under his sash who will leave everything and come up here is the problem. What do we have to offer? Three hots and a cot?"

The old man smiled gently, his face lit by the fire. "Students are what you got to offer. If he's a teacher he'll want students above all."

"Yeah. 'When the student is ready, the teacher will appear.' I've heard that one a lot. All I've got to say is we must be goddamn unready, 'cause no one's appeared."

The ghost raised one eyebrow. "You're in a bad mood, Raven. Nothing gets done that way. I'll take my leave." And Sidney Sundown faded, along with the forest.

Ewen puttered around the school. He cleaned the toilets in the changing rooms. He doodled in the grime on the windows.

A year ago life had been simple, and all things under control. It hadn't been exactly happy, but it had been under control.

It was the end of April, and the bamboo began to break the ground with its new growth, the shoots covering the stubs left by last winter's bizarre souvenir hunt. The young shoots were thicker than ever, and Ewen had slipped a rubber band over one of the old stems as a guide to how much they were growing per day. It was a fearful amount—almost an inch—and he remembered all the old stories about people staked out over growing bamboo, to be slowly impaled. Of course that was timber bamboo, not the ornamental kind. At least he assumed it was not the ornamental kind. His bamboo didn't used to make him queasy.

He did an ink-brush painting of the new growth, and it turned out to be one of the most abstract, dynamic and unpleasant works he had done in years. He put it in a corner, facing the wall.

He called Susan, hoping she would not be under a horse's belly when the phone went off. He worried about that. Luckily, she was at lunch, and though he had trouble hearing what she said through her mouthful of salad, at least she wasn't going to be kicked. He told her about his interview with her great-uncle.

Susan Sundown had no problems accepting that Ewen talked to ghosts, but something in what he said had her choking, gulping iced tea, and breaking out into her trademark raucous laughs. Like a braying mule, he thought, with a touch of impatience. "So what's so funny about it?" he asked her.

"The two of you is what's so funny," she said. "Talking on and on. The pronoun. Accepted without question by you both."

"What pronoun?"

She swallowed again and took a breath. "The pronoun 'he.' Would 'he' be willing to do this or that? What do we have to offer 'him'?"

It took Ewen a few moments to follow her, but then he felt his face go red. He was glad she could not see it. "Oh."

"Maybe you can't find your teacher because you're looking in the wrong . . . the wrong restroom!"

"Oh."

"Betcha can find an old lady with less to lose and more to gain joining up with you guys. And gals."

Ewen didn't want to say "oh" again, so he was silent for a moment. Then he mentioned that Barbie hadn't said a thing about a woman teacher.

"Not every woman is as rude as I am," said Susan, and she snorted.

Ewen saw Susan only a couple evenings a week, plus maybe a whole Sunday. It was a far drive into the Cascades to her clinic and back again, and they both had things that were important to them. He missed her constantly, though: every part of her from her oak-colored, very female body, to her flawless courage and her stupid laugh. If push came to shove, Ewen knew he could move more easily than she could. A painter can paint anywhere, as long as he's willing to commute to do portraits.

He had family here, but he couldn't blame Lynn for that. He hadn't seen his twin sister for years at a time while they were in school, and she had her own life. More troublesome, he had a school to run. That was the problem that involved a lot of pushing coming to shoving.

One more reason to find a teacher.

Ewen picked up the phone because his sister was going to call. "Hi, Lynn," he said. Lynn did not ask how he knew it was she, or why he picked up before the phone had rung. She just began, "It's Jacob again, Ewen."

"I thought you weren't seeing him anymore."

"No. Not for months. But they've got him up in the Snohomish Hospital's detox center and he asked for me. It was against their rules for him to call, but he managed to sneak a message."

There was too much in this to be quickly understood. "Detox? For biting himself? And why did he have to sneak . . . "

Lynn sighed. "I guess he's been looking for comfort in other ways since I saw him. And as for not letting him call . . . well, that's only his story, and perhaps he's not entirely on-center at the moment.

"Whatever the case, I would like to go see him. Find out what's up."

Ewen waited for more and then said, "And you'd like me to come with you."

There was more silence and then Lynn said, "I never could do for him what you could."

Ewen felt pulled in one too many directions that day, but he did not consider refusing. "All right," he said. "Gotta find someone to take a class, but okay."

The detox center was a little brick box with shrubs around it. At first it looked attractive enough but Ewen felt there was something odd—cheap—in the appearance of it. As they went up the walk he realized that the tall shrubs, which looked like they shaded the windows, concealed nothing at all. It had no windows. A row of narrow clerestories, far above head height, looked out over spindly pines, but that was all.

There was some bother about their getting in. Lynn spoke to a nurse behind a desk, who kept repeating the words "hospital policy." Ewen grinned a moment at his sister's frustration, for her own receptionist was equally irritating. Finally Lynn pulled out Jacob's file, and from it took a yellowing slip signed by Jacob's parents more than two years before. As Lynn shoved it across the desk at the nurse, a guard lounged closer to the group.

Ewen lounged closer to the guard.

A telephone call was made to a doctor—no, to a nurse practitioner—and Lynn was given permission to enter—accompanied by the guard. The man attempted to walk between Ewen and his sister and was confused to find Ewen already past him and through the automatically locking door.

Inside, the little box of a building was gray. All gray. Walls, doors, floors—gray. Ewen found it very strange—a hospital painted gray. Baby blue, peach, soft green, even beige he had seen in hospitals, but never gray. It offended his painterly sensibilities. There was a desk with two women behind it, and two corridors extending at right angles to the desk. As Lynn strode up to the desk, Ewen glanced quickly down the corridors, unsettled but not knowing why. The guard was still very close.

There were three patients that he could see. One was a woman, wrapped in a terry-cloth robe and seated in a plastic chair, her head hanging down. The others were both men, wearing hospital johnnies, and they stared at him. Neither had shaven in some days. They walked slowly toward him, legs wide and feet spread, as though they stood on a ship's deck. Or on the set of a B-grade zombie movie. One older man, with a heavily lined face, leaned forward toward Ewen and opened his mouth. Ewen also leaned forward to hear what he would say, but the woman closest to the desk said, "Alan. You remember what you were told. Leave people alone. Mind your own recovery."

The old guy looked like he could use some of that: recovery. Still he looked at Ewen and said very clearly, "Drugs."

"I guess so," answered Ewen. The man's eyes were so glassy Ewen could see himself reflected in them, as in a convex mirror.

"I mean they *give* me drugs," said the old-timer. "Here. Would you believe it?" His breath was very bad.

The near woman rose from her seat, taking off a receptionist's headphone and took the man by the arm. He swayed off with her, down the corridor. "Recovery, Alan," she said. "Take care of your own recovery."

It was the way the kids used to say, "Mind your own business." Or "beeswax." *Mind your own beeswax.* It had never been a very friendly thing to say. The younger man also stood braced as on the deck of a ship, but he wiped his hands up and down the sides of his face and focused on Ewen. As he stared, he took a long, careful breath. Ewen felt his consciousness sliding.

Despite his odd rapport with Rez, Ewen had never been in the mind of another human being, and his contact with this stranger was much like his sporadic communications with Rez. He saw himself standing there—looking shorter and slighter than he thought of himself—and he felt the breath moving in and out of the stranger's nose. He smelled what the stranger smelled, coming from him, and it was beautiful.

I smell like the outside world to him. I smell like someone who can go through that door behind me.

While this went on in silence, there was some discussion between Lynn and the nurse. Ewen overheard the phrases "professional courtesy" and "not appropriate for a new patient to be using the . . ." He heard his sister say, "I'm sure you are very courteous, and very professional. And my seeing Jacob could scarcely be considered inappropriate." Lynn spoke in her blandest voice. His attention picked up, because Lynn's blandest voice was her most dangerous. "Now I'd like to see Jacob," she concluded serenely.

It worked. They went through a gray door into a room with four beds, each shrouded behind gray curtains. The curtains were almost green, he was pleased to see. Ewen glanced left and right. He could see nothing through the fabric, but some other sense told him there were people behind two of the curtains. The floor nurse was looking closely at Ewen, as was the guard who had accompanied them. Ewen said nothing to explain his presence.

The nurse slid between the drapes and Lynn followed, Ewen trailing behind. As he entered the tiny cubicle, he pushed the curtain open. The guard walking behind him closed it again. "Jake," said the nurse to Jacob. "Are you awake?"

There the boy was, flat on his back, his arms spread out and tied to the bedrails. The sight of this raised the hair on Ewen's arms, possibly because a crucifix was hanging above the bed. Jacob had spittle dried on the left side of his face. He opened his heavy green eyes. "Hi, Doc," he said. "And hi, Doc's Brother."

"Hi, Jacob," said Lynn, warmly, and then, less warmly to the nurse, "Why is he tied to the bed?"

She looked at Lynn in surprise and said, "He bites himself. Didn't you know?"

"I know he used to. He quit. A long time ago."

"Not any more," said Jacob, and he giggled. "Now I just booze."

Lynn leaned forward and examined Jacob's arms. Jacob was wearing a hospital johnny and Ewen could see only old scars. Lynn opened her purse and took out a pair of gold scissors, which had handles shaped like the head of a crane. With these she snipped the gauze restraints. Ewen felt the nurse in front of him shift from foot to foot, and the guard also moved. Ewen also tested his balance, but not so that any other would notice. "Wow, that's better, Doc," said Jacob.

"So you've taken up drinking as your hobby since I saw you last, Jacob?"

He grinned at Lynn, his eyes very glassy. "Yeah, I did. A lot of us guys did. Three of us kicked off the wrestling team at once. Ruined the season."

Lynn looked over her shoulder at the floor nurse and the guard. "Please give us some privacy," she said. The nurse looked surprised and the guard looked stubborn. "Professional courtesy?" Lynn added. After a silent moment, the two swept out of the cubicle, belling the curtains out around them.

Ewen breathed easier.

"So why did you call me, Jacob?"

The boy scrambled up against the headboard. He was very clumsy, and it seemed his left hand was asleep. "Get me out of here, Doc. Doctor. Please. This was a mistake."

Lynn stared closely at him. "How did you get here? Courts? The school?"

"Naw. It was my own idea. And Dad's. After I got kicked off the wrestling team. I got him so worried I said I wannata . . . wanted to do something about it. I was thinking I should go to meetings or something. You know . . . AA, or like that? I've heard a lot about that, and so has Dad. He called this place and they said I had to come here before I did anything else, because that was the way things were done these days, and you know what they did? They took away my wallet and keys and everything, and stuffed me full of drugs. Drugs! When I never did drugs in my life; not even pot."

"It's pheno-fuckin'-barbital they got me on. 'Scuse my language. And Librium. I didn't know they still made phenobarbital, did you? It's like that old movie *Valley of the Dolls*. For the first day I thought it was great—I mean, heavy drugs for free and all—but yesterday I damn near wet the bed! Guy next to me does it a couple of times a day. Wet the bed, I mean. It pisses them off. No pun intended."

"How much were you drinking, Jacob?"

He smirked and ran one clumsy hand through his hair. "That's another thing. They keep calling me Jake. Where'd they get that?"

"How much were you drinking?"

Jacob leaned forward, a loose grin on his face. His johnny slipped off his shoulders. "Hell. I was putting away a six-pack most Friday and Saturday nights. By myself! But I'm not going to go into seizures from stopping, like they said I would. I stopped once before, for a couple'a weeks, and didn't have any seizures. Just a hangover. See, I wanted to prove I could stop drinking, and I did. See?"

Lynn sat on the bed and lifted his eyelids, first one and then the other. "What do you want from me right now, Jacob?" Her face was very closed. Not even Ewen could read her expression.

His eyes clarified and focused, suddenly. "I want you to spring me. Get me out of here. I mean, look at the place. Look at me. This is hell. Get me out of here!"

She settled back and sighed. "I don't have the power to do that, Jacob. Not if your father signed you in. He must have thought you needed . . . "

"No! That's the thing! It was my idea. But it's his insurance, ya know? And I'm not allowed to get in touch with him, and even if I did, he's not allowed to come here to see me. He can't find out what's going on. You were the only one I knew who could get in. That's why I called you."

Lynn sat on the bed and looked fixedly at nothing. Her voice was perplexed. "I can tell him how you feel. But even if he signs you out, there could be some trouble with the insurance covering it."

Jacob's brow furrowed. "How much trouble?"

"I'd guess about ten thousand dollar's worth."

The amount slammed Jacob back into the headboard. "Ten thousand . . . " He stared at Lynn for a few seconds and then said, "I'll pay him back if I have to. Doc—I'm really in hell! There are so many things not right here. And after a week of this they want to send me somewhere else for a month. I'd rather be dead!" More calmly he repeated, "I'd rather be dead."

Ewen stepped up beside his sister. He didn't have as much sympathy with Jacob as he might have, because he had always had such contempt for drugs, alcohol included. But he, too, was feeling freaked about the clinic. "Maybe we can at least get you a vacation, Jacob. A short vacation from all this gray."

Lynn turned severely to him. "Don't promise things you can't . . . " She suddenly understood. "Oh."

He sat at the head of the bed, pushing aside the rolling table. Jacob, who understood at about the same time as Lynn, gave him a nervous grin. "You know you're not supposed to sit on someone's bed, Doc's Bro. If they saw you you'd be in trouble." Then he shook his greasy head. "But no, you wouldn't be. Not old Ewen. Not cool as a cucumber Ewen. You could lay them all out—couldn't you?" He licked his lips nervously. "But would it still work with us, that little trance thing? After all this time?"

"Let's find out," said Ewen, and he leaned forward and touched the boy's temples with his fingertips.

Ewen was an old hand at getting to the small grassy place with Jacob. He'd done it maybe eight times in the last few years, and he approached the matter with some confidence. So he was surprised to find himself battered by storms when he linked with the boy. He felt Jacob in front of him, and he called up in memory the grassy spot by the wall and the trickle of water, but for thirty seconds there was nothing. There was only Ewen's open mind, invaded with images of the gray hallways and the confinement of the plastic curtains. He was about to agree with Jacob; no, this wasn't going to work.

Then he felt them both falling into his own vision.

He focused his concentration on the simplicity of the picture: grass, limestone, water. It flickered and was gone again, and he grabbed onto it instinctively by switching from the quiet meditation he usually used into the explosive concentration he had developed in martial arts. Perhaps he shouted. Perhaps it was only force in his mind and he made no sound at all.

There was the picture he called forth behind his eyes and he put Jacob into it. Immediately the scene skewed like a piece of film gone off its reel.

He was flummoxed for a moment, and then—*It's drugs* he realized. *I have no experience with minds on drugs. What do I do?* He sat still and let the scene be, drugs or no, and slowly the spinning and the confusion resolved itself into his safe-place again, with Jacob sprawled over the grass, one arm on the limestone wall. He was still wearing his hospital johnny. Ewen made an adjustment and put Jacob into wrestling shorts and top.

Better? He said in his mind and Jacob looked up. Ewen wasn't there on the grass, of course. Not in person. "It's better as all hell!" Jacob giggled, speaking to the sky as though to God, and he got to his feet. He put his hands behind his neck and though the entire experience was immaterial he gave a left and a right crack to his back. He was grinning.

You're safe, said Ewen, and Jacob raised his arms and crowed. "More than *safe*, Doc's Bro. I'm free. Totally free!" He started trotting toward the line of cypress, behind which stretched nothing but a flat, modern cemetery in Santa Barbara.

Not totally, said Ewen, as clearly as he could. *This is temporary. Freedom you can win yourself.*

"*You* can win it, you mean," said Jacob. "You're magical Ewen Young and I'm just a high school dweeb that made a really big mistake. Right now, I'll take this for freedom." And he was gone, through the trees and out into a fantasy world that existed only in Ewen's head.

Ewen felt like a complete fool.

"He's sleeping," said Lynn quietly, unaware of the strange quality of the event that had just happened.

"Please get off the bed," said the nurse behind her, irritably. "It really interferes with a patient's recovery."

Ewen stood, slightly muddled. How much time had passed? "It interferes with . . . what?"

"They want us to leave now, is what she's saying," Lynn whispered into his ear.

On his way out, Ewen, still feeling off balance, turned to the nurse and asked, "Why gray?"

She looked at him sharply and put her hand to her hair, which had the roots of age showing. "I mean the walls, the floor, the doors—why gray?"

Her sparrow features tightened. "I'm sorry we offend your ideas of . . . of feng shui!" She pronounced it wrong.

"It offends my sense of color," he said calmly, and followed his sister out the door. Behind him he heard the guard mutter, "Fuckin' interior decorator."

"That was uncomfortable, I know," said Lynn, once behind the wheel of her car.

"You don't know the half of it," answered Ewen, massaging the back of his neck.

Lynn sighed. "I'm aware the place is dingy, and of the fact that there are no windows . . . " She paused a moment and added, "And I'm not sure about the kinds and amounts of medications they use.

Phenobarbital is very old stuff. I guess it's cheap. Same with Librium. But they must have a tight budget; we all do. And some of those people come in there with severe problems. In danger of death. It's a necessary service."

"That's not what I mean," said Ewen. "Except that I think it does have something to do with the drugs. What I mean is that Jacob sprang up and ran away."

"Away? Away from where? We left him just lying there."

"He ran away from the place I took him, and that was the same place as always."

"Well, well . . . " Lynn knew about Ewen's private interior realm. She knew the grassy place as a real one, from when they were kids together in Santa Barbara. She accepted his use of it on trust. Twin-trust, is how she thought of it. Now she sputtered, "Then he went where this time? *Into where?*"

He shrugged. "Into Santa Barbara? I don't know. I just wish I'd had more time to pull him out. Always before, he just went to sleep. Always before, there was time."

"He did go to sleep," she ventured.

"Not in that world he didn't."

Lynn got onto the freeway in silence. After a few minutes of driving she asked Ewen, "So what do we do?"

He shrugged again and folded his arms in front of him, playing restlessly with the seat-belt cord. "We just make sure he wakes up, I guess." He ruminated a minute, and then added, "I think what happened was that he had gotten used to being deep under, because of the drugs. And the booze. I think that my little sleep-nudge didn't mean anything to him today. Drug tolerance."

"I'm sure he'll be okay," said Lynn, sounding anything but sure. This disturbed Ewen all the more, for Lynn was the psychiatrist, and he relied on her knowledge. He was only "Doc's Brother."

"Call the hospital later, would you?" he asked. She nodded and said, "And maybe you can visit your . . . place . . . and make sure he's not still there?"

"You bet I will," he said, and having nothing else constructive to offer, he put the question of Jacob aside and thought about the school.

Chapter Twenty-three

EWEN BROUGHT the matter of Rose Wing up to the senior students' council that evening. There was a largish silence.

"I think I remember hearing her name," said Ryan, finally. "She's in Santa Barbara, right?"

Ewen nodded. "She was a senior student of Al Lo when Uncle Jimmy was there. She was about at his level. In fact, after he got divorced . . . " Ewen cleared his throat and decided not to go there. "Anyway, she's someone we haven't thought of before. I don't think she has any close family back in Santa Barbara. I know she's still teaching, but I don't think she ever got her own school."

"Did she ever want her own school, I wonder," murmured Perry, shifting his long legs. "It seems nobody does, these days."

Ryan sat upright. "I never thought of a lady," he said. "Never occurred to me." He caught Barbie Cowell glaring at him. "Well, you didn't, either. Or never spoke up about it."

Barbie rolled her head around, thoughtfully, holding her elbows in her opposite hands. "It's because of the boys, I didn't."

"'Scuse me?" said Ewen. "What about the boys? What boys?"

"The little boys. The ones who come in because they're making trouble at home. Or because they don't have a male role model—whatever. Do you think you'll be able to fire *them* up with an old woman teaching?"

Ewen had seen Rose Wing in action and the others hadn't. He wondered how to communicate the flavor of her work, which was impressive. Instead he said to Barbie, "You teach them sometimes."

She smiled bitterly. "I avoid it when I can. And when I have to teach the boys I have to be a lot rougher with them than a guy has to be. Constant push, push, push, just to maintain discipline."

Perry leaned over and looked Barbie in the face quite seriously.

"Sounds like they *need* that push, push, push if they're ever going to respect a woman. It might not be fun for you, but if they don't learn now . . . "

Ewen was feeling very uncomfortable. He should have been aware of this problem because he was, however unwillingly, the head of the school. "Maybe we should arrange more sessions where you clobber some large guy repeatedly. Big falls. Make an impression on them. I'll help."

Elliot Anson, one of the older brown belts, muttered, "I thought you said a large guy." Ewen presumed he was not supposed to have heard that.

Ryan was sitting on the edge of his chair in taut concentration. "Better yet would be for the kids to see all the teachers taking orders from an *old* woman. I hope she is an old woman?"

Ewen smiled at that. "Old enough, at any rate. As old as Uncle Jimmy. And she has really clean technique. In fact, her background is a lot like Uncle Jimmy's. I wish you could see her! And there wouldn't be that much compromise between her style and ours, which would be great."

"And she's interested?" asked Barbie, one eyebrow cocked.

"I have no idea," said Ewen, and the whole crew sank back in their chairs, sighing. "But I'll ask her."

"Call tonight," suggested Elliot. "We can't take much more of your totalitarian rule."

"I can't call," Ewen answered. "That would be very rude. I'll have to go down to Santa Barbara and see her."

The idea of going down to Santa Barbara was exciting. Ewen hadn't been there in a long time, and Susan never had. He could show her a piece of his past. He began to look forward to it.

But Susan could not leave for the weekend. She had taken emergency duty for a friend and that was not something she could cancel for a trip to California. Ewen was disappointed. She'd certainly have liked it. Anyone would like Santa Barbara, and the two might have even been able to go snorkeling. He would enjoy showing her the colors beneath the California waters: the pink and orange and lavender of the anemones and the gold light through the kelp forest. He had an image of the dog, Resurrection, wearing a mask and snorkel, her big paws cutting the water like fins. He drew a cartoon of it, and perhaps that could work up to an ink painting if the image stuck in his head.

He called Rose Wing that evening and asked if he could fly down for a conversation. Wing seemed bemused by the idea he wanted to talk with her and was flying down for no other purpose, but she told him he was welcome and asked no questions. He wondered if Rose—he thought of her as "Old Rose" in private—had any inkling of his motive. She must still think of him as a kid in his mid-twenties.

Had she any idea of the oddities that had happened in his life this past year? She probably knew about his being shot, and about . . . about Uncle Jimmy. There was a certain amount of gossip endemic to the West Coast kung fu world. As for bloody confrontation with the "Canadian terrorists," well, that had been widely and inaccurately covered in all media. About the rest, he decided he was being grandiose. Who cared that Ewen Young had changed inside, except Ewen Young?

On the airplane early Saturday morning, Ewen looked out the window and contrasted this flight with the one he had taken with Susan last winter. This plane was much higher up. There was less snow. The flight was quick, comfortable, and quite sterile compared with puddle jumping with a wolf-dog harnessed in the cargo hold and a gorgeous cowgirl Indian pilot. Ewen heard her laughter in his mind as it had sounded when they skidded down a runway in Oregon, avoiding the police. A person needed earplugs when Susan laughed. He wished he had Susan beside him now, earplugs or no. "Most weekends" was not enough time to be with her. She swooped down on him, or he swooped down on her (airplanes, again) but they were locked into their separate lives.

If I could find a teacher to take the school, I wouldn't need to live in Redmond. A painter can work anywhere.

It was still early in the day when they landed. Perfect weather for the spring season. Wind off the ocean. Ewen felt a moment of nostalgia so strong he leaned against the wall of the airport corridor. Here he had been thinking of leaving Redmond for the mountains and now he felt entirely like staying in Santa Barbara. Snorkeling. Long walks on the beach. Ewen put his unruly emotions away and hailed a cab.

———

Rose Wing looked just as he remembered her from five years ago: slight, strong and with only a few gray strands in her shining black hair. He had painted her back then and he hoped to get in at least one good drawing during his visit.

He had never been in her little house, which was beautiful in scale but filled with a strange combination of stores and ornament. The walls were hung with textiles: not all Chinese but all lovely. There were heaps of cloth piled up on chairs and in corners as well—blankets mostly—and these were of very different quality: warm but cheap and the most that could be said about the colors was they would not be likely to show dirt.

In the center of her parlor stood what Ewen first saw as the guts of a piano, but quickly turned in his eyes into a large loom, warped with a silken and very complex weave. This was of natural color but wide ranging in the shades created by the various textures.

She grinned as she saw his glance darting from the assorted elegance to the gray piles. "One tapestry buys a lot of simple warmth," she said, and let her shuttle down on the bench. Then she adorned herself with her trademark half-smile until he was forced to speak. He told her the whole of his intentions.

She had no objections to sitting for a sketch once again, but serious reservations about adopting an orphan school. "Right now, I'm rather looking to avoid new responsibilities than to seek them out," she said, smiling ruefully.

Ewen was not a salesman by nature, but he did his best. "You're not seeking them out, Master Wing. We're seeking you out. And we're looking for guidance, not a nine-to-five slog. We really need a head teacher."

She continued to smile, saying, "And you ran out of male prospects—is that it?"

Ewen hoped he was not blushing, for he was very embarrassed at her quick assessment of the situation. "At first we were looking for a man, but that was only . . . only stupidity on our part. On my part, really. A friend called me on it, and I saw what I had been doing. Or not doing. The truth is that you are the most qualified teacher around, and also the closest to my uncle's style. A lot of the senior students are afraid of finding someone who will try to spin them in a completely different direction. Making them feel their years of work have been compromised. After you're thirty that means more. Worse, they're afraid the school will close completely and they will have to start over again as white belts in Aikido or something."

Rose's smile became gentler. "And would that be a bad thing? Starting over as a white belt? What would you lose—prestige? Surely you would not lose your skills or your spirit."

He bowed his head. "True. But after Uncle Jimmy's death they— we—have found ourselves feeling more united than ever. Like a family. But a family needs a leader." Ewen raised his eyes to her. "Or at least a school does. I think you'd like us," he said. "Most of us have been there regularly for years. And we've got some great little kids coming up."

Rose Wing sat back down on her bench, surrounded by tiny tools and shining silks. She rocked back ever so slightly as though she were still weaving, her eyes fixed on Ewen. "I remember one of those great little kids and I've heard the teacher they want is you, Ewen. That seems the most likely answer to your problem. You pick up for your uncle."

"*But I have no teacher! I need a teacher myself!*" Ewen found he was almost shouting. Rose continued to rock. The gentle light of a Santa Barbara spring shone sideways over her.

"Well, you certainly don't need daily monitoring, Ewen. You haven't needed that for years, and you weren't getting it from James, anyway. If you need advice, or an eye to watch your own progress, you can fly down here and I'll be glad to give you the benefit of my 'advanced' years. Though I don't have all your skills. I haven't yet returned from the dead. And the plain truth is I have no magic powers. What the great delog needs from me, I don't quite know."

Ewen was struck speechless for half a minute. "Magic . . . what do you mean, Rose? What have people been telling you about me?"

She sighed and rocked. "Well, if I believed half of what I've heard I would have done nine prostrations as you entered my door." As Ewen continued to stare she added "But I only believe a little of what I hear. Not half. Still, Ewen, it sounds like this is your school. That it's meant to be."

He blurted out, "I don't want it!"

"The magic power or the school? No matter. I don't want either one myself."

He stared at her with such defeat and disappointment, it made her start to laugh.

"But I'll tell you what I'll do. If you people can pay my fare, I'll fly up there every few months and work with you. I'll even allow you to make a big deal about me, if that's what the beginners want. I'll sit there on a cushion like a Buddha and observe your senior belt tests—students love that. But I'll show up only every few months. I couldn't stand your weather more often than that. Now why do you still look dissatisfied?"

Ewen was reduced to honesty. "I'm in love with a doctor. A horse doctor, to be exact. And she can't move down from the foothills and I can't move up into them. Because of the school."

Rose slapped her hand on her thigh and rocked harder. "Oho! Now I get it. True love. But that will work out."

"It will?"

"Certainly," said Rose Wing, and Ewen sat at her feet and believed her.

Chapter Twenty-four

EWEN HAD RESERVED a hotel room, on the chance that none of the friends left from his years in Santa Barbara were home, or were not inclined to let him bunk with them. But Rose Wing assumed he would stay in her guest room—it was only necessary to push *that* room's loom to one side—and he was glad to let things go that way. Once settled in, he called his sister at her office; Lynn turned her cell phone off during work hours. As always he had to navigate the minefield of her receptionist, who could not or would not learn that Ewen Young was a privileged person. At last he got through to Lynn, who had only a moment between appointments.

"Did you call the detox unit?" he asked her. "Did Jacob come out of it?" Through all his entertainment in the flight and anxiety concerning Master Wing he had not lost his worry over the boy.

She answered, "I called them. They said he was fine." She answered promptly but sounded less than certain.

"But did they say he woke up?"

Lynn repeated, "They said he was doing fine. I couldn't make an interrogation out of it."

This was not the answer Ewen wanted, but he couldn't make an interrogation out of it either. Not with his sister. Ewen asked her to call if she heard anything more about Jacob.

"Are you really that worried, Ewen?" she asked.

"Not . . . really. It's just that no one ever ran away from me before." Lynn got a laugh out of that. "I mean, when I was trying to help them."

She told Ewen to give her best to Rose.

Later that afternoon, Ewen took a stroll down the palm-edged boulevard and watched the perfect sea break against the sand. He walked on until he came to the house where he had grown up, where no Youngs lived now. He thought it looked a bit shabby, and wondered if that was how it had always looked. The garden was certainly less appealing than it had been, having been turned from the complex, slightly cluttered home of two children (complete with a tiny tree house that only lacked a tree beneath it) into a perfect, unadorned green rectangle of Bermuda grass. The house had been painted beige.

Beige. Gray. Why did people want to live that way?

He went past his old middle school, which looked much the same. He walked and thought, not paying much attention to his steps, and found his feet had taken him (like an old horse circling its accustomed route) to the cemetery.

There it was: a place he had not seen for many years, but which remained pictured in his mind always. The trees had grown taller, and that was good, but the flat rectangular stones in their rows looked as impersonal as ever. He walked diagonally into the cemetery, stepping right at the bottoms of the rows, so that he would not actually be walking on anybody. He used to walk the cemetery this way, years before. Being polite to the dead. Ewen was still trying to be polite to the dead, especially now that they had started to talk back.

He passed through the screen of cypress, which had become much thicker and more resistant to passage. Here was the small space of grass, looking weedier than he remembered, and there was the little limestone wall and the trickle of water running over concrete behind it. Over the years the concrete had become discolored with the minerals in the water, and the trickle was very slight indeed. Ewen folded himself down beside the wall. He listened for the water, and heard the cars on the road three hundred yards away.

He thought how once a man had stepped into the tangle of cypress trees and found not a cemetery, but an endless forest. He saw the area in the grass where he had left Jacob (at least in his mind) so many times before. The grass bore no imprint. But then it was grass, and would not have shown wear anyway. Ewen sat very still, and he began to hear the little sound of the water.

Without any disturbance of mind or body he slid from the grass underneath him to the same grass in his mind, and the trickle was now louder, sparkling, and merry. A gentle wind shifted silver stripes in the green grass. For the first time in over a week he was not homesick: not for Redmond, for Santa Barbara, or even for Susan. He took a grateful breath, unfolded himself, and glanced around for Jacob.

There was no boy to be seen, but there was a trail: an obvious, almost comic trail of wet sneaker prints. They slid through the tall grass and appeared again on the other side of the trees. They were long-strided, irregular—dancey. They were the prints of a young man having fun. Jacob had here been jumping from tombstone to tombstone. There was a waffle pattern on a slick piece of red granite, and then a toe-mark with a big circle outlining the ball of the foot on top of the words "Beloved Father." Black granite stone. Ewen followed, grinning slightly. It occurred to him that no one buried anyone under limestone anymore. It was soft, as stone goes, and these simple granite blocks would last longer than most cities.

What Ewen knew about tracking he had learned from Susan Sundown, and was connected to teaching him to handle—assist— Rez. So far this spring he had gone on two searches and found the bones of one long-lost hiker. Following Jacob's tracks in this world was not challenging. Why should it be, when Ewen had created the world?

He passed the empty field to where the old middle school stood, looking quite a bit newer and more polished than it had when he had passed it for real just an hour before. The entire street looked newer, except for one old decrepit grocery which. as he now remembered, had been a car wash earlier this afternoon. Jacob's prints were still dewy, though the grass behind them was overgrown. They were not, however, still dancey. It seemed Jacob had gone into a more focused, seeking behavior, darting from one building to another, across silent crosswalks and down the middle of a street without traffic. Even a beginner didn't need Rez for this one.

Ewen found Jacob lying on somebody's lawn, his hands behind his head. He was still wearing the wrestling togs Ewen had thought to clothe him in, and his scars showed along his gangly arms. He watched Ewen approach without expression.

Ewen dumped himself down on the grass beside the kid. He was not tired, but he felt he ought to be, after the trip south and the tracking. He waited for Jacob to speak.

"It's just another trap," said Jacob, staring at the sky. "There's no one—nothing here."

Ewen took a slow breath. "I *told* you it was temporary. Just a place to rest in for a while. I remembered it from a long time ago, and I made a picture in my mind that I transferred to you. I'm not God. I'm not a world maker. In fact . . . " and he glanced around at the middle-class residential street in Santa Barbara, circa 1982, "I'm surprised I remember this much." He got his feet under him.

"C'mon. It's time for you to go back." He stood up and held out his hand to Jacob.

"Back there! No. I won't go back there. You've seen it; that place is nothing but a piece of hell!"

Ewen stood still and thought about the place. He didn't entirely disagree, but Jacob had done nothing to make him care overmuch. "It's for less than a week, Jacob. Just a few more days. I mean, you can just sit there and read for a few days, right? Or watch TV?"

Now Jacob, too, thrust himself off the ground, and his pale thin face was suffused with blood. Ewen noticed the small scars and blotches of teenage acne asserting themselves over the boy's skin and, without thinking about it, erased them, as he would do for a client whose portrait he was painting. They returned again, stronger, as though Jacob himself was insisting on his adolescent substance. Ewen gave up and let his subject be.

"I can't fucking watch TV when the door to the TV room is locked. My wallet is gone and the doors are locked and since I noticed that—well, nothing is bearable anymore. There's nothing I can do but get out. I'll stay here in this twilight-zone place if I have to. For a few days, it's better than the hole!"

Ewen shook his head. "No. No, Jacob. While you're here you're not awake there. And if you don't wake up they'll never let you go. You'll find yourself in a worse place, eventually. In a psychiatric back ward, or whatever they call it now."

The kid slapped one hand into the other. "They're *going* to put me in a worse place already. I'm supposed to go from here . . . uh, I mean there, the detox center . . . to a rehab place for a whole month. And that will be locked, too!"

Ewen sighed, rubbed his neck, and shifted from foot to foot. "Well, it'll be better than the hole—I mean, the hospital. I'll bet it will. I'll bet you'll get to go outside, do things, talk to interesting people . . . " He thought about this and added, "Very interesting people, probably. Very interesting stories—like your own. I did some drawing classes in a rehab center, once. It was kinda neat."

Better than being in a hospice, kid. You don't leave a hospice with a thirty-day coin.

"No!" screamed Jacob. "I just want to go home. Home! All I have to do is not drink, right? Swear to God I won't drink. I'll go to school. I'll do fucking trigonometry. Just let me go home!"

Just let me go home, thought Ewen, and for a moment his sympathy was complete. "Listen, Jacob. I'll call your father. I'll tell him how much you want to go home. He can probably get you out; you're underage."

"He won't." Jacob gritted his teeth alarmingly. "Doc said if I leave before they say so he'll get socked ten grand by the hospital and the insurance won't cover it. But if I stay the week and then thirty days they will cover the whole thirty grand of the treatment. We can't afford ten grand . . . I'd really rather be dead," said Jacob, with cold sincerity.

Ewen didn't have ten grand to spare either. Not easily. But he had some years under his belt. "I'll bet the money's not that certain, Jacob. I mean, the insurance can't particularly *want* to pay out the extra thirty grand. Especially if you can show you don't need the treatment. We'll get your father on your side. Maybe a specialist lawyer. Things like this are done all the time. Compromises."

"Yeah," said Jacob, looking at Ewen with defeated resentment. His immaterial nose was running. "By you, they are. The great, the famous, the unkillable Ewen Young. I'm just a piece of shit kid, drinking beer in empty basements."

Sympathy dissolved. "Goddam, that's enough, Jacob! I've done my best and now I'm leaving. You can come with me or stay here and be a vegetable in the real world. I can't change you." He held out his hand for the second time and Jacob took it.

Ewen was stung by the boy's attitude. He was unused to being the focus of someone else's resentment. He was also worried about Jacob, regardless of his personality, because he had gotten Jacob into this particular situation. He also hated the gray into which he was sending the kid.

He had never worked his little world from two different places before: the real and the mental. And Jacob was a wrestler.

Ewen came back with Jacob, and then they separated. But before they separated, Ewen felt himself flipped over. He recognized the sensation of being flipped, just like that in martial arts, and then everything got very strange.

Chapter Twenty-four

HE WAS TIED to the bed. They had threatened to tie him to the bed, because they thought he was pulling his IV out, but he hadn't been pulling it out, and besides, they never did tie him to the bed. That was the better part of a year ago. Ewen tried to clear his head.

It was Jacob who had been tied to the bed. Ewen's eyelids were stuck together with sleep. He opened them with effort, first the right, then the left, and they came unglued with a Velcro sort of sound. He looked over and saw Jacob's gangling, teenage hand tied to the bed. Turning his head to the other side he saw the other one. Ewen was terrified beyond screaming.

He was all alone in a greenish light; the plastic curtains were drawn. His arms were not pulled tight out to his sides because the bed was narrow, but he thought that even if they had been, it would not have hurt. Nothing seemed to hurt. He could feel the sheet bunched under his back, but the feeling was distant and unimportant. In fact, Ewen's terror became distant and unimportant. He lay there in Jacob's imprisoned body and began to yawn.

Then he grunted. He chuckled, heavily. The kid had gotten him—gotten him really good. And right after his lecture to Jacob on just surviving the days. "Easy for you . . . " Jacob had said. Now it didn't seem anything was going to be easy.

He listened. There were soft footsteps in the hallway. Somewhere in the room someone turned the page of a magazine. A big, glossy magazine, by the sound of it. Ewen considered his situation.

He was the wrong person in this bed. That was problem number one. He was tied up. That was number two. And now that he polled the provinces of this body, he needed very strongly to piss. That was "three." Three-and-a-half, maybe.

He could call for someone to let him loose. Surely they would understand the immediate need. But Ewen was reluctant to call attention to himself right now. He didn't know how best to behave. Honesty would not work. It was not as though he could shout out that he was not "Jacob the Beer-Abuser," but "Ewen the Cleanly Living." He would only get put in a different sort of locked ward.

He looked at "his" right wrist. The hand was bony and the wrist fairly narrow, but whoever wound the gauze had not been punitive about it. He turned his arm over (with more difficulty than expected, as Jacob was nowhere near as flexible as Ewen) and gained a little slack. He pressed in the big thumb and turned the arm back. More slack. It took him only a few minutes of this finger-dance to get his hand out of the bonds. The left hand was a matter of pulling loose a bow. Ewen, wearing Jacob around him, darted into the bathroom and took a pee.

Jacob's underwear was foul. So was his body. Ewen scrabbled in the bedside locker and found a clean set of sweats and jockeys. Whatever else he did, he could not begin in this state. He began to tiptoe to the door, holding his clothes in his arms, when a bored voice behind one of the other curtains said, "Slippers. They'll ding you for bare feet."

He glanced down at his impossibly pale, impossibly large feet and scuttled back to the bed. Nothing there. The locker. There was a pair of paper slippers into which he burrowed his feet. The slippers were very large. Ewen flapped back out to the door and confronted the hallway.

To the left and down a perpendicular hall was the desk, which he remembered. To the right was a tall set of shelves bearing white towels. Ewen grabbed one. He thought a moment and grabbed another, and a washcloth for good measure. He walked purposefully down the almost empty hall, passing a few other people without connection of word or eye. He hoped there was a shower room along this hall, or he would be forced to walk purposefully back again and turn down another.

There was a shower, and he turned into it and locked the door behind him. It was a simple sort of affair, but he had showered in worse. He turned the dial to the mid range and waited for the water to warm. When he had waited a good long time without much result, he stepped into the flow and turned the dial all the way to "hot."

It was a quick and freezing shower. Ewen scrubbed every part of Jacob's body, hating both it and the shower. When he was done, he bounced out, dried off and donned Jacob's sweats. As he dumped the wet towels into a hamper he noticed a small, handwritten sign over the bin:

Note: Hot Means Cold and Cold Means Hot

Ewen stared at this for a long minute, his mind spinning without traction. He began to giggle, then laughed outright, but the laugh soon turned into a yawn. He leaned against the door.

Back in the room he made an inventory of his possessions. Besides the sweats he had two other clean briefs and a burgundy terry-cloth robe. There was also a pair of beat-up gray sneakers on the floor of the locker. A stick of deodorant. A toothbrush. No toothpaste.

No wallet, no car keys (did Jacob even drive?), no picklocks or pocket change. No pockets, in fact. As he sat on the bed and thought about his inventory, he considered it unfortunate he was not a super-spy. A super-spy could use these things and escape like the wind. Maybe even a person who had read a lot of books about spies could. Ewen had not read many spy novels.

He sat on the bed and began to zone out again, and thought that it was not too uncomfortable to be caught in the body of a teenager in a secure place, stuffed full of Librium and phenobarbital. Then he suddenly remembered that Jacob was caught in the body of thirty-three-year-old Ewen Young in a cemetery in the outskirts of Santa Barbara, California, where he didn't know a soul, and he became truly frightened.

How much money had been in his wallet? Only one hundred dollars or so. There would be no more to draw on, because Ewen didn't carry a credit card, but only a debit card, and the PIN was written nowhere. Ewen's return flight was e-ticketed. Would Jacob know how to use the print-out to get himself back to Seattle, Washington?

Probably he would. Kids these days knew more about computers than the average Microsoft programmer. But would he want to go back to Bellevue? Jacob was on the run; would he return to the place where his stolen "vehicle" was registered? And if he did return to Ewen's home, what kind of unimaginable trouble would he get Ewen into?

As he thought he stared at the wall, and began to droop, and to yawn like a saber-tooth tiger. Suddenly the green curtain was thrust back with a squeal and a cute little nurse came in, wheeling a pillar of a machine with knobs, screens, and a blood-pressure cuff. She smiled and greeted him as "Sleeping Beauty," complimented him on his hygiene, stuffed the cuff around his left arm and a tethered thermometer into his open mouth.

The cuff didn't like its readings; it repeated its task three times. The thermometer just beeped. "All done," sang the little nurse, and then her place was taken by a larger version, carrying only a small cup. This one also sang, and "Time for your pills" was the burden of her song.

"I don't think I need them right now," said Ewen, and was surprised to hear Jacob's voice responding, but with Ewen's own, more mature inflection. The nurse looked disappointed in him but unsurprised. "Do I have to talk about seizures again, Jake?"

Ewen almost opened his mouth to object to the name. Not to say, "I'm not Jake; I'm Ewen," but to say, "He's not Jake; he's Jacob." Instead he said nothing. He took the pills and then a drink of water from the bedside carafe. He put the pills into his cheek beside his gums and made a big thing of swallowing. For a moment he thought she might force his mouth open to see, or stroke his throat, like that of a cat being dosed, but she just smiled and left, squealing the curtains closed. "Remember, the AA people come for an hour tonight at seven-thirty, if you feel up to it. No pressure: just if you feel up to it."

"Dung hungh," replied Ewen, almost swallowing a Librium. After her steps receded into the hall he dashed into the bathroom and flushed both pills. A capsule had started to melt in his mouth, so he rinsed out under the sink. His gum was stained red from the capsule.

Dinner came, and it was an immense helping of chicken, rice, and Brussels sprouts. The sprouts were gray. Ewen was staring at them in disbelief when a face appeared around the edge of the curtain. It was that of a young man—though older than Jacob—with lean cheeks and an attempt at a beard. "Oh, sorry, man. The Brussels sprouts are what they give you when you're too out of it to fill out your menu."

"I like Brussels sprouts," said Ewen uncertainly, and he picked up one grey thing on the end of his fork. It slid off again.

"Okay, but I thought we're supposed to be done with self-destructive behavior," said the other, and he disappeared again.

The Brussels sprout tasted like it had been marinated in old, soapy dishwater. Marinated for days upon days. Ewen spat it out again. The chicken tasted like nothing on earth. The rice, however, tasted only of aluminum, and rice often tasted that way when badly cooked. Ewen distrusted all rice cooked by white people. It was probably not poisonous, however, so he ate it. He stared at the food and wondered the old wonder—is what food tastes like to me the same as what it tastes like to someone else? It usually was voiced more like *Is what I call blue the same color to me as what you call blue is to you?* Except he couldn't answer that question in a place where most everything was gray. Including the Brussels sprouts.

He called out "Hello? Is it just me, or is the food really . . . "

"That bad? Yes, it is. I dunno why. But I've got some M&Ms I've been hoarding, if you're really desperate . . . "

With M&Ms Ewen could at least get an idea whether colors were the same in this new body, but before he could answer the call came for AA group. Perhaps they would be taken somewhere and there would be opportunity to slip away and . . . and do something. He wasn't sure what. Ewen went.

Where they were taken was down the hall again, to a room with imitation windows painted on the walls. They were cute, cottage-y windows with gardens behind them. Badly done. He sat in an easy chair and watched a half-dozen other people scuffle in, mostly in hospital johnnies. None of them spoke to each other.

Behind the padded arm of Ewen's chair was some graffiti done in fiber-tip pen. It was quite naughty and involved nurses and a medieval dungeon. It was also quite talented. Ewen shoved his chair closer to the wall, lest it be discovered and erased.

Far down the hall came the snap of a door, followed by a tiny gust of wind. It made Ewen look up. His nose twitched. There were heavy footsteps and two men strode into the little room. They were somewhat battered-looking and wore motorcycle leathers. The smell of leather and oil filled the room and Ewen realized that he was staring at the two men, fascinated. *It is the smell of the outside,* he thought. *They smell of liberty.*

They spoke of AA and NA for about a half hour, telling their own stories and how the Twelve Steps had changed them. Though it was very interesting and Ewen tried to listen, he spent most of the time memorizing the looks of the two strangers. One was thin to the point of gauntness and the other wore the traditional Harley potbelly with pride. The lean one had a beard through which a scar ran diagonally and a barbed wire tattoo around one wrist. The heavy one was younger, and the knuckles of his right hand had at some time been broken and had healed imperfectly. Ewen reached in the pocket he didn't have for the tiny sketchbook, which was not even in this state of the Union, and in the end he simply memorized their faces, forms, and attitudes.

By now they were taking questions, and a couple of patients had them, mostly to the tune of how AA could get them out of detox, or out of jail. Ewen was taken unawares when the discussion devolved upon him. He started. "What? Oh. I don't have anything to add. You all said it very well."

His roommate—he of the beard attempt—smiled slowly and said, "We usually at least say our name."

Before he could guard his tongue Ewen said, "If I thought there was a chance in hell you'd believe me, I would."

Laughter. "I've heard almost everything," said the lean man. "And it's not my job to judge anyone else's story."

Ewen almost believed him. He almost said something real, but in the end he said only, "I'll just listen, tonight."

At the end of the hour, a nurse appeared in the door and the two men rose to go. As they passed by the nurse, the lean one's pale eyes shifted around and beyond her, and Ewen knew at once the stare of an old con around a guard. It was striking to see, and all the more so since the man obviously did not know he was doing it. The nurse, too, cooperated in the vignette without knowing. Ewen didn't need to memorize this, for it was snapshot into his brain.

The boots went down the hall, the door opened upon darkness, the two men stepped out, the brief free air came in, was cut off again, and it was all over. Ewen felt his heart racing.

He sat down on one of the row of plastic chairs just opposite the long desk, and he concentrated. If he could contact Lynn, he was sure he could convince her of his identity. Especially if she didn't see Jacob's body. On the phone he could do it.

Lynn probably knew something was wrong with him already. There must be a thousand things he could say to his sister that Jacob could not know: birthdays, favorite flavors. Childhood embarrassments. That was it—the time she had gotten stuck in the tree house with her dress over her . . .

"Jake? Jake? Are you listening?"

Ewen lifted Jacob's head in confusion. The evening nurse was looking at him sternly. "You know you can't sit there overhearing our conversation. It's a violation of other patients' privacy."

Ewen stood up and moved to the far end of the room, where jigsaw puzzles were littered over a plastic table. He saw parts of a tugboat scattered amidst an African savanna. He could still hear the nurse and her assistant conversing. They were discussing how best to obtain a coffeemaker to brew a better cup of coffee for the staff in the detox unit. The nurse called out "Jake? Jake?" again and Ewen fiddled with the cardboard pieces and did not look up.

"He can't hear us," said the nurse and went on talking about good coffee.

He needed coins. Lots of coins. He didn't have any. This problem seemed enormous to Ewen, and it was stupid that it should be enormous. Getting change for a phone call was a simple thing for an adult man. It shouldn't make one sweat. Ewen *was* sweating. He got up and walked into his room.

The other man was reading *Rolling Stone*. He had pulled back his drapes, and (so far) had gotten away with it. Ewen asked him if he happened to have any change. The fellow dropped his paper into his lap. "You know I don't. I didn't have any this morning, so how would I have any now?"

"Sorry," said Ewen. "I just forgot."

The young man sat up straighter in bed and looked curiously at Ewen. "Jacob? Since when did you start apologizing for things? And why didn't you say 'fuck'? You always say 'fuck.' This rehabilitation shit must be powerful stuff!"

Ewen wished he knew his roommate's name. "Yeah. Must be." He started toward his own bed and then turned on his heel. Very politely he added, "Fuck."

The man with no name was still laughing when Ewen pulled his own curtains closed. He took his pillows, piled them at the head of the bed, and sat on them. Pain in his knees informed him that this body was not built for the full lotus. Not even for the half lotus. As he placed his hands in his lap it further told him it had no idea how to meditate. Nor even to sit still.

He was sweating, though it was not warm. He guessed he was getting rid of the toxins created by all the booze and medication, and he and Jacob's body would just have to endure it for a while. *What were Jacob and Ewen's body enduring right now? If they walked in front of a moving truck right now, would it be Jacob or Ewen who would die?*

He took a deep breath and pulled his mind to center. He did it again and again. Suddenly his mouth and nose were flooded with a hallucination of beer. He felt the bubbles on his tongue and smelled the sharp bitterness of hops in his nose. He was salivating. He wanted that beer more than he wanted the next breath of air.

Ewen had never cared at all for beer.

This was not fair. As Ewen felt this he knew the meaninglessness of the statement, and he grinned to himself. But he still felt it.

His wildly leaping mind hit on the thought of Sid Sundown. He had never needed a phone to call Sid. But was his ability to visit the old dead man a property of his body or of his mind? Was there a split between the two: body and mind? Not according to Buddhism. But there was something; why else was he here, sweating onto a stiff hospital bed sheet, without change to make a phone call?

"Sid?" he called, almost silently. He reached for the grove of cedars.

"This is the kind of problem Raven gets into," said the old man, sitting by his little fire. "Raven is too damn clever for his own good."

Ewen looked down at his own hand. It *was* his own hand. Here, at least, he was Ewen. "How do I get back?" he asked.

Sid shrugged. "I dunno. I never said *I* was clever." Sid Sundown and the clearing in Idaho faded away, leaving Ewen sitting on the bed, sweating.

Finally he had an idea. He padded barefoot to his roommate's bed and said, "I forget. When is staff shift change?"

It was 9:48 p.m., and Ewen was standing by the nurse's station, drawing the evening nurse with a fiber-tip pen on computer paper. It was an odd experiment, because the muscles of his hand were not quite in tune with his brain, so the result looked a bit shakier than it would have under normal circumstances. Still, it impressed the nurse enough (and flattered her enough) that she made no complaint about Ewen's nearness to the sacred desk.

While he sketched, he listened for the steps of the next shift coming down the corridor. The metal door was heavy, but not soundproof. He had his foot negligently hooked through the pillar of the blood-pressure machine, which was lounging by the desk like a very skinny human.

They were not alone. Two men in bathrobes, towels over their arms, were gazing at his little portrait. "Man," said one unshaven fellow, "you could do that for a living." Ewen smiled and said nothing. He was hearing the footsteps.

Four feet behind him the latch of the door rattled and the guard stepped in. Ewen spun around and brought the pillar with him. "Look out!" he cried in seeming distress, as it toppled at the surprised man. The guard grabbed the piece of equipment as though it was a fainting damsel, and through the crack between his body and the frame of the door Ewen slid away. Guard and expensive machine crashed to the floor and Ewen was through. Behind him he heard one patient shout "Wha-hoo! Go, boy!" and then the sound of a buzzer.

This was not the way in which he had entered with his sister yesterday. He was in the main body of the hospital, in a broad and open room containing a Starbuck's, a gift shop and a huge salt-water fish tank. The fish seemed amazed to see him streak through, but then, they were fish and possibly always looked that way. At the end of the long lobby he had to choose right or left and he chose left. He found himself at a dead end with elevators on either side. The buzzer kept sounding and there was someone stamping down the vinyl flooring behind him.

It was another guard: this one taller and more slender than the one he had floored. The guard seemed to have no weapon other than a short baton, which he did not draw. He put his arms out to the sides, as though Ewen were a horse on the edge of bolting. "Easy, kid," the guard said warily. "It's not as bad as you think."

It's worse. And I'm not a kid.

Ewen approached him as though it were the guard who was frightened. Then the guard from the Detox Unit, the one he had flattened, came around the same corner, and this man was noticeably upset by his little accident. His baton was out and ready. The younger guard turned and looked behind him.

Ewen took his moment. He shoved one of Jacob's shoulders into the young guard's solar plexus and knocked him against the angry one. They both went down, the angry guard padding the other's fall. Ewen spared an instant to be glad it had happened in exactly that way. He was not fond of the angry guard. He darted out of the elevator hall and toward the front door. Jacob's legs were gangly and not terribly coordinated, but they were long and useful for darting.

The front entrance was dark and there were only a few straggling visitors. One woman with a child in arms shrank back from him. The buzzer from the violated Detox Unit was still sounding.

Before Ewen made the door, a third guard appeared, standing by the wastebasket at the side of the door. He was grizzled and short and looked like he had done something else with his life before retiring to become a hospital guard. Ewen paused before the door, reluctant to mix it up with the old man. "Just let me by," he said quietly, but the guard spread his legs, put one hand on his baton, and shook his graying head. Ewen sighed, hearing more footfalls behind him. "Then hold this," he suggested, and tossed the wastebasket lightly at the man, who grabbed and staggered under the weight of the thing, opening the door as he backed away for balance. Ewen slid through.

It worked twice in a row, he thought, as he ran into the chilly dark. *Just ask a guy to do something for you and don't give him a chance to say no. What a discovery!*

After a brief moment it occurred to him that people had been doing as much to him his whole life.

He was running down a street of shops—a Pony Express, a convenience store, a beauty parlor with a smudgy window. Everything looked slightly seedy, slightly past its prime, but he saw it all in a rush, not daring to turn to see whether the stubborn, unlucky hospital guard was still following him. He turned off at the first opportunity, where a construction site was standing still in the moonlit stage. He clambered over its chain-link fence and hid in the gloom cast by a large Caterpillar tractor.

Ewen concentrated again, coming up with nothing new. He needed to make a phone call. He needed sanctuary. He needed to get back to Jacob.

Perhaps he could return to his "home" place by the cemetery, and as he had found the shining footprints, perhaps he could find the place—the site, the "crack"—where Jacob had left with Ewen's body. Once before, he had been able to force his immaterial nature back into his body when he was lost. That had been in a golden temple, in a room full of blood. He'd had Rick Petersen's help. But even if he could displace Jacob now, what would happen to the boy? He'd be where Ewen was now, and though Ewen was furious at the kid, he knew that Jacob, dropped here suddenly, might not make it till morning. And he was Lynn's patient.

No. Ewen needed a phone call and a place to stay, and he needed to find Jacob again, face to face.

First things first. The phone call.

Ewen sat very still, though Jacob's body was tormented with itches and twitches, souvenirs of an ill-spent year. He watched the row of clapboard houses that backed the building site. He saw a slump-shouldered young man walk through a hole in the fence of one of those yards. Five minutes later, the man ducked out again, standing a little straighter and walking a little larger. This was interesting. Ewen scuttled from his shadow to another one that ran over a section of the fence. He emerged on the other side of the fence, still concealed. There was no sound of pursuit from the road behind him. No flashing lights. Maybe an escaping patient was not such an unusual thing to Snohomish Hospital.

It was chilly, but Ewen had felt much worse weather, especially since traveling with Susan Sundown and Rez. He moved his arms and legs slowly, to make sure they would still work, and then he sat still again.

Another figure came into the alley, this time an older man. He scrambled through the small hole in the plank fence with difficulty as Ewen watched. Ewen heard some talking and voices were raised, but only a little. After a minute the man squeezed out between the planks and he, too, departed.

Over his left shoulder Ewen could see the upper floors of the hospital from which he had run, and he grinned tightly. Where better to have a crack house than on the block where the customers did their hospital rehab? At least Ewen assumed it was a crack house; he had heard of crack houses on television. He knew very little of illegal drugs through experience.

He crossed the alley and leaned against the fence of the neighboring yard. There was no dog noise, but then there wouldn't be. Noise would be bad for business. He vaulted this fence.

Or tried to. He slid down the way he came, feeling silly and with his shirt caught on the wood. What had Jacob been doing with his fine, young wrestler's body? Ewen tried again, clambering over as silently as possible.

The yard was ratty, but the house before him didn't seem abandoned. There was the reflected glow of a TV in the other end. No lights in the kitchen. Ewen bent down and peeked through an open knot in the fir planking at his destination.

This house was not occupied, or not usually occupied. Half the back-porch stairs were missing. The kitchen door was not quite in true, and through the crack Ewen could see a lamp burning. Not electric light, though, a Coleman. Then the door opened, scraping over the porch flooring, and someone stepped out, stretching and yawning.

To Ewen's surprise it was just a kid. It was a short-haired, beardless boy of about fifteen, blondish, wearing a baseball jacket and cap. The cap, of course, was turned backwards. He had a roll of greenbacks in his hands and casually juggled it from hand to hand. Ewen crawled toward him against the side of the broken porch trellis, almost on all fours.

The kid made stalking easy for him. He was paying no attention. He stepped down the two remaining steps and bounced over the missing ones, with the easy energy of childhood. He looked at the hole in the plank fence and cracked his back, looking for all the world like a salesman in a car dealership who was waiting for the next lucky customer.

Ewen came up from behind and put one hand over the boy's mouth. He put one foot against the back of the boy's knees and forced him to kneel. "I need something from you," said Ewen quietly into his ear.

The boy nodded as forcefully as Ewen's hand allowed him and reached readily toward his jacket pocket. Ewen was in the pocket before the boy got there and took out a little .22, which he put on the ground behind him. He hoisted the boy up again, to put him further from the gun. "That wasn't what I meant." He tried to think how to explain things without scaring the boy into something stupid and without telling too much. "I just got out of the hospital, there," he began, "and I've got nothing."

The boy relaxed in relief. He tried to talk through Ewen's hand. Ewen gave him a little room and he said. "I got it. I know what you mean, and I've got anything you could need. Just don't hurt me. I got cocaine, ice, dope, whatever you want."

"You got a phone?" asked Ewen.

The boy tried to turn his head around, unsuccessfully. "Yeah. I got a phone."

"Well, I'm sorry, but I'm going to have to take it."

"Why? You think I'm going to call the police on you?"

Even as the boy was mumbling into his hand, Ewen heard movement in the house behind him. He swivelled, putting his captive between himself and the house. There, in the broken doorway was outlined a girl. "Don't hurt him!" she whispered. "Don't hurt him!"

Ewen looked closely and asked her very politely to take a few steps backwards. When she had done so he could see her by the light of the gas mantle lantern. She was one of the cutest little teenagers he had ever seen. She was wearing tights and an oversized men's sweatshirt that came down to her knees. She had rosy cheeks and a rosebud mouth and eyes that took up a large part of her little face. She, too, wore a baseball cap turned around backwards. "I don't plan to hurt him," he told her. "I just need his phone. And maybe a little cash, too."

At this the boy stiffened. "That . . . that money isn't mine. If you take it, they'll kill me."

Ewen felt around the pockets of the jacket for the large roll of bills. They seemed to be mostly twenties. One-handed, he peeled one off the roll. This was harder to do than he expected, and the boy had begun squirming in earnest. Ewen put one foot firmly down on the gun in the grass and the other around the boy's neck. He got one twenty off the roll and others floated down to the ground. He let them lie.

"Now your cell phone." He shifted to investigate the other pocket.

"Take mine. It's better," said the young girl on the porch, and she threw a sliver of pink at Ewen's head. Having used this dodge twice in the past hour, Ewen was not fooled by it. He swivelled and let the thing hit his captive in the head, while he found the phone he had been looking for. Holding the phone and the balled twenty in his free hand, he shoved the boy forcefully away while he bent to pick up the gun. He backed away, holding the gun aimed vaguely between the two and in that manner he reached the hole in the fence.

He considered the scene before him: the sullen, embryonic hustler and the girl. "You could do better than him," he called to the girl on the porch. "Lots better." He disappeared into the dark.

Back out in the dim alley he encountered a very thin woman, who had been approaching the dealer's entrance. He held the gun down at his side, away from her. "You should give them a couple minutes before going in," he said quietly. "They're in a sort of disarray right now." She stopped and regarded him warily. He thought of telling her that she, too, could do better than this, but there was no hope behind his thought.

Ewen couldn't climb back over the chain-link fence with his treasures in one hand and the gun in the other, so he skulked down the street a bit further. There was a fence between yards that led to what seemed to be a wooded lot, and had he been entirely Ewen he would have vaulted up and walked along the top railing. Being partially Jacob, he didn't dare try. "Oh what have you done to your young body, Jacob?" he asked the hands he was wearing. With some bitterness, he added, "Or should I just call you Jake?"

There was a damp cardboard box from a giant TV leaning against the back wall of a store. Ewen started to duck into it when he was stopped by the smell, feel or other unknown sense of a presence near him. "Somebody there?" he asked.

"And why wouldn't I be?" came the answer, along with a blast of sweet wine and old cigarettes.

What a neighborhood, he thought. *Or is this the world's norm and I live in an exceptional neighborhood?* "I just wanted a place to use the phone," he said aloud.

"Well, use it in your own room," said the irritated voice.

Ewen backed out and kept walking. The gun in his left hand bothered him. He could imagine far more trouble than help coming to him from this gun.

It was a little .22 caliber revolver. He had seen on TV that they were a popular weapon among the gangster crowd, but he didn't remember why. It didn't matter. He flicked open the cylinder and dropped the cartridges on the ground. Putting the open revolver on its back on the concrete, he tried to stamp the cylinder off. He hurt his foot; it seemed guns were made more sturdily than he'd thought.

He returned to the construction yard and jammed the cylinder between two of the steel uprights of the fence, and yanked on the thing. The gun was extremely well built, but he got the mechanism of the cylinder warped to the point where it would not easily retract into the body of the gun, and would definitely not revolve when the trigger was pulled. Wiping the gun all over his sweatshirt to remove his fingerprints, he dropped it on the ground.

He went on, seeing no one else in the shoddy alley. Finding no good hiding place in sight, he squatted down between two garbage cans, where the smell was different but considerably worse.

Would he have to convince Lynn of his true identity, or would her twin sense immediately know? Had she known something was off with Ewen for hours already? What if he got Theo? That might actually be easier.

What if no one was home at all? Ewen began to regret the quixotic gesture that had made him steal only twenty dollars. He might need more.

He flicked open the phone. The keypad was tiny and the light terrible, but he picked out the number and waited. On the third ring it was picked up and a treble voice answered, "This is the Young-Thurmond residence and this is Teddy speaking."

Ewen took a deep breath. "Teddy. I know I don't sound like it but this is your Uncle Ewen."

"Okay," said Teddy, reasonably. "Did you do something spiritual again, Uncle Ewen?"

Ewen was silenced by the question for a moment. "Something spiritual?"

"Daddy says I shouldn't call what you do 'magic.' He says it's spiritual stuff."

"Oh. Well then, yeah. I've made a big spiritual mess and I need to talk to Mommy."

"Okay."

"Tell her it's Uncle Ewen calling. Tell her you're *sure* it's Uncle Ewen."

"Okay," said Teddy.

Chapter Twenty-five

JACOB FELT THE STRUGGLE and the flip and then he was down on the grass again. He lay there on his stomach, and looked around at the trees and the little limestone wall.

All that planning and for nothing. Here he was, back in the pretty little trap into which Ewen had put him and the only way he was going to get out was to return to Snohomish Hospital Detox Unit. To hell, in other words. He cursed, using his favorite word again and again and felt very sorry for himself.

Then he noticed a strange thing. He had his hands fisted and jammed into the grass and his arms were tightened with his rage. And his whole body, toes to fingers, was off the ground. Jacob looked under himself and saw light between his body and the grass. There was something wrong with gravity.

There was also something wrong with his clothes, for instead of wearing his hospital johnny or his wrestling uniform he was neatly clothed in chinos and a Hawaiian shirt in a green ferny pattern. He looked at his hand, filled with crushed grass, and it wasn't his hand at all. That forearm, solid as a tree-bough, could never have been his. It was also considerably tanner than he had ever been. He sprang to his feet and actually left the ground for a moment, coming down in perfect balance. He ran one hand through his hair, which was heavier, straighter and longer than his.

So part of the plan had gone right. He had managed to flip Ewen. He just wound up stuck in the same stupid place as before. He noticed something on the ground and picked up an eel-skin wallet, a large ring of keys with a heavy blue tube for a keychain—that was odd—and a small pack of Kleenex. He put them in the pocket of his (Ewen's) trousers and marveled at what a prepared kind of guy Ewen was. There was even a pocket comb in the right back pocket. Well now: prepared old Ewen was going to have to deal with Detox Hell for a few days. And maybe a month of rehab after that.

Unless he came back for Jacob. Could he do that, in Jacob's less-than-prepared body? Jacob decided he would make it as hard as possible to be found.

He walked toward the trees that divided this spot from the cemetery proper, and was surprised to found it took more steps to get there. Even in this fine-tuned body. Jacob laughed, realizing for the first time that Ewen was shorter than he was. When he had first met Doc's brother, Jacob had been quite a bit shorter, and in the past couple years he hadn't noticed things changing. As he thrust himself between the cypresses, he laughed sharply, with a resonance that wasn't quite his own.

Hey wow! I'm Chinese! he thought, and then he was brought up short by the traffic in the distance, beyond the wrought iron cemetery fence. This place he was in was only Ewen's imagination. It was made-up. It didn't have traffic. It didn't even have people.

Or it never did before.

Jacob scuffed his sneakers through the grass, jingling Ewen's keys in his pockets. He passed by a woman who was peering at the ground, looking for one rectangular stone among the many. He smelled earth, and saw there was a black rectangular hole in the grass at the other side of the field, with a backhoe busy at work. A grave. They were digging a grave. Jacob had never seen a grave being dug. He peered at it as he jogged along. Now he was at the gate of the cemetery, and the air around him was sour with diesel exhaust.

Where the hell was he? Jacob let out an excited chuff, which was in a different tonal register than he expected. Earlier, when wandering around the empty streets of Ewen's mind, he had seen signs indicating the city was Santa Barbara. One man's idea of Santa Barbara. But this . . . this was a louder more confusing place. This was more Jacob's kind of place. He guessed this actually *was* Santa Barbara. He leaned against the wrought iron palings, giggling to himself.

Jacob had no idea what to do now. But he was all on fire to do it. He began to jog right along the outside of the cemetery fence, cutting left and right around other pedestrians.

This body he was wearing was a trip; both heavier than his and lighter in movement. He dodged around a woman with a baby stroller, and she gave a slight "eek" as he passed. That sound and other passing things vanished in his wake.

Jacob was reminded of the movie *Big*. He had been a little kid last time he saw it and hadn't understood why it was supposed to be so sad. But he was fifteen, not twelve, like in the movie, and Tom Hanks hadn't gotten to be in the body of a magical martial artist. Jacob did not undervalue Ewen Young at all, though he knew now that he could play old Ewen for a sucker. He even liked the guy. But Ewen had had all the luck up until now and today it was Jacob's turn.

He'd give the body back, in time. Jacob reassured himself that he was no car-thief. Just a joy rider. And what joy.

He passed under a hanging sign, belonging to some kind of fern bar. He leaped up and slapped it, and to his surprise the wooden board swung up to the horizontal, and the force of the slap stung his hand. Ewen's hand. He stared at that brown hand for a moment and then giggled again.

"Having fun?" asked somebody. "I always like to see somebody having fun."

It was an old guy in a pea coat; he was really old—maybe sixty. His face was stubbly and he leaned against the fake adobe wall of the building. He was holding a thing like a small flute, made of wood. Jacob wondered why he was wearing a pea coat in the Santa Barbara sunshine and then he glanced down and saw the miserable shoes and broken-cuffed trousers. A homeless man. He gave up wondering because there was no sense in anything they did. They were crazy.

But Jacob was in a great mood. "Yeah. I'm having fun," he said, and he reached into his chinos' pocket. He gave the guy a handful of change and one bill. He didn't look to see what denomination.

The man looked faintly surprised. "Kind of you," he said, and the money disappeared.

Jacob could not be standing in front of a bar all this time and not be aware of what it was. He had a moment of indecision, for he had just (one way or another) gotten out of detox and he hadn't been feeling that well for a while before. But this was Ewen Young's body, and Ewen wasn't an alcoholic. This was a freebie. And there was so much money in Ewen's pocket. He could feel it.

He went into the pleasant room lit by the green light coming through the ferns. Jacob stared at that light for a few moments, as though Ewen's eyes themselves were drawn to it. Then he went to the bar.

Jacob had never been in a bar before, but he knew how it was done. The light shining off the myriad of bottles behind the polished wood bar caught Jacob's eyes as the light from the window had not. They were of so many colors and shapes, and the names seemed like magic incantations: Sambuca, Amaretto, Drambuie. He was still staring, rapt, when the bartender came up to him. "Lunch?" she said.

He caught himself up and processed her word again. "No. I'll have . . . I'll have a beer." He took out his wallet and began to sort through the plastic cards.

"What beer?" she asked amiably, because she was not at all busy, and Jacob (Ewen) was a good-looking man.

"Uh . . . uh . . . Bud." He took out the driver's license, noting that Ewen had been born in 1979.

She was blond, and at least thirty years old. Yet she seemed to be flirting with him. "Okay, but we have fourteen different kinds. You ought to try something new."

"Oh, I am. I am trying something new," he answered, amazed at his own wit. "I'll have . . . what should I have?"

"How 'bout Becks?" He nodded, and she brought him a green bottle with keys on the label. She poured it and it looked like Bud. He took a taste and was terribly disappointed.

The bartender was watching his face. "Well. That wasn't a success, was it? Let me get you your Budweiser. No charge."

Jacob had a sudden flash that it wasn't he who was turned off by the taste but Ewen. Ewen's mouth. "No. Wait. I think I'm just not in the mood for beer. Let me try . . . try a Long Island Ice Tea." He'd heard of these. Knew a girl who filched them from her father's private stash of little cans. Diane—that was her name, and she was really hot—was strongly in favor of them.

"So be it," said the bartender, blinking just once. "But it's heavy stuff on an empty stomach; we make a hefty Long Island. Just hope you're not driving."

"I'm not," said Jacob, primly, and he watched the bartender at her witchcraft. When she was finished with the tall glass and had added two cherries, one slice of orange and an umbrella, she glanced up to see Jacob there, still holding Ewen's driver's license out on the bar.

"You look young, fella," she said, grinning. "But not *that* young."

The drink was amazing. It took his full attention. He could not imagine what was in it, but guessed that tea was not any part of it. He forgot about the blond bartender and her flirting in his total concentration in the taste and feel of the Long Island Ice Tea.

Later, when the color in the glass was paler—more indicative of ice than ice tea—he noticed the guy in the pea coat sitting at the end of the bar, holding a coffee cup in both hands. The blond bartender was chatting with him, which surprised Jacob, as that was not the usual reception homeless men got in bars. He also noticed that the light was dimmer and there were a few more people in the place.

Jacob felt very fine, but a little seasick, too. He decided he needed better air. He almost forgot to pay for the drink, and in the poor light he could not easily read the amount written on his bill. He left a twenty. Why not?

Santa Barbara at twilight was a marvelous place, and all roads led down to the sea. The cool breeze came up (almost too cool) and Jacob leaned over a rail and watched the mild surf melt into the sand. There was a thin sound of music—old-style music—maybe the man with the flute. The setting sun was turning the water improbable colors and he knew there were things he was going to have to do. He was going to have to let the people up north know what happened to Ewen's body. If Ewen hadn't already told them. He grinned at the thought of his own pimply pale face and uncertain voice trying to convince the Doc he was her brother. A weak and nasty place in his own mind rejoiced at the lack of success *that* attempt would have, but Jacob didn't really wish Ewen ill. He'd have to call. He'd also have to find a place to eat dinner. And to spend the night. And most immediately, to pee.

Now that he thought about it, that need was intense. Behind him rose a row of shops and restaurants. In front were the stairs down to the sand. Jacob decided for the sand.

Peeing with another man's penis was the strangest part of the escapade so far. He tried not to make comparisons. As he zipped up and headed back up the concrete stairs to the boulevard he came face to face with the man in the pea coat. The flute was sticking out of one of the side pockets. Jacob gave back a step.

"They're pretty strict about that," the man said casually, gesturing down at the wet patch in the sand. "Especially downtown here. You could get a ticket."

Jacob grinned despite himself. "Yeah, but it wouldn't be *my* ticket."

The old man just stared for a few moments. Then he turned aside to let Jacob up and off the stairs. "On vacation, then?"

Jacob gave him a startled look, but then decided he had read too much into a simple comment. People did go to Santa Barbara for vacation.

The breeze had turned a bit sharp and his Hawaiian shirt flapped against his body. "Yeah. I'm on vacation. And by the way, where's a good place to eat around here?"

He thought perhaps he shouldn't have asked this man such a question. He probably didn't eat in a lot of good restaurants himself. He might even be offended. But the man said, "That depends on what you like to eat."

In a moment of mischief Jacob said, "Chinese food."

Still no change in the old man's serious expression. "There's a place up two streets. But the Thai place right yonder is better, and cheaper, too." Very slowly, as though not to frighten, he put his worn hand down on Jacob's arm. "And, friend—I can see by the glassy look in your eyes you're not used to being on vacation. Not used to drinking things with umbrellas in them, maybe I mean. Now Santa Barbara is a great town. Best place in the world. But if you don't know it . . . if you're just on vacation, as it were . . . it's best to be careful where you do your drinking. And how much."

Jacob's first reaction was to be impressed by the man's evident sincerity. And by the fact that the old man was, definitely, not on vacation here himself. But riding over this was a blast of anger left over from Snohomish Detox. He flexed Ewen's shoulders and arms. "You don't know me," he said.

The man backed away, still calm, his pea coat stirring in the increasing wind. He raised both hands peacefully. "That's right. I sure don't."

Jacob crossed the boulevard, feeling anger like a pleasant energy. He got honked at once. He found the Thai place right away.

There was a moment of unease when he discovered that Ewen Young carried only a debit card. Most restaurants treated these as credit cards, but there was always a chance . . . And there was only so many twenties left in the eel-skin wallet. Luckily this place was like many others and he was able to sign for the bill and the tip. He slurped the last of this Long Island Ice Tea loudly and got up to go. The Tea wasn't up to the standard of his first.

To go, yes, but where? It was completely dark now. Up north it would not have been dark yet. These were the months of long light. He felt a sting of resentment; he was a Washingtonian and should have had that long evening. He'd paid for it all the dark winter. And where were all the hotels of Santa Barbara? They should be down here by the ocean. That's where people wanted to go, right? Jacob was getting damned chilly now, and tired.

Or maybe it was Ewen who was tired. Ewen wasn't used to all this drinking. And Ewen's stomach was now so full. Jacob turned up a dark street away from the ocean. Away from the wind. He was looking for a "vacancy" sign. Instead he found a sporting goods store and looked longingly at a windbreaker in the window. The store was closed.

The street seemed to be going uphill. He made a right angle turn, but that street also seemed to be going uphill. He was very weary now, and quite sick, and he sat down between two storefronts and held his head in his hands. He found he had his left hand in his mouth and was biting down on it. He stopped, both because he was determined to be finished with that obsession and because this body didn't belong to him. He didn't want to give it back to Ewen Young all bitten up. Bad enough to joyride it, and get it cold and dizzy.

Jacob needed to find a hotel. There would be a phone by the bed and he could call north, and the whole thing would be taken care of.

What he found, instead of a hotel, was another bar. It wasn't what he wanted, but it was warm inside.

He decided that as long as he kept to beer he wouldn't be sick. Beer never had made him sick. It was the fancy stuff that had done him in.

And beer didn't taste so strange anymore. Perhaps that was because it was Bud or because he'd stopped tasting it.

Jacob looked around at the people at the bar. These guys were certainly not on vacation in Santa Barbara. Not unless they did construction work on their vacations. Maybe that was it. The rest of the year they were lawyers, but on their summer vacations they did roofing. Jacob smirked and made a snorkelish noise at the thought of that.

"Who're you smilin' at?" asked the guy he'd been looking at that moment, a redhead, very sunburned and weathered. Old. Fairly old: maybe forty. "I'm thinking you might be a lawyer," he found himself saying to the guy. "And that's such a riot."

The sunburned man stared without expression. "And what's funny about that?" he asked. "Maybe I am. Are you? A lawyer?"

Jacob's father was a lawyer. Patent law. Jacob thought he knew something about the matter. "I could be." He made a vague gesture at the Hawaiian shirt, the chinos, the impeccable Nikes. He tried to explain his joke. "This looks more like a lawyer than you do."

There was another man standing beside the sunburned guy. He was darker, but much the same in Jacob's eyes. "And I think what *you* look like is a drunk," he flatly stated.

Well, here we go again. Just out of detox and it seemed the whole world was a big judgmental AA meeting. "I think *you* look like a drunk," he replied, and to him it seemed the height of wit. "I think you all look like drunks in here. I mean, why'd you come here except to get drunk? Is there any other reason to sit in a dive like this but that you're drunks?"

Jacob felt he was being open. He was sharing. He was startled when the redhead's fist swung for his face and more startled to find his own arm had blocked it—blocked the punch and gone on to deliver his own stinger to the guy's nose. Jacob had not even seen it happening. He stared at his arm—Ewen's arm—as though he was not sure whether the thing was a traitor or a savior, but quite certain it was nothing that belonged to him.

"That's just about enough over there," said the bartender, but he made no move to come around or over the bar.

"Ish *more* than enough. Is too fuckin' mush," replied the darker guy beside the redhead, who was now holding his gushing nose in both hands. He moved warily around Jacob, out of arm's length, and when he tried to slip a choke hold around him, Jacob was startled and sent Ewen's hand to hit the man in the groin.

Now there were a number of people approaching the scene, anger in their eyes. Jacob was scared out of his wits and left matters entirely to Ewen's reflexes. He hit two more men and kicked someone in the knee.

"I'm calling the cops now," the bartender announced, and at that moment someone slammed a chair down on Jacob's head.

Had he not been drunk he might have gone cleanly unconscious, but the borders of awareness had gone so muddy that he remained on his feet and went plodding toward the door. It seemed everyone else had similar intent. Five men intersected in the one narrow doorway and Ewen's arms and shoulders tossed them out like bowling pins, except for the redhead, who got miserably squished into the doorjamb itself. From under his bloody hands the man mumbled, "You Hawaiian asshole, I'm going to breag you inna pieces!"

Outside it was cold, it was dark, and people were still trying to hit Jacob, who ploughed on up the street, away from the ocean and toward nowhere. Back in the bar there was only the bartender—who had not called the cops—and Ewen's wallet, left on the bar. Soon there was only the bartender, who never did call the cops.

Somewhere in the night a thin tune repeated itself on a wooden flute.

Chapter Twenty-six

EWEN ALMOST didn't call Susan to tell her about his problem. He didn't want to disturb her was his surface thought, but as he was riding home to Redmond in Lynn's Toyota he realized that his reluctance was more embarrassment than consideration. He had not had too much reluctance to put his sister and her son through this marathon of coastal driving, so obviously he was not being overly considerate tonight. It was just that he didn't want to be seen by Susan looking like this.

Teddy was staring at Uncle Ewen. Avidly staring. "Uncle Ewen? You got a pimple." His mother told him that Uncle Ewen didn't need to hear that.

"Uncle Ewen? You gonna stay this way?" Mother told Teddy that Uncle Ewen was not going to stay that way. She told Teddy to stop bothering Ewen, but she couldn't stop him from staring.

"This is all my fault," said Lynn, unexpectedly.

"Your fault?" Ewen's Jacob voice nearly cracked. "How yours?"

"Entirely my fault. I got you involved with Jacob to begin with. Like Uncle Jimmy, I've had you working for me without recompense for years, and like Uncle Jimmy, I've gotten you in trouble."

"Who could know? I mean, I certainly didn't predict Jacob would be able to flip me into his body and take off in mine. Nor that he'd want to."

"I'm so disappointed in him," sighed Lynn. For her, this was a pretty severe stricture. "I don't even know why he chose to engage in this self-destructive drinking this year. To not call me, too . . . he had been doing so well. I guess adolescence just hit. Hit pretty hard, maybe."

"Yeah." Ewen took a deep breath and let it out slowly, running one hand over his blemished chin. "But it's not supposed to hit a person twice."

"I'm sorry," said Lynn again. She bit her lip.

Ewen made up his mind. "Can I have your cell phone? To call Susan?"

"Will she believe it's you, Ewen?"

He thought about it, and slowly smiled. "Sure. I'll just use my 'true name.' She knows it."

Lynn snorted. "True name! I'm your twin and I don't know any 'true name' for you."

"That's right." Ewen was beginning to smirk. It was an oddly "Jacob" expression. "And you're not going to."

Susan was not that hard to convince. It was, however, hard to get her to stop roaring with laughter.

"Is that Dr. Sundown?" asked Teddy, leaning toward the phone, which Ewen was holding away from his ear. "She sounds like a donkey!"

Late in the night, four of them were heading back south in Susan's Cessna. There was Susan piloting and Lynn in the copilot's seat. Behind them rode Ewen—in a fold-down seat that was uncomfortable under his long, skinny body—and Rez in her harness. Below them California rolled away, sometimes twinkling and sometimes asleep.

Occasionally Susan still erupted in brays of laughter. "I wish you wouldn't do that, Susan," said Ewen. He was resting his face against the window, gazing at the lights dejectedly.

She went silent, but only for a few moments. "If I thought you couldn't fix this right up, sweetie, I wouldn't be laughing." Another few seconds went by with no sound but the roar of the engine. "You *can* fix this right up? Can't you?"

He sighed. "Just let me get my hands on him," Ewen said in a dire voice. In truth, he had no idea how to repair the situation, but the women didn't have to know that.

"Well—remember, when you do catch up, you'll be getting your hands on *you*!" She began to chuckle again. Lynn Young-Thurmond stared at her, wide-eyed.

Rez was staring at Ewen, her nose working nervously. Their meeting had not gone smoothly, and Ewen had had a chance to see how the big dog reacted to most men. He had worked to open his mind to her, happy to find he had that ability even as Jacob, and that had made a great difference, but she had let him know she was looking for the proper moment to tear that disfiguring body off her dear friend Ewen. He hoped they could find the boy before Rez found the moment.

"What does Theo say about this whole thing, Lynn?" asked Susan.

Lynn shrugged. "He says it's not Tibetan."

"Not Nez Perce, either. Have you tried getting in touch with Uncle Sid, Ewen?"

Ewen lifted his head off the window. "Once. He thought it was funny."

"It is funny. But call him again. He might know something."

"Maybe. But he's too much like you, Sue. He'd just die laughing. That is, if he weren't . . . "

"Already dead. I know."

Ewen scratched a pimple. "Besides. I hope we have this . . . fixed up tomorrow. Or is it today already?"

Lynn looked around the seat at her red-eyed brother. "You're tired. I'm so sorry."

"Please don't say that again." Ewen let his head bang against the window again. More moments passed, filled with engine noise. "You know what's really weird?" he asked.

"Everything, right now," answered Lynn.

Susan spoke. "What's weird is the fact that if I touched you right now I could be convicted of aiding and abetting the delinquency of a minor. Or whatever it's called." She giggled again.

"It's called child molestation," said Lynn tartly. She dealt with molested children too often to make jokes of this nature.

Ewen spoke louder than either woman. "That was a rhetorical question. I'm going to tell you what's weird. I keep having taste hallucinations of alcohol. Nose hallucinations, too."

They both turned and stared at him. "That's amazing," said Lynn. "You always despised the taste of alcohol."

"Still do. But boy do I want some! And even weirder, I don't know what kind of liquor I'm hallucinating. When it's not beer, or wine, that is. It's sharp and herbal and . . . something like mouthwash."

"Maybe you're hallucinating Listerine," said Lynn.

"Are you hallucinating smoke?" Susan asked. "Or cough syrup?"

"No. Neither one. What would those be?"

"Well, smoke could be Irish whisky or Scotch. Bourbon is a bit like cough syrup. Rye is like . . . mmmm. Let me see . . . "

"Rye bread?" suggested Lynn.

Susan showed her teeth in a grin. "Boy. You two are both babes in the woods. Nothing like that. I can't think of a good analogy. It's kind of a spoiled sugary taste."

Ewen leaned forward. "I didn't know you knew so much about the stuff either. I've never seen you drink it."

"I hope you never do," said Susan Sundown. They flew on through the dark with engine noise punctuating the silence. She didn't laugh again for a long while.

Chapter Twenty-seven

JACOB MUST have been asleep for a while, because he was now wrapped in a woolen blanket and huddled against a wall. But no, this wasn't a blanket. It was a pea coat. The grizzled old man was squatting next to him, patiently watching.

"How'd I get . . . " He looked around and saw he was in an alley, not too dirty an alley, under moonlight.

"You got here by yourself, boyo, and then you sat down. Sleepin' and shiverin', sleepin' and shiverin'."

Memories flooded back and few of them were pleasant. "I got in a fight." He put his hand to the top of his head and pulled it back very quickly, wincing.

"Yeah, but you should see the other guys," said the old man, grinning. "Which I did. You cut a swath through that old workingman's club back there. What were you fighting about, anyway?"

"I kept hitting people," said Jacob, in pure wonderment.

"Got that part. But why?"

"No. I mean we were fighting *because* I kept hitting people. I got scared about something and it just went off."

"It?"

"The body," said Jacob in tones of grievance. He looked at Ewen's tan hands. They looked perfectly ordinary.

The old guy leaned back. "Friend," he said. "It's just advice from a stranger, but you should lay off the hooch."

This irritated Jacob for a moment, but only for a moment. "That's what I've been hearing," he admitted. "From all sides."

He stood up, propping himself against the fake adobe wall. Only his head seemed to be hurt. But he was tired, and he was cold, even though he was wearing another man's coat (among many other things.) "I've got to get in touch with some people," he said. "I need to call home."

As he said these words, a new sort of peace settled over Jacob. He needed to call home. Washington. His father. But most of all, he needed to find Dr. Young. To tell her about her brother.

"I need to start doing things right," he said to the old guy without the coat. And, though he had to be without a clue what Jacob was talking about, he nodded wisely.

"Can you tell me where to find a phone?" he asked, and fished into the back pocket of his chinos. The wallet was gone and so was the new peace he had found.

"Oh, shit!" said Jacob.

Four people and a dog found themselves at the cemetery and it was locked.

"I expected that," said Susan. "They wouldn't be able to keep a cemetery open all night. It would be a mess in the morning."

"It's not like kids could kick over the flat tombstones," said Ewen, wearily. "But I suppose they could spray graffiti over them."

"What they'd do is shoot up on them," said Lynn. "And what better place to spread HIV than a cemetery." Both her companions looked at her in surprise. She was almost a perfect stranger to cynicism.

"It won't matter," Susan said, and she bent down to the dog. "Rez. Find Ewen. Ewen."

Ewen himself snorted as the dog looked uncertainly from her handler to him. Susan put her hand to the concrete in front of the wrought-iron gates. "Here. Find Ewen."

Rez put her long nose to the spot and began to sniff. She paused only for a second, thrust her muzzle between the railings and drew it out again. She turned to her left along the sidewalk, not even lowering her head to the scent. She pulled against her tracking harness. "Good going!" said Susan, leaning back for balance. They trotted down the street in Resurrection's wake.

"About thirty years ago," the old man was saying, "I was in Arizona. Me and a friend knew a guy who was gonna die of booze and dope. This wasn't something that was gonna happen eventually, you understand. He was gonna die maybe that day or the next day. My buddy and I were really good at spotting where a guy was, on that path. But we weren't his family or anything, so we didn't have what you'd call authority to do anything about it. Especially not thirty years ago. Especially not in Arizona."

The old man was striding along under the streetlamps, with Jacob walking behind him. Jacob's head was hurting like a very bitch. "So, what we did was, we waited for him to shoot up and while he's nodding we tie him up."

"Tie him up?"

"Yeah. Tied his arms behind his back and put a gag in his mouth, and put him in the back seat of the car. Now, at that time the nearest treatment center was about a hundred twenty-five miles away, and so we start driving. But it was April, and already hot down there, and of course we ain't got air-conditioning, so we're drivin' with the windows open and hot air blastin' over us and the guy comes to and starts makin' noise. Tries to butt me with his head, too. We've had about enough of him already when we come to a river that runs under the highway, so . . ."

"You didn't!" said Jacob, aghast. The old man turned and glanced at him in surprise. "Sure we did. We just got out and took a swim in the river, leaving him there."

"Oh," said Jacob. "I thought . . ."

"Hell! We left the windows open. Like for a dog. He wasn't gonna die of heatstroke. And the second part of that trip was much more pleasant, what with our clothes soaked and our mood improved. And we'd planned it just right. By the time we got to the treatment center—where was that? Tempe, maybe?—he was so strung out and out of control they felt it necessary to certify him."

They walked on, and Jacob didn't ask where they were going. He had never asked. "Last I heard about the guy, he was nine years clean and sober. But I heard he still wanted to bust my chops.

"There's no pleasin' some people."

The old man suddenly grinned. "You know, while we were swimming and the guy pokin' his head out the window, gag and all, there were a number of people drivin' the other way—passed us right by. They waved. We waved. Only in Arizona!"

They were on a residential street and the old man walked up the driveway that belonged to a very small, concrete brick house. He knocked on the door, waited a few minutes in the dark and then knocked again.

Jacob was very much aware that he was wearing the old man's coat, and he wished he had the courage to take it off and give it back. But he was cold and tired, and he didn't have that much courage.

"Used to be they wouldn't take in alcoholics at most hospitals. This was before my time, and I'm not sure why. Maybe they thought they weren't really sick. Maybe they thought we deserved to die." Jacob caught the change to the word "we" and looked up at the guy more intently. "Anyhow, this old guy told me he once took a friend in, having seizures and all, and the people said they wouldn't admit him because it was alcohol withdrawal. So my friend hauls off and punches his friend. Fractures his jaw. 'Now he's got something else wrong with him,' he says. 'Now you can admit him.'"

"And did that guy want to fracture *his* jaw when he got out?" Jacob asked, interested despite himself.

"Not that I heard."

The door was opened by a young woman with stubbly pink hair. She was about five feet tall and drop-dead gorgeous. From what they could see she was wearing only a long men's T-shirt. "Wha—?" she asked the old man, squinting and blinking, and then she focused on Jacob behind him. She said nothing else.

"We got a guy here on vacation, Em. Thought you might want to get your feet wet in Step Twelve."

She glanced from one man to the other. She practiced keeping her eyes open. "Sure thing," she said. "C'm in."

She was so short and so cute she reminded Jacob of Frodo the hobbit. A girl Frodo. With pink hair. Under the ceiling light the living room was dusty and overflowing with books. She had the habit of putting the books down open, which Jacob's father had never permitted him to do, on account of the spines. The indoor air was warm, and smelled dusty. Bookish. She did not, however, look bookish. Her hair stood up in sleep-flattened spikes. She wore a nose ring.

"May I present Jacob the Vacationer," said the old man. "He got in a bit of a rumble in that bucket of blood downtown."

Jacob didn't remember that the place had been called The Bucket of Blood. He vaguely remembered it was something like The Pier House, or Private Dock, or something marine. Bucket of Blood seemed to fit it better, though.

The pink-haired girl was looking at him carefully. Jacob avoided her stare and thought he might be blushing. Could she tell, through Ewen's coloring?

"You don't look too bad," she said, thoughtfully.

"Got hit with a chair, that's all," said Jacob, and immediately felt himself a fool. He added, "My name is Jacob—but then he told you that. Jacob Fischbein."

She stared at him. "Not really! Jacob Fischbein? You're kidding me!"

He responded, "No. Really. Why . . . ?" Then he remembered appearances. "It's a long story," he added lamely.

"I'll have to hear it sometime," she said, and then put out one of her fragile-seeming hands. "I'm Em. Short for Emma."

"Or maybe its 'M' for membrane. Or magic," added the man. "Em is our local expert in the eleventh dimension. She's our 'brane' trust." He stretched out the word for emphasis.

Pink Em shot him a chiding glance. "This man's already got enough on his mind right now without your impossible puns," she said.

Jacob was very happy to be able to say, "Oh, but I get it. Superstrings. Rippling membranes colliding. Pre-Big-Bang stuff."

Em held on to his hand for a few moments. "You're a physicist, Mr. Fischbein?"

He wished he could say he was. He wished she hadn't called him "Mr. Fischbein." He wished she hadn't let go of his hand. "No. Not yet, anyway. I watch the Science Channel, though. You should quiz me on the Indonesian hobbit fossil."

She stared at him.

"*The Hobbit*," he repeated, staring at her.

"I was thinkin'," said the old guy, " . . . that maybe you could put us in your Kia and drive us somewhere. Like to the Lady Rose's place."

"I would," said Em, "but it's in the shop. Brakes and rotor worn through."

The old man shrugged and scuffed his feet on her old carpet. "Bummer for you. And sorry we woke you up."

"I don't mind. I'm ready for some 'twelfth dimension' study anyway. We can walk." She looked at Jacob closely and added "It'll clear your head."

He asked if he could use her phone. After some trouble they found the thing under an old Richard Feynman book. Em went off to change.

As Jacob picked up the cell phone, his friend spoke a word into his ear. The word was, "Almost sixteen. Almost." Jacob turned. "Almost sixteen what?"

"That lovely little thing is fifteen years young. She drives on a learner's permit. You want to remember that."

"Fifteen's a great . . . " Jacob had a revelation. "Oh. I see." As he tapped the number for the Thurmond residence in Redmond, Washington, Jacob felt a sudden increase in his drive to recover his own fifteen-year-old body.

There was no one at home at the Thurmond house. The office was closed, of course. He couldn't remember his doctor's cell phone number. He sat on a dusty pile of books and looked at the streetlight shining through the window shade, very dim and yellow.

"By the way, I'm Raymond," said the old guy, who was poking a cotton hankie down the length of his little flute.

"Oh." Jacob was embarrassed, because he certainly should have asked by now. He felt all sorts of awkward, sitting there, and his head was beginning to throb in the warmth of the house. He unbuttoned the pea coat and shrugged it off. "Sorry. I forgot I still had your coat."

"Keep it for now, Jacob. I'm good against the cold. You get what I was saying about Em?" Raymond looked almost fierce.

"Sure. She's a kid."

"She's a precious kid, and smarter than any two people together would have the right to be. She's also one of us."

Jacob lowered his head. He had caught on to what "one of us" meant. The "twelfth dimension" had made it certain, for him. But he had trouble connecting little Em with anything as low as a detox center. Anything as low as Jacob.

Chapter Twenty-eight

Alex Bell had a broken nose, and the doctor in the ER had said he could either have it reset (later) or spend the rest of life with his face pointing in a direction fifteen degrees off from where his feet were heading. He was in a bad mood because of this. He had also had an interaction with the Santa Barbara Police, which he had instigated in an attempt to obtain justice, but had later regretted. A man who had been in a bar fight, and who was undeniably—well, tipsy—had a hard time convincing the boys in blue that he was a wronged party. Even though he wasn't *driving* drunk, or causing a public ruckus or anything, they seemed reluctant to take his complaint about the whacked-out Chinese guy who had damaged his whole crew as well as himself. He was in a bad mood because of this, too. He was also quite seriously feeling the Vicodin they had given him, and still a little bit drunk. Just a little bit. All this put him in a bad mood.

Fernando, who had taken a shot to the groin, was moving a bit stiffly. He had accompanied Alex to the hospital, but had not asked to see a doctor. It was a bit too personal an injury for Fernando to share with a stranger. Jack walked beside the two, holding his head in his hand. They had said there was nothing they could do about the loose tooth, or the bruise on his face beside it. He, like Fernando, had mooched one of Alex's pills.

Fernando was driving, which the police would not have appreciated. It would have been just like the police to pull Nando in for a DUI while refusing to take action against the Chinese guy, who really *was* dangerous. But the three had things to do and Fernando wasn't feeling sober enough to walk right now.

He cruised down the boulevard with a drunk's cautious driving, five miles under the speed limit. He made the right turn toward The Private Dock successfully, except for cutting it a little close and hopping the curb. The bar was now closed, but none of the crew were sure they would have gone in there anyway. Ed, the owner, kept a baseball bat under the counter and no one could remember whether his chair had broken when they used it on the Chinese guy's head. Besides, they weren't looking for another drink. They were looking for the guy.

Em had been right about the cold and his head. She had also given him some aspirin. "Don't mix alcohol with Tylenol," she had said. "Don't mix alcohol with anything, really. In fact, don't mix alcohol with your body."

"Em," Raymond had said, "Don't be a pain in the butt."

They marched along, Em's legs moving faster than the men's. Jacob was filled with self-recrimination and self-pity. He scarcely noticed the beautiful California scenery and the dazzling California stars. "Who's the lady we're going to see?" he asked. "She some kind of AA honcho?"

"AA doesn't have honchos," said Em. Raymond said, "She's a weaver. And a bodhisattva. She helps people."

Jacob said, "Whatever," and was immediately aware that was an asshole remark. Before he could qualify or apologize, however, Raymond had put his lips to the little wooden flute.

Jacob caught Em's eyes and said, "Sorry I said that. But I think I need more help than what a rehab thing can give me. Maybe you'll understand, because you know about the eleven dimensions and stuff like that. The truth is . . . " and he thought how best to put it. How to tell the whole story. "The truth is I don't belong in this body."

Em stopped in place. Raymond, watching his fingering, bumped into her. "You'd make a really lousy girl!" she blurted.

Rez followed the trace as though it were a line drawn in the air above the sidewalk. The difficulty was for the others keeping up with her. The three humans trotted down the stairs to the sand in the dark, only to be brushed aside by the dog coming back up, snorting out the concentrated scent of urine.

They stopped momentarily at the locked door of the restaurant. "At least you ate well, Ewen," said Susan.

"I wish I had," Ewen answered. "Jacob's belly is growling."

"It's not the only one," answered his sister. "But at least your belly's warm. I forgot just how nice Santa Barbara was. Is."

Ewen sometimes kicked his long legs into the back of Susan's feet, and apologized. Each time he did, she giggled.

"Things aren't so funny right now," he told her. "Something's wrong. I can feel it."

"You mean something's *more* wrong than an hour ago?" Lynn, the shortest of the three, was working harder keeping up and her tone was slightly acerbic.

"Getting steadily wronger. I'm . . . he's in trouble. Been in trouble for a while, now."

"Oh crap," said Lynn. Susan said, "Shit!" Rez pulled harder.

They came to the darkened bar, where Rez sniffed intently at the crack of the door. She stood on her hind legs and leaned against the glass. Ewen put his eyes to the glass and peered. There was nothing to be seen, except a chair upended on the counter. It was missing a leg. He cleared his throat. "This could be very bad," he said quietly.

"The fucking drunk!" said Susan with more feeling. Rez emitted an almost subsonic growl. Falling back to the sidewalk, she went on, dragging the humans behind her. Ewen glanced sharply at Susan, because that was not her kind of language.

Jacob stopped to look out at the ocean, which was breaking in phosphorescent froth over a broken table of rocks. It was really neat looking, and he wished he could appreciate it, but right now he thought he might throw up again. If he did, he didn't want Em to see. He felt her small hand around his arm. At the same moment, he heard a car drive up, cross the center line and park jerkily beside them.

Raymond was fingering his little flute nervously as the redhead with the metal splint on his nose got out. The smell of alcohol was strong in the clean ocean air. Jacob took a step backwards. Em just looked blankly at the car.

"Found you, you son-of-a-bitch," said the redhead. Fernando stepped out of the car, and there was also the sound of a slamming door from the other side.

Raymond stepped forward, his hand up, palm out in front of him in the universal gesture. "Hey! Peace!" he called out.

The redhead cut the air dismissively. "Out of the way, geezer. Our fight's with this piece of shit!"

Raymond raised his other hand, holding the flute. "I'm sure there doesn't have to be a fight, brothers."

"Yeah, there fuckin' does!" Alex slammed his fist into Raymond's arm. The little flute hit the pavement, where it split along its length. "My recorder," said Raymond, mildly. He bent to pick up the fragments and Alex Bell kicked him aside. Now both Raymond and his flute were sprawled on the sidewalk.

Jacob waded in. He knew more about wrestling than punching, but this body was splendidly equipped for either and he had gone suddenly red with rage. He threw a punch at the redhead's broken nose, from which the redhead flinched away. The punch caught Alex in the cheek. It broke his cheekbone with a chicken-bone snap. He howled.

Around the front of the car came the guy he had groined in the bar. He was carrying a bottle of Bacardi in his hand that he swung at Jacob's head. Jacob ducked and grabbed the man's wrist as it went over. He pulled the bottle out of the man's hand and poked it, narrow tip first, into the man's throat.

While all this was going on, Jack, the one who had hit Jacob with a chair, was also approaching. He was somewhat more cautious than the others. He was no less drunk than they, but he was less angry, having won his first encounter. He was also not on pain pills.

Beneath his line of sight stood Em with her thin arms held out. "Stop!" she cried, but no one heard her at all. She raised her right hand into the face of Jacob's assailant. "Violence is not the solution," she declared forcefully, and he hit her, backhand.

Em's little antique glasses shattered, and the splinters stood out from her skin all around her eyes, which filled with blood. They were, unfortunately, not real corrective glasses, but part of her 'look,' like the pink hair. Her look suddenly became something from a horror movie. Her pink skin, her white windbreaker and her shirt (which was pink to match her hair) all went black in the lamplight. She sank to her knees, all around her black, black—except for the spots where the streetlight winked off her broken glasses.

The attacker stared, his hand still in the position in which he had ended his strike, looking like a tennis player without a racket.

Jacob stared, equally frozen. Everyone at the scene stared, motionless, including Raymond on the sidewalk. Then, slowly, Alex, Fernando and Jack retreated toward their car, walking backwards. Jacob put one hand out toward Em, but Raymond stooped in before him. Em collapsed into Raymond's arms. "Leave her alone, you fucking drunks!" he shouted. "You bunch of fucking drunks!" He began picking pieces of glass out from around her eyes.

Raymond picked the girl up; in his adrenaline-fueled terror she seemed to weigh nothing. He turned in a circle and then approached the car, which was just revving its engine. "Hospital!" he cried. "We've got to get her to a hospital!" Alex, Fernando, and Jack listened to him closely. They each nodded wisely, but then they piled into their car, drove off and left them on the bloody sidewalk.

"Does she have her cell in her purse?" Jacob asked, but Raymond made no answer. A large dark sedan drove by and Raymond stepped into the road in front of it, holding the girl up in his arms. An elderly man, well dressed, stepped out of the driver's side and spoke with Raymond. His wife put her hands to the sides of her elderly face in distress. The man opened the rear door of the car and Raymond crawled in, still carrying Em. Then they drove off.

Jacob stood there by himself. The street was very quiet. There were some sparkles of glass on the pavement, and a lot of black blood. To his surprise, he found he was still holding the bottle of Bacardi in his shaking hand. It was intact. It was half-full.

This seemed like a small miracle to Jacob.

Chapter Twenty-nine

IT WAS a long trail in the middle of the night, but no one doubted the nose of the dog. When she came up a planted walk to a small house in a neighborhood of no distinction she paused and sniffed the door. Then she turned around to return to the sidewalk. There she stopped for a moment, stared over her shoulder at her pack of humans and whined.

"I wish the dog could talk," said Lynn, soldiering on.

"She says there's a change in the trail. Someone new added, probably," said Susan.

"It's a bitch they added," said Ewen. "I mean a female human."

His sister gazed at him, open mouthed. "You can talk to the dog?"

"Anyone can talk to Resurrection, and she can answer," Susan said. "But only Ewen knows exactly what she's saying."

"And even in . . . that!" Lynn pointed at Jacob's lanky body and sounded as though she were commenting on Ewen's poor choice in clothes. They went on.

The trail led them back to the ocean, where the air was very brisk, but movement kept them warm. The surf crashed loudly against rocks, and there was a touch of spray in their faces. Suddenly Rez tilted her head back and emitted a howl, soft and deep as the tone of an oboe. She glanced from Ewen to the dark ocean and back again. With a great heave she tore free from Susan's grip and dragged her leash along the sidewalk and under a roadside barrier. They could hear her heavy claws scrabbling over rock.

Susan clambered after her, with Ewen close behind. Lynn, left back on the sidewalk, tried to shout over the waves. "Wait! Look! There's broken glass here. And—I think—blood." She peered over the rail and wondered about the wisdom of following them, in such darkness and over the wet crags. There were three of them out there, all crawling on all fours over the nearer rocks. Only the dog looked confident.

Then Lynn lifted her head and saw another figure outlined very slightly against the night sky. There was a glint of glass as a bottle moved back and forth and she recognized the body of her brother, balanced on a jagged peak of rock, his legs soaked with the waves. He was holding a liquor bottle in one slack hand. Lynn felt a sudden sweat grow cold on her face. She climbed over the rail.

Susan was closest to him. "Ewen? I mean Jacob?" she called. "Be careful, Jacob. Please be careful."

Eyes she loved very much turned toward her and there was someone else behind them. "Do I know you?" he said, slurring his words. As he turned on his heels to look at her he swayed and one foot slipped. He recovered his balance and stared owlishly. "I don't think I do know you. Do I?"

"I'm Susan, and this is Rez," shouted Susan over the noise of the sea. She tried to sound calm. Calm and confident. The dog beside her was grappling the rock's wet surface with her toes spread in a very feline way. She looked at Ewen's body and thumped her tail once, uncertainly.

"Nice dog," said Jacob, offhand. "I always liked shepherds." He swayed again.

"Please, Jacob. Please come off that rock," Susan pleaded. Behind her, Ewen clung to his own rock and thought it best to be invisible.

"No," said Jacob, thoughtfully, swirling the little that was left inside his bottle. "No. I've done enough damage already."

"That's why you should come in." Susan heard herself pleading, and knew that was not the way. Not what a hostage negotiator would say. And what else was she, but a hostage negotiator?

Jacob lifted his eyes past the rocks to the sidewalk, where there was some lamplight. "There's my doctor," he said conversationally. He glanced closely at Susan. "You a doctor, too? That why you're here?"

"I . . . I'm a veterinarian."

He raised his eyebrows. "That's mush . . . much better. I always like veter'narians . . . I'm going to drown myself, you know," he added to this. "I've done enough damage."

Ewen stood upright. "No, Jacob. You're not going to drown yourself. You're going to drown *me*!"

Jacob looked canny. "I knew you were there, Doc's Bro! Had to be. Where the ol' Doc is, an' all . . . And I'm not going to drown you because you're there and I'm here. So there. Here, I mean." He laughed unevenly.

Ewen slid around Susan and placed his foot against an outcrop just above the waterline. He looked up at himself, standing high above him. "Jacob. This isn't fair."

He couldn't see his own face. It was just an oval outline against the stars. "Yes it is," it said. "Just look at it this way: that bod you're wearing is almos' twenty years younger than your own. Longer life span. Also . . . " and he pointed out with his bottle, "it's *taller*. Hah!"

Now Ewen could see a shade of expression on the face that should have been his. It was full of self-disgust. "Let me tell ya why I'm going to drown myself. Know what I did tonight?"

Ewen nodded. "Yeah. Got drunk. Got into a bar fight. We saw the chair. But you seem to have come out of it alright."

"Killed someone, is what I did."

Susan closed her eyes and groaned. Ewen said nothing.

"I killed a beautiful girl. A physist. Physicist."

"How'd you do that?" asked Susan in horror, knowing she should not even speak.

"She got into my bar fight, is how. I mean the guys I hit came after us and got us right back there on the street. And Em tried to stop the fight and got in between us and the guy slammed her right across the face and she went down, dead."

Simultaneously Susan and Ewen spoke. She said, "Then *you* didn't do it." He said, "Are you sure she's dead?"

Jacob considered. "Pretty sure. She's gotta be blind, at least. They smashed her glasses right into her eyes. Raymond took her off to the hospital in some guy's car."

"That sounds like there's really hope," said Susan.

"Bullshit."

Ewen was cold and wet and desperate. "Jacob," he called. "Lift up your shirt."

"Wha?"

"I said lift up your shirt. You've got a hand free. Just do that one thing."

Jacob looked down, remembered what was in his other hand, and started to raise the bottle to his mouth. Then he shook his head and released the thing. The Bacardi bottle hit the rock, still did not break, and bobbed away on a wave. "Now I've got two hands," he said, and he lifted the Hawaiian shirt up and looked at his own (borrowed) chest. "Jeez Louise," he said, looking at the puckered central scar. "What the hell happened to you? Oh, I remember. You got shot. Looks like you ought to be dead already."

Ewen nodded. "You're right. I ought to be. I got shot in that heart. I think it was the week I worked with you last, before you stopped seeing Lynn. So—please—think for a minute. That body got shot in the heart and it's still alive. Think how much that body wants to live!" He sighed and sobbed and his teenager's voice broke. "Let me have it back, Jacob. It's mine. You can have your younger, taller body and do whatever you want to with it. The whole rest of your life can be yours."

Jacob shook an admonishing finger at Ewen. "Not true. You're lying to me, Doc's Bro. We switch back and I'm going to get locked up again, for even longer this time. Maybe forever! I know that much about the law!"

"They can't keep you locked up forever when all you want to do is die, Jacob. That can be over right away."

"Hell with that. They can make damn sure you don't kill yourself. No shoelaces. Belts. The lights left on all night! Don't you watch TV shows?"

Ewen sank lower on his slippery little foothold and shook his dripping head. "The truth is, Jacob, no one can keep you alive if you want to die. That's the honest truth. Not for long. Even people who want to live can't keep doing it forever. And if you die in that body you'll make unhappy not only everyone who cares about you, but everyone who cares about me, too." Ewen slipped and caught himself again. Susan let out a gasp. Lynn clung to the black face of a rock.

Ewen continued. "Please. I'm wet and shivering and scared and I'm begging you. Come in, Jacob."

Jacob looked into his own face and saw the terror. Slowly, with much help and with many terrifying slips, he came in.

The women stared at Ewen's face. Ewen's face as they had never known it, muddy, slack, and very red-eyed. They both shook their heads. "You look like you did in the hospital," said Lynn, glancing from

Jacob to Ewen and back again. "When we didn't know whether . . . "
Susan stroked his wet and salty hair and said nothing. The dog sniffed,
stared and growled low to herself.

Ewen himself put his hands to the sides of Jacob's—of his own—
head. Jacob only stood there, feet braced, looking at the sidewalk.
Looking at splinters of glass. "Please sit down," said Ewen, and pulled
the other with him. They sat in the drying blood.

He held his hand to the other's forehead, but it wasn't working.
Nothing happened except he felt the cold sweat of his own skin.

Perhaps Jacob's body was wrong for the task because of the damage
he had done to it. Perhaps the difference was in the years of training
Ewen's body had undergone, which had made this strange trick
possible to begin with. Perhaps the problem was a genetic difference.
It could be one of any number of things, but Ewen sat there using
Jacob's hands and it wasn't working. He felt a panic sweat begin on his
face. "Put your hands on my head," he whispered to Jacob, his voice
shaking, and Jacob did.

He felt a touch, dark and fleeting, and Ewen realized that Jacob was
only a hairsbreadth from passing out. He might easily have passed out
on that rock in another few seconds. Ewen threw himself into that
deadened mind with desperation and found once again the grass by
the runnel of water.

Here it was daylight, for it was Ewen's Santa Barbara, which never
changed nor grew older. He wasted no time talking to the man in the
Hawaiian shirt but flipped him as he had been flipped before. He had
a moment to think *How is it I get thrown twice and Jacob not at all?*
When it was done, he was Ewen again, sitting in the cold and dark,
thoroughly soaked and thoroughly drunk. He staggered to his feet,
leaned over the beach barrier and began throwing up.

Chapter Thirty

EWEN HAD never been drunk before and he did not like the sensations a bit. In spite of it all he was happy. He was a happy drunk, trying to walk down the Santa Barbara street at night without passing out, two women and a kid propping him up.

"You probably won't remember any of this tomorrow," said Jacob, striding along with his lanky body hunched against the cold and his gangly hands in his pockets. He walked so fast Lynn was holding on to his belt loops to keep up.

"Who won't? You or Ewen?" asked Susan bitterly.

Jacob managed a grin. "I think it's going to be him," he said. "I feel fine. Except I'm hungry."

Hearing this, Ewen bent over and tried to heave again, almost overbalancing them all.

Rez growled at Jacob decisively, pleased to have the pack mate and the stranger sorted out properly once again. "Your dog doesn't like me," he mentioned to Susan.

"*I* don't like you," said Susan.

Jacob had temporarily forgotten that he was essentially worthless and had been planning to kill himself, but Susan's words brought it all back to him. He stopped so suddenly his doctor ploughed into his back. "That's right," he said with force. "You shouldn't. *I* don't like myself."

They were on their way to the closest hospital, which Lynn hoped was still where it had been when she left Santa Barbara and residency, years before. They were going there to see how Em was. With only a first name, they had been able to get no information by cell phone. They would have been in a cab, if there had been cabs roaming the early morning streets, and if any that had come along would have been willing to accept four people and a huge dog.

As it happened, the hospital had not moved and, as they saw its lights shining over the buildings that surrounded it, their weary pace picked up. "Ewen, we should have you seen to, also," she said, taking her brother's arm. "You could use something for your stomach, at least."

"Don't do it!" Jacob warned in a voice of authority. "He'll just wind up locked up somewhere. Besides. If Em is . . . still alive . . . she won't want to see him."

"I thought you said she was certainly blind now," Susan said tartly. She honestly did not like Jacob and was having a hard time concealing the fact.

"Well, Raymond wouldn't want to see me. I mean, him."

It was very quiet outside the ER doors. Susan stayed outside with Rez, but the rest of them walked into the lobby. Sudden light and warmth almost put Ewen out on his feet. He deposited himself on a chair by the door to the examination rooms, letting Lynn and Jacob go ahead to find information. A voice he recognized floated out of the swinging door. He stood up, surprised.

"Wait!" he said to no one in particular. "That sounds like . . . " He stood, swayed once, and strode through that door.

"Master Wing!" he called out. "Master Wing? Rose?"

"Here," came the quiet answer.

An orderly and a nurse's aid followed him, along with the effluvia of Bacardi and bile on his breath. Ewen found Master Rose Wing standing by the bedside of a small person he did not know. Her face was wrapped in bandages, but her large dark eyes peeped through. She was saying, "Nine months clean and sober and here I am, flat on my back and high as a kite on morphine."

"I think it's Demerol," replied a man of middle age, wearing a pea coat and leaning against the wall. He looked up to see Ewen standing there, and his eyes narrowed for a moment. Then he sighed. "I'm sorry I just left you back there, Jacob. But you've gotta know I am angry."

Ewen stared at him. "Hello, Ewen," said Rose Wing. "I had this wild idea it was you they were talking about. Though why 'Jacob' I can't understand."

The hospital personnel had caught up with Ewen, who disengaged himself from them without knowing he was doing it. "I am totally at a loss, Master Wing," he said. It came out "atta losh."

Jacob came up beside him, struggling with the orderly less successfully. "It wasn't him," Jacob declared. "It was me." He barged forward and hung over the girl's bed, staring down. "Em. I'm sorry. I am so sorry for everything. But I'm Jacob. Like I said before, that body wasn't really mine."

Em blinked through her bandages. She began to giggle. "I think I believe you. You look much more like Jacob Fishbone. Fischbein!" She giggled again. "Don't worry. I'm not mad at you, Jacob. It wasn't you who hit me."

Raymond listened to this, looked blank, and then muttered. "On vacation. Christ on a crutch! *That's* being on vacation?"

"There are too many people in this room," announced a nurse.

Outside in the waiting room there were only a few weary people, one of whom was Alex Bell. His face was now misshapen on one side, and his nose protector sat askew. Jacob glared at him and got only a generic look of resentment in return. He stalked over to the admissions desk and announced to the attendee, "That man there was with that guy who put that girl in the hospital."

The attendee wasn't sure what to make of Jacob's series of "that's," but she pressed a button and the single cop in the lobby hustled over. Seeing this, Alex rethought his desire for more medical attention and started for the door, but he did not make it. As he felt the restraining hand on his shoulder, Alex turned, only to see the face of Ewen holding him there. Alex didn't notice the odor of alcohol on Ewen's breath because he had an equal fog surrounding his own. He cringed at the touch.

Ewen marveled at this reaction, as a Santa Barbara police officer came up and took his place by Alex. "Do I know you?" asked Ewen Young, with woozy curiosity. Alex only showed his teeth.

Raymond came in to defuse the situation. "Officer, I think that if you find this man's car, you may find my little friend's assailant still in it. Passed out, perhaps. Miss Woolcott can probably identify him here and now."

Alex turned left and right, realizing his decision to come here once again had been a bad one. "But this guy . . . " He pointed at Ewen. "But this guy . . . "

"Do I know you?" Ewen asked again, with such curiosity and transparent innocence that Alex gave up the fight. He was showing the cop his identification when the troop walked out into the early morning.

"Tell me about this," said Rose Wing. "I missed most of a night's sleep for these shenanigans. I should be rewarded with some entertainment."

Ewen began. "I can't tell you much, Master Wing. Rose. I spent most of the afternoon in Redmond and most of the night riding in a car and then in a private plane, coming back."

"Anyone else I would doubt," said Rose Wing. She threw on a red silk shawl embroidered with flowers, which she wore after the style of Gandhi. It looked good on her. "Especially if they were as drunk as you are right now."

"What'd you call her?" asked Raymond, glancing brightly between the two. "What'd you call the Lady Rose?"

"Master Wing," said Ewen. "Do you know her, too?"

"Wow. Things are unfolding into a Calabi-Yau shape, as Em would say."

Ewen peered owlishly at Raymond. "Whatever that means," he said.

Jacob intervened. "Ewen isn't drunk ma'am . . . uh, Master Wing Lady. At least he didn't do the drinking. I did. I made all the trouble." He lowered his eyes, remembering the quantity and quality of his sins. " 'Fact, I really screwed the pooch," he said in a voice he thought no one else would hear.

Lynn spoke up. "Rose, Ewen helps me sometimes with my patients. In . . . untraditional ways."

"Like doing their drinking for them?" the older woman asked dryly, but added, "No, that was a joke. I don't really think that." She shrugged. "If the mind can depart from the body and then come back, why can't it depart and go into another body? Once we believe Ewen is as strange as he seems to be, the rest is easy."

"I didn't do it on purpose," said Jacob, as Ewen was explaining. "It was just supposed to be a trade. An even trade."

"Supposed to be a trade?" Ewen echoed him softly. For a moment, he seemed very dangerous in his drunkenness. Jacob shrank back.

Susan came up to them, with Rez at her side. Susan seemed the more tired of the two. Rez larked and gamboled in front of Master Rose Wing—The Lady Rose. They separated into groups. Jacob, Susan, and Rez went to Rose's Jetta, while Ewen and Lynn caught a cab. Raymond returned to Em.

Jacob told the whole story in a rush to Rose Wing, not skipping over the parts where he had done badly. "Quite a twenty-four hours, Jake," she said. He did not correct her over the name. "But let it stop there. The night after a drunk is no time for an entire fifth step, and the two of us are strangers to you. Sorry—three of us." She glanced over at the dog. "And I don't think you have to 'never forgive yourself' about what happened to Emma. She doesn't seem to hold it against you. In fact, she *had* said she was sorry Jacob was such an old guy."

"She *did?*"

"Yes. But she was under the influence of narcotics when she said it. And you might want to make some amends to Ewen Young."

"Better believe it!" muttered Susan. Rez growled like an engine.

"How? I mean how can I possibly . . . "

"You have all your life for that," said Rose. "A life he saved—remember? And you don't still want to die, do you?"

Almost sullenly, Jacob answered, "No."

"Now *there's* a stubborn alcoholic talking," said Rose, adding to Susan "I'm sorry if this conversation is just Greek to you, Dr. Sundown."

"Oh, I'm fluent in Greek," she answered.

In the cab, Lynn saw that her brother was deeply asleep, his head against the door window, so it was to the driver that she said, "Look! The sun is coming up."

The Puget Sound high summer hit between one day and the next: a short spell of dry and hot weather. Rez left clots of brown hair around the house, and in the yard the bamboo had dropped its brown sheathing.

Jacob Fischbein's father received a story that was plausible and completely false, except for the bits concerning conditions at the

Snohomish Hospital Detox Unit. He was angry, but not only with his son.

Jacob began to volunteer at Sangye Menla hospice and never spoke again about committing suicide.

Rose Wing did like the students at the little school. Ryan Watanabe, in turn, was enthralled by Master Wing, from her weapons style to the way she wore her self-woven and embroidered shawl. He called her "Sifa."

PART IV: Autumn Returns with the Tale of Lynn and Puppies

Chapter Thirty

EWEN WAS DOING "Northern Dragon" in his back yard when Susan came up the driveway with Rez trotting beside her.

As a child, Ewen had always thought of the form called "Northern Dragon" as being furry like a wooly mammoth, or like the creature in *The Neverending Story*, so he was smiling a little as he moved from movement to movement. Then he saw Susan. He saw Susan's face. He stopped in place, his heart beating hard in his chest.

"We need you," she said. "We've been called in and we—I—would really like you to come along this time. Because of the way you can listen to Rez."

Ewen had accompanied them at their work before. It was interesting, and, once, he had been of some help. But he had never seen his sweetheart's face this taut—this somber—because of Rez's recovery work. Not even when they found the body of her uncle frozen beneath the snow. Her face was a terrible signal. It made Ewen's ears ring and his nose fill with the smell of the autumn's first cold rains on the grass. He didn't want this—whatever it was. He had a cowardly feeling that if he could stay in this still moment he could avoid some unbearable future.

"Called into what?" he heard himself ask. "Called by whom?"

Susan stepped the rest of the way to him, the wolf dog at her side moving with military precision. Rez, he saw, was as serious as his mistress. "You haven't been listening to the news? You really don't know?" He shook his head slowly. "Well, you at least heard the sirens last night, didn't you?"

"I didn't get home till late." His mouth was so dry he could hardly talk. *How did a mouth dry out so quickly, between one moment and the next?* "Classes."

"It was just up Novelty Hill Road. They found the remains of a child. She had been gnawed. Eaten."

Ewen opened his mouth to say something—perhaps, "Oh my God"—but nothing came out. He found that his arms were still outswept in the air from Northern Dragon, and he put them carefully down.

"There's reason to believe there may be more," she said hesitantly.

"More remains? More people's remains, you mean? Then it's not . . ."

"Not an attack by a bear. Or coyotes. No. That's why they want Rez. That's why I want you . . . And I'm so sorry to do this to you," she concluded, and she just stood there.

Ewen lived just off 236th Avenue NE. It was only a few miles to Novelty Hill. Hardly any distance. For a moment his self-pride rose up and asked him how this had happened without Ewen Young knowing about it. How had Ewen Young—protector of humanity, "Raven, He-Who-Goes-Between-Worlds"—failed so badly. In his own neighborhood, goddammit. Then that self-pride was blown away by the late October wind, which was wet and cold. Ewen, too, was suddenly wet and cold.

"Poor child!" he said. "Poor Redmond. Poor . . . everybody!"

"Yes," said Susan. "Poor everybody." Resurrection scuttled forward, still sitting, and licked his cold hand.

He had a moment when wild excuses rushed into his mind and almost out of his mouth. He could not go with Susan because his sister was expecting him to go over to her office and bench test her new BrainMaster biofeedback trainer with gamma-wave sensitivity. This activity seemed of cosmic importance. He was also planning on doing some layering on an oil he had begun, and after all, wasn't he a professional painter? Didn't that count? Wasn't that the most important thing, after all? Then the moment of his excuses passed and Ewen followed Susan back down the driveway.

In front of his house Ewen glanced over to find Mr. Kelly on his own lawn, both arms wrapped around his own burly body. Mr. Kelly looked at Ewen with his eyes fixed and opened too wide. "You heard? Isn't this somethin'?" he asked Ewen. His voice was gravelly. "Isn't this really somethin'? And me with three kids!" Ewen said nothing. The wind was blowing into his ears.

Susan had parked her battered old Suburban in front of the house. She opened the door for Rez and the dog followed her sharp graying muzzle onto the floor behind the seats. Ewen, too, felt gray as he slid into the shotgun seat. For once he moved without grace. Susan pulled the big vehicle out onto 236th and headed for Novelty Hill Road.

He expected her to say more, but when the silence went on for more than a mile, he asked Susan exactly what she wanted him to do.

"Just the usual. Follow after me and tell me what Rez shows you. In her mind."

The weather was cruelly beautiful for such an errand. The sunlight shone pale and the color of peridot gems, first under the heavy forest and then through the sweet gardening of Redmond Ridge housing complex, where one side street of new houses followed another, all huddled against the forest around them and all looking the same. When they reached Novelty Hill Road itself, the country opened out and the road went on in pleasant wide sweeps. On the far side of a large pond of aging water lilies there was a graveled drive where people stood in small groups. They were hugging themselves as Kelly had done. A policeman in uniform was stationed at the foot of the drive. Susan pulled over and began to take out her wallet, but the officer saw Rez in the back and waved them on.

"My dog's got more of a reputation than most cops," Susan murmured, and they bumped their way onto the drive.

Ewen did not reply to this. He was shaking his head slowly and forcefully, left and right. "No. No, Susan. This can't be right. This is the back way in to Sangye Menla. Medicine Buddha!"

"Theo's hospice? Oh Christ!" The Suburban climbed over the badly rutted and lumpy drive and through second-growth trees with heavy undergrowth. "Your poor family! Death can't seem to leave you alone!"

"I'm not sure Theo would want it to," said Ewen with some bitterness. He noticed that Rez had her nostrils out the left rear window, not blowing goofily, like that of the average dog, but daintily sampling. With only the slightest effort, he found his mind pulled to that of the dog. She was becoming taut—focused. *There's work here* was her message.

Ewen was glad to let her be the boss.

They pulled out into a field torn with old ruts from heavy machinery and threatened by a few years' encroaching briars. Dead thistles emitted a white cloud as he opened the door into them. To his right was a wall of poplars that had been intended to screen this area from the gardens behind Sangye Menla. Ewen himself, a few years ago, had helped hack some of these paths from the grounds into the untouched woods. Other people, either patients long gone or staff, had kept a half-hearted effort toward maintaining them. There were police standing here and there, still as garden gnomes. One young officer, looking like a statue of St. Francis, was quietly sneaking peanuts to a squirrel.

Rez leaped out from behind him, exploding a cloud of the thistles. She landed with a small *umph*, but did not falter. She darted to Susan Sundown's side. A detective—one whom Ewen did not recognize—walked carefully over the bad ground to her and said something to Susan, pointing at Ewen. "He's with the dog," she replied.

This struck Ewen as funny. *He's with the dog.* But the credentials seemed sufficient to the detective, a stocky, young African-American. Ewen obediently followed Rez, whom Susan sent out with the command, "Quarter!"

Ewen knew Resurrection did not need the command; she knew her work from top to bottom. The command had been issued to communicate authority to the surrounding police officers. Ewen looked over beyond the poplars and saw Dr. Willy, along with a patient sitting in a chair. This young man looked weary, and was wearing a breathing mask attached to an oxygen cylinder. Dr. Willy looked as intent as always: more houndlike than Rez. They met eyes for an instant, and Dr. Willy gave Ewen one slow, curious nod.

Rez, meanwhile, had made a desultory sweep of the ground and then looked up at her owner, asking very clearly whether she had to go on pretending not to know all the things she did know—whether she had to go step by baby-training step. Susan Sundown glanced down at the dog and flipped her hand up in a "go ahead" gesture. The dog echoed that gesture with her head. She trotted off to show the nose-blind humans what was up.

Ewen saw, heard, and smelled what the dog sensed. Unlike the dog, he was afraid of the knowledge. He followed after Resurrection like an acolyte. He stopped in place when she stopped, knowing the exact spot in the thistles to which they were heading. When the dog sat down formally, put her head up and began her slow song he closed his eyes and let a trace of moisture leak down his face. Perhaps he was howling, too, inside.

"What's she doing?" asked the detective, looking both alarmed and suspicious, and pointing at the moaning dog.

Ewen stared at him as though the man were speaking a foreign language. "She's saying there's someone dead here," he explained very carefully to the detective.

Susan came up beside them. "She's saying *dig*, dammit! Could she be more clear?"

The man stepped back from her anger. "Yeah, sure. But I never heard of a dog that responded to a scent by howling like some wolf!" he added, her emotion waking his own.

Ewen, feeling only half-human himself, spoke very slowly. "She doesn't like it when people die. Especially puppies. Children, I mean. She doesn't like it."

Susan took a stick out of her large handbag. The end was painted red. She stabbed it into the earth in front of where Rez was sitting. "Quarter," she commanded the dog again, more quietly this time.

"This ground hasn't been dug up," said the detective, kicking at it lightly. "Look at all the stuff growing on it." Susan Sundown growled "city boy" under her breath. Resurrection, for once, wasn't influenced by her owner's mood. She calmly stood up, walked forty feet and sat down again. After a moment she howled again. Ewen followed her, immersed in the same bad dream.

Right in front of his feet he sensed all the ingredients of a human child, and through Resurrection's very strange mind these ingredients were assembled for him to understand.

There was a girl here, arms stuffed beside her head, one leg over the other, hips twisted in the carelessness of death. She had been wearing cotton, though no colors came through the dog's mind to his. It had been wrapped into a ball and buried on top of her. She was older than the first one that had been found, and more recently put under ground. Her body's rot was a history of great complexity, involving many plants and animals. He saw it all behind his closed eyes.

Once her skull's emptiness had been occupied by a family of field rats, but they left at the end of summer. Ants had written a neat and careful smell map of the inside of her braincase, making highways through the crushed hole in the back of the skull, and convolvulus wrapped roots around her throat, feeding on flesh gone to soil. Ewen could see the rags of the plant's leaves, which had once borne white flowers, and he heard the red-tipped stake being driven in amongst them. Perhaps he got all this from the dog, or perhaps it was the combination of Ewen the painter and Rez the nose-artist that completed the picture. "Schoolgirl," he whispered into Susan's ear. "She's just a schoolgirl. Maybe dead a year."

Susan didn't look well. In the same hushed tones she asked, "Are there more?"

"The first one was an older girl. Longer under the ground. I think she was the one who lost her head—her skull . . . I think there'll be another," he said, but he let his eyes drop from Susan's face. "But not for me. I'm through." Ewen was too ashamed to look at her as he said. "I can't go on with Rez today. This last one . . . "

She put her hand softly on his arm. "Oh, no, Ewen. Don't apologize. I can't imagine what you're seeing."

He shrugged. "It's not what I'm seeing. It's what Rez is feeling. But she's gutsier than I am." He turned and left the crime scene, heading toward Sangye Menla, feeling ashamed. He heard them go on about their work behind him as he left. He had a fairly clear idea where Rez would stop next, but he closed his mind to it.

Ewen sat himself down on the ground between Dr. Willy and the patient. "Do those sticks mean bodies?" asked the young man with the facemask. Ewen said nothing; he was trying to rid himself of all traces of his link with Resurrection.

Dr. Willy, hawk-like, gazed out between the poplars at the ongoing work and nodded. "Learning to handle tracking dogs, Ewen?" he asked. Dr. Willy spoke very fast. He was from New York. "Or just keeping your girlfriend company?"

Ewen made a noncommittal sound.

"Greg, here, is the one who found the skull. The first one, I guess. Rolled right down onto the grass yesterday evening. Had a big hole in the back of it, but . . . " Dr. Willy flopped his arms helplessly. "I'm not an M.E. Could be a coyote's gnawing. Or could be a hammer."

"Yesterday evening's only when I found it," the young man said. "It could have been there a while. It's not great weather for hanging out.

And I didn't even notice if there was a hole." His voice was muffled. "I thought maybe I'd discovered where this place's graduates all go."

Dr. Willy smiled, being very used to the gallows humor of the people who came and went at Sangye Menla. Ewen just stared at the grass. Behind his eyes went a slideshow of images: the brat, the runaway, the boy with two teeth missing seen on a milk carton, never noticed by him before. He no longer had any idea whether he was getting signals from the dog or making this all up out of his own imagination. "How many stakes now?" he asked Dr. Willy.

"I see three," said the storklike doctor, leaning on a poplar trunk and hopping, tiptoe. "No, behind the blackberries that looks like . . . I take it back. There's still only three. And now they've moved into the woods." He sounded oddly like a sports announcer.

"They won't find any in the woods," Ewen told them brusquely, and then, feeling their stares, added, "That place is all roots. Douglas firs and hemlock. I . . . remember trying to cut a way into it. For the pathways."

"That's right," said Dr. Willy. "You built the walkways originally; didn't you? That was kind of you, Picasso. I remember a lot of manual labor was involved."

Ewen craned his neck around and saw the stakes himself. He knew they were where they belonged and that each of them marked a human being to be dug up. He knew, along with the dog, that their job was finished.

"Goddamn," Ewen said to Dr. Willy, who was an old friend. "For all these months, I knew her name was Resurrection. I knew why that was her name, too. I had every reason to know, but it never hit me until now."

"A somber job," said Dr. Willy.

"You bet," said the man in the mask, as though the subject of death was completely unrelated to him. "Wow."

"She's really something; that dog is," said Dr. Willy. Ewen also leaned against a poplar. It swayed with his weight. Dr. Willy was still gazing intently through the high hedge. "She just threw up, I think," he said. Both the young man and Ewen stared at him. "The handler, I mean. Not the dog."

Ewen straightened. "Susan threw up?"

"If that's the dog handler's name. I can't say I blame her," he added. The man in the mask agreed with him, nodding. The plastic mask bobbed.

Ewen crossed the broken ground in a series of almost balletic leaps, still landing—as he had been schooled—only in his own or in Susan's footsteps. When he reached her she looked wan and very embarrassed. "See. You're not the only one who had too much of this, today." He took her arm and gave her his pocket-pack of Kleenex.

"The boy scout," she said, grinning a little tightly. "Always prepared." Rez whined at Susan's side and stroked her leg awkwardly with the side of her heavy-clawed paw. "It's okay, babe," Susan said, either to Rez or to Ewen. "I should be used to this. It's nothing."

A few last flies were buzzing in the autumn air. She flapped them away. "We're done here, anyway. Now they dig."

The short detective was waiting at the edge of the briar jungle. He glanced askance at Rez, who growled back half-heartedly. "Have to tell ya," he said to Susan. "I think your dog's full of shit. Or maybe she found a little bit of bone here and there and each time she sits you think you've got a new body. You'd have us convinced there's a new Gary Ridgeway running around Redmond, when she's probably smelling rabbits."

"City boy," said Susan, this time not under her breath.

From behind them came a very deep voice which said, "Or maybe there is a new Gary Ridgeway running around Redmond." Detective Rick Petersen turned to Susan. He looked at her wan face but said nothing about it. "You say she made a clear signal for each of those three stakes?"

"Clear," said Susan to Petersen. The tall detective slid his glance over to Ewen. "You working with Rez on this, Mr. Young?"

Ewen felt a rush of gratitude toward Petersen, just for being there. With the team of Petersen and Ryde at the crime scene, things would begin to make sense. Even if they did not, it would no longer be Ewen's problem. Nor Susan's. But where was Ryde?

He was standing beside the black detective, ignoring the man's very indignant expression. Ryde came closer, peering into Susan's face. "You don't look like you feel so good, Dr. Sundown," he said, stepping forward. She mumbled something and shrugged.

Very clearly the black detective said, "This is *my* case, Brigham Young."

It took a few moments for Ewen to figure out the insult contained in that remark. Rez needed no such time. She showed every one of her teeth. She licked them. Petersen lifted his head and laughed out loud. "In your *dreams* it is, Cromwell," he laughed.

Ewen took Susan by the hand and led her away from the broken ground, the briars and all the various kinds of nastiness.

As they returned to the Suburban, Ewen noticed Rez favoring the one leg again. "Did she sprain something?" he asked Susan. His own connection with her had given him no information about this; the dog had been too intent on her work. Susan answered, "No. It's just arthritis. She's getting old."

Without thinking he replied "Old? How can she be old? She wasn't old before!"

He rubbed his hand over his eyes and sighed at his own idiot remark. Then they both laughed, Susan rather ruefully. "Things change, don't they?" As she started the car, Susan and Ewen turned to each other and said, in complete unison, "I'm really sorry about this." She broke the resultant silence first. "I mean I'm sorry I got you involved. I can guess what she showed you."

"And I meant I'm sorry you had to be the one to do it in the first place, Susan. I'm sorry it made you sick."

She smiled wanly. "It seems to have made even ol' Rez miserable. She hates dead . . . dead . . . "

"Puppies?"

"Yeah." They nosed back onto Novelty Hill Road again, past the onlookers, who were still standing in small groups, still holding themselves by the elbows as though they might otherwise fall apart. "Rez was spayed late, after reaching puberty. I didn't get her until then, and I should have spayed her immediately, because of the wolf genes. Because she was so talented I waited and made excuses. And because . . . Well, I did it at last. Couldn't breed that temperament. But I think she always missed puppies. The only humans she really likes, as a group, are little kids." Susan was clearly upset, saying all this. Despite the cold, her face was sweaty.

Ewen leaned over the seatback, trying to think what to say that would make everything right. Something that would show how he appreciated Rez as she was, and assure Susan she had done everything perfectly. He couldn't come up with anything as fluent as he wanted, and found himself just roughing up the top of the big dog's head. "I'm sure ol' Rez has better sense than to miss having a pup! Puppies are worse than kids, and look at kids! Yeah, big girl!" He laughed, half-forcedly. "Little tail-pullers. Eye pokers." Rez sighed and stretched out on the long cargo hold of the Suburban. Ewen did not want to explore her mind any more, so he just reached further and continued stroking her head.

"Kids aren't so bad," Susan muttered.

Ewen didn't rise to this bait, because his mind was leaning back toward the terrible field behind them and he was trying to compose his field report to Susan, the official handler.

"And as for puppies," she went on, "well, there's a puppy coming in the near future. Coming to my little pack, if I want to keep working search and recovery. Rez is eleven."

Ewen was only half-attentive. He gave Rez another playful tweak. "This pack won't need another tracker for years, yet. Not while Super Dog here is still breathing!" He put his face close to hers and whispered, "Puppies! Yuck!"

Then he took a breath to clear his mind and got down to the business at hand. He began to recite, counting on his fingers: "Here's what we got, back there. One teenage girl, not yet a skeleton. One toddler, all bones. A boy, younger than the teenage girl, I think. But that's when I gave up. On the third. My attention started to fail me. But we had Rez, and she didn't give up."

"No. She never does. And she's sure there's nothing else under the trees." She waited a bit and then added, "She *is* sure, isn't she? I mean, if you know . . ."

"There's no one under the trees," said Ewen. "It's just the three. And now the guys are there. Petersen and Ryde. Now it's up to them." Less forcefully he added, "Now we can let it go, Susan. Now we can go back to being just us." Ewen leaned back in his seat and tried to remember what he'd been doing earlier today. Northern Dragon. That's what it had been. He almost smiled.

"Now *you* can let it go," whispered Susan Sundown to herself, and she drove him home.

Chapter Thirty-one

LYNN YOUNG-THURMOND KNEW her brother was having a bad afternoon. She knew it as clearly as she would have known she had an itch between her shoulder blades. But she no longer reacted strongly to such feelings leaking from her brother, for Ewen Young led an eventful life and she had her own.

The Young twins were thirty-three. *Thirty-three, goddammit. Hard to believe.* He could take care of himself. She was a bit surprised when he did show up to help her with her coherence trials. The reason he was late, however, did more than surprise her. She was overwhelmed.

"Bodies? Children's bodies, at Sangye Menla?"

"No one told you?" Ewen realized that he had blurted the whole thing out—more brusquely than the way Susan had told him.

Lynn sat on the edge of her desk. She had to scoot her hips up with her hands to reach this high. "Who would? I haven't touched the TV. Theo's with the Dalai Lama . . . I mean not personally, but at the Mind and Life Conference. Who's at the hospice now? Are they all upset? Oh, dear! How many bodies . . . ?"

"Dr. Willy," he said, to her first question. "And no: I don't think the patients are . . . No. The guy who found them was more or less just curious.

"And three. Rez found three."

We found three.

"Don't start worrying about Teddy," he added, seeing her eyes flash to the picture cube on the desk. "You know he's safe at school."

"At soccer practice," she said distantly. "It's four o'clock. School's out. I should go and pick him up now." She slid down to her feet, her high heels clicking sharply on the floor. "I should go pick him up now," she repeated robotically.

Ewen walked behind her to the door. "You know this doesn't have anything to do with Teddy. Teddy's fine. If you drive the Toyota screeching up to the field you'll just scare him . . . "

She gave a small snort. "I'm not going to 'screech.' But I'm alone here with him and Theo's all the way over in the other Washington talking with bigwigs and I do have to go pick up Teddy. It's time. It's time." Her voice rattled and her face was tight.

Ewen held the door. He plucked the car keys from her shivering hand. "You're not alone, Lynn. I'm here. And I'm going to stay with you and Teddy for a little while. If I'm not enough to make you feel secure, we can borrow Rez." He felt a momentary inner wince at the sudden image of Resurrection that flooded over him, a superhuman wolf-dog and monster killer howling over old dead puppies she never had. Limping into the car. But still she was Rez, and she was a member of his own little pack. The protectiveness he felt astonished him, considering he had never known a dog before.

It was all family.

"Besides," he continued to Lynn, "the team of Petersen and Ryde are on the case. You know that means all is well."

Lynn stood on the sidewalk beside her little Toyota and looked at the keys in her brother's hand. "Maybe you should drive me," she said, and tears welled down her golden-ivory cheeks.

"So much death," Lynn said, her breath shuddering, leaning against the car window. "I don't know when I signed on for so much death."

Ewen blinked at this but said nothing. He had never heard a word of criticism from his sister concerning Theo's time-consuming hospice work, or his bardo studies. He wasn't even sure Lynn was complaining about those things now, though Ewen thought she had every reason to. Diplomatically he said, "You could probably use a vacation, Sis. And I don't mean a seminar with the Dalai Lama. Something like Club Med."

She scratched her head. Dark brown hair fell over her eyes. "That kind of fun takes a lot of preparation, Ewen. When you've got a practice. A family."

"Leave Teddy with me," he said, knowing she would never do it, and hoping only to distract her. "We can go up the mountains to see Susan. He can learn how to ride a mustang. Or stick five gallons of oil down a mustang's nose. Or hotwire a Mustang. She can do all three."

"Hotwire? You mean she can really . . . that she really has . . . "

His sister was recovering already. Good. "Oh yeah," said Ewen complacently. "Susan's my *b-a-a-a-d* girl! She used to be hell on wheels."

Teddy was, of course, just fine and very muddy from what soccer practice means to a little kid. He was too young to be embarrassed by his mother's extravagant public hug. Ewen drove them back home and closed himself into the downstairs bathroom to call Susan on his cell phone. She answered immediately and began talking right away.

"Did Ricky get to you already? I told him to try you before getting in touch with your sister, because, you know . . . "

"My sister!" Ewen felt a moment's blankness, then a cold prickle over his arms and neck. He made sure the door was closed. "Why does Petersen need to get hold of Lynn?" *Teddy's all right. We know that. Teddy's all right.*

Susan cleared her throat, and Ewen had a mental image of her adjusting her phone on her shoulder. He heard the clatter of what might be dog's claws. "It's because they got an ID. On the first body, while we were out in the field. Found the parents—thank God, *that's* never my job. Turns out that Lynn was their doctor."

Ewen pressed his hand against one wall of the bathroom, and it started to bow outwards. He was unaware a crack in the drywall had begun to spread. "*Whose* doctor? How? Lynn's a psychiatrist. Susan—please make sense!" He was almost shouting now, and stopped to swallow.

In a chastised, small voice Susan said. "I know. But she was still the girl's doctor. Her therapist. You see, everyone thought she ran away. The girl, I mean. That was over a year ago." There was silence, broken by the static of her phone against her polo shirt. "The name—her name—was Ellie Frankel."

He mumbled the name back to her to show he understood, and then turned off the phone without saying goodbye. Ewen prepared himself for the message he would have to relay, but as he stepped into the hall he saw that Lynn was already on the phone—the kitchen phone—returning a message she had found on the machine. The job he was just now dreading had been done for him.

Lynn stood with her hands braced against the kitchen counter, staring through a layer of cabinet glass at the dinner plates on the bottom shelf. Ewen moved up beside her and waited for her to speak. It seemed to him he waited for a long time.

"I was surprised she'd run away," Lynn said flatly. "But not *that* surprised. Her home situation wasn't very good." She seemed fascinated by the blue ring around the edge of the stoneware plates. Ewen glanced at them and thought of a line of poetry, "White plates and cups . . . blue-ringed." What was that from? Rupert Brooke, he thought. A World War I poem. About death, of course. It would have to be about death.

Anger started to grow in the soil of Ewen's shock and confusion. He'd had just about enough. There was some doubt in his mind as to the appropriate subject of his anger. Reasonably, it should be against the unknown horror that had done these things to children in the back yard of the hospice. To children. Also to Lynn, to Susan. Even to old Rez. There was enough anger to spread around. But somehow it was easier to angry with Theo, out gallivanting with the Dalai Lama. Together, he and his sister could get really angry with Theo. Royally angry. Before Theodore Thurmond, life had not been like this for Lynn, or for him. Before Theo, Buddhism had been little more than a Young family tradition—his mother's influence—expressed mainly in art and incense. Now it was all a different sort of thing, expressed by a house filled with dying people, and at this moment Ewen wasn't sure it was an improvement.

He opened his mouth to express some home truths about Lynn's husband, but she spoke first. She said, "Teddy."

That seemed to be the perfect refutation of Ewen's unspoken argument. Without Theo there could not have been Teddy. Ewen was used to having his thoughts anticipated by his sister, so he misunderstood this one word and was confused when she continued, "Where is he? Teddy. I don't remember where I left him."

This was something he could help with. The red flowers of anger blooming behind his eyes faded. "You didn't *leave* him anywhere, Sis. He's not a package. When we got in he took himself up to his room. I heard him playing *Wild Divine* just a moment ago." Ewen put his hand gingerly on Lynn's shoulder, and left it there for only a moment. They were not a touchy-feely family. "Teddy's one thing you don't have to worry about, Lynn. I'm here, and in the unlikely event of . . . of a water landing . . . of an intruder, I mean, I would be simply overjoyed to take someone apart. Into little pieces." He gave her shoulder a quick squeeze and quickly released it. "I'd make each piece the same size."

She turned in place, blinking often, looking inward. "No, Ewen. Thanks, but I'm past my hysteria. Teddy doesn't need a bodyguard. I just want to know what he heard. I want him not involved. As much as possible, not involved."

Lynn Young-Thurmond looked into her brother's eyes with sudden hard focus. "Occupy him, please. Entertain him. Anyway you like. I've got to look into my records."

They were playing the biofeedback game together, Teddy and Ewen, when the detectives rang the bell for Lynn downstairs. Ewen had not been doing as well with the game as usual, and with the sound of the bell he broke into a sweat that knocked a large Montgolfier balloon up into the computer graphics air: ropes, gondola, and all. Teddy gave his uncle a superior glance.

"I just wish I could know . . . " said Ewen to the boy somewhat shamefacedly. "You know—what they're going to talk about."

"You can't listen when Mommy's talking about her patients," said the boy, didactically. "Never."

This girl isn't going to care at all about her privacy, he thought. Aloud he said, "I know that, Teddy," and he gave up his electronic finger-rings to the boy, who brought the balloon back down with great composure and docked it at the wharf. Teddy continued expertly along the CG hallways, past the pear tree and the row of doors to the cobra, which was Teddy's favorite event. Teddy loved outsmarting the cobra and always played the game on "extra hard" mode.

Children learn so very quickly. Kids!

His uncle watched Teddy and tried not to listen to the sounds below. *He is a beautiful boy,* Ewen thought. *Already he's becoming all arms and legs like Theo, but he has his mother's face.*

Teddy's glossy hair was darker than his mother's. The front of it hung over his face and it was a wonder he could see at all that way, but he would not have it cut. Occasionally he would blow upwards to clear his vision for a moment. Theo, too, wore his hair very long, but that seemed to be for different reasons. Ewen had found that men like Theo often grew their hair long down the sides because they were losing it on top.

Ewen was still studying Teddy when a soft rap came at the door. He thought he handled his nervousness at this fairly well, but when Detective Gideon Ryde creaked the door open he looked in at Ewen's face and grinned. "Somehow you're reminding me of Resurrection herself, sitting there by the boy, Mr. Young. Resurrection the dog, I mean."

Ewen grinned wider. "Like I'm about to take a piece out of your leg, Detective?"

"If I look at young Theodore wrong, yes."

Teddy yanked off the finger-rings and slapped the game closed in a few, very practiced moves. He greeted Ryde brightly, because Ryde was "the detective who wanted to play with him." This had been Teddy's memory of Gideon Ryde since their first meeting. As on their first meeting, Ryde slid down the wall to sit beside him now, bunching up a suit jacket that was always slightly rumpled. "And how's the great computer gamer today, Theodore?"

Teddy put up with being called Theodore because Detective Ryde was "company," and one had to be polite to company. "It's really a neat game, sir. It's not like other computer games."

Ryde looked over the boy's head at Ewen for a moment and then back again. "I guess that means no one gets killed in it."

Teddy made an expression that in any adult would involve a furrowed brow. As he was very young, it resulted only in a slight narrowing of the eyes. "That's not what I meant about it being different. It works in a sort of magical way. Things happen because you *want* them to happen, and the magic in your fingers makes them happen."

Ewen bobbed forward and caught Ryde's eyes. "How's it going?" he asked the detective. "Are you allowed to tell me anything?"

Ryde shrugged, raising his jacket shoulders up next to his blond head. "How *could* it be going, Mr. Young?" He looked at Ewen intently. "This is the worst case I've had to deal with in my whole professional life. That thing last winter, in the temple—that was nasty. You know that better than anyone. But this . . . " He glanced quickly at Teddy and did not say: *All those children . . . !*

"Is Lynn . . . " He wanted to ask: *Is Lynn all right? Is this going to be unbearable for her?* But what he said was, "Is she able to help?"

Ryde nodded. "Oh, yes, I think so." He looked at Ewen some more. "We all do our bit: your sister, Rick, that wonderful lady of yours, Dr. Sundown. (And by the way—you make sure you take good care of that lady, Mr. Young.) And you also do your bit, Mr. Young. Even the dog does her bit."

The dog and even me *is the right way to phrase it. I'm an assistant to the dog. My boss is a bitch.* That thought rang unexpectedly cheerful to Ewen. The grin fled once more across his face.

"We'll get the bad guy," said Ryde, and he grunted as he slid himself up the wall and went out the door. Ewen feared to look back at Teddy. He feared to know how much of this interchange the boy had understood.

Teddy watched Ryde go and said to Ewen, "They're gonna catch a murderer." He smiled broadly and unplugged his laptop. "That's so neat!"

Chapter Thirty-two

LYNN WAS FAIRLY DRAINED when the detectives left. She sat by the living room coffee table, arranging all the manila folders and turned off the laptop. In the kitchen she heard Ewen stir-frying something up for dinner and Teddy's continuing line of chatter rising above the noise. She began to stand up and then she sat down again, dizzy, with a strange disconnection. It was, she reflected, a sort of opposite of *déjà vu*. It was more like a *veja*—a never-was. She couldn't think who would be getting up to walk into the kitchen: Dr. Young-Thurmond: child psychiatrist, Lynn the twin sister, Lynn the helpmeet of Theo of Great Compassion, or simply Mommy.

She looked down at her hands: thin, long-boned, well-groomed, with moderately short nails and clear polish. Once they had been chubby hands and she had bit those nails. Then they had gone through long periods of grubbiness from climbing trees and riding ponies. Then there had been many shades of polish, some decals and a few rhinestones. There had been a henna-dots period and she had drifted dangerously close to a tattoo until medical school excised both the motivation and the energy for such things. Now those hands seemed cold, competent and totally unrelated to Lynn.

Dr. Young-Thurmond had been a willful construct, because Lynn had always known she couldn't carry the immense stories of her patients into her home life, both for self-preservation and because of ethics. And she couldn't show her rhinestoned, hennaed, or otherwise zany side to the kids. They wanted help, not just another wild friend. So the careful, thoughtful doctor persona had been created. But where had these other Lynns come from, and why did they seem so unrelated to one another?

I've always been thought of as a happy sort of person, she said to herself. *Me and Ewen. Just the "Anime Twins." How long ago that was . . .*

And it's all "what I've been thought of." Have I been "what I've been thought of?" She considered that question in two senses, and at that moment had no idea whether it was true in either sense.

I've been an anchor to people. Through death and destruction and midnight colic, I kept it all together. I chanted with Theo, broke boards for Uncle Jimmy, kept a hundred trivial secrets with my teenage brother and a thousand non-trivial ones for strangers. Even my mischief years, so long ago, were fairly harmless. I'm the half of the twins who got no ribbons, no magic, no adventures. I'm the half that had a baby and spent a lot of nights worrying about other people.

"What I've been thought of" is due for a change, she said to herself, having no idea what she meant by that.

She stood up, stretched, popped her right knee as her weight slid back onto it and walked into the kitchen, feeling older than thirty-three.

"Her mother was dead," said Lynn to her brother as he cleaned the spots of sauce off the table. "That was part of the reason Ellie came to me. And her father . . . I don't know where he is, now. Six months after she disappeared he left town. There was nothing shady about that; he had no family here, and it wasn't hard for him to find a software job that allowed him to leave the scene of such misery. Of course, we didn't know it was *such* misery, then. We only knew his fourteen-year-old girl ran away, after a few years of being in trouble in school."

Ewen was trying not to speckle the manila folders with soy sauce. "And you're sure you can speak to me about all this . . . "

Lynn shrugged. With her slight shoulders the movement was oddly like lifting and dropping a three-by-five file card into the box. "Who's left to sue me? Besides—don't you know most everything about me and what I do already?"

"No," he said ruefully, wiping the table. "That just works from me to you. You know what I'm doing or feeling. Not vice-versa. Hardly fair to you, is it? You get all the worry and bother."

She gave him a startled glance but said nothing. She returned to her subject.

"Ellie was street smart. Like many unhappy kids. So you'd think that would make her harder to trap than the more innocent. But I find it actually works in the opposite direction. When a kid thinks she knows more about life than the adults around her, she makes her own decisions and keeps her mouth shut about them. Most of the time it works out okay, but when she's made the *wrong* decision about someone, there'll be fewer people knowing what happened."

"What'd you mean 'most of the time it works out okay'? It seems to me that usually it's a load of trouble . . . "

Lynn cut him off with a wave of her slight hand. "Let's be real. Sometimes kids *do* know more than the adults around them. Ellie was certainly more in tune with things than her father was. She was very bright. Very bright and very angry."

Ewen sat down and thought about this, a piece of speckled paper towel in his hand. "Maybe it had nothing to do with who Ellie was or how she behaved. If the bad guy simply snatched her off the street . . . ?

"If this had to do with one kid, I'd be more likely to believe it. With three there has to have been more premeditation involved. That's my guess. Even today, in our sad society, if children disappear against all expectations, there's a great ruckus made. But there are the kids who *might* be expected to run away, or be stolen by a noncustodial parent . . . I think we're going to that find each of these children who disappeared was, well, I guess 'unsettled' is the best word. They could pass as runaways. I think—no, I'm sure—there was premeditation involved in this. Some sort of stalking."

Ewen rocked back and forth in his chair and looked at his sister. Her hair was falling in her face as Teddy's had done. He had almost forgotten that look of concentrated intelligence that was hers alone. And that slight shade of bitterness, unseen since the birth of Teddy.

He wanted it to go away again. "What do you mean 'we're going to find'?" His voice was sharp. "How does this terrible thing become a 'we?' The police are the finders-out, here. You were just the girl's shrink, and that was a while ago. My connection with it lasted about an hour and a half." He looked around the Thurmond house and thought, *This is my reality. The cabinet with the plates, blue-ringed. My sister with her hair over her face. That horror in the bramble-field does not have to be my reality.* He raised his eyes and looked around him at his sister's house. It was slightly cluttered, with a number of plastic trucks in the living room. He loved it as much as his own home. *This is my reality*.

"But I'm part of what happened," said Lynn very calmly. "Because I touched her life. I was part of her life when she was murdered, and at the time I never knew. I know now. I will not just do as everyone expects and let it all go."

Oh, no, said Ewen to himself, knowing his sister very well. *Oh, no*.

"It's a great misfortune for a teenager to be a lot smarter than the adults around her," Lynn said again, later, as she set Ewen up with a pretty cup of silver needle tea and some gingersnaps on a leaf-shaped plate. Her own tea she dumped into a chipped mug. She snitched her brother's cookies as she talked. "First off, the kids don't simply *think* they're being misunderstood, like all of us; these kids know it for a simple fact.

"Imagine if our parents had been blindly negative about us. If they had been . . . people with only a few categories in their minds. If everything had been black or white?"

"You mean if they had been stupid," said Ewen. "With Dad it was close enough to black and white, and God knows he's not stupid."

Her smirk was identical to his, but was aimed at Ewen. "You didn't have it so bad! You just never appreciated Dad."

He shrugged and took a large bite of cookie, mumbling, "You were always his favorite!"

Lynn just rolled her eyes exaggeratedly. Though it was true. In at least this Chinese-American family, the girl had been the favorite. The "doctor" girl.

"Ellie was driven half-crazy by her father's form of discipline . . . Don't ever tell anyone I used the word 'crazy.' 'Crazy' is not a technical term . . . She believed he had simply refused to understand his debate club, sherry-sipping daughter. Truth was, he really *couldn't* understand her, and that's why he nagged her constantly. He was worried."

"Or maybe he was just a nag." Ewen grabbed for the last cookie. Lynn beat him to the gingersnap, but broke it down the middle and shared. "You just don't like fathers, Ewen. Admit it."

Ewen kept his mouth shut and chewed, but eventually he muttered, "Obviously there turned out to be something for the guy to worry about." He settled back with the teacup balanced on the palm of his hand.

"Yes, but not what he thought. He worried unproductively. He worried that when she said she was at the library researching old *Newsweeks* that she was actually out somewhere in the back seat of a Chevy. He would call the library, with excuse after excuse, to make sure she was actually there doing strategy with her debate team partner."

"And she was? In the library, I mean?"

"Oh yeah. Or at a friend's house where the computer ran faster. But whatever she was and whatever he did, he embarrassed her. He was a BASIC programmer, which is sort of like being a manual laborer in Redmond or Bellevue. Worse, a BASIC programmer is almost extinct, like a mammoth."

"And that made him an 'untouchable?'" asked Ewen, who spoke no computer languages and was mediocre at using Windows. Other than a certain skill with Photoshop, he was not very technical.

Lynn nodded and cleaned her lips with a paper towel. "None of that matters, really. But what I'm leading to is that Ellie had learned to keep secrets. By the time she got sent to me she had become very good at it. Would have made a damn fine lawyer, some day."

Lynn made louder noises with her tea and dunked the last fragment of gingersnap. "The worst thing about a kid who is more intelligent than her family is that she assumes she knows more than any other adult, too. That included me. She made it clear she didn't think much of my brain."

Ewen made the inevitable brotherly sarcastic remark and got the inevitable sisterly punch in the upper arm.

"But I let her get away with that," Lynn continued. "When I should have called her on it. Because it was that kind of attitude that made her a sitting duck. It doesn't take an adult genius to hoodwink a genius thirteen-year-old."

"And that's what you think happened to Ellie Frankel? She was 'hoodwinked?'"

Lynn slammed her mug down between stacks of files. "I'm sure of it. She . . . she had older friends, she said. She was very proud that most of her friends were older."

"Like 'dirty old man' older?"

"Naw. Anything over twenty-five would be in the geriatric category with her. But I remember some stories about a friend old enough to buy liquor. Ellie was also in one of my group classes. She met a lot of other kids that way. That was my goal. None old enough to buy liquor though."

Ewen reflected on the matter. "Your group classes . . . ? Wasn't Jacob doing that for a while?"

Lynn nodded. She stared at her tea.

"You . . . gave up that idea after a while, as I recall?"

She grinned at Ewen, becoming his twin sister for a moment again. "Yeah. The kids started to gang up on me. Think of Jacob and what he did to you! And I was pretty young myself, when I first thought of that. Full of ideas."

"You still are," he said. "Young and full of ideas." He rose, balancing all the tea dishes on one arm. Ewen left his sister to ruminate over her old records.

Chapter Thirty-three

SUSAN FINISHED her paperwork with the police, and went out to look at a litter of pups that had been recommended to her third-hand. No one knew she was doing this, Ewen least of all, because she knew it would lead to more acrimony. She needed to be looking for Rez's replacement. She wouldn't have to be replaced today, and Susan hoped not this year, but dog's lives were pitifully short and she was going to need another partner. Another very special tracking dog.

She had already been disappointed by one Redbone Coonhound pup that had been built up to her as a very promising nose. Hounds—except for bloodhounds—don't usually make the best search and rescue dogs, but this bitch had been touted as an exception.

In person, the young bitch pup they were looking at had just impressed Susan as a fool. Susan was probably biased in that, because she was famous as Rez's handler, and no dog on God's green Earth could have looked or acted less like Rez than this fawning russet stripling with its oversized ears and soft brown eyes. But Susan had known from the beginning that she must not even try to find the equal of her bitter, loyal wolf-dog. It was Rez herself who let her know the hound pup wouldn't cut it. Although the dog was tolerant of the pup, as she was of most babies, she had made her lack of interest clear. Some dogs are simply dull dogs, however good the nose, and there's not much search and recovery use for a dull dog. Rez had made it clear she thought the pup stupid. That had been two weeks ago, and since then Susan had been doing only telephone research.

She had called a friend who had a well-known tracking Golden Retriever bitch. He was the best man she knew at starting the blind and deaf little newborns and socializing them. His pups were all they *could* be by the time he had placed them, and she had heard he had an up-and-coming litter. After the events of this terrible day she wanted to see something young and alive, so she was now standing the man's doorway with no appointment and the fog creeping in around her as though she was being pushed forward by the dark.

She knocked, and after some barking and scuffling noises the door was opened. "We hear you got some pups," Susan said to Lenny Boatman. The squeals in the background and the general milky smell of old Boatman's living room verified her statement. "I've been looking for a pup, because my girl here is getting a little stiff, and . . . are they all spoken for?"

Boatman was wearing a worn plaid bathrobe and he had a bag of frozen raw scraps in his hand. "Spoken for? No, Susan, they're not spoken for, but I'm not sure you'd be interested. You'd be looking for a male tracking dog, preferably a recovery dog, right? All I got is puppies." He realized he was standing in the doorway and backed off to let Susan in. Rez moved to follow, but Susan signed her to wait on the concrete front patio.

"Yes. But I'll have time to start my own now. I *think*." For a moment she stopped and looked worried. "Yes. I think so. And as for tracking skill, well, your Zelda's found more lost hikers in the Seattle Area than any other local dog. As well as a few bodies."

Boathouse beamed at the praise. He was a stocky Muckleshoot-tribe man standing in a house that looked from within as though it was made up of the spare parts and pieces of other people's houses. The room was thoroughly puppy-chewed, even parts of the tabletops. "Yes, she has, good old girl. But these pups aren't Zelda's. They're my new dog's. They might not be your cup of tea, Susie."

"Why not, Lenny? You know I don't care about the AKC thing."

He grinned, slightly embarrassed. "Well, they're certainly not AKC. They're Oz doodles."

Susan stood motionless on the torn linoleum flooring, staring at the rumpled Indian man in front of her. "Oz doodles?"

"Yeah. 'Oz' as in Australia. They were bred out of Labs and poodles. Starting in the eighties. Added other breeds since—I don't know what all. They're good for lots of things, though they started out to be guide dogs. I've had great luck with tracking, though. And one of my Lily's earlier pups is doing epilepsy assistance. One of her grandparents is doing research at cancer-sniffing. Have you heard of that? Can't say how that's working out; medicine's not my thing." He furrowed his brow for a moment. "Only thing I wouldn't use them for is arson detection, really, because of all the hair." He snickered and prodded Susan with a spare elbow. "All that hair. Get it?"

She kept staring at him.

He added nervously "Lily, the mother, is a good dog: out of Rutland lines, very healthy. Good temperament. Good nose. Wait'll you see the size of her nose, actually. Wow."

When Susan still said nothing, he babbled on, gesturing with the bag of dog meat. "Don't look at me like that. Aussie Labradoodles are actually very practical dogs. They can be clipped short if you want and of course they don't shed. People like that. And they've kept the breeding very clean."

Susan shook herself. Cleared her head. "I know about Labradoodles, Lenny. I treat a few. I just never thought that *you* . . . "

Rumpled Muckleshoot man that he was, Lenny Boatman hung his head, but only for a moment. Like all good breeders, he was proud of his dogs. "You should at least take a gander at them before giving me that—that look!"

She became aware she *had* been giving Lenny "that look." "I'm sorry. Of course: show me your pups," said Susan.

They were seven weeks old, and in the time Lenny had been in the front of the house they had knocked the puppy-pen over on its side and spread themselves across the kitchen. Mother was lying on her furry chocolate side, not quite relaxed in the presence of this human but not concerned enough to rise up. Her coat was light and fleecy. Angora. Around the legs of the table lurched, pounced, and tottered six unlikely balls of fluff and color, marked with round eyes like raisins. Two were brown, one light gold, one cream and one solid black.

Carefully Susan sat herself down on a clean spot on the kitchen vinyl. She watched the puppies watch her, and out of long experience felt the personalities of each of them display themselves to her. The cream guy was the biggest of the litter. By his lolloping movement he seemed slowest to develop, which was to be expected. He fixed his eyes on her and made her into the goal of his travels. His pencil tail wagged, held straight over his back.

"He'll be a real go-getter," said Lenny, blandly. "He's got some growth comin' in him." He watched the woman watching his puppies. He knew at least as much about puppy maturation as the veterinarian did, and knew much more about these special ones he was selling, but he was a salesman and also knew when to keep his trap shut.

One of the browns also made for Susan, and being of a lighter build, she made it to Susan's lap first, where she made a puddle. Susan took an offered sheet of Bounty, sopped up the mess and didn't otherwise react. The other brown—a male—looked at her, yelped once and sat down hard on his tail. The dark gold bitch puppy stayed under the kitchen table.

The dark one came halfway from his mother to the stranger, sat down and gazed at her. He tilted his head left, and then adjusted it to the right. He took another step forward, made a half-hearted play-bow at Susan and sat again, examining her some more.

I wish Ewen were here, she found herself thinking, though she had not forgotten for a moment how he'd reacted to her talk of puppies. She put her hand out for the puppy to sniff. He stuck his cold nose into the palm of it and gave her one lick. Then he examined her some more.

Old Boatman watched all this out of the corner of his eye. "He'll be a wise dog, that one," he said, looking in the opposite direction as he spoke. Looking completely unconcerned. "Of course, he's the most expensive one, too. Because he's the best. I bet he'll be a body recovery dog, if you still are looking for one to do that. He could be a rescue dog, too. He'll have the muscle. And of course he'll swim." Boatman made a wide sweep of his hand. "And then, these're all bred to be service dogs." Lenny sucked on his lower lip. "A lot of market for service dogs, these days."

She ran her hand through the puppy's soft pelt of curls. "I can just see the briars in this," she said.

"Not so much the fleecy ones like him. The wooly ones do collect 'em, though. You clip the coat short. They look like whatever you want them to. Underneath they look like a sporting dog." He cleared his throat and said, "Even if you're not interested in what many people call a mutt, you can still . . . "

"Oh, Lenny, shut up about the 'mutt' business," she said. She was looking at the puppy with her head tilted much as it was looking at her. "Can I take him to the window for just a moment for Rez to see? And can I do the usual tests? I mean, if you've got the time."

Very, very casually Lenny Boatman said, "I got the time. And it's good experience for the pup. New person. Even a new dog. If Lily doesn't mind, I don't." Lily lay there and seemed not to mind as Susan picked up her puppy.

Boatman walked behind, saying. "And I understand has to have some say in this. By the way, you *are* going to keep . . . "

"Rez has a home with me as long as she lives," Susan said coldly.

Together they took the blocky puppy out into the cooler front room, where the wolf-dog sat waiting by the picture window. She got up when Susan came toward her, and the puppy was carefully and slowly extended in front of the glass. Rez was very polite and waited for an invitation to come closer. At last she leaned forward and sniffed courteously at the puppy's side, as though the layers of glass between made no difference The sniffing went on a long time as she pretended to sample the pup, and it was punctuated by a few appreciative snorts.

The mime was so good that Susan had to wonder whether her dog could get some scent through the double-paned window. If so, that wasn't good, because the little thing hadn't had its last vaccinations and wasn't supposed to meet strange dogs. But maybe Rez was receiving something else from the pup that wasn't smell. Perhaps the connection between Ewen and Rez wasn't simply on Ewen's side.

The puppy looked through the glass at Rez as he had at her owner, with its little head cocked. Susan saw that Resurrection's eyes were soft, and her tail slowly brushing from side to side. The old dog was feeling contentment from the pup, just as Susan herself had received, as she felt the soft, wiggling, black thing in her hands.

"Bitch takes to a boy pup quicker," commented Lenny, standing behind them, one dark eyebrow wisely raised. "Male dogs like the little bitches. It's just nature."

"Maybe you're right. She sure didn't like the coonhound bitch pup I showed her last week," Susan remarked.

Lenny shrugged. "That don't really prove nothing. I don't like coon dogs much myself. But then, lots o' folks do."

Susan stood on the porch fifteen minutes later, an uncertain smile on her face. She had just put down five hundred deposit on a puppy, which seemed to be the opposite of every dog she had ever had. How unlike her! She hardly understood her own reactions this past month. If things continued in this direction, she might be buying the little thing a rhinestone collar in a week or so. Buying Prada shoes. (Was it shoes Prada made? She scarcely knew.) She looked down at Rez for reassurance, and the old dog was grinning up at her through her gray muzzle and despite her sore joints and the weather throbbing in every elderly inch of her, Susan knew that Rez would have been content to take the pup home that very evening. So maybe she'd done the right thing by buying what was so often called a "designer dog." If only for Rez.

Either the creature would be a tracker or it wouldn't, and the designer dog appellation would have nothing to do with that. You couldn't be sure about any dog, not even a bloodhound.

The real problem coming up in the future, she thought, was Ewen. He'd made his attitude about a new dog clear. About a new anything. She remembered him hanging up the phone last time she called without even a "goodbye." Was this a sign of the future? Susan thought about this future and tried to blow it away by blowing frost-rings with her breath under the light of the porch. As always, the frost-rings didn't come out right.

Ewen just didn't want things to change. Oh, when they first got together he had, or had claimed to. He had wanted her to leave her practice and come down to Redmond with him. But that idea had faded after a few disagreements—really very minor disagreements, in her opinion—and he had told her he took her career seriously and would push no more. And, admittedly, he did take her career seriously—maybe more seriously than she did herself. It's what she'd always wanted in a man and she'd gotten it. Whoopee for her.

But if he didn't want even a new puppy, how was he going to feel about any really big change? She thought of his placid, balanced life, with paints and kung fu and meditation each keeping its place, and of his house, which despite all the oil paint was on the verge of being neat. Strange house for a man.

Susan's own life had never been so perfectly balanced. Things happened around her in great surges. Gains and losses. She feared her surging life would soon find itself losing Ewen Young. She wished he had shown more gumption about wanting her to move down the mountains.

But still there were some good times coming up, whether or no . . . There would be the puppy for them to train through the dark winter: Not her and Ewen, maybe, but at least her and Rez. To train and to be silly with. That would be better than nothing. And then would come spring and summer, with long, bright days and other changes.

Susan stepped off the porch, thinking about new names.

Chapter Thirty-four

EWEN HAD PULLED the seat cushion from Lynn's living room couch and placed it across the head of the upstairs hall by the stairs. Behind him Teddy slept in one of the rooms and Lynn in the other. Ewen had had to re-insert the boy's floppy limbs under the covers, one by one, because Teddy had had a hard time falling asleep. (It must have taken him eight minutes.) He hadn't seemed upset; it was just the excitement of the detectives being there, and of course part of it was just that Uncle Ewen was sleeping over, and Daddy was not.

Behind the other bedroom door he could still hear the shuffling of papers. He wondered if it was his responsibility to barge in and tell Lynn that it was past time to put those away and go to sleep. That such an act was foredoomed to failure didn't make it any less stuck amidst his nagging thoughts.

He closed his eyes and let those thoughts go. Immediately his mind was filled with the image of Rez. Rez flinching as she put weight on that leg.

The winter had not really begun, and already he felt covered with winter darkness. Darkness and aching bones. How could they all make it through until spring—especially old Rez? He thought of Susan's prospect of a puppy and wished he had not snapped at her as he had done. A puppy, at least, would be alive. A new living being amidst their lives. And if Rez didn't like it—if she felt displaced—she could move to his house and live with him. He'd take her everywhere with him, as Susan did now. He'd take her to the school and she could sit by the side of the mat. She could almost be his dog.

Fat chance. Rez was Rez, and Susan was the only master she admitted.

Besides, he knew so little about dogs. His father had never allowed them to have one.

He turned on his back and looked up at the shadowed tin-stamped ceiling. Was it his father's voice that had been causing all this upset about a puppy? About hating things to change, really. Ewen thought he had kicked the more negative messages of his father out of his mind years ago. But the reason he recoiled at the thought of puppies—was ignorant of puppies—was probably his father.

It was also connected with the difficulty he had felt physically comforting his sister earlier today. His father's shackles of coldness, which Ewen had thought he'd escaped by all the sweat and bodywork he'd done, and by all the oil-paint smears on the floor. Not entirely escaped, he guessed. These were things he wanted to share with Susan. Along with an apology, of course. If it weren't so late he would call her now.

Sweat and paint had been Ewen's rebellion against his father. Pink hair and Theo Thurmond had been Lynn's. Poor man, Dr. Young. Ewen was sure he had never consciously intended putting shackles on anyone. But there was no reason to feel especially sorry for Dad. He'd lost a beloved wife but raised two kids he couldn't be ashamed of. And he had one really great grandson.

> *May all be happy.*
> *May all be peaceful and at ease.*
> *May all be safe.*
> *May all be free from fear.*
> *May all know the truth of their own nature.*

Ewen said these words and in another moment of concentration he began to feel them. He fell asleep smiling slightly, wrapped in an old quilt on the musty carpet of the upper hall floor.

The next morning Lynn got Teddy off to school and then asked her brother if he was available for a few hours that morning. She had rescheduled her sessions and thought she could use some company in the interview she was planning.

Ewen had at last begun to find it easier to delegate his school teaching duties. Now that he had begun to accept himself as head of the school it seemed his sense of responsibility to it was less oppressive. Had he had a portrait sitting, that would have been a more difficult matter, but his only painting was later that day. So he said, "Sure. Who're we going to interview?"

Lynn was pulling on her gloves, for it was moist and chilly. "I was thinking of the tooth marks on the bone. We're going to have a talk with Jacob."

Ewen stopped in the doorway, slamming his hands against the jambs. "No. No! It's not Jacob!"

Lynn stared a moment in shock and then shook her head dismissively. "Don't worry, Ewen. I wasn't thinking of it that way. He's just a lead. He has memories."

Still, Ewen felt he was becoming a traitor. "Why do you need me along?"

"To whom would he feel closer? Who would he feel more desire to please?"

"That's what I mean," Ewen said. "I don't want to use him."

Lynn stepped around him, very neat in her princess-waist tan leather coat. She was angry. "He wasn't so careful about you! He wanted to take your two precious lungs and fill them with salt water!"

He muttered, "Jacob was drunk."

Lynn shot him a look of disgust. "Yes, he was. Now he's not drunk. So? Why would he object to talking about the meetings? Do you think he's the murderer after all? Or that he doesn't want to help find the killer?" She met her brother's eyes and hers flashed. When he bent his head and started toward the door again she followed him out and locked it behind them.

Jacob was changing another sheet. There was a lot of sheet-changing at Sangye Menla every day, but perhaps not usually so many volunteers doing the changing as today. There were a lot of volunteers in the hospice, even after the reporters in disguise had been turned away. Even amongst the legitimates there was a lot of staring out the back windows toward the ragged line of poplars, where people dressed in official tan and people dressed in official blue were pacing back and forth. If one opened the back doors the air was filled with the scent of turned dirt. Inside, there was a lot of smothered gossip, which involved both the volunteers and the dying patients themselves. Odd, but it seemed to cheer them up. The patient in Jacob's room was sitting in the bedside chair, waiting for her bed to be made. This lady was too sick to bother with serial murders.

Ewen and Lynn helped Jacob with the room, and the work was done with the speed of a NASCAR tire-change. Then they retired to the library, which was at the front of the building. It looked out on the reporters rather than the police. Lynn closed the curtains.

She turned to the mystified youth. "I want you to remember, Jacob, back a few years ago."

"A few years? That's forever to me," said Jacob. His face had a ruddy glow and his eyes were bright. Even his complexion was improved. Most of this was a result of love. It had been conducted mostly by email and phones calls to Em, but as she was currently in town visiting, the Fischbein mood was high. But now Ewen was beginning to think that some of this glow was like that of the patients'—the common reaction of people whose lives had lightly brushed against the works of a murderer. Ewen had seen it a lot in the past year. Lives just lightly brushed . . . Like a violent movie, it could be an interesting memory.

He sighed as he inserted the last pillow into its case. *Lightly* brushed. He envied that distinction, for he had had his skin brushed thin in the past year.

Jacob folded into a small chair with teen-aged, Pinocchio-hinged looseness. He seemed both larger and younger than he had been the summer before. The whites of his eyes were clear. Sometimes Ewen could forget for a half-hour at a time that Jacob had stolen his body and come close to snuffing it. Perhaps by next year Ewen would be able to forget for longer periods. Theirs had been an unusual relationship.

"Back when Dad first took me to meet you, Doc? That far back?" He still had his own last pillowcase in his hand, and idly he snapped it back and forth.

"Almost that far back. Back when we started groups of kids to talk to each other once a week." Lynn leaned her elbows on the chair arms and rested her little chin on her laced fingers.

Jacob thought for a moment. Ewen heard the sound of gossip that hissed along an adjoining corridor. It seemed odd to him—gossip in a hospice—but why not?

Lynn described the girl who died.

He shook his head. "Sorry, Doc. I never met this Ellie girl."

"I know, Jacob. It's the others who were around her that interest me."

He stared at her. "The others . . . Oh, you mean . . . Oh, wow, Doc. You think it was one of your own that did it?"

Lynn shrugged her butterfly shoulders. "Probably not. But I don't know what to think."

Jacob sat bolt upright. "You mean—because of the biting? I heard from one of the attendants that there were tooth marks . . . Ohmigod, Doc! You can't think it was *me*!"

Ewen felt obliged to squeeze in here. "I'm sure she doesn't, Jacob. Jake. But just to please 'Doc's Bro,' just say out loud for us that it wasn't."

"It wasn't," said Jacob, quite loudly. "And you, of all people, should know that it wasn't me. Having *been* me, and all. And with your special tricks . . . "

"I'm not a mindreader," said Ewen, repeating Lynn's shrug with his more robust shoulders. "But I didn't really think it was you. We were wondering if maybe you have a few special mindreading tricks of your own. Could you have met a monster a few years ago? And, would you have the instincts to recognize a monster if you meet one?"

Jacob let his gaze slide down from Ewen's face to the tile flooring. "Yeah, I think I might. Have a little bit of the instinct. Maybe everybody does." He raised his eyes brightly to Lynn's face for a moment. "I guess my being another patient takes out the patient-doctor privacy thing."

"Serial murder takes out the patient-doctor privacy thing," said Lynn. "At least in my mind."

Jacob told them all he remembered. It was much less than they had hoped for.

Petersen pulled out a chair for Lynn. Ewen squatted on the floor at her side. "Okay. Good. We're glad for any help we can get. But Dr. Thurmond, er . . . Young, is it? Dr. Young?"

"Usually Young, when I'm being a psychiatrist. I don't care right now, Detective."

"Dr. Young. We would really rather have questioned Jacob Fischbein ourselves."

"Well, you still can. Of course."

Petersen rocked back and forth slowly in his own chair. Lynn hid a smile, because so many of her patients did that: rocked back and forth in their chairs. "But we would rather have inter . . . talked to him first. Before you did."

Lynn let her smile escape. "Suddenly he's a suspect? But you hadn't even thought of him before this minute. Why not just take what I can give you now? And if it leaves you suspecting young Jacob, I'm sure you can still break down a fifteen-year-old."

Jacob had just turned sixteen and Lynn knew that, but she was suddenly feeling combative. Suddenly she wasn't so sure about the tall, Indian detective being a family friend. There was something in his eyes. And there was the matter of Ewen and Susan Sundown to be considered. Hadn't Petersen been her boyfriend?

Petersen didn't know about Jacob's escapade of the past summer, as far as Lynn knew. Though Petersen had been involved in a few of Ewen's more unusual escapades, she doubted Ewen would have told him about this one, which involved Ewen (at least in body) breaking the law.

Petersen let his chair thump down and he rearranged his sharp, dark features into a more amiable expression. She recognized it as a "professional" expression. She had a few of her own and she put one on. "Okay. Shoot," he said.

"Jacob was in a group of my kids a couple of years ago. A socialization group, though I never called it that in front of them. They shot the breeze. Hung out together."

"And what was wrong with these kids? Or can't you tell me?"

Lynn sniffed. "I can tell you many of them were brought to me by parents who were looking for more perfect children. They're middle-class kids who get sent to tutors when they get Cs in classes, or trainers when they don't make the soccer team. They all get special help for their Washington State Tests and SATs. I'm one of the professionals they use when the other professionals don't work and the kids still aren't perfect."

"You sound a bit bitter, Dr. Young."

"I know . . . and I shouldn't be, because at least I get a chance to help the kids get out from under the pressure cooker they live in. And because these kids make it financially possible for me to help some others with worse problems and no well-off parents."

"Not to mention pay your own mortgage, Doctor. No offense meant by that, but being a psychiatrist is not the worst way to make a living."

"No offense meant." Odd, that was what was always said when offense was meant.

"No, it isn't," said Lynn, smiling frostily. "You caught me, there."

"And it all goes to help the hospice, too. Doesn't it?" asked Petersen. "That's got to be a terrible drain on you."

Lynn looked at Petersen and thought how strange it was the detective should say exactly that. "A terrible drain." And he didn't even mean it in the way it was most true: emotionally. Or did he? Lynn looked at the huge man looming over her, eagle-eyed, now sitting very still as he regarded her.

"Sangye Menla is supported by a foundation. The food on our table—or our mortgage—wouldn't be a drop in the bucket." Lynn gave him her half-smile, the one that established who was in charge. "Let me tell you what Jacob told me about the groups."

He let her tell him.

There was the boy who bragged he had been beating up his wheelchair-bound grandfather. No, of course Lynn hadn't known that was going on at the time. She would have done something about it. And Jacob hadn't believed the boy, either. Probably it was never true. But it was something of interest.

There was the girl who showed great resentment toward her younger sister. She was a top-rung student, high science marks, good soccer player. Wouldn't have been brought in for help at all if she hadn't been seen with her hands around the younger girl's throat . . .

Petersen interrupted. "It won't be a girl," he said. "Females don't engage in this sort of serial killing."

Even in Washington State? Ewen thought, remembering Petersen's odd stories. But he didn't want to break in.

There was the Goth kid. Jacob had remembered this one best. He said he was a Satanist. He wore the usual white make-up. The reversed crucifix earrings. He was a compulsive manga reader.

"Compulsive *what?*"

"Manga. Japanese comic books. In his case, the hyper-violent ones. Surely, Detective, you've heard of manga?"

Petersen shrugged. "No. But I'll bet Gid has. If it has to do with kids . . . "

"People of all ages read manga. And all socio-economic backgrounds. Anyway, I'm not telling you anything here that Louis held as secret. He loved shocking his stodgy elders. Probably still does. I haven't seen him in a year. He dropped out of school, I think. Or was sent to a bigger, better set of trainers than they could find in Redmond. This was a very rich family. Old money."

Petersen's eyebrows rose. "'Old money'? What does that mean, out here in Washington State?"

She shrugged. "I guess I should have said 'pre-Microsoft.' "

"Oh. Yeah." He nodded.

Chapter Thirty-five

SUSAN HAD BEEN at Ewen's Redmond house for a half-hour, waiting to meet Ewen when he returned from doing a portrait. She was making lunch in his little kitchen, when Rez let out her single, sharp warning bark. Susan took the cheese sandwich off the burner and walked to the front door where a pretty, child-faced blond woman stood staring through the glass side-panels of the door at the huge dog. Susan opened the door.

"Don't tell me Ewen has a dog!" said the woman. "That I *won't* believe."

Susan thought of a half-dozen things to say, but decided on, "Why wouldn't you believe it?"

The blonde just stood there and shook her head. "It's just not Ewen. If I had ever *dared* bringing up such an idea . . . But with his allergy to commitment I didn't dare!"

Another half-dozen things sprang to life in Susan's mind, none of which got said. But Rez did start to growl, very quietly.

"Would you like to come in?" asked Susan, knowing the woman wouldn't. Not with the big dog growling. But asking did sort of establish Susan's own rights to the place and so she asked. She was very surprised when the woman did come in, brushing past both Susan and Rez.

The visitor glanced briefly at Susan, from her slightly manure-stained sneakers to the kitchen apron covering her shirt and cords. After the glance she said, "Good. I was always after him to get someone to come in here and clean up every week. I guess having to be independent made him face reality." The woman, unasked, sat down on the couch and with an air of old familiarity she opened the drawer of the end table where Ewen kept his stationary. She got out a pad and began to fill it with neat handwriting. She used a Cross pen she'd taken from her expensive-looking purse. "Or maybe it was the extra mess that came with the dog he used to object to." Pausing in her writing, she glanced over at Rez, who was still making that steady, quiet, very threatening sound. "I could have, at least, helped him pick out a more suitable puppy. Better looking. Better behaved."

Susan put Rez into a firm down-stay.

The woman finished her missive, folded it, dug around in the drawer and found an envelope. Thoughtfully she put the letter in the envelope and then, looking distrustfully up at Susan, licked the envelope and sealed it firmly. "If you're still here when he comes back," she said, "tell him Karen stopped by."

As the terrible woman rose to leave, Susan caught a whiff of her very expensive perfume. All she could think of to say was, "I'm not a house-cleaner. I'm a vet!"

When she was alone again Susan sat down on the couch, where the perfume still hung in the air. Why hadn't she just picked up the creature and thrown her off the porch? Why hadn't she destroyed her in a couple well-chosen sentences? She'd always been good at finding such sentences. She discovered she was sniffling. She knew damn well why she hadn't defended herself appropriately. She wrapped her hands over her middle and hugged herself, letting the tears fall on the tattered, flowery apron. "Puppy!" she said, half-laughing and half-crying. "A more suitable puppy!"

Rez didn't break stay. Exactly. She weaseled forward on her belly over the floorboards and put her huge graying head in Susan's lap. She licked Susan's hands and stomach.

Ewen found her weeping into her apron, mascara streaked down her face, holding an envelope in her hands. He gave a small involuntary leap backwards, which—along with the expression of shock on his face—didn't help the situation. Yet Ewen had rarely seen Susan in mascara, let alone wearing it in vertical stripes.

"What the . . . what? What?" He stood there feeling like a fool and the dog growled at him. Rez growled at *him*. Ewen was dumbstruck.

"I can't help it!" Susan shouted. "And I'm sorry if you're sorry, but actually I'm not! Not sorry a bit!" She thrust the envelope at him. "Here. I'm still here, so I'm supposed to give it to you."

He took the envelope, recognized the writing of his name as the penmanship of Karen, whom he had not seen in person for the better part of a year. From deep inside himself came the simple warning: *Uh oh. Uh Oh.*

"And as for the puppy, it's an ASD Labradoodle from the best lines and even if we're not pretty enough for you, he will be!"

This is all about the puppy she was talking about. That's all it is. I snapped at her about the puppy. I mean, I bitched at her about . . . Oh hell. "I'm sorry, Susan. I shouldn't have opened my stupid mouth about the puppy. I was just surprised and things have been so heavy around here lately . . . I was about to apologize to you about that anyway."

She might as well not have heard him. Perhaps she hadn't. "And I'm sorry about you being allergic to commitment, but then I'm not making it your commitment. It's mine and I've wanted one for so long . . . " She broke off, jaw quivering too much to talk.

"Allergic to commitment? No. Jeez, no, I'll help with the puppy. That's no problem. As long as he doesn't eat paint and get sick, it's all fine with me. I didn't know you'd wanted one for a long time . . . " Ewen sat down on the couch beside her and took her strong and beautiful shoulders into a big bear hug. Bear hugs of that sort were not natural to him, but he was determined to get better at them.

Susan looked at him through her raccoon mask and gave a great sigh. "Oh, Ewen. I don't mean *that* puppy. Not the Labradoodle. I mean *this* one. Ours. Mine." She cradled her not quite flat stomach in her hands and Rez shoved her long nose between the two humans. Ewen had no clue until the dog shoved her own canine mind and canine nose into his and showed him what he, the great observer, should have noticed weeks ago. What Gideon Ryde had noticed. What had Ryde said? *She was a wonderful lady and he should take care of her?* And then Ewen remembered that Susan had thrown up at the crime scene. Susan Sundown did not throw up at crime scenes. Ewen put his hand over her slender one and both upon her still slender middle. "Puppy?" he said in a tone of complete astonishment. "*Ours?*"

She turned her face away and sucked in a great sniffle. "Well, yeah. Ours, of course. But I'm not putting anything on you. You didn't ask for this."

Ewen pulled her to her feet. He rested his head on her shoulder, embraced her, and spun her around. He thought of the passion hiding in the strong and beautiful body beside him. He marveled at that, and at the thought of his heroic, ass-kicking, wolf-leading lady dissolving in tears. Ewen had never seen her in tears and, truth to tell, had never thought to see her so. He shook his head at his own stupidity.

Ewen the superman, the magical traveler between worlds, the artist . . . Ewen the completely flummoxed. Ewen the ordinary man . . .

Ewen the father. Between one moment and the next Ewen's brain reset itself. Ewen's heart reset itself. Ewen the father.

"Oh, Susan, Susie. You can't know how I feel this moment!"

"I think I can," she sobbed. "And it's not your fault!"

He snorted gently. "Yes it is. For being a fool. A fool who was content to remain a fool!" He tried to get his thoughts in order. "Let me tell you, girl, what life's been like, for me this year. Will you hear it? The whole story?"

Susan nodded. She wiped her nose on one of his ever-present tissues. That being insufficient, she wiped it again on her sleeve.

"In this past year or so I've been bounced between life and death more times than seems really fair. I've been on first name terms with death so often I should maybe say we've been on 'nickname terms.' And maybe I do call it by its nickname. Maybe its nickname is 'fear.'"

Susan sniffled, wetly. "You're *never* afraid, Ewen. You're always the one in complete control of things."

Ewen made a look of disgust and bunched his fists. His powerful muscles stretched under his shirt so much that Susan was almost afraid of him. Almost. "That's complete bullshit. Just because some quirk of fate gave me the power to travel between worlds, to talk to the dead, or at least your Uncle Sid—And I know he's not exactly like anyone's idea of a ghost, but he is dead . . . Maybe there are people who would get off on that kind of stuff. Superheroes. Not me. Especially not me at the age of thirty-three! But one thing of value has come to me this past year, and you know very well what that was."

Susan hoped she did, but she shook her head, in case she was wrong.

"I met you, Susan. Susie. My crazy Indian wise-woman. Boot-toe kicker of bad guys. Finder of lost people. Wolf-leader. I've spent the last six months figuring out the best way to go about leaving my little perfect house and my little perfect schedule to follow you, and now it seems I don't have to worry about it any more: I just do it. And the idea that we're going to have a baby in the springtime and a puppy in . . . whenever . . . is just the sweetest thing. For once, a victory for regular life. And it's ours!"

He raised his head from her shoulder and his eyes, too, were sparkling with tears. "Susan, I am *so happy!*"

"You are?" she asked incredulously, as he used another of his tissues to dab away at her face. It seemed the mascara was the heavy-duty kind. "You are?"

"Oh yeah! I am."

Susan took a deep breath. "Well," she began, and took another deep breath. "Well, I have to tell you that the baby will probably be more like early summer than spring . . . "

"That's just as wonderful."

"And as far as leaving your perfect little house—maybe it's better if we don't. I probably can't continue being a mountain vet and being a good mother at the same time. Not as good a mother as I want to be."

Ewen sat back in delighted surprise. "That's great. You move in down here and don't be a vet at all for as long as you like. Just a mom. We can afford it. Really."

"Just like that?"

"Just like that. Except . . . "

"Except what?" Susan looked like a dog—or perhaps a raccoon— that expected to get hit.

"I think we should get married."

"Oh," she said softly. "Yeah. If you want to. And if you don't mind."

"Mind what?"

"Marrying an Indian."

Ewen laughed until he cried again.

Chapter Thirty-six

PETERSEN HAD BROUGHT Jacob Fischbein into the interrogation room, knowing Dr. Young would be irritated that he had done so, instead of visiting the young guy at his home, or in some neutral place. But Dr. Young was not the detective here. Jacob was not offended. He only wished his damn father did not have to be in the next room with the door cracked open. Some legal necessity or other. It put Jacob's enthusiasm on leash.

"So, Jake. After all that acting out at the detox center last summer you wound up with no charges pressed against you. That's quite a feat, considering what you did."

Jacob had been looking around the clean and simple box of a room and thinking how much less depressing this place was than the Snohomish Detox Center, and Petersen's words caught him by surprise. He had to think.

What Jacob did last summer? He meant what Ewen did, in Jacob's skin. As Jacob had been told by the Youngs, and had had to memorize, that wasn't so bad. He'd scuttled out from some guards and just left.

The big cop couldn't have any idea what Jacob *had* done, really. Jacob bet this whole approach was just trying to get under his skin. Like calling him "Jake," repeatedly, when he'd been told he preferred Jacob. Petersen must have seen him flinch at the name. Well, he wouldn't see him do it again. Jacob had seen his share of cop movies.

And he knew he hadn't killed anyone. Sooner or later—he hoped sooner—they'd discover that. (That belief also came from watching cop movies.)

"What I did was be held against my will in a hell-hole and manage to escape. That isn't against any law I know of."

"But you weren't being held against your father's will. And you're a minor. Good thing, too—being a minor—considering how you knocked those cops around."

For a moment Jacob wanted to tell the tall cop that he knew the difference between a cop and a hospital guard. He also wanted, so badly, to announce that it wasn't he, Jacob, who had knocked the guards around, but Petersen's buddy, Ewen Young. But nothing good would come from that direction. He'd learned some discretion in the last few months.

"If it had been my father's will that I was there, and that I was treated like that, then I don't think he'd have been so committed to the lawsuit."

Petersen's eyebrows rose sardonically. "Nothing said about a lawsuit, here."

"Naturally. They don't want it spread around. When it comes up there will be a lot to read about in the papers. Dad wants the place closed down."

Petersen himself had not heard a whole lot of good about the Snohomish Hospital Detox Unit. But he also wasn't too sympathetic to junkies in general. As for spoiled kids, they were maybe at the bottom of his list. He looked at the gangling boy in front of him, legs propped out sideways in the metal chair, and he wondered what the story was.

He started over again, looking for what would hurt most. "So you . . . bite . . . yourself."

Jacob very carefully didn't flinch. "I did when I was a kid. Not recently, though. And I never bit anyone else."

"Why'd you do it? I mean, it seems completely beyond me, why a guy would lean down and take a chunk out of himself like that. Drugs, gambling—I might not like those things, but at least I see the attraction. But self-mutilation? I thought that was just for girls."

Jacob felt the breath knocked out of him and for a second he thought he was going to give Detective Petersen what he wanted. A physical assault on a cop. Or worse, a display of tears. But at that moment he seemed to feel the presence of Ewen sitting beside him. Old Doc's Bro would not let himself be pushed like this, to emotion beyond self-control. And Jacob had this funny, almost superstitious idea that Ewen had left a little bit of his splendid self behind in Jacob's body last summer. Then he had used Ewen against his will, but this time he felt he was using him very differently.

He breathed deeply, as he had seen Ewen breathing, with eyes half-closed, and he said, "I bit myself to distract myself from emotional pain, which had to do with being the disappointing oldest son of Leonard Fischbein, my father, who does everything flawlessly." Damn that Dad was listening. But he'd heard it all before. Jacob continued.

"It was an infantile reaction. And then I discovered drinking beer, which served the same function with less bloodshed. It was also immature. And *now* I have discovered AA. So far that's working a lot better than either alcohol or self-mutilation." He sat up straighter and watched Petersen watching him. "Is my girlfriend still waiting out there?" he asked politely.

Petersen straightened. "The little girl with the pink hair? Yeah, She's waiting, but I don't know for what. For you?" Petersen tried to look doubtful, but when that didn't work he added, "She has no business in the station."

Jacob clasped his hands together on the metal desk. "She thinks she does. Besides, she's visiting me from Santa Barbara. Where should she go?"

Petersen shrugged, expressing sudden disinterest in the whole question. The interview did not seem to be going as he'd wanted.

Jacob grinned inside.

Emma Woollcott was sitting in the dingy lobby next to Mr. Fischbein, who was apologizing to her once again. "This isn't at all how I imagined your visit to the sunny Northwest to go, Emma," he said. "And it's so very nonsensical for them to think Jacob is involved in such a terrible crime just because he used to have a . . . a bad habit. A habit not much different than biting your fingernails!"

This was the second time Em had visited Jacob's home since last summer, and she was becoming attuned to Mr. Fischbein's way of re-writing the past. Attuned, but not accepting. She knew the self-inflicted scars on his poor body better than his father did, but she would never have characterized them as "biting your fingernails." Nor would she ever call Jacob's leap into self-destructive alcoholism "teen-age acting out," as Mr. Fischbein had. But neither did she believe, for a moment, that Jacob had been spending the past few years cannibalizing children.

Still, it was good, she thought, to have a father who would at least go to bat for you with the law, however inadequate he was in other respects. And it was probably a damn good thing for Jacob right now to have a father who was a lawyer. She played idly with the tiny silver triangle pendant around her neck.

Mr. Fischbein, watching the pink-haired girl, was again relieved to remember that that triangle within a circle meant Alcoholics Anonymous, and not some sort of lesbian group. He wasn't sure about Jacob hooking up with an alcoholic—after all, the boy at one time drank a wee bit too much himself, and all this talking they did about alcohol couldn't be a good influence. And the stripy pink hair wasn't exactly the look he'd like to see around Jacob Jr. (Though he had to admit, the girl was very, very hot.) And boys would be boys.

And it was good, at least, to have a girlfriend who would go to bat for you when you were in difficulties, however unsuitable she was in other respects.

"I don't like him for it at all," said Gideon Ryde to Rick Petersen, outside the interrogation room. "Despite the habit of self-biting. Nothing else fits." He dropped a file flat on his desk and gave his partner a disapproving look.

"I didn't say I like him for it either," said Petersen imperturbably. "I just think he's a baby asshole and full of himself. Comes in here like he's God's gift. Sent by Dr. Lynn Thurmond-Young, who in turn thinks she's Mother Theresa."

Ryde stared at his partner, open mouthed, as he suddenly understood the personal layers involved between this gangling, slightly pimply kid and Detective Richard Petersen. Why the kid was being bullied by Petersen.

It wasn't about Jacob. It wasn't even about Dr. Young, who had been as helpful as a cop could want from a witness.

It was about Susan Sundown.

Until last year, Gid had thought that the on-again, off-again affair between his partner and the glamorous Indian vet would end in a loving marriage. It would just take time. But now it was surely going to be Mr. Young and Susan in the loving marriage. Gideon saw the signs, and perhaps now Ricky saw them, too.

Giddy Ryde wanted his partner to be happy for once, but if it wasn't to be in this manner, he was at least glad *some* people were going to be happy. Dr. Sundown would be a very good mother; that was obvious. And Ewen Young, once he got it through his thick head that his lady was pregnant, would probably be the best of fathers. Gid was confident of this. He had *faith* in it.

He wished he were standing in front of Dr. Sundown right now instead of a miserably moody Rick Petersen. "Well, Rick," he said slowly, navigating the currents of his partner's temper. "Perhaps the kid is. God's gift to us, I mean. We certainly deserve a leg up in this case. And since one of these poor kids was Young's patient . . . "

"One so far. They might all be."

Ryde ignored this improbability. "And since he knows a number of the kids Ellie Frankel knew, as kid to kid, rather than as doctor to kid, perhaps we should value the information he has for us."

Petersen had been leaning against the enamel-painted wall. He thrust his body forward aggressively. "Yeah. Well, *you* go value it from him!"

Rick Petersen stalked down the hall and was gone.

Gideon Ryde entered the interrogation room, where he smiled at Jacob. "I'd like to ask you a few questions, Jacob," he began, smiling easily. "About those kids from the therapy group. But first—again— are you sure you don't want your father in here with you?"

Jacob snorted, but he tried to minimize the snort, as this fellow didn't seem to be looking for a fight with him. Very quietly he said, "I'm sure I won't feel free to speak with him in the room. I had this interview-thing out with Dad the moment he got here, and he finally accepts it as the simplest way out. If he were in here I wouldn't get in a word edgewise. He'd be telling me to shut up every ten seconds, no matter what you asked. I'm happier with him out in the lobby. And he accepts that. But—Em is out there, too. Isn't she? Could I see her for a moment?"

"Em? That's the beautiful young lady with the AA medallion around her neck?"

Jacob nodded.

"Well, she's there, and I'll let her see you for a minute, but it wouldn't be appropriate to allow her to stay . . . "

"Right. I wouldn't want her to. All this stuff about murder; it must be freaking her out. I just want her to know I'm all right."

Detective Ryde nodded, and as he was stepping out the door, he turned and said, "By the bye, I don't drink alcohol either."

Jacob was remembering what he could for Detective Ryde. Almost free-associating, as once he had done for Dr. Young.

"There were two Lous in the group. Lou Two, the guy who came in later, was the guy the Doc was talking about. With the Satanism thing," Jacob said. "Though I don't think Lou Two would have really known Satan if he got bit in the tush by him."

"In the 'tush'?" echoed Ryde bemusedly. "I haven't heard that word in awhile."

Jacob Fischbein looked up. "You haven't?" He looked closely at Ryde. "It's probably just one of those words that welled up from the underclass. Most changes in the American English language, you know, come from youth slang, or other oppressed minorities." Jacob was glad to have had this thought. He felt he had been competent in his expression of it. The blond detective seemed to be really listening to him. Jacob's heart swelled.

"I guess so," Ryde replied, keeping deadpan. "So Louis—er, Lou Two—wouldn't know if the devil bit him on the tush. By that I guess you mean he wasn't really . . . malicious. Go on, please."

Jacob nodded. "He was just your standard Goth. I mean, he was fourteen and hadn't had time to figure out a more original personality. Something that would get the same attention as a Goth but be his own—you know? And his system was slow."

"His system was slow? He wasn't too bright, you mean? A few bricks short of a load?"

"No. I mean he didn't even have the latest version of Windows." Jacob leaned back on the hind legs of his chair, but this time it was not a gesture of challenge. He was just thinking. He scratched his scalp meditatively. "He couldn't come up with anything more interesting than Satanism. Oh, he did the pancake makeup thing, and the eyeliner. Owl earrings, as I recall. But Lou Two's problem was he didn't have anyone to *do* it all with. He wasn't in the right crowd. Or any crowd. He bought his earrings from his girlfriend's *Gaelsong* catalog, if you can believe it."

"It's a stretch," said Ryde, who had no idea what the boy was talking about. "But I'll believe it if you say so."

Jacob tilted his head left in thought for a moment and then went on. "I mean, well, at least his anger was authentic. I give him that." Jacob tilted his head right to balance things. "With those parents and all those zits . . . "

"And when you say he was Goth, Mr. Fischbein . . . "

"Call me Jake," said Jacob, astonishing himself.

"When you say he was Goth, you mean he was death-obsessed. Right?"

"Yes, but then so was . . . John Keats, for example."

"Keats the poet? But Keats *was* dying. He had TB."

Jacob hadn't expected the detective to know about Keats. His respect grew. "Yeah, but what I mean is that his death-imagery shouldn't make you think Keats was a mass murderer. My hit on Lou Two was the same. All brooding, but as far as I know, he never kicked a cat in his life. Now Katherine, on the other hand . . . They were talking about taking Katie's kitten away from her because of the way she was treating it. But then she had an excuse, I guess. She *was* dying, or at least very sick. Cancer of the . . . the bones, I think. It's been so long I don't really remember much, but I remembered that. I had never met anyone who was dying. I thought somehow they'd be more likeable." He sighed heavily. "I've learned better, since . . . Anyway, it was all over eighteen months ago."

Eighteen months ago. A very long time when one was a kid. Ryde looked at the list of names by his left hand. "She was in the same group as Lou Two?"

"For a little while. Dr. Young took her out of Community, because of the kitten. And then later she went to a hospital somewhere. I haven't thought about her in ages." He shook his head again. "I was really narcissistic in those days, Detective. Just a mixed-up kid."

Ryde snuck a glance at the narcissistic, mixed-up kid in front of him now. "And how did Lou Two get along with Katherine, for example?"

A shrug. "I don't remember them ever talking."

Ryde returned to his list. "Let's move on, then. How about George Merski? Do you remember him?"

Another shrug, this time dismissive. "Georgie the bully. He *was* a few bricks short of a load, Detective. And there wasn't much use from the beginning in putting him in with other kids for therapy. A bully who is happy being a bully is going to stay what he is. In fact, I'm not sure what value there was in putting a bunch of kids with behavior problems in together to work things out. I mean—working things out is exactly what they're . . . I mean, we're . . . no good at."

Ryde tapped the list. "But can you go on about Georgie?"

"Do I think he's the monster? The cannibal?" Jacob wiggled in his cheap chair. "I think George Merski might have taken those kids and beaten them into the ground, no problem. But chewing on them afterwards? Not likely. Not even if he'd seen *Silence of the Lambs* five times in a row."

Ryde agreed that Merski was out of it, mostly because he knew George Merski had been incarcerated at Monroe for more than a year. But he said nothing of this to Jacob. "Well then, Jacob—er, I mean Jake. I guess we're done."

Cordially, Ryde slapped him on the shoulder, rose and left the room.

Jacob got up to leave the room and wondered if he'd just been played "bad cop, good cop." And if he had been, what they thought they got out of it. He didn't think he had either incriminated himself or done much good incriminating anyone else. He ruminated for another few moments about the meetings of Dr. Young's kid-groups, which had been pretty boring, all in all, and his years of sessions with Dr. Young herself, which had not been boring at all.

He thought about Ewen Young, and his debt to him. He would spend the rest of his life apologizing to ol' Doc's Bro. Then he had the enormous realization that he had never really thanked Doc herself.

Thanked her for being the one adult he could talk to, for three hard years. For coming to see him when he called, after he had walked out on her. For still being there, even now.

Jacob had thought Ewen had the magic. He grinned as he strode out of the interrogation room. There was magic and there was *magic*.

Neither the boy nor Gideon Ryde knew that Petersen followed Jacob secretly from the station.

Rick Petersen was very good at surveillance, especially considering the disadvantage of his height. He was near enough to witness Fischbein reclaiming his girlfriend in the lobby and being reclaimed by his father. Petersen was inclined to dislike Mr. Fischbein, senior, because he was a lawyer, and his dislike for the son lessened as he heard the disagreement between the two as they walked out. Seems Fischbein, senior, would have preferred for his son to refuse to talk to the police at all, and only remained in the lobby because of Jacob's insistence. It seems years of Jacob's insistence had worn the man down.

Petersen heard Fischbein raise his voice. Fischbein, junior, kept his very cute girlfriend's hand in his and kept his voice down. He carried his girlfriend's book—something by the physicist Richard Feynman—under his arm and walked out to the car, where they managed, politely, to lose the father.

They did not lose Petersen. He followed them leisurely in his personal CR-V and was intrigued that they returned to Sangye Menla, the hospice within sight of the crime scene. But after a half hour of watching them through binoculars as they changed sheets and scrubbed down a room, he started his engine again and left them to their work.

Chapter Thirty-seven

"Wow!" Dr. Lynn Thurmond-Young hugged Dr. Susan Sundown and spun her around. The effect was much like that of a whippet spinning a wolf. "Oh, I'm so glad. So glad for both of you. We were waiting and waiting to be told . . . !"

"Waiting?" repeated Ewen. "You mean everyone was expecting us to get married? We've been slow off the line?" He was attempting to embrace both women at the same time, with moderate success.

"Not *everyone* was expecting you to get married," said Teddy, matter-of-factly. "Only us. Mommy. Daddy. Me. And Granddad, of course."

Ewen squeezed more tightly and the whole spinning circle came to a stop. He looked in amazement at his sister. "Dad, too?"

"Your father doesn't mind?" Susan looked a bit anxious. "About me not being Chinese?"

"It didn't even occur to me that Dad gave me a thought any more, one way or another," said Ewen in wonderment.

Lynn giggled. "Oh, of course he gives you a thought! And though—I don't know—he might have liked to have at least one all-Chinese grandkid, there is something about Susan much more important to him!"

Susan frowned. "Which is . . . ?"

Together Ewen and Lynn said it. "You're a doctor!"

"A vet," said Susan in a small voice.

"That's still a big plus, to him." Lynn noticed a mangled envelope in Ewen's pocket. "What's that? Congrats from someone?"

"From Karen the Creep," said Ewen.

"She's *still* trying to get you back again? Even though you chose painting over her version of your future together years ago?"

Ewen rolled his eyes. "She only gets in touch every time she breaks up with the latest guy. And no, it's not congrats. It's the nasty little message that finally—indirectly—let me know what I was too stupid to figure out myself. It's a note Karen left with Susan for me. A note that left her in tears!"

Lynn grabbed for the envelope, but then looked to Susan's face for permission. Getting that permission, she ripped it open. After a second she raised her eyes again. "It just says . . . "

"It says 'I was by this afternoon. Keep in touch.'" He quoted from memory.

"That left you in tears?"

Susan, who had cleaned and refurbished her face an hour ago, murmured, "It was the way she said it."

It seemed so simple and obvious when Susan suggested they let Ryan Watanabe know they were going to get married. After all, it had been simple when they had let Lynn know. It had been superfluous, in fact, and Lynn had been relieved to get the news of the pregnancy out in the open, so she could coo and sympathize. Of course she had suspected Susan was pregnant—everyone except Ewen seemed to have known— and she had accepted their marriage as inevitable since last winter. She expressed how happy she was for them, but then immediately asked if they would please watch Teddy for a few hours, grabbed her purse and drove off. This was less courteous than Lynn's standard behavior, but they were in no mood to say no. They were left with Teddy and his large box of Tonka toys, feeling the need to spread their news further.

It had still been simple when Susan called her grandmother. "I hope she doesn't mind I'm not an Indian," Ewen had said nervously, but Susan had only shrugged and said, "You're a Santa Barbara Indian, remember." And then Grandma further stepped on their announcement by claiming she already knew, because her brother had told her in a dream.

So it should have been simple when they told Ryan Watanabe. Instead, it had opened the floodgates of school spirit.

It would be a wedding for the sifu.

"I'm not a sifu, Ryan," said Ewen. "Except in your tiny little head. I'm just Ewen."

"You're *our* sifu!" replied Ryan loyally, and hung up to tell all the others. Ewen, who would perhaps have liked to tell the others himself, was left standing there with the phone in his hand and a frozen smile on his face. A half-hour later, as they were explaining to Teddy that they were not going to start parking the airplane in Ewen's back yard, Ewen got a call from Barbie Cowell asking whether it was true they were all going to be wearing their silk uniforms.

"Uniforms? To what?" he asked her. "To the wedding," came her answer. "During the procession."

Barbie was assured they would not be wearing uniforms of any kind, and that no procession had been planned. She admitted relief.

When Perry called, it was to ask whether it was true that the ceremony would be held in the Buddhist temple where Ewen had seen the butchered monk the winter before. He was evidently glad to find there was no truth in this rumor. He was, on the other hand, disappointed about the lack of silk uniforms.

"We'll just have to have two weddings," said Susan, after he hung up. "One for my eccentric family and one for your eccentric school."

"Three," amended Ewen. "You forgot the eccentric 'doctors' in my family."

"That's the one that will cost money," murmured Susan, kissing him.

When the phone rang again they both stared at it. Out of some intuition, their minds flew from planning their joyful ritual to the police investigation. This would be about the police investigation.

The faces of Susan and Ewen produced identical expressions of rebellion. Susan prevented Teddy from answering the phone at all. "I have an idea," she said. "Let's all go out and see a puppy."

"Hi, Lou," said Dr. Young. The young man was standing at his door, his dun hair in his eyes and his gray hoodie crooked over his shoulders. He had evidently been napping. He was certainly not wearing makeup or earrings.

"Dr. Young. Wow. It's you. I mean, it's been a long time." She nodded and he stood in his family's colonial fluted doorway for a few moments before it occurred to him to invite her in. "My mom's not home from work yet," he said, as he guided her to a seat in the similarly colonial living room.

Lynn was amazed once more at how much growing a boy did in these years between thirteen and sixteen. This blondish, blandish figure was so tall next to her that she might have been intimidated, if he had not been so obviously intimidated by her.

He sat down across from her, on a Thomasville colonial chair that had seen better days. The whole house was like that, Lynn noticed now. Very expensive stuff that had seen better days. It suffered from more than just time, too; it was neglected. She noticed a certain lack of "house pride" she didn't remember from before with Mrs. Cameron. The dining set must have run many thousands of dollars, but the braid rug beneath it was sun-faded L.L. Bean. Lynn knew that because she herself had L.L. Bean rugs. Nothing wrong with them, but this was the kind of inconsistency she was born to notice.

She heard rain pattering on the window somewhere. The boy— the young man—sat very still and stared at her. He was obviously wondering why she was there. She herself was wondering why she was there. She had a son of her own. And a brother getting married. She got no thrill out of realizing that she was risking herself.

"I know why you're here," he said suddenly, and so closely did those words follow her own thoughts that her heart skipped a painful beat.

"You do, Louis? Then tell me, because I'm not sure."

He gave her a sideways smile. In his quiet, rawboned way, this youngster was going to be very attractive to women. "Jeez, Dr. Young," he said. "You sound more like a shrink than you used to! You used to be so . . . open. Not like the other authority figures from my checkered past." He shuffled his feet. "I remember how you accepted me. I mean, with all my quirks and silly makeup. And the body piercings." His smile grew more rueful. "Back then I thought I had miseries." He snorted and rubbed his nose with his hand. "Back then! I didn't know what miseries were."

"If you know why I've come here, Louis, please tell me," she said again, looking up at him. *Because I can't remember myself. Not one clue. And I'm getting very nervous.*

"It's because of the bill."

Lynn's mind stopped on a dime. " . . . because of the . . . "

"The bill. Like every other bill outstanding when my father cut out on us: the utilities, the mortgages, the cars we used to own. I have no idea how much money we owed you when I had to stop things like tutors and coaches and therapists. Usually those places just sold the debt and we got to deal with greasy little collection services, but I guess you don't operate on such a large scale . . . And about that all I can tell you is that I'll pay you when I can. I appreciate all you did—all the time you took—but it's going to take me lots *more* time to make it right."

It was very dreary in this large, cold, colonial room. Lynn felt the sorrow of unexpected poverty, which no amount of psychiatry could cure. She repeated silently to herself the prayer her mother had taught them. *May all beings be happy. May all beings be peaceful and at ease.* At last she shook her head. "Oh, Louis, I'm so sorry to hear all that. I'm sorry you think that's why I'm here. What a mistake! I wish you had told me at the time why you were quitting. We didn't have to drop our conversations. Especially if you were so unhappy. We could have . . . "

"We didn't need to run up any *new* debts, doctor!" he said, his tone a little sharp.

"There would have been no issue of money. Many times my patients don't have any money."

His smile grew more lopsided than ever. "I thought about asking—for a schedule or something, but Mom wouldn't have it. Pride, you know. We were very proud of ourselves."

Were very proud. Lynn noted the past tense. She didn't know what she was going to say in response, and what came out was a surprise to Lynn, herself. "Life can really suck, can't it, Louie?" She heard her own note of dissatisfaction and wondered who she was talking about.

However unprofessional, it seemed that this was the right thing to say. His blue-green eyes shifted focus. They took on a spark of humor. Her fear began to dissolve. "Yeah. It can and does. So—why *did* you show up today, Doctor Young? If it wasn't about the money?"

"I was worried," she said. "Haven't you been reading the paper? Watching TV?"

He shook his head. "Two jobs. Why? What's been happening?"

Lynn stood up and took a deep breath. She heard the rain falling harder. "Three kids have been found dead around here; rather, their skeletons have been found. One of them was my patient, and she was a kid I hadn't heard from for a while but never followed up on, you know? Now, more than a year later, I discover . . . "

His fair face lit up. "Oh! And you were worried. About *me!*" He looked quite touched.

You're almost exactly right, thought Lynn, but she didn't correct him.

"And here I'm bitching off at you as though all my problems are your fault . . . "

As they faced each other in the dim room there came the sound of a key in the front lock, followed by a shoulder shoved against a door that had swollen from the autumn moisture. Mrs. Cameron came in, a heavy bag on one arm and groceries on the other. She was wearing some sort of pink uniform.

Always before Mrs. Cameron had worn Peruvian Connection-type clothes. Alpaca. Ikat patterns. Lynn was suddenly very conscious of her own silk-wool ruanna and Talbot moleskin trousers. "Hello, Mrs. Cameron!" she called out, as naturally as she could.

Mrs. Cameron flinched. She tried to hide her uniform behind her packages. "Dr. Young? What . . . ?"

Lynn caught Louis's eye and nodded to him in comradely fashion. "I'm sorry to show up on your doorstep like this. I was . . . trying to find someone else, and we were just catching up on things, Lou and I."

As the woman went toward the kitchen to deposit her bags, Lynn shook Louis' hand. "Call me sometime," she said to the young man. "But only if and when you want to! No bill. No therapy. Just—like I said—to keep in touch." And she retreated over the scuffed wood floor of the foyer and made her own assault upon the rain-warped colonial door.

He followed her and lent his strength against the squeaky hinges. "Thanks, Dr. Young," he whispered as she went through. "Thanks for everything."

Once more Susan descended upon Lenny Boatman without giving warning. He blinked to see them all. Perhaps he thought this was Susan's way of making sure the puppies were being treated right. Showing up without warning. He could not know that the truth was that they were just in hiding from the "celebration" that seemed to engulf them.

The pups were asleep in a heap around their big mama, who resembled a sleepy haystack on the kitchen linoleum. Ewen looked at them all and his jaw dropped. Susan hadn't stopped to describe what they looked like, and he hadn't really spared any thought to it. Teddy looked at all the puppies and put both his hands over his own mouth, making a gasp like that of a jeweler unexpectedly confronted by the Hope diamond. Susan and Lenny watched their faces watching his dogs, and Lily flopped her long tail lazily against the floor.

"I can't believe . . . " began Ewen, and he shook his head in wonderment. "They are *so* cute! I didn't imagine they could *be* so cute!" His fingers began to twitch with an imaginary brush and his mind filled with shades of pigment. "Which one is ours?"

For a moment Susan felt guilty. "You hadn't seemed interested, so I had to choose by myself."

"Okay, but which one is ours?"

She pointed. "The little black guy," she said in a small voice. The shiny dark puppy lifted his head as though he understood.

"May I touch him?" Ewen spoke not to Susan, nor Lenny Boatman, but to Lily, plush haystack with dark brown eyes. Lily allowed it.

Teddy had a cream-colored puppy butting against his legs. His eyes darted from one chocolate bundle to the cream, to a gold, and then to another brown. His face was as pink as the nose of the cream-colored puppy. Then it crumpled. "But . . . but . . . Which one's *mine?*" he whimpered. He repeated his plea louder. Completely on overload, Teddy stood there and began to cry.

"We can't all have new puppies at the same time," said Ewen to the disconsolate boy. They had moved into Boatman's shabby living room so Teddy's tantrum wouldn't frighten the puppies, or—worse—the mother.

"Why not! Why not! You got two puppies and I don't got any. I don't got nothin'!"

This was so far from the truth that Ewen reeled back in his seat. Teddy, of all boys on this Earth, having nothing? "You've got two great parents, Teddy, and a great grandfather and an uncle and . . . and

328 | R.A. MacAvoy

even an aunt. Aunt Susan. And you've got computer games and biofeedback and soccer . . . "

"Pish!" said Teddy very clearly. "Pish!" Ewen wondered where he had gotten that word.

Susan leaned into Ewen's ear. "None of that means anything to him right now, Ewen. He's tired and hungry and besides, Theo *is* out of town." What she did not say aloud was that Teddy was right in crying because he didn't have a puppy. To Susan, that situation was quite naturally painful.

Ewen was trying to understand. He was going to be a father and therefore he had to understand. "But Teddy's not like this. Never. He's always been a really special kid."

"And he still is," she whispered, and took Ewen's hand in hers. "Special includes throwing a fit, sometimes."

Lenny Boatman was standing beside the little family group, rubbing one hand over his raspy chin. "It's the puppies, too," he said diffidently. "Don't forget the puppies are involved in it. Boy's never really *seen* a litter of puppies before, has he? Well, that'll do it to a kid, every time." Boatman glanced over his shoulder at the kitchen, where the puppies were squealing. "It's something special between kids and puppies. His wrinkled eyes opened slightly. "Hey! I don't suppose . . . "

"No," said Susan and Ewen, together.

Chapter Thirty-eight

LYNN SAT in her car in the fading light. She watched the runnels of rain coming down the windshield. She had not been surprised to learn about Georgie Merski. She had never gotten the boy to see that anything he did which turned out wrong—and that was most anything he tried—went wrong by his own doing. His parents taught him in perfect agreement (even if they agreed on nothing else in their calamitous lives) that nothing was his fault.

The boy had believed two things very firmly: first was that the world owed him everything by right, and second, that it would try to withhold from him each and every one of those rights. So it had been for the parents all their lives, and so it became for each of their five children. Of course, being five-ten and two hundred twenty pounds in grammar school had not done Georgie's socialization much good, either.

So it was with no amazement Lynn had learned that Georgie was now a guest of the State of Washington: armed assault. He'd put a man in a wheelchair and himself in a prison cell. All by the age of fifteen. George Merski was out of this particular terrible picture: he'd been incarcerated when the last child had disappeared into the field.

George had been one of the kids she had never charged a penny to help. As best Lynn could remember, neither Georgie nor his parents had ever expressed any surprise about that or felt any sense of obligation. Even just now, his mother had said nothing about George's time in mandated therapy in the past, except that Lynn Young must not have been a very good therapist for it all to have turned out so wrong.

There was one more thing Lynn thought she was supposed to do now. It hovered in the back of her mind as the rain pelted on the roof. It bothered her that she had forgotten it, but it did not bother her excessively, because she knew it wasn't to do with Teddy. She'd left Teddy with Ewen and Susan. Having Susan around would be a relief, she thought, with a little smile. Not enough women in this family.

Whatever it was she had forgotten couldn't matter right now, though, because Lynn now had the answer to the terrible question of the week, and she had only one more stop to make before these hellish few days would be over. She leaned over to look again at her last set of MapQuest directions, flicking on the overhead light for a better look.

This bleak certainty she felt now must be what Ewen felt when the knowledge of death or danger settled into his mind. How Resurrection must feel when she got the scent that made her raise her grey muzzle and howl at the sky.

There was only one stop left to make. Lynn called first.

After making the call, Lynn turned the key, strapped her seat belt and drove.

Mr. and Mrs. Conner were standing by the door together, ready to let her in and take her umbrella. For a few seconds there was this un-expected moment of normality as the Chinese-American professional woman in her raincoat and sensible shoes was welcomed by the couple into their little house in Kirkland. Then Lynn stopped in place in the middle of the living room carpet and simply looked at them.

Mr. Connor returned her gaze for a few seconds before letting his slide down. Mrs. Conner looked only at the fireplace, where the first maple logs of the season were sizzling merrily. "We thought it would be the police, when you called," she said in her sad, Midwestern accent.

It had been a year since Lynn had heard that voice and those hopeless tones, but she remembered them well. "So you were already expecting this?"

Mr. Connor shrugged his bear-like shoulders. "After the news a couple a days ago, of course we were."

"So you knew already? Before they found the bodies?" Lynn listened very closely for the answer, and she used her eyes.

He rubbed his grizzled head. Mrs. Conner continued to stare at the mantelpiece. "Not exactly. Not all this." He raised his face, offended. "You don't think we would have just sat on it: our knowing what she did, if there was anything we could do to help, do you? *Do you, Dr. Young?*"

"I don't know you well enough to guess," said Lynn quite bravely, and without being invited, she sat on the living room armchair. She was a very slight person, and its chintz stuffing seemed to swallow her. "Why don't you tell me? All about it?"

He cleared his throat. "We found out only after Katie was so sick. Too sick to hurt anyone anymore, I mean. Then what could we do about it?"

"Save some other children's families a great deal of pain?"

He turned to her, angry. "Which families? Do you think she gave us names? A map to a burial plot? Swear to God I never knew what to believe of the things she said! There's still our little Brenda to consider, and besides, Katie was out of her mind by that time."

"Don't say that about Katie," said Mrs. Conner, wearily. "That she was out of her mind. She had tumors. She wasn't crazy. She had tumors and she was killing those children purely in an effort to live!"

Lynn tried to make sense of what Mrs. Connor was saying. She ended by shaking her head from side to side. "What on Earth, Mrs. Connor . . . ? In an effort to live? "

Mrs. Connor was not much thicker-built than Lynn, but with her it wasn't natural slimness. As she sat down on the couch across from Lynn, the skin was hanging loosely off the backs of her thighs, and suffering had given her round face bulldog jowls. She gave the longest sigh Lynn Thurmond-Young had ever heard. "If Katie hadn't been so smart to begin with. So good in science. None of this might have happened."

Lynn just waited.

"Have you ever heard of telomeres, Dr. Young? Or mitochondria?"

"Of course," said Lynn dismissively, and then realized that the dismissal was not kind and that it might not be wise to be rude to the Connors.

"Well, we never did. But Katie had been studying them in school. Telomeres, she said, are the plug-ends of our genes. As we get old they get worn away. That's *why* we get old." She glanced at Lynn for a moment, as though fearing she might argue the point, and then she added, "That's what Katie said, anyway. While she could still talk. And the mitochondria, they must have something to do with life force. Life force! Katie talked about it all the time. She didn't have any left, she said. Her telomeres were all worn off early, or her mitochondria were, or some such. She needed—help—from healthier children."

Mr. Connor strode over and stood above Lynn, but though he was still a big man all the threat seemed washed out of him. "Poor little thing thought she was some kind of vampire, only a scientific kind, and if she could . . . consume other lives, she would live. But she wasn't responsible for what she did. You knew Katie from before. She was a good child. She just went out of her mind."

"She wasn't out of her mind," Mrs. Conner repeated bitterly. "She just had tumors in her brain."

Lynn said nothing; she scarcely breathed.

"And she never hurt those kids, you know," added Mrs. Connor. "Never put them in pain. She just hit them from behind with a hammer. Never felt a thing. It wasn't like she was one of *those!*"

Lynn sat there for what seemed like a long time. She didn't know what one of "those" was. Nor did she care.

No one said anything. At last Lynn noticed that the ornament on the fireplace mantle at which Mrs. Connor was staring was a fancy porcelain urn. Katie was still in the room with them. The maple logs underneath continued to burn merrily.

"You *will* call the police now—won't you?" Lynn asked, rising.

"You can do that for us," grunted Mr. Conner.

"It would look so much better if you did it yourselves," said Lynn, and she went out to find her umbrella. "And it's not my job," she added, angrily. No one walked to the door with her.

On her way back to the car she heard her cell phone calling from inside her purse and she suddenly remembered what she had been supposed to do. She was supposed to be at the airport, picking up Theo. Lynn smiled slightly, bitterly, as she flipped open the phone

It wasn't Theo, but Jacob Fischbein. The events of the week caught up with her and instead of greeting him she blurted, "What happened now?"

"Oh, Jeez," came his voice contritely. "I didn't stop to think it might be a bad time, with all the . . . with all of it."

"I'm sorry, Jacob. I'm just strung out. What can I do for you?"

"I just wanted to thank you, Doc. That's all. I just couldn't wait." His voice was so earnest it broke in the middle.

She stood there in the rain in front of that dreadful little house, one hand on the door handle of her car. "Thank me for what, Jacob?"

"For everything," he said. "For absolutely everything!"

As she got in and pulled off the wet coat, she thought of Jacob and Louis. Two "thanks" in one day. From teenage boys. Not bad. Sometimes she said to herself as she started the engine, a person actually *can* win the grand prize!

Theo Thurmond came home filled with inspiration and stories about the Dalai Lama, only to find no one was interested. Ewen and Susan were getting married, and Theo felt that was good, but to his mind somewhat pedestrian. They were having a baby and they were going to be living in Redmond. That was good too, but again, uninteresting, compared to his insights into the dharma!

There had been three bodies discovered next to Sangye Menla and he could only shake his head at that and think gently of impermanence. He knew Lynn had suffered some anxiety because of this and he wished he had been here for her. In fact, he promised Lynn he would not go off alone again. Not for a long time. A year. But the murderer had really not been a murderer at all but only a sick child, so he meditated deeply on the truth of suffering and the truth of the cessation of suffering. He was glad the patients at the hospice had not been more upset by the discovery of the bones.

What was most alarming to Theo was that his well-mannered son had spent the weekend developing a terrible temper and a demand for (of all things) a large, apricot-colored puppy. On this he meditated long, seeking understanding.

Winter sank in with heavy rain again, as the Northwest paid with darkness for its long summer days. It wasn't a dreary winter, however, but a hectic one, with three weddings occurring before Christmas (all involving the same bride and groom) and a baby shower before the first day of spring.

The black puppy turned bigger and curlier as he grew and he surpassed all expectations, both in size and personality. Teddy was his official godfather and was allowed to name him.

He was called "Happy."

About the Author

R.A. MacAvoy is the author of twelve novels. Her debut, *Tea with the Black Dragon*, won the John W. Campbell Award, the Locus Award for best first novel, and a Philip K. Dick Award special citation. It was also nominated for the Nebula Award, the Hugo Award, the Ditmar Award, and listed in David Pringle's *Modern Fantasy: The Hundred Best Novels*. Born in Cleveland, Ohio, she has been married for thirty-three years to Ronald Cain. They live in the Cascade Foothills of Washington State.